Divas Don't Cry

Hollywood High Series
Hollywood High
Get Ready for War
Put Your Diamonds Up
Lights, Love & Lip Gloss
Heels, Heartache & Headlines

Also by Ni-Ni Simone
The Ni-Ni Girl Chronicles
Shortie Like Mine
If I Was Your Girl
A Girl Like Me
Teenage Love Affair
Upgrade U
No Boyz Allowed
True Story

The Throwback Diaries
Down By Law
Dear Yvette

Also by Amir Abrams
Crazy Love
The Girl of His Dreams
Caught Up
Diva Rules
Chasing Butterflies

Published by Kensington Publishing Corp.

Divas Don't Cry

Hollywood HIGH

NI-NI SIMONE
AMIR ABRAMS

KENSINGTON PUBLISHING CORP.
www.kensingtonbooks.com

DAFINA BOOKS are published by

Kensington Publishing Corp.
119 West 40th Street
New York, NY 10018

All Kensington titles, imprints, and distributed lines are available at special quantity discounts for bulk purchases for sales promotion, premiums, fund-raising, and educational or institutional use.

Special book excerpts or customized printings can also be created to fit specific needs. For details, write or phone the office of the Kensington Sales Manager: Kensington Publishing Corp., 119 West 40th Street, New York, NY 10018. Attn. Sales Department. Phone: 1-800-221-2647.

Dafina and the Dafina logo Reg. U.S. Pat. & TM Off.

ISBN-13: 978-0-7582-8858-5
ISBN-10: 0-7582-8858-1
First Kensington Trade Paperback Printing: April 2018

eISBN-13: 978-0-7582-8859-2
eISBN-10: 0-7582-8859-X
First Kensington Electronic Edition: April 2018

10 9 8 7 6 5 4 3 2 1

Printed in the United States of America

1

Spencer

Is trashy-ratchet the new chic? Well, my little *daaaablings*...ask Heather Cummings. The sixteen-soon-to-be-seventeen-year-old reality-TV star was spotted coming out of Thug Hitz, a recording studio on Martin Luther King Jr. Boulevard (known for giving birth to some of hip-hop's grimiest beats) last night, show-casing her porn-star body in an extremely daring low-cut cheetah-print bodysuit. Boobs and booty spilled out of the skimpy outfit. Can we say...camel toe and yeast?

The teen star, most remembered for her role as Wu-Wu on the now-defunct television series *The Wu-Wu Tanner Show*, paired the risqué ensemble with a pair of mink-fur thigh-high boots and had what appeared to be a blunt—or one very long, very fat cigar—dangling from her purple-painted lips, which appeared heavily shellacked with loads of gloss. Heather's sidekick, Co-Co Ming, known for his flamboyant fashion sense and over-the-top theatrics, wore a cheetah-print thong with a bolero-type jacket and a pair of animal print mules. The two cohorts gave onlookers and passersby an impromptu show filled with raunchy hip shaking, rhythmic foot stomping, pelvis thrusting, and lots of booty clapping in the middle of the street, stopping traffic and causing what police in the Baldwin Village section of Los Angeles County labeled a mini-riot.

When Heather and her entourage were asked to disperse from the streets, the reality-TV star gave police her middle fingers then turned her back to the cameras and brazenly bent over and slapped her voluptuous derriere and yelled, "Kiss what my ex-friend paid for."

A source closest to the teen confirmed that said *ex-friend* was none other than teen socialite Spencer Ellington, the daughter of famed TV producer and host of the internationally popular talk show *Dish the Dirt*, who'd generously donated ten grand to sponsor Heather's comeback from flat-back to Baby Got Back...

"Why that little *tramp!*" I heard Kitty hiss as I sauntered into the kitchen, where I found her—uh, my *so-called* mother—sitting at the table sipping a cup of coffee as she slung a magazine across the room. Lawdgawdjeezus. It was simply too early in the morning to have to share air space with her, but I was willing to pardon her antics—this time. God, she was such a...a...a dang joy kill.

But being the loving and kind daughter that I was, I rolled

my eyes and snidely asked, "What tramp trampled on your little peanut patch now, Mother?"

I tilted my head and stared her down.

There was a long pause.

She eyed me, nostrils flaring like a wild bear ready to eat its prey alive. Ooh, I loved it when Kitty had that rabid look in her eyes, snarling and gnashing her teeth. It made me want to dial 9-1-1 and Animal Control, then sit back and watch them tranquilize her before dragging her into a cage, and then taking her out into the desert and letting her out into the wild, where she belonged.

Oh, Kitty, Kitty, Kitty...

It was no secret around these parts that she and I had a very ugly and tumultuous relationship. She didn't know how to be gracious and kind. Nor did she know how to be—or *ever* had want to be—a mother. So her role as one was nonexistent. And, clearly, I'd been her meal ticket right after she'd married Daddy, Dr. Ellington, nearly seventeen years ago. She reeled him in with all of her cunning seduction and bedroom trickery, then sank her fangs into his loins. *Mmmph.* Kitty was nothing but a laundry bag of soiled panty-sets. Yet I had to give it to the conniving hag. She was wealthy, powerful, and—almost—beautiful if she wasn't so dang ugly inside. But I wasn't one to be messy. Heeheehee. So I wasn't going to slay her for the dragon she was. No, no, no. I was going to stay loving and kind.

Anyway, from what I've sorted through from all of Daddy's muddled rumblings (these days his mind is getting muddier and muddier with delusions, thanks to that nasty Alzheimer's disease snatching his brain cells and stripping him of his sanity) over the last several weeks, Kitty had been nothing but a broke-down nobody before he'd rescued her from her meager beginnings, somewhere deep in the swamps. Kitty never liked talking about her past, so I was doing my own family tree, raking up leaves and digging up roots. So far, I'd come up with nothing! Zilch! Nada! It was like the woman never existed. But that was another dirty, laborious story.

Ooh. I had to remember to lay a few good coins across the collection plate the next time I drove by Pastor Too Fly's house of worship. Ooh, he was some kind of fine, hunky man-wolf. He liked them young, hot, and tender. He even had my ex-bestie, Rich Montgomery, penned up in his confession booth a few times. She walked in a saint but wobbled out a sinner.

Amen.

Amen.

Amen.

Mmmph.

Kitty kept her gaze locked on mine. And I'd had enough. I had to get to school, before Rich started her red-carpet ritual of holding court—a press conference she had every morning in front of Hollywood High, where she droned on and on about (*yawn*) nothing or no one except herself in front of anyone who'd be bored enough to listen. And right about now, I'd rather be there with my ears bleeding out than standing here.

I stamped my foot, then slammed my manicured hands up on my fabulous hips. "Well, goshdangit! Are you going to answer me or not? Or are we going to play the stare-down game this morning? You know looking at you for any extended period of time wears my retinas out and makes my eyeballs ache."

Kitty sneered at me. "Shut it, Spencer. I'm not in the mood for your craziness this morning. That damn Heather is back at it again. Every time I turn around, that demon child is somewhere turning up with her goddamn trickery."

I narrowed my eyes. "And whose fault is that? I told you not to give that junkyard junkie a television show, but *nooooooooo!* Kitty thinks she's the cat's *meeeeeeooow* and does what she wants to do. Now look at you. All tore up because your little trash project is doing what she does best. Be trashy. She's nothing but a hapless buffoon. And *you*, Kitty, are nothing but the court jester."

Kitty rolled her eyes. "Spencer, darling, isn't it your feeding time?" She put a hand up. "Oh, wait, dear. Sssh. Do you hear it?" She cupped her ear with a hand. "Wait for it. Hear it? It's the sound of a belt buckle hitting the ground somewhere across the border." Her diamond bangles clinked as she clapped her hands. "Yes, my darling, yes. It's your feeding time. And there's some horny boy wearing a sombrero and cowboy boots under some stairwell waiting to—"

"You wait one flimflam*flucking* moment, Kitty. Don't you dare disrespect me! I don't feed until after two p.m., so get it right! And I *don't* do it under—"

She slammed her coffee mug down on the table. "You little twit," she snapped. "Don't start. For once in your spoiled, self-absorbed life, can you show your mother a little compassion? Can I get a moment of solitude so I can think? I've been nothing but good to you and that damn pill-popping trick, Heather. And time after time, all you do is disrespect me and test me. Both of you have done nothing but try to ruin my good name."

Now it was my turn to do the eye roll. "Oh, Kitty, lick mothballs." I smacked my Chanel-glossed lips together. "What has that junkie whore done this time?" I asked, feigning ignorance. But unaware I was not. I was Spencer Ellington, for heaven's sake! *Mmmph.* As if the universe didn't already know. It was my life's mission to know everything good and dirty about tramps like Heather.

As usual, Little Miss Train Wreck was all things foul and foolish. Just hungry for attention any way she could get it. Her self-esteem was just a-floating around in the toilet. Poor thing. It'd been bad enough she pulled that desperate stunt at Rich's sweet seventeen (although there was nothing sweet about that troll) birthday bash several weeks ago. *Mmmph.*

Up on stage rapping about Richard Montgomery being her father. *Ha!* Lies! Rich's dad was an old, nasty horndog, spreading his loin juice all across the seven continents.

Heather Suzanne Cummings and Rich Fat Girl Montgomery sisters?

Bwahahahaha. What a mismatch if I ever saw one. One was light bright like a knockoff Rainbow Brite doll. And the other was...well, she was...well, uh, she was an oversized Barbie with wide hips and a kangaroo pouch. Cute though. Real cute, like one of those cuddly little koala bears.

But I wasn't the one to spill any good tea, so I was going to leave that brew right in the kettle and let it steep. Still, the highlight of that night was seeing Rich's ole fluffy butt cheeks hit the floor in dramatic, over-the-top fashion. That trick would do anything for a photo op. Even fake a faint.

God, she was so shameless!

Mmmph. All I needed that night was a box of lightly buttered popcorn, a bag of Twizzlers, some gummy bears, and a Sprite and my sugar and butter rush would have been on fleek. I'd already had the front-row seat. People oohing and aahing and pointing. Cameras clicking. Lights flashing. The paparazzi rushing toward the stage for close-ups. Logan Montgomery, Rich's ratchet mother, snatching Heather by her long, booty-sweeping ponytail and slinging her to the floor, with one red-bottomed heel pressed down on Heather's neck, her arm extended back, hand in a closed fist—ready to punch ole Miss Heather's eyeballs in.

Ooh wee, *yass!* It was pandemonium at its best. I loved it. You should have seen the caption in the next day's news:

FIRST LADY OF HIP-HOP, WIFE OF HIP-HOP MOGUL RICHARD MONTGOMERY, AKA THE LEGENDARY M.C. WICKEDNESS, READY TO KNUCKLE UP IN A BIRTHDAY BRAWL WITH TEEN REALITY-TV STAR AT DAUGHTER'S 17TH BIRTHDAY BASH!

Ooooh, *yassss, yasss!* The scene that unfolded before everyone's eyes that night was a delicious sight. I couldn't wait to get home so I could sit back and light up one of my cherry-flavored hookah pens and sip a chocolate martini while I watched the videos that had been splattered all over social media. Rich's mom's—with her ole roguish self—had gone viral. And the slow-motion versions of Rich hitting the floor with sound effects were ridiculously hilarious.

Kitty huffed. "Are you that dense, Spencer?" she asked, yanking me from my reverie. "Have you not been following her? It's all over the blogs."

I shrugged. "I don't care enough to want to know," I lied. "Heather and I aren't friends anymore. She turned her back on me. Gave *me*—the one who'd been the most loving and kind to her—her precious booty cheeks to kiss, the ones *I* paid for."

Kitty sighed. "Oh, Spencer, get over it. Be thankful you were able to give back to the flat-assed and less fortunate. It was a charitable act, a tax write-off. So woman up! Stop quivering over a few measly coins and count your blessings, darling. You gave that wretched girl hope. A new lease on life, a reason to carry on.

"See," Kitty continued, picking up her cell phone and punching in her password, "that's what happens when drunkards spawn children. They give birth to a generation of churlish, unruly demons. And Heather Cummings is just that—a wild, heathenish, attention-whore; just like her mother, Camille, had been all those many years ago, when the world cared enough about her once-glorious movie career. Now look at her. A woman who spends her days and nights wearing sheer nightgowns and six-inch mules with a bottle in one hand, a cigarette in the other, and an Oscar covered in dust and cobwebs on the mantelpiece. She's an old, dusty relic, Spencer dear. So don't harbor ill will toward her daughter. Heather is who she is thanks to her drunken mammy and her invisible daddy.

The poor girl is broken. And you should never kick a wounded bird in the neck when it's already down."

She dialed Heather's number. The phone rang three times, then went straight to voice mail. Kitty called again and got the same thing. She called a third time, left a scathing voice message. Then called again.

"This stinking troll," she hissed. "I know the little tramp is ducking my calls, but I will drag her by her edges and roast her on an open pit the moment I lay eyes on her. I. Am. Not. The. One. I will destroy what little career the junkie twit might *think* she has."

I rolled my eyes.

Kitty could be real stalkerish, almost cuckoo-crazy with intent when she sank her teeth into something she wanted. The media mogul hadn't become a worldwide brand by putting up with shenanigans. No. She'd gotten to the proverbial top by slicing throats and chopping off heads. And sleeping with a few dirty old men—but I'm not messy and I don't gossip, so moving along. Heeheehee. But, anyway... I wanted to be the one to hand her the hatchet and watch her hacksaw Heather's scalp clean off her head.

But wait...

"Camille, Kitty here," I heard her say as I poured myself a glass of orange juice. I took a sip, then plucked two large strawberries from a ceramic bowl on the table in the breakfast nook. I bit into the delicious fruit, then swiped my tongue over my lips to catch its sweet juices. My body shook. And I felt—

"I don't know what kind of games that tricked-out daughter of yours is pulling," Kitty continued, "but she's not answering her phone. And now neither are you. It's about seven-oh-one in the morning. I do hope you're not somewhere drunk and drooling. But, anyway, I need you and Heather at my office today. This afternoon. Three p.m., *sharp!* Not three-oh-one, not three-oh-two. Three p.m. Got it? Now get up. Wring out your liver. Fluff your hair. Powder your pasty cheeks. And get your-self in gear! I've already invested too much of my time and my goddamn coins on Heather. And, my darling Camille, know this: I will *not* keep sponsoring some slutty wild child. I already have one of my own."

What the—

Slutty? Wild?

Moi?

Oh, how dare she!

I plucked another strawberry and popped it in my mouth, then sashayed over toward Kitty and tossed my orange juice in her face.

2

London

Fine, fly, and forever fabulous...

That was the mantra I'd lived by for most of my life. I'd lived and breathed it. And in my mind's eye, that was what I used to be. Or at least what I thought I was. Because I'd been told that I had to be. That it was expected of me. So I embraced the lie.

And yet no matter how many times I repeated those words, no matter how many times they spun around in my head, until I finally thought I believed every word, it was still never enough. I'd still feel like there was something missing. And then the lights came on, and I began to see my life clearly for the very first time. Everything I thought I was, everything I pretended to be...it was all make-believe. I'd been pretending to be something I didn't feel and didn't believe.

And still I walked European runways and through the marbled halls of my elite school with my head held high, back straight, pelvis thrust, one foot in front of the other, poised and ready. Always ready.

My mother, Jade Phillips—yeah, *that* Jade Phillips. Re-

nowned supermodel. Yeah, her. Anyway, she'd drill into my
head from when I was a little girl that a girl had to always stay
ready. Be ready to snatch the moment. The spotlight. The
click of the camera. And she'd taught me, very well, how to
live the illusion, how to *be* the illusion.

Fine, fly, and forever fabulous...

At that moment, my phone rang.

I stared at the screen for a second, then pressed IGNORE. It
was Spencer. Why on earth would Spencer Ellington be calling me? That girl loathed me. And I wasn't any fan of hers either.
She was as cunning and sly as she was crazy. And someone I
would never, *ever*, trust.

From the moment I stepped foot into Hollywood High,
Spencer and I hadn't seen eye to eye. She was too obsessed
with Rich and hated the fact that Rich and I had been close
friends—for a very short while. Until that meddling *bish*,
Spencer, ruined it.

I'd had Rich wrapped around my manicured fingers, and
Spencer couldn't stand it. She'd be somewhere lurking, always in Rich's ear, filling her pumpkin head up with lies and
speculations. Okay, well, maybe not all lies. Well, okay, okay.
There'd been no lies told. But I hadn't been all that forth-
right with Rich either.

But heck—neither had she.

This was Hollywood, for Christ's sakes. Everyone was dis-
honest and disloyal to a fault. Tinseltown was wrapped in the
glitter of lies and deceit and illusions of happily-ever-after.

A minute later, my phone beeped. A message. I sighed,
rolling my eyes. But decided to replay it anyway.

Spencer's voice blared through my speakers, nearly piercing my eardrums. "*Lonnnnnn*don. Ohhh, *Lonnnnnn*don. I
know you saw me calling you. Is that your hearse in front of
me, driving like three-point-five miles a minute? Where are
you off to now, the cemetery? Do you have another playdate
with the grim reaper?"

I held my breath.

"Godjeezus! You're so dang ugly, London. A travesty. A—"

A horn blew. Then Spencer yelled obscenities at whomever had wronged her on the road. "Anyway, back to you, troll doll. Tell your driver I said pull onto the side of the road and let a real driver show him how it's done. Oooh, Miss Low Money... Little Miss Broke Down Girl, I can't wait to catch you slipping again so I can claw your eye sockets out."

Click.

I pressed DELETE, hung up, and exhaled.

Seconds later, a black, two-door Bentley coupe, with pink interior, sped by in the lane for traffic going in the opposite direction, horn blaring as it swerved, then cut in front of us. The last thing I saw before the car disappeared was the back of Spencer's license plate.

KISS IT.

Now, I knew I had my own issues, which I was happily working on in therapy. My therapist, Dr. Kickaloo, was *every*-thing. She was showing me how to heal *me*, how to like me—and, most importantly, how to love me. And I knew I still had a lot more work to do.

But, baby, *mmmph*. Spencer needed a permanent stay in a padded room. She was straitjacket cuckoo. I just didn't quite understand how no one else saw it, except me.

Here was the weird thing. Spencer had been the only one who'd been there for me at the lowest point of my life, when I'd felt broken. When everything inside of me had cracked open.

God, what had I been thinking? Attempting suicide had been the craziest thing I'd ever done. And yes, that was a to-tally reckless and insensitive thing to do. But at that unbear-able moment, I'd felt like I'd had no other way out of all of my hurt. I'd felt trapped. And all I'd wanted at that time was an easy escape. But what I really needed was for someone to listen, to hear me. And, for once, really see *me*.

London Elona Phillips.

Not the illusion.

Not the mink lashes and hair extensions.

Not the model on runways.

Not the face on fashion magazine covers or print ads.

Not the designer clothes and expensive handbags and heels.

Just *me*.

A teenage girl who wanted acceptance and love and friendships, who wanted to fit in and belong. A teenage girl who still yearned for her mother's arms wrapped lovingly around her and craved her father's attention. A teenage girl who was flawed, who struggled with body image and weight issues, and yet had dreams and fantasies of being swept up in romance.

I was all of those things.

And all I'd ever wanted was for people around me to see me for me. But what I hadn't known then that I knew now was, all I ever really needed to do was open my eyes and really look at the girl staring back at me. I'd been right there, all along.

I looked out the window, suddenly thinking about Rich. Part of me still hoped that maybe, one day, she and I wouldn't be estranged, that we'd both discover a new way of being friends again. Although I really didn't know how that would work out since she was now dating my ex. My past. My worst mistake. The boy I'd kept hidden from my parents and the world, the boy who had been my secret love for almost three years of my life.

Justice Banks.

The two of them—long story—were now all hot and heavy. At first, I'd been devastated. Hurt. That he'd dumped *me* for her. I'd driven myself nearly insane trying to figure out what it was that she'd had that I didn't. But in the end, it never really mattered. What mattered then, and mattered now, was that he didn't want me. So I had to learn to let him go. I had to stop obsessing over him and holding onto his lies and his abuse and all of his broken promises and just let it all go.

Whew. It wasn't easy. But now I can see the two of them together in a magazine or read about them on social media and not break down in tears. I haven't seen them together publicly yet, so who knows how I'll be then. But for right now, I'm no longer pissed at Rich, envious of her, for having what I thought should have been mine.

So whatever.

The so-called Pampered Princesses of Hollywood High were all in shambles. And from where I was sitting, Rich Montgomery was the biggest mess of us all. But she couldn't see that. And maybe she never would. Whatever. Not my problem. I had to keep my focus on what I wanted my life to look like, not anyone else's.

I settled into the backseat of the chauffeur-driven Benz and scrolled through my newsfeeds. So far, there was nothing exciting or worthy of my interest happening in Twitterland or on Snapchat. The blogs were all atwitter with the news that Heather had been spotted giving an impromptu concert in the middle of the street as she was caught coming out of some ghetto-hood studio with a blunt and a forty-ounce. The gossip sites and tabloids had speculated that Heather was backsliding quicker than a California mudslide. And they were all probably right.

Repulsed, I clicked into *Come Get This Tea*, a teen blog site that had all the dirty deeds of any-and-every-body who was somebody in the world.

My lashes fluttered. I narrowed my eyes as one caption caught my attention. I scrolled on in the story...in...utter disgust as I read.

The Bad Girl of hip-hop royalty, Rich Montgomery, seems to have been bitten by the green-eyed monster we all know as jealousy. Yaaaas, my little chickadees, yasss. The boom-bop-and-drop-don't-stop-get-it-get-it party girl, in all of her exquisite jewels and Parisian couture, was seen late last night, during the bewitching hour, being dragged out of her mouthwatering beau's Manhattan Beach condo by men in blue, yelling out obscenities and making threats of violence toward anyone she catches the hunky heartthrob looking at.

A source noted that Rich and the bare-chested lounge-singing R&B crooner were spotted struggling in the hallway over a cell phone. The couple could be heard arguing over his Facebook account, with Rich demanding access to his webpage and accusing him of giving all of his stud-boy eggplant to someone else.

The anonymous source reported that the Brooklyn transplant tried to flee from Rich's tirade. The source alleges Rich Montgomery clawed at her lover's face during the 1:00 a.m. altercation and he'd mushed her. Police were called, but so far no charges have been filed.

Fighting over Facebook? What's next, busting windows out his car? Oh, wait. She's done that already, too. Can we say, psycho lover?

A check this morning of the love-crazed Turn Up girl's Twitter and Facebook pages revealed posts of a girl madly in love without a care in the world. So tell me, my sweet chickadees . . . what's love got to do with it?

Suddenly Justice's voice haunted my headspace. "...*you dumber than dumb, yo. Real spit, London...you don't love me. You don't even love ya'self...You crazy, London...You make me sick, yo...you so effen worthless, yo...Pig. Hog... wit' ya ugly self. You insecure. Fat. Nasty...stupid-azz trick... Look at you, six-foot-tall giraffe-neck self. Big-foot amazon. Don't nobody want you. I was the best thing you'll ever have...*"

I grimaced. What a nightmare it had been being with him, trying to love him. Sadly, I'd almost believed his every word. Almost.

I took a deep breath and shook his foiled attempts at trying to brainwash me from my thoughts, clicking out of the blog's browser before shoving my phone back into my handbag as my driver turned into the entrance for Hollywood High.

I ran a hand along the nape of my stylishly tapered hair, then took my hand and swept my bangs from out of my eye. Long gone were the weaves and hair extensions. These days, the new me embraced a short, sassy do.

Deep in thought, I stared out the back seat window, taking in the campus's beautiful scenery. The grounds were immaculate. On the outside, the world looked calm, and all was right.

My driver neared the school's circular drop-off area.

And then I saw *her*.

Rich.

Standing up at a podium—hair done, face done, in her sparkly jewels and all of her fabulousness. And then went the flash of several zealous photographers' cameras, momentarily blinding her. But Rich kept smiling, as though everything in her world was picture-perfect.

The driver stopped where the red carpet met the curb, and I waited.

Moments later, the car door swung open, and I stepped out.

"London! London! Over here, beautiful!"

In a flash, the attention flew from Rich to me. All the paparazzi were shouting for me, wanting me to turn in their direction.

"What are your thoughts on Heather Cummings's latest iTunes hit, *Hoes Gone Wild?*"

I shrugged. "She is what she sings."

"London! Over here, darling!"

"Is there another catfight brewing between you and Spencer Ellington?" one of the paps barked.

I tossed my bangs. "Only if she strikes first," I replied, allowing the handle of my one-of-a-kind Dior handbag to drop into the crook of my arm.

"What about you and Rich? Will the two of you ever make up and be besties again?"

At that moment, my eyes caught Rich's. I forced a smile, tossing my bangs again, and strutting up the red carpet as though it were a runway. She returned a fake smile of her own. And then the cameras clicked.

3

Rich

Click!
Flash!

"Your thoughts on the state of the Pampered Princesses, Rich!" said a reporter from *Glamdalous* magazine as she turned her back to London and faced me.

Click!
Flash!

"Everyone wants to know!" shouted a *Ni-Ni Girlz*'s correspondent. "Will you, Spencer, London, and Heather ever be friends again?"

I blinked.

Blinked again.

Then shivered and gripped the sides of my dazzling pink podium, making a daunting attempt not to step out of these six-inch, cobra skin, red bottoms, take off my diamond hoops, and beat these raggedy reporters to the ground! 'Cause I know freakin' well these silly tricks didn't just click and flash all over that bald-headed bird London *and then* turn to me.

Like I was nothing.

Sloppy seconds.

Something to be dismissed, then picked up when London, scratch that, when Leyoncé was done with them.

Oh, hell to the no! Never to the not!

I am *the* Rich Gabrielle Montgomery! Socialite. Role model. Fashionista. Made of brown sugar, locker room magic, black glitter, and gold!

Hip-hop royalty!

Bluer blood than Blue Ivy.

Better direction than North West.

From the loins of all loins.

The DNA of hood style and street grace.

A unicorn, baby!

My mother, Logan Montgomery, née Shakeesha Gatling, is the fearless leader of *all* the groupies. Better game than Blac Chyna, Amber Rose, or Melania Trump could ever dream to play. Hailed from the streets of Watts to backstage after backstage after backstage, until she laid and slayed my daddy— hip-hop sire turned founder and CEO of Grand Records, M.C. Wickedness, better known as Richard Montgomery Senior. All of which makes me a what? A who?

Well, I'll tell you: the seventeen-year-old queen of these Pampered Princesses, baby!

El lady of these Hollywood streets.

Boom!

Bam!

Snap, snap!

And *these* reporters that *I* called here better recognize and put some *respeck* on it!

Gon' talk to London *and then* speak to me!

I don't think so.

Do they not see that London's freak-wear is overrated, outdated, and straight from The Gap? And that my hot pink D&G blazer with my personal crest (an embroidered music note with a blingin' tiara on it, centered on the left breast pocket), Gucci wife beater, and navy-blue Secret Circus jeans, has bodied every tramp on *this* scene.

Plus,

I got a ring on it.

London is man hungry. Parched mouth. And thirsty.

I'm well rounded.

She's insecure. Unsure.

I have edges.

Her dome is a half globe.

You see where I'm goin' with this?

Zero comparison between Lon*dog* and me.

But you know what...

Inhale.

Exhale.

I'ma be the bigger person and let it go.

'Cause clearly Satan is trying to bring the Petty LaBelle out of me.

However.

Don't sleep.

Though I may worship in the church of Love-and-kindness, I ain't Jesus.

He forgives.

I don't.

I batted my extended lashes, cleared my throat, and forced another smile to bloom onto my round face. Then I curved my right hand over my button brown eyes, and looked out and into the sea of paparazzi gawking at me. "What is that I hear on the wire, honey? Will I partake in a friendship with whom? With what? Chile, cheese! Boo, please! Clutchin' pearls!" I paused and took them in again. "Did you all miss the memo?"

Before any of them could answer, I turned to the left, where the vice president of my red-carpet committee stood. "Clara, will you let the people know that I no longer discuss tacky and ill-mannered hoes. That I have turned over a new

freakin' leaf, and all I want around me is positivity. That the
new Rich is all about balance and synthetic energy. Puhlease,
make the people aware of my new and improved malnutri-
tion."

"It's mantra, Rich," Clara whispered.

I gritted my teeth. "That's your problem, Clara. You stay
reachin', these people don't speak French." I pulled in a
deep breath. Pushed it out. "Know what, I'll speak for myself." I flipped my fabulous mane of thirty-two-inch, grade
8A, Malaysian kinky curl over my shoulders, and said to the
paps, "I have called you here to denounce a *Trashy Teen
Trend*'s headline, where they have come for my throat, again.
This time by saying that washed-up and cracked-out Heather
Cummings is my sister."

"Well, Rich," a *Vogue'alicious* reporter jumped in, "we
have all seen the video of Heather giving one of her infamous
and impromptu concerts at your birthday party, where she
delivered this information on the mic. What do you have to
say about that? What does your father have to say about
that?"

The hairs on the back of my neck pricked. I shoved both
hands up on my hips and spat, "Lies and deceit! How dare
you drag my upstanding daddy into this! Have you seen
Heather's mother, that musty dragon! Mmmph, before she
and Heather go around spreading lies, tell Camille Cummings
I said to step her slut level up, 'cause my daddy doesn't do low
budget or curbside!"

The *Vogue'alicious* reporter continued, "But you're not
saying no. Which means there's a possibility?"

"Didn't I just tell your whack azz?" I paused.

Breathe, queen, breathe.

My eyes scanned the crowd, then settled on London, who
posed in the center of the red carpet, with her chin held up
and one long foot in front of the other, like she awaited
drum rolls, rose petals, and a serenade.

Our eyes locked, and Londumb took her big mouth and smiled. It took everything in me—or, better yet, out of me—not to jump over this podium and stomp out her gag reflexes. The only reason why I didn't leap was because today's media marquee was to be my statement about how Heather played herself at my party, and how *Trashy Teen Trend* needed to stop coming for me. Therefore, *moi* was not about to give another ounce of my shine to this self-absorbed and deranged amazon.

I took my right hand and brushed invisible dust from my shoulder.

London's smile grew wider. Then she hit me with a small wave.

Deep breath in.

Deep breath out.

I returned my attention to the *Vogue'alicious* reporter and said, "Looka here, homie. I'm trying to get my kind lady on, but you're working my nerves.

"Now, check this: All of y'all need to hear me, and hear me well. My daddy, Richard Montgomery Senior, may be a gigantic-energizer-Romeo, but I can assure you that that over-the-rainbow, vile, sloppy spawn of a drunk, Heather, who shall remain nameless, is not one of my daddy's bastard by-products. Now tell Camille I said to call Maury and try again. Moving on, as I—"

"Rich!" The *Glamdalous* reporter interrupted me, "Tell us what happened the other night when you and JB got into one of your wicked fights! The police were called. Sources say you were arrested. Can you confirm or deny?"

Breathe.

Breathe.

Breathe.

I snapped, "Lies!" I peered at London and did my best to burn a hole through her face. "*My baby, my man, my lover, my trick daddy* and I have never been better." I blessed her with a sinister smile, then looked over to the reporter and said, "And *anyway*, why are you all up in *my* crotch life?"

The reporter continued, "A source close to you says that, in fact, there *was* a fight, that you *were* arrested, and that you're fully aware JB is no good for you, but you're too busy, and I quote, 'being a low-self-esteem, Jenny Craig dissin', buffalo wing eatin', beer drinking, trashy ball-eater' to better yourself."

My mouth fell open.

The blood in my face boiled.

My warm chocolate cheeks turned beet red.

There were a few gigglers in the crowd, and London had the nerve to be one of them! I zoomed in on her face. "Excuse, you, *Londog*? You find that funny? A second ago, I thought perhaps milk-mouth Spencer had flapped her Saturday night special. But maybe it was you, witcha jealous self. Always hatin'! Gon' pull up in a stretch, like it's prom time—girl, please! I swear this pampered ho wears me out! First, the suicide mission for attention, now this!"

London stepped closer to the podium. She was now a hair away. "Let me tell you something, I know you're out here trying to impress these reporters with your low-grade church basement Easter speech—!"

"Not today, Satan." I slammed my hand into the podium. "Not. To. Day."

The reporters' cameras clicked and flashed as they buzzed about, vying for the best angle of our dead-heat.

I couldn't believe this. Destroying Heather was to be the new headline. The social media sites and magazines had already covered me dragging London—once in Heather's driveway, another time in Club Tantrum, and the last time out of her deathbed to the grave...well, almost. At least I was about to, until the original ball-guzzler, my ex-ex-ex-ex-BFF, Spencer, got involved...long story. But you get the point, me beatin' down London was old news.

London pointed her extra-long index finger into my face, and her hot gaze lit into me. "First of all, ghetto-tramp, I don't even *think* about you, let alone waste my time *talking* about you. You're not worth my breath."

I plucked London's finger out of my face and spat, "Don't get deep fried and slapped, hooker!" I took my earrings off and laid them on the podium. "For the last few months, you been on the sick and shut in list, and now you wanna come for me? Girl, I will clothesline the life out of you, again!"

London didn't bat an eye. "Oh, puhlease, spare me, what you need to do is clothesline the life out of that beer-belly muffin top hanging over your pants!"

Beer belly muffin top?! "Chile, cheese! At least I eat. Something you should try! Instead of pouring your guts in the toilet, you need to take your stitched-up wrists, pick up a fork, and practice holding down a meal. Or are you still enslaved to an IV drip?!" I paused, giving her a moment to soak that in. Then I popped my fingers in her face and continued, "And *attention whore?* Who's more of an attention whore than you?!"

"Your mother!"

"My mother—"

London's chiseled chin was practically midway to my nose, as she snaked her neck, looked down at me, and said, "You *heard me*, your mother, Shakeesha Slut-Bucket Gatling!"

Hell no, she didn't!

I pushed up the sleeves of my blazer and stepped out of my heels, dropping six inches. London towered over me, but I didn't give a damn. I stepped deeper into her space and said, "Let me get you together, son. Don't you worry about my mother; worry about that raggedy, runway tramp of an egg donor you got, Miss Orphan! Your mother doesn't even like you, and last I heard, she absolutely couldn't stand your fat and funky father!"

London snapped, "If he's fat and funky, he got it from your mother when he was snappin' her legs back!"

Oh, hell no! Lies and deceit! My mother would never sleep with a bearilla like Turner Phillips! Not when she has the king of all kings, my daddy, spread across her sheets!

I took a step back, lifted my fist into the air, and just as I was about to hook this ho into another time zone, somebody caught my hand and yanked me around.

Westwick!

"*Rich Montgomery!*" he shouted, his eyes blazing and his mouth clenched. He stood in between London and me. "*Stop this madness this instant!*" he yelled. He tugged at the hem of his suit jacket, yanking invisible wrinkles out. "I'm so sick of you dragging the good name of this institution down!"

Mr. Westwick pointed into my face, his jaw clenched. "How dare you even have a press conference after I specifically told you last week that there'd be no further 'red carpet' events. Hollywood High Academy was built on intelligence, elegance, refinement, and pride. Not hood-bugger theatrics! This is a fine institution, not Skeezerville High! Yet you are single-handedly turning it into a pigeon's nest with one beak-brawl after the next! We have become the laughingstock of the educational community. I told you this was to be no more!"

I sucked my teeth and parked my neck to the left. "Excuse you, but I have a duty to inform the community—!"

He gave a snort and shook his finger in my face. "Inform the what? The community? How about this, since you wanna inform the community. How about we let the good people know how you are dumber than all the doorknobs Spencer Ellington keeps in her mouth! That your IQ is lower than Heather Cummings's bank account, and that if it were not for your parents' black card you'd be in high school longer than London Phillips wants to be alive.

"Now get your things, and let's go! These shenanigans are *over! Done! Finished!*" He snatched London and me by our wrists, forcing her to high-step and almost trip and me to stumble barefoot up the steps, leaving behind my shoes, my earrings, and the media's camera clicks.

4

London

"**M**r. Westwick, why am I here?" I asked, narrowing my eyes. I was annoyed. Very, very annoyed. And it was taking everything in me to remember my manners and bite my tongue. He had had me in his office with the door shut for the last ten minutes, sitting in one of the leather chairs situated in front of his desk.

Staring me down.

He straightened his paisley ascot, his gaze piercing through me as he pursed his lips, then clasped his hands together. "Well, let's see, here, Miss Phillips, Miss Rambo Ratchet. *Why* are you here?" He cleared his throat. "If memory serves me correctly, you are here because you are weak and incompetent. You are here because you lack direction and sensibility. You, Miss Phillips, are here because you can't seem to keep your ghetto antics at home . . . where they belong."

I blinked. How dare he!

I huffed. "I'm not *ghetto*. And I'm definitely *not* ratchet, either. Wrong girl. Try again."

"Oh, no, Miss Flop Tart. I have the right girl, all right. And the only thing you're trying is my patience."

I sucked my teeth. "I didn't do anything wrong."

He snorted. "And therein lies problem *numero uno:* denial. Should I dial the Jesus Network to lay hands on you, to heal you from your waywardness—now or later? Or should I request a lifeline to hell for you? You're not living in reality, London. And since you want to backtalk, that'll be another ten grand—a discount, no less—for—"

"*Ten grand?*" I shrieked, giving him an incredulous look. Mr. Westwick was such a crook. He was always trying to squeeze hard-working taxpayers out of money with his dumb fines. There was a fine for being late—aka late fees. A fine for being disruptive—a disruptive tax fee, as he called it. A fine for sneezing—a clean air tax fee. A fine for this, a fine for that—fines, fines, fines, and more fines.

He squinted at me for a moment, then scowled. "Yes. *Ten. Grand.* That's a ten with a comma followed by three zeroes."

"For *what?*"

"For waking up this morning, then coming to school with the intention of creating a disturbance. Umm, let's see. For looking lost and lonely and being desperate for friends. What, your mommy didn't give you enough hugs? She didn't nurse you properly? Is that it, London? What, you have attachment issues? Abandonment issues?"

I blinked again. "How dare you," I snapped, "disrespect *me.*" I stood to my feet. "I will not sit here and be insulted or ridiculed by you or anyone else. I've done nothing but be respectful to you, Mr. Westwick. And yet you try to offend me at every turn. My parents—"

"Your parents aren't even together, Little Miss Orphan Annie, so sit your little hot box back in that chair or find yourself tossed out of the building on your forehead."

I blinked, taken aback by his remarks. They stung.

"Oh, what? You think I don't read the gossip mags? You think all I do all day is sit around and be fabulous? No, Miss Phillips...I sit around being fabulous, reigning over one of the country's most prestigious schools, while staying abreast of all current events—the real, the raw, and the trashy."

I rolled my eyes, sinking back onto my seat. I angrily folded my arms over my chest. "Fine. But you don't have to disrespect me."

"No, little girl," he retorted, reaching over his desk and extending an arm out, putting one of his pudgy hands up like a stop sign, mere inches from my face. "*You* don't have to disrespect yourself!" He plopped his butt back in his chair and slammed his hand down on his desk. "But all you do is disregard Hollywood High's policy on etiquette and social grace. I keep warning you, Miss Phillips, that I will not tolerate your antics up on this campus. I'm not playing out here in these streets, Miss Phillips. And yet you continue to test me. You continue to be defiant and belligerent. Being aggressive and inciting a riot on school grounds is grounds for suspension—no, expulsion. And criminal char—"

"*A riot?*"

"Yes. You heard me. R-I-O-T, riot! And I will not stand for it."

"Are you *frickin'* kidding me?"

"Watch your tone and your language, Miss Phillips. Better yet, that's going to cost you another ten thousand dollars—for using aggressive language."

My nose flared. "This is bull crap, Mr. Westwick."

"Make that another five grand," he snapped, snatching open his desk drawer and pulling out a digital calculator. He began punching in numbers, his stumpy fingers quickly moving over the keys. "You're racking up a nice bill, London Phillips. Shall I run Daddy's black card now, or just keep a tab going?"

I *tsked*. "This is so not fair, Mr. Westwick. And you know it."

"No, Miss Phillips. What I know is that you are a disgrace to your parents, your peers, your headmaster, and this fine institution. Hollywood High was built on the principles of class, sophistication, honor, and integrity. And you and that

Rich Montgomery have done nothing but drag down this school's reputation with all of your hood-boogie shenanigans."

He gave me a stern look, raising one of his bushy eyebrows. He tilted his head. "Go 'head. Say something so I can tack on another fine. Your disrespect for my authority is appalling. And, quite frankly, Miss Phillips, I'm a split second from having you hauled off in handcuffs..."

I felt a flash of anger. "*Handcuffs?*"

"Yes. H-A-N-D-C-U-F-F-S. You do know what they are, don't you? Silver wristlets. Seems like that's the only way you little ruffians in heels learn—in shackles and restraints."

I gasped. "Are you serious right now?"

"Oh, I'm 'bout as serious as a bad case of herpes."

I huffed, shifting in my seat. "Fine. I'll just sit here and keep my mouth shut. Let you do *alllll* the talking. It's your world, Mr. Westwick."

Mr. Westwick suddenly smiled. "Good answer. Now we're finally getting somewhere." He reached into his top drawer and pulled out a compact mirror, then flipped it open. "You know, Miss Phillips, it hurts me to say this"—he reached for what looked like a tiny toothbrush and started brushing his eyebrows—"but I'm utterly disappointed and ashamed for you..." He peered over the mirror and eyed me. "I thought you had better sense than trying to associate yourself with the likes of Rich Montgomery. I'd thought you'd learned from the last time she shunned you. She dragged your name through the toilets every chance she got, has wished you nothing but ill will, and still you grovel for her friendship."

"I do no such thing," I stated defensively, my voice not nearly as convincing as I hoped. I swallowed hard and turned my head and glanced around the office as I fumbled with the tangle of pearls at my throat.

Mr. Westwick laughed, bringing my gaze back to his. "And

there goes that nasty denial thing again. You're drowning in it, Miss Phillips. Deny, deny, den*iiiiii...al*. Have you no shame? No dignity? Rich Montgomery is a disgrace to this institution. She's a prime example of what a cheap motel on two feet looks like. She's the triple T's..."

I gave him a perplexed look, but said nothing.

"Trifling, trashy, and trouble," he continued, snapping his compact shut. "I pride myself on maintaining the upmost discretion when it comes to the students here at Hollywood High, but Rich Montgomery is the walking definition of classless. And the human billboard for what sloppy seconds looks like. And you want to be friends with *that?* You're walking around here crying, slinging snot, and wringing your hands, to be embraced by some reckless little floozie."

My eyes widened. I opened my mouth to say something, but then quickly shut it, deciding it was best not to add any more fuel to his already lit fire.

Mr. Westwick gave me a deadpan stare. Then he shook his head. "Why on earth would you want to be linked to *that?* I mean. I understand your self-esteem is low and your self-worth is nonexistent, but that still doesn't excuse your choice in peers, Miss Phillips. Rich Montgomery is going nowhere fast. She's a pink helmet special. She's the black Honey Boo Boo of the *ghet...toe* with the IQ of an army ant. She's borderline crazy. And she's hotter than a hot chili pepper. And would you like to know what they say about her on the men's—I mean, boys'—locker room walls?"

"I—"

"Well, I'll tell you," he said, cutting me off. "They say she's better than an Easy Bake oven. Always hot, always ready, always easy to stuff. Is this the type of girl you want to be associated with, huh, Miss Phillips? Some whorish little troll?"

I shrugged. "Rich and I are no longer friends," I finally said, moving my bangs to the side and staring directly at him.

Everything he was saying was true. And yet, for some reason, I almost wanted to take up for her. Almost. I knew enough to know that Rich would never return the courtesy. I owed her nothing. So I said *nothing*.

Mr. Westwick grunted. "*Mmmph*. Lucky you. Count your blessings and get on with your life, Miss Phillips. There's still hope for you. I mean—of course, we all know you've failed at being the next top supermodel, so there's no need for the world to relive that epic fail all over again. But at least you can, hopefully, make an honest living wearing a black smock at some makeup counter popping pimples and applying concealer in one of the local department stores."

"*Excuse* you?" I snapped incredulously. "I'm not *ever* going to be standing on my feet applying makeup to anyone's face or cleaning out some woman's pus pockets. A counter girl is *not* what I aspire to be."

He chortled. "And you're obviously not aspiring to upgrade the company you keep either, Miss Phillips. So let me give you some friendly advice: Pick a side. Either toe the line or get towed out of here. You're ice-skating on some very thin ice, young lady. So let me help you save yourself from another white coat visit."

He wrote out a pass, then slid it over the desk toward me. "Stay. Away. From. Rich Montgomery. Or suffer the consequences." He raised a brow. "Do I make myself clear?"

I reached for the pass and nodded. "Yes. *Very.*"

"Good." Mr. Westwick stood to his feet and whisked around his desk, then sat on its edge, crossing his feet at the ankles. He ran his hands through his thick, blond man weave. Or maybe it was a man wig. Whatever it was, from the neck up, it made him look like a fifty-five-year-old version of Justin Bieber.

I stood to my feet as Mr. Westwick eyed me.

"I trust we won't have to have this conversation again, Miss Phillips. Will we?"

I rolled my eyes and gave him a tight smile. "Absolutely not."

"Good, Miss Phillips." Mr. Westwick squinted at me. Then he lifted himself from his desk and sashayed toward the door, swinging it open. "Now get your snooty butt out of my office."

5

Heather

10:30 a.m.

Calculus.
I was thirty minutes late.

The classroom was packed.

Though I usually sat *waaaaay* in the back, tucked away in the cut, some powder-face Goth chick had plopped her Dracula-ass in my seat. And if that wasn't bad enough, she took her coal-black bravado, looked at me, and smiled.

I shot her the finger. And begrudgingly took the only seat left, in the front row, directly before Mrs. James, who pursed her lips into a tight frown, then leaned against her mahogany bureau, and unleashed, "Class, if you desire to be something in this life, you must learn to be on time and show up for your success."

Whatever.

I wasn't about to give this old bird the pleasure of me flipping out, just so she could command me to Westwick's dungeon.

Screw her. And screw him too!

Instead, I looked straight ahead, stared out of one of the floor-to-ceiling windows that framed Mrs. James's desk, and watched the fresh raindrops hit the glass, then melt away.

Besides, this was all bullshit anyway.

This class.

This subject.

This school.

Dreams.

Sweetness.

Memories.

Love.

Sobriety.

Parents.

Friendships.

Second chances.

All. Of. It.

Bull. Shit.

You know what's real?

Time.

And no, time doesn't heal all wounds. That's a widespread lie. Like the tagline of some priest granting you forgiveness, it sounds good, but it don't mean nothin'.

Time is gangster.

Thorough.

Boss.

Time has no time.

It ain't gon' stop and wait. Or give you a minute to catch your breath, to think, or to see how you can redo a moment and make a new memory.

You gon' have to take whatever time gives you, and that's it. 'Cause it don't rewind. Otherwise, I'd jet back a year and never let anybody drag me off my hit Wu-Wu Tanner television show.

Revert eight months and be a ride or die for the Luda Tutor comedy series, instead of letting Disney snatch the role from me, all because I had a tiny little skittles party that ended with a paddy wagon ride to jail.

Summersault back six months, and instead of dropping two number one iTune hits, I'd slam 'em wit' three.

I'd damn sure fall back two months, two weeks, five days, twelve hours, and thirty-one minutes, to the moment before I met Nikki and never look her way. Never give her a chance to touch my shoulder, line my nervous belly with butterflies, or my cheeks with flushed heat, or hear her say, "...you look pretty...let's take a selfie...my number's in your phone."

Never spend time with her.

Kiss her.

Fall for her.

Share secrets with her.

Long to spend the rest of my life with her.

Never hear her sob, *"Heather! Reporters are all over campus! My family is calling me, demanding that I come home and explain what's going on! My friends are questioning me! Why would you do this to me?!"*

"I didn't do anything!"

"Liar! You did! How else would the blogs and everybody know what we've been doing...when it was only the two of us! I'm finished with you!"

I wouldn't go through any of that.

I'd make sure Nikki was reduced to my peripheral view— something I could see but really couldn't see, all at the same time. A passing flash, a puff of fading color, worthy of nothing more than a sideway glance.

But.

I gotta deal with the crumbs of the clock. And be a heartbroken, D-list, reality-TV star, owned by the oracle of all things trashy, Kitty Ellington. Who for whatever sick and twisted reason thought it was a good idea to call me at six in the morning and piss on every ounce of my get-right high, by demanding to know why I'd given an "...extemporized concert in the middle of L.A., for free!"

I couldn't believe that pussy came at me all crazy. So I raised my head from my line of crushed Adderall, affectionately known as Black Beauty, sat up in bed, and gave Kitty what she called looking for. I said, "I gave the concert because I goddamn-mother freakin' could, and what?! I gave the concert because that's what I do, give concerts! Didn't nobody stop me. *Ain't nobody* ever gonna stop me. And guess what? When the mood hits me, I'ma do it again, and again. That's why I did it, trick!"

Click.

Five minutes later, as I lay back against my goose-down pillow, being lifted up where I belonged, courtesy of Black Beauty, my mother, Camille, charged into my room. Like she paid the rent. A glass of scotch in her hand, spilling over her fingertips. The hem of her white, see-through nightie swished from side to side, and her matted mink slippers banged into the wood floor with every step she took.

She stopped at the foot of my bed and screamed, "What did you say to Kitty?!"

I blinked—not once, but three times. Then I said, "First of all, did you knock?" I paused, giving her a moment to reflect on her behavior. Then I pointed to the door and continued: "Now you wanna try that again?"

Camille's porcelain-colored face turned blotchy red. She took a sip of her scotch, then said, "I'm in no mood to drag your ungrateful and junkie behind out of that bed and stomp on it. I'll let Kitty do the honors." She took another sip. "I swear, you just don't know when to quit, do you?! Somehow you have managed to piss Kitty off, twice in one week! Now she wants us to report to her office by three o'clock sharp this afternoon! And you had better be there, or else."

Now the "or else" is where Camille and Kitty had me effed up at.

Let me be clear: I didn't do threats.

Furthermore, *if* I decided to make an appearance at the Litter Lounge, aka Kitty's office, neither she nor Camille would see me at three o'clock. Mmmph, maybe at four o'clock. Maybe even four thirty. But three o'clock? Never. 'Cause don't nobody tell me what to do!

"Excuse you, Miss Cummings." Mrs. James called my name, like getting my attention had been a struggle. "Are you going to answer the question or not?"

I hesitated. "What question?"

She pursed her thin lips. "The one on the board, beneath the graph."

I looked at the graph, then scanned the question: Is the graph of $g(y)$ and that of $g(y+2)$ the same?

"No," I said. *Now move along.*

"And why is it different?" Mrs. James asked, clearly just to annoy me.

I took in a deep breath, let it out, and said, "It's not true because the graph of $g(y+2)$ is that of $g(y)$ shifted two units to the left." Then I bugged my eyes, like duh! Mostly because I knew she thought I would get it wrong, but I didn't.

Now she was really pissed, and instead of smiling and calling on me again, like she usually did when a student answered one of her dumb questions correctly, she shot me a soft eye roll, scowled, and said, "Luck was on your side that time. But you need to pay attention."

Bish, please.

I returned Mrs. James's nasty look and she moved on to the next student.

I twisted in my seat.

Then sniffed.

Sniffed again.

Dang, I need some get-right.

No, you don't.

Yes, I do. Just a pinch.

You had some this morning... wait for the afternoon.

Bzzz... bzzz

I reached into my gold-studded black-rabbit clutch and took out my vibrating iPhone. I had five texts. All from Co-Co Ming, my BFF, my main chicka, my homie himself!

His first text read, "WHERE ARE YOU, DIVA? I'M IN THE LIBRARY WAITING FOR YOU."

I looked up at the clock on the wall: 11 a.m.

Dang!

For months now, I'd met Co-Co in the library at 10:45. It was my job to slang to the stoners, who slipped out of class for their daily bag of Lolita, Co-Co's name for his bomb weed sprinkled with dope dust. But ever since things fell apart between me and Nikki, I'd been slippin' on my slangin'.

The second text: "UMM. WHERE ARE YOU? IT'S TIME TO TAKE YOUR POST."

Maybe I can still make it.

I looked at clock again.

11:05.

Too late.

I read the third text: "HO, IZ YOU SERIOUS?"

Ho? Oh, he got me messed up!

Fourth text: "I'M DONE WITH YOU, HO. D TO THE O TO THE N TO THE E. DONE! YOU HAVE PLAYED ME FOR THE LAST TIME!"

Up yours too, Co-Co!

Fifth text: middle finger emoji, followed by, "YOU AIN'T ISH, HEATHER! AND YOU AIN'T GON' NEVER BE ISH! YOU'RE FIRED, TRICK! I DON'T WANT NOR NEED YOU SELLING FOR ME NO MORE! IT'S OVER FOR YOU! LIFE AS YOU KNOW IT HAS BEEN SHUT DOWN, HO!"

Oh, hell no!

Co-Co got me all the way twisted! Wait 'til I see this queen, I'ma get him straight!

He should be in the girls' lounge, counting his money.

"Excuse me, Miss Cummings!" Mrs. James slapped a hand on my desk, snapping me out of my thoughts. "First, you're late, then you're not paying attention to today's lesson, and now you're being outright disrespectful by texting in the middle of my class!"

I've had enough of this tramp!

"Girl, bye!" I stood up.

Mrs. James snapped, "Heather Cummings, sit back down! I did not give you permission to leave!"

I didn't even respond to that. I returned my iPhone to my clutch, then tucked my clutch under my arm, and sashayed out the room. My zebra catsuit clung to my curves, as my Cinderella stilettos clicked against the white marble floor, while my forty-two-inch, silky black, Korean ponytail rustled in the wind, and my ten-thousand-dollar booty bounced, one jiggling cheek at a time!

6

Spencer

"**Y**ou dirty *whore*," Rich hissed the moment I sauntered through Déjeuner Café and slid my booty cheeks onto the plush chair across the table from her. It was fourth period and I was famished, and so not in the mood for Rich's foolery.

I slid my manicured hand over the crisp linen tablecloth and stared at her.

Hard.

Long.

"Don't sit there and give me that dumb look, *trick*," Rich sneered. "I should sling this drink in your face." She slid the straw between her greedy lips and sipped her frothy concoction, then flicked her tongue over her lips to catch the drippings.

She let out an obnoxiously loud, foul-smelling burp. It smelled like sewer. Like skunk booty. Goshdiggitydangit! Rich was so dang uncouth. Rancid. Toxic. But I dared myself still. Refused to flinch, frown, or fuss.

"I swear, Spencer, I don't know why I ever wasted my

whole fabulous life and my entire soul being a good-good friend to you, when all you've ever done is whore and lie and turn your back on me."

Finally, I blinked. Tilted my head. And blinked again. Obviously, the belching twerk queen was having a moment. And right now, all of her moments were colliding together. She clearly needed me to reach over and slap her face. Whap, whap…pow! Slap her right back into reality. But instead, I reached over and laid a hand over hers.

"Umm, Rich. Have you taken your meds today?" I patted her hand. "Do you need another round of shock treatment?"

She yanked her hand away. "I don't *need* treatment. I need to know why you can't ever be what I've been to you— a good, loving friend."

I rolled my eyes up in my head.

She sighed, then licked cocktail sauce from her fingertips. "All my life I've had to fight, Spencer…"

"And you loves Harpo, too. Don't you, Miss Sophia?"

Rich slammed a shrimp down on her plate, her brown orbs widening. "*Harpo?* Who the hell is *Harpo?* How dare you try'n play me! I've never been with…wait. Is that the name of that cute boy with the curly chest hairs I met one night down on the beach?"

"The *beach*," I repeated, surprised. "When were you on the beach with some curly-chest-haired boy?" Rich was such a smut.

"Girl, one night when I was waiting all night for my man to come home"—she reached for her linen napkin and dabbed at her lips—"there was an angel that came down from the sky and comforted me. But that was so two weeks ago." She narrowed her eyes. "And none of your dang business, you nosy troll."

My lips curled into a sly smile. "Oh, another one-night anonymous romp."

"Clutching pearls! I don't do romps, you dingbat! And I don't do one-night stands! I'm a lady, Spencer. I do rendezvous. I do quickies. I do overnighters. I lay down on my back. I don't stand up for nothing! Not even for a night."

I smirked. "Uh-huh. And you'll do anything with a pulse."

"Lies and deceit! Don't get punched in the throat, Spencer. You know who my man is. And you know he is the only man I will ever be true to! I subscribe to the prescription of good loving and being with *one* good man. And Justice fills my prescriptions and satisfies my every need."

I laughed. "Ooh, the trickery. The lies. You can't even spell *one*, Rich."

"Lies and deceit," Rich snapped. "Double you-*ohh*-enn. Won. Now what, slore?"

I snickered and clapped my hands. "Good girl, Rich. Good girl." I scooted my chair back and crossed my legs. "Once again, you've proven my point."

Rich shot me a nasty look. "And what point is that, *Speeeencer?*"

"That you are not the brightest of us all," I said snidely.

Rich pinned me with a hard stare. "*Exaaaactly.* I am not *bright*. I got melanin. Don't do me. And don't try to tear down my skin color. And I'm glad to see you finally know your place. Beneath. *Me.*"

I chuckled, but the old me would have hopped up and slapped her with my flyswatter. But today was a good day, and I wasn't about to let this Jezebel steal my joy.

"Oh, Rich." I shook my head. "Rich, Rich, Rich. Don't flatter yourself, hon. Even if I were a bedsheet, I wouldn't want to be beneath you. You soil easily. And I don't do stains."

"Clutching pearls! *Hooker*, what are you tryna say? I always keep a clean pair of sheets in my travel bag."

"You mean *ho* bag," I corrected over a snicker. "And it's a *set* of sheets, not a pair."

She frowned. "Ohmygod, Spencer. You're such a dumbo, an airhead...but whatever. Your hate for all of my fabulousness is atrocious. Sickening. Embarrassing. Why don't you face it, Spencer: You'll never be me. But I'm sure you'll die trying, so let me get out my black gloves and veil and start working on my eulogy, because it's over for you. You'll be stretched out in your coffin in no time.

"And why are *you* sitting here, all up in my beautiful face, anyway?" Rich continued, not realizing I hadn't made one caustic remark back to her. "Ruining my appetite. I can't be with you hoes. You bobblehead trolls stay testing me."

I dropped my eyes to her almost empty platter of shrimp, jumbo crab cakes, and calamari, then fluttered my gaze back to her as she bit into another shrimp, then swirled it into more sauce.

I pressed my lips together and glanced around the café, taking in the white leather sofas, lava-topped tables, and white-gloved service. *Mmmph.* I took in the table where all the jocks sat, then rolled my eyes when I spotted Corey. Ugh.

I slid my eyes over to the cheerleaders' table right next to theirs. The cheerleaders in their little skimpy skorts were laughing and leaning into someone else's ear, whispering their dirty deeds. Next, I glanced over at the geek squad table, the doofy and the goofy table. Heeheehee.

The café was alive with chaos and chatter.

I slid my hand down into my handbag and pulled out a pair of mother-of-pearl binoculars and peered through them. I grunted out my disgust at the sight of Co-Co Ming, slinking through the café's sliding glass doors donned in a black cat-suit and a pair of silver—what looked to be peep-toe—pumps, along with a pillbox hat atop his little peanut head.

"*Ugh.* Motherofsweetbuttermilk! That wet noodle is a hot mess."

"*Trick,*" Rich hissed. "Who are you stalking now?"

I turned my attention to her and screamed. "Aaah!" I clutched my chest, staring through my binoculars. "Ohmygod, you have a big face," I said, feigning fright. "There should be a law against faces that huge. And your eyeballs! Ohmygod! They look like golf balls."

"Oh, shut up, Spencer," Rich spat. "You birdbrain. And tell me who you were eyeballing through them binoculars."

I sighed, dramatically, removing the binoculars from my face. "Co-Co."

Rich rolled her eyes. "That *thing*. Please. *Next.*" She looked over at him as he talked and laughed and waved his pageant wave at anyone who would pay him attention.

"I see he doesn't have his pet, Heather, with him."

Rich laughed. "She's probably under some rock, drooling."

"Real crackhead-*ish*," I said over a giggle.

Rich snickered. "Yasss, honey, yasss. Real ashy-lipped."

"Hood booger-*ish*."

"Ghetto-tramp-*ish*," she countered.

"Ooh, ooh," I said, excitedly. "Trashy-ratchet-*ish*."

Rich frowned, then narrowed her eyes to thin slits. "That's not nice, Spencer. Talking about Heather like that. You are so dang phony. Two-faced. Heather's done nothing to you for you to drag her like that. I can only imagine what *you* say about *me* behind *my* back."

"Girl, choke on a breath mint," I snapped. "I don't say no more than what you say about *me* behind *mine*. So get over yourself. The only one two-faced is *you*."

Rich pounded her fist on the table, rattling plates and cutlery. "Lies and deceit! I have only one face, trick! The face of fabulousness, and I resent you trying to defile my character and ruin my good name. Wait. Are you coming out for cocktails later? I need to let my hair down and just relax. You know school stresses me out."

I gave her a long, hard stare, then reached over and grabbed her hand. "I can only imagine how stressful failing would be."

She tsked. "Failing? Girl, lies. I stay winning. There's no fails over here."

Blank stare.

"Anyway," she prattled on, "I have *never* talked about you, slore."

"Rich, lies. You—"

"Tramp, can *I* help you?" Rich snapped, cutting me off, her eyes flashing with anger.

I glanced over my shoulder and looked into the face of Rich's new source of agitation. London. Heeheehee.

"Oh, hey, Cruella," I said casually. "Where are your one-hundred-and-one Dalmatians?"

Rich grunted. "*Mmmph*. Beast girl probably ate 'em. All those cute li'l puppies floating in her stomach acid."

"Whatever, Rich," London replied, pulling out a chair.

"Oh no, ohhh nooo," Rich said, tilting her head. "Did we invite you over here? Did we send you a telegram saying it was okay for you to be in our company?"

London swiped her bangs from out of her eyes and took a seat. "Rich, I'm not here to fight. But, sweetie, I sit where I want. You don't own this table. And last I checked, you didn't own *me*. If you don't want me sitting here, then *you* leave."

Rich's nose flared. "*Beeeyotch*, you're so pathetic! Desperate for friends."

"Yeah, says the drunk driver," London spat back.

I bit back a snicker. Oh, how I wished I could have been a butterfly fluttering in the wind the night Rich had gotten pulled over by the cops for being intoxicated behind the wheel. I warned her to not drive home. Offered her the comforts of the pool house. But she'd snubbed me. Turned her nose up to my good accommodations.

So I'd done what any good-good friend would have done. I called the police on her.

"Clutching pearls! Tramp, you're out of order," Rich snapped. "I have never been drunk. Tipsy, yes. Slurring my words, maybe. Staggering, just a bit. But I don't ever drink and drive far, whore. I find the nearest hotel and get a room!"

I couldn't help but laugh out loud.

"Spencer, I don't know what the heck is so funny. Don't do me, tramp!"

I tossed my hair, then reached inside my bag. "Wolf, don't get ugly. Here, I've been holding onto these," I said as I slid her two AA pamphlets.

She narrowed her eyes. "*Whaaaat?* Clutching pearls!" She slung the Alcoholics Anonymous brochures back at me. "I know all about being an *AA*—African American. I don't need you trying to give me a history lesson on being black and beautiful. I'm a European queen with Indian running all through my blood, honey. Don't do me."

London laughed, and I shot her a nasty look.

"Something funny, Miss Humpback? I know you're not laughing at my good-good ex-bestie." Even if she is dumber than a California mudslide.

"Ha!" Rich said. "Tell her, Spencer. That slore knows she doesn't wanna see you with those hands. I should hop up and molly-whop her upside that big pumpkin head."

"And I'd like to see you try it, Rich," London stated calmly.

Rich jumped to her feet, snatching a fork and pointing it at London. "Ho, I will prong your forehead up! You skank! You cheap, pathetic wannabe!"

Suddenly a hush fell over the café, and I saw cell phones being held up in our direction.

"Um, Rich," I said calmly. "Put the fork down, girlie. You're about to be on the next *Snapped*."

"Screw *Snapped*," she hissed. "Screw Jenny Craig! Screw The Gap! Screw all their whack-azz endorsements. And screw this skank-face. Nobody asked you over here, London. We all know how ugly you are. What, you lonely, too? *Bish*, get a life and stop trying to live mine!"

Now London was up on her feet. "*Really*, Rich? Is that the best you can do? You think I want *your* life? Girl, bye! Your life is a catastrophic mess! You're flunking all your classes...!"

"Lies and deceit!" Rich shouted. "I don't do failure! I'm getting all *D's*, ho! So come again, tramp! The only thing that's failed is you, boo-boo! You want everything I have!"

Click, click, click...

Cameras flashed.

I reached for my shades inside my bag and slid them on. Then I made sure I angled my face just right to catch the light. Heeheehee.

Click, click, click...

"Yeah, right!" London retorted. "What you are is sloppy! All used up! All run through! You're a man's toilet, Rich, one flush after the next! Yeah, you're fabulous all right! But riddle me *this*, Rich, since you think you're all that: Has Justice called you fat yet? Has he told you how insecure you are? Has he told you how worthless and lazy you are yet? Well, guess what, sweetie. He will! Justice is going to strangle your soul. And you know what, Rich? You deserve everything you get!"

Click, click, click...

I blinked. Shifted in my seat. Then locked my eyes on Rich. I saw her shudder slightly, saw her lip quiver, just a bit. Ole Miss London had banged a hammer down on a nerve, and I loved every bit of it. Still, I had to take up for Rich. I always did. But before I could get a word in, Rich had turned into the Incredible *Hulk*tress.

Click, click, click...

"You ugly *bish!*" Rich shouted, grabbing a handful of half-bitten shrimps from her plate and throwing them at London. Then she grabbed the bowl of cocktail sauce and slung it in London's face, causing a messy food fight between the two of them to erupt.

7

Heather

"*Heather, I don't know what kind of junkie-trash games you're playing, but you had better clean your act up and get with the program, or you will find yourself picking trash and collecting aluminum cans for your next payday. I need you at my office this afternoon. Three p.m., sharp! Not three-oh-one, not three-oh-two...*"

3:06 p.m.

I glanced at the time again and rolled my eyes.

This old trick was late! The nerve of her! Threatening me. *Me*, for Christ's sake! Did she not know who I was? Did she not know what I was?

Apparently not!

I was Heather Cummings, baby! A star! An iTunes sensation! A YouTube celebrity! The queen of one-of-a-kind Korean couture!

I was...

3:08 p.m.

I shifted in my seat. Crossed my legs, then uncrossed them. Then shifted in my chair again. I was getting fidgety. I needed a pinch, just a taste, to keep my mind right. I wasn't an addict or anything. I knew my limit. But there wasn't anything wrong with having a little get-right from time to time. Heck. Everyone had a vice, a thing.

And my thing...my occasional use of crushed Adderall with a pinch of this and a pinch of that—usually molly, though—was under control. There wasn't anything wrong with a having a little party favor at your fingertips to kick up the party even when there really wasn't one being had.

I was a free spirit.

Not some junkie.

I wasn't some wayward child.

So who the heck did Kitty think I was, summoning me like I was some effen stray? Leaving me some damn nasty-gram on my cell, demanding my presence. Disrespecting my time, my life.

So what if I liked to turn up a little?

I worked hard, and I loved to play harder.

So what if I liked to bend over and give the world my greatest *ass*et to kiss every now and again? It was mine. It was paid for. And I had a whole lot of it. So they—and *she*, could kiss...

Camille grunted, snatching me from my inner rant. "Where the hell is this damn woman?" She glanced at her bejeweled timepiece. "This is so like Kitty. Selfish. Inconsiderate. She's always been a selfish whore. Always only thinking of herself, cutting into my happy hour like this."

"*Mmmph*. Sounds like someone else I know," I muttered.

"Excuse *you*. Is there a problem here?"

Eye roll. "Oh, *nooo*, Mother. Everything's just peachy. It's a beautiful day in the neighborhood."

"And I'm missing my midday cocktail hour," Camille retorted as she stood to her feet, glancing at the time again. She started pacing Kitty's office, her one good pair of Chanel pumps sinking deep into the plush carpet fibers.

I rolled my eyes and sucked my teeth. "Didn't you have your liquid snack before we left the house?"

Camille stopped her pacing and shot me a nasty look. "Little girl, I know your pill-snorting behind isn't sitting over there judging me. Don't try me. So what if I had a cocktail? I can drink out a whole damn bar if I want to. I'm a grown woman, not some little girl tryna play grown-up."

I looked her up and down. My mother was a hot mess. Always. Standing here all dolled up in what looked like a Marilyn Monroe halter dress—in black, though with a vintage fox stole draped over her bare shoulders.

A mink shawl in almost eighty-degree weather!

"Ain't no one thinking about you," I said flatly. "And, anyway, you might be grown, but I'm the one sponsoring all of your booze binges."

"*Binges?*" she rang out incredulously.

"Yeah, binges?" I repeated. "B-I-N-G-E-S. Your hourly need for a scotch on the rocks to ward off those nasty shakes."

She stalked over toward me and reached over and grabbed my hair, yanking my head back.

"*Ow!*" I yelped, grabbing her hand at the wrist and trying to free my hair from her grip. "Get off of me!"

She leaned in, her face mere inches from mine, pulling my hair harder. "You little ungrateful snot," she hissed, her hot breath singeing my nose hairs. "You had better watch your tone"—hair tug—"and watch what you say to me." She tightened her grip on my hair.

I cringed. "Ow."

"Don't *ow* me, you little turn-up queen. Because of you and your hoochie-mama antics, I'm stuck here with you instead of being in the comforts of my home. All you have to do is stay off the drugs, lay off the ratchetness, and follow the damn yellow brick road to success. But nooo. You wanna be difficult. Wanna be ratchet. You wanna have me living back in some nasty flea trap again."

I swallowed, hard. "Yeah. Okay. Forgive me for taking you out of your comfort zone, Mother. For taking you out of your nasty see-through nightgown and kitten heels. Forgive me for ruining your access to a bar that *I* keep stocked, just to keep you drunk and out of my business. Yup, this is all my fault, Camille."

"*Camille?*" my mother screeched. "Oh, so now we're on a first-name basis, huh, Heather Suzanne? Is that how we're doing it now? Calling me *Camille*, huh? Do I need to remind you of what the inside of a hospital looks like? Do I?"

I saw the fire flash in Camille's blue eyes, and I knew then she was on the edge. And if I pushed her over it, I'd be in the back of another ambulance, beat up from head to toe, like before. Oh, no, I had things to do this weekend. I couldn't be laid up in a hospital bed.

"N-no," I finally stammered out.

She yanked my head again. "I didn't think so, little girl. Contrary to what you may think of me, I am *still* your mother. And I will lay hands on you, snatch your breath right from out of your chest. I will take your whole scalp off. You hear me, Heather Suzanne? I will take. You. Out. So you had better check your self-esteem and check your damn attitude. Do you understand me?"

Defiantly, I said nothing, just stared this crazy lady down.

I wanted to punch her in her throat. Wanted to kick a hole in her chest for yanking on my three-hundred-dollar, thirty-inch 7A. This was four bundles of deep wave goodness, and she was trying to pull it out of my scalp.

She was so frickin'—

Slap!

My eyes widened. My whole face stung, my ears rung.

"I *said*, do you hear me?" She yanked my hair harder and swung her arm back to slap me again.

"Yess," I cried out. "I hear you."

"Good."

She slapped me again, then let go of my hair, mushing me in the head.

"Now sit up straight and fix your damn face before that lecherous woman comes up in here."

She narrowed her eyes and watched me through thin slits as I begrudgingly straightened myself in my seat, then held the side of my face.

"And when Kitty finally shows her hideous face, you had better not open your trifling mouth to say one damn word. You let me do the talking." She started pacing again. "You'll catch more flies with honey when dealing with that trick. So you let me handle her. I don't need you screwing up our money." She huffed. "I need a cigarette. Got my nerves all tore up. You just can't seem to do anything right, can you, Heather?"

Screw this crap! I didn't need Camille's abuse. And I didn't need Kitty's judgment. I was outta here!

I stood, shouldering my monogrammed hobo bag. "I'm out of here."

"Oh, no you're not," she countered.

"Let me see you stop me," I challenged, fighting back tears. "I've kept my end of the bargain. I came at three like the good ole slave master ordered. And"—I glanced down at my watch again—"she's kept me waiting long enough. Who does that?"

Camille yanked off her mink and charged over toward me. "You sit back in that chair"—she hit me with her fur—"before I beat you into the grave."

I plunked down in the chair and crossed my arms tightly over my chest.

"I've done nothing but dedicate my whole life to you," my mother continued. "I've sacrificed everything for you, you little witch! I've denied myself the comfort of a man, a career. A life. All for you! For what? So you can piss it all away for a good time? So you can become the next new trap queen, twerk your way into some low-budget rap video? Is that what you want for yourself, Heather? Huh? To be some video ho?"

She swung her fox wrap at me again, its tail hitting me in the face. "You will not ruin everything I've worked so hard for. It's bad enough you destroyed your Wu-Wu television career with all of your junkie antics. And now you're about to kill your reality-TV career. Mediocre or not, it's still a career. A start to something greater, but all you wanna do is snort it away." She huffed. "Didn't you learn anything in that high-priced rehab you were locked away in? Perhaps you need a return stay, a longer one, to help you get your mind together."

She was referring to my twenty-eight-day stay that she'd practically had me committed to, pretending to be the concerned mother. Oh, please. Miss me with that. But it was either a jail stay or rehab. So I took the lesser of the evils.

Always Hope.

I scoffed. "Always Hope was nothing but a joke, just like you pretending to have my best interest at heart. We both know the only thing you're interested in is your next drink. You're the one who needs rehab!"

"Why you little..." She raised her hand to slap me again just as the door swung open.

"Oh, how sweet. A mother-daughter moment. Am I missing all the fun?"

Camille dropped her hand. "You're late, Kitty. And I don't appreciate you making me wait, like I'm one of your flunkies. You said three o'clock, and yet you don't waltz up in here until twenty after? Really?"

Kitty whisked around her sleek mahogany desk, then took a seat. Her flowery scent wafted around the room. "You wait for *me* because *I* write the checks around here," she calmly stated, sitting in her leather high-back chair. "*You* wait for *me* because *I'm* the one who keeps your daughter working. In a flash, I'm the one who can shut your daughter's whole career down. So I suggest you don't forget it. Now take a seat,

Camille, so we can get down to business. Better yet"—she pressed a button on her desk and a mirrored wall slid open, displaying shelves of liquor—"shall I offer you a drink?"

Camille huffed, swinging her stole over her left shoulder, then taking a seat. "I don't need a damn drink, Kitty. What I need is for you to tell me why we're here. And why you're wasting my time with this foolery."

Kitty turned her attention to me. "You're a hot mess, Heather, real messy. And I love it. But I need for you to dial down the turn-up. You need to learn discretion. That stunt you pulled the other night was just short of a catastrophe. So what do you have to say for yourself?"

"I-I..." I stammered, feeling myself slowly shrinking into my chair.

She tapped her manicured nails against her desk.

"Well?"

I shrugged. "Nothing. I don't know what the big deal is. All I was doing was giving my fans what they love. A show. You said you wanted me to stay in the headlines. And I have."

"You bumbling idiot," Kitty snarled. "Are you brain dead? I said keep them talking, not for you to keep looking like a damn fool, like some slut-bucket junkie. What type of dope are you snorting now, Heather? Because from where I'm sitting, you need to be back in rehab—indefinitely."

"Now wait one goddamn minute, Kitty," Camille snapped, placing a hand up on her hip and leaning up in her seat. "Don't you dare talk about my daughter like she's some derelict, some reject. Heather is not an addict! And she doesn't need some damn *rehab*. What she needs is your support, *not* your haranguing. We both know my baby is a free spirit..."

Baby?

I blinked. Wasn't this lady about to clobber me? Wasn't she just threatening to rip out my lungs? To take my life?

And now I was her *baby*. *Mmmph.*

"Oh, Camille, shut it. Is your brain that soaked in whiskey?

Are you that much of a wet brain to see?" She let out a disgusted sigh. "What Heather is, is a train speeding down the wrong track. And I seem to be the only one trying to keep her from a crash and burn."

I shifted in my seat.

Camille snorted. "Oh, Kitty. Stop with the theatrics. You've always been so melodramatic. We both know Heather's a star. Her ratings alone speak for her. Her fans love her. And every iTunes song she drops becomes an instant hit." Camille reached over and grabbed my hand. "My baby is the real deal, Kitty. And I suggest you recognize it."

Camille smoothed her hands over imaginary wrinkles at the hem of her dress, then crossed her hands in her lap. "Now I suggest you back up off her and tell me what you plan on doing to keep her star shining brightly. And not another word about some rehab; she doesn't need it."

I cut my eyes at Camille and smirked as she crossed her legs.

You go, boo! Yass, honey, yass! Let her know! Check her, boo!
She slayed.

Kitty let out a mocking laugh. "So says the woman who can't go a day without a drink." She scoffed. "What a Hallmark moment. An alcoholic mother defending her pill-snorting daughter's honor, how sweet."

Camille jumped out of her seat. "How dare you judge my child, or *me*, when you have a daughter who's walking around with permanent kneepads on and a battery pack in her neck...!"

I eased up in my chair. A catfight! *Yassss*, honey, *yassss!* This was too good to be true. And I had a front-row seat. I slipped my hand in my bag and felt for my phone; then a sly grin eased over my face.

"That Bobblehead is the biggest knob gobbler in Hollywood!" Camille exclaimed. "And don't even let me get started on you, tramping around, preying on old, lonely men. You've been whoring since you were thirteen, Kitty—maybe even longer than that. But you don't hear me trashing you or your slutty daughter, do you?"

Kitty's lashes flapped as she clapped her hands. "Bravo, darling, *braaaa...vo!* Give it to me, Camille. Let's get down and dirty, the way I like it. And of course you'd know all about whoring, darling, considering how you spent your whole career on your back. You've been spread eagle with every Hollywood celebrity who'd have you. It's no wonder you never made it in the porn business. I hear you were quite the naughty girl. But, of course, you couldn't even do that right. And then when you got yourself knocked up by someone else's man..."

"He was *my* man first, Kitty!"

"*Which* one, Camille? Who, Harry? Tom? Bill? Lionel? Ray? Joe? Do tell, dear. Because we both know you had to pull a name out of the hat just to pin it on someone."

Camille jabbed a finger through the air. "You shut your filthy mouth with your lies!" she shouted. "You know who my man was, Kitty. Richard, that's who. So don't you dare go there! That man was mine. And you know it. I gave him *every*thing."

I blinked. Took in the heated exchange between Kitty and my mother, my hand tightly gripping my phone.

"And look at you now, Camille. With nothing," Kitty declared. "No career. No life. No money. Milking off your daughter's measly earnings. Stuck in a time capsule wearing old relics from some forgotten movie set. It's no wonder Heather is such a mess. Look at who her role model has been: a damn drunk whose spent her life chasing a lie!

"And no matter how many head nods you garnered back in your heyday, no matter how much dust has collected on that nineteen-nineties Oscar you covet, you're still a nobody! Nothing more than lily-white trash, Camille. So spare me the I Know Who I Am monologue because no matter how many bottles of scotch you try to drown your sorrows in, you will always be the same dirty, snotty-nosed Norma Marie Schumacher with the dingy panties whose hick daddy loved crawling—"

Slap!

Camille's hand landed across Kitty's face.

I blinked. Ohmygod! I couldn't believe—

"How dare you?!" Camille shouted as her body shook. "You seem to have forgotten that you're from the same backwoods of Mississippi as—"

Slap!

Kitty's hand seared into Camille's left cheek. "Get *out!*" she yelled. "You and your bastard child get the hell out of my office! Or, so help me God—"

"You evil *biiiiiiitch!*" Camille stepped out of her left shoe and threw it at Kitty. It flew over Kitty's head and hit the wall in back of her. "Screw you! Screw your television show! And screw your damn money!" Camille yanked me by the arm, pulling me out of my seat. "Let's go, Heather. We're outta this hellhole."

She stormed toward the door, hobbling on one heel while dragging me in tow.

My heart sank. My career with Kitty Productions was officially over.

Thanks to my mother.

And all I kept thinking as I was being dragged out of Kitty's office was, *"Way to go, Camille."*

8

Spencer

"I think I know you," Daddy said as he turned his head toward me and narrowed his eyes. He did that sometimes...well, um, most times. Forgot. Then miraculously remembered.

This afternoon was obviously another one of those days when his mind jumped from thought to thought. Scatterbrained, that's what he'd become. His brain was one big scrambled egg. Oh, it was horrid.

Daddy's Alzheimer's was chewing out his memory. And I hated seeing him like this. Vacant. One big parking lot full of jumbled recollections.

I stared at him. He was donned in a black velvet smoking jacket and red silk ascot stretched across the sofa. A fire blazed in the hearth of his sitting area despite it being a deliciously warm eighty-seven degrees outside.

I blinked four times.

What in the heebie jeebies?!

From the waist down, Daddy was in a pair of striped boxers, with his black dress socks on pulled up over his calves and a pair of burgundy dress shoes.

I sighed inwardly. "Daddy, where are your pants?"

"Now that's none of your business, gal," he said tersely. He stretched an arm and pointed his finger at me. "I *do* know you."

"I know, Daddy, you already told me."

"Ooh wee," he said, slapping his knee, "you were one sassy gal. Fast, too."

I blinked. "*Excu—*"

"Never could keep your skirt down," he continued. "Always somewhere tryna show your pocketbook."

"To show my *whaaaat?* My pocketbook? Daddy, lies! I don't go around showing anyone my, my…"

Ohmygod! Realization bloomed. Daddy wasn't talking about one of my coveted Chanel or Dior bags, he was talking about—

Ewww.

I stomped a heeled foot with perhaps more vigor than needed. *Danggit, I could have broken my heel!* "Lies!" I snapped. "You ole nasty goat! I will scrub your mouth out with bleach. You filthy heathen!"

Daddy laughed. "Simmer down, kitten. The truth don't tell no lies, and a lie don't tell no truths."

My lashes flapped. I wasn't in the mood for any of Daddy's riddles today. I took a deep breath and counted to fifteen in my head. I had to remind myself that he wasn't really Daddy. I mean, he was, but then he wasn't. He looked like Daddy. But he didn't act like him. Most times I didn't know who he was.

He was becoming more and more of a stranger with each passing day. And obviously I was becoming more of one to him as well.

"Daddy, are you taking your medications?"

"Duh, no."

I frowned. "And why not? You know you need them to stay sane."

"I'm already sane," he said over a laugh. "I'm the most

lucid one in this entire gated prison. It's you and the rest of the world who are crazy. Keeping an old man under lock and key."

I let out an exaggerated sigh. "Oh, Daddy, stop. You're not in prison. And no one's keeping you under lock and key."

He glanced over at the two hired orderlies with bulging muscles stuffed in white uniforms on the other side of the room.

"Oh, well. Not really. They're here for your safety. To keep an eye on you."

"Dammit!" he swore as the fire hissed and crackled. "I don't need to be eyed! I need to be entertained! Lock me up with three strippers in sparkly bikini bottoms. Not those"—he flicked a thumb over in the orderlies' direction—"two hunky dorks."

I looked over at the two men, who both pretended not to be fazed by Daddy's ramblings. They both acted as if they weren't in the room with us.

"Well, there'll be no topless hoochies watching over you," I stated firmly.

"Fine, Joy Kill. Be like that. Deprive a dying old man of his last wishes."

I swallowed hard. "Daddy, stop talking foolery. You're not dying. And you still need to be taking your meds."

He snorted. "Hush, li'l darling," he stage-whispered, placing his finger to his lips. "The walls have ears. Everything you say, everything you do, they're recording."

"Who?" I asked, glancing around his ginormous suite. "Who's recording us?"

"Big Brother. Martians. The feds. CIA. The po-po," he rattled off, adding a sly wink. "They see"—he lowered his voice to nearly an inaudible whisper—"and hear everything."

I rolled my eyes up in my head. I counted to sixteen this time, then backward. I was so, so confused. How could Daddy be so fascinating and frustrating at the same time? How could I love him and yet be so angry with him?

I swept my eyes around his suite, locking my gaze on the wall of priceless artwork. I needed a distraction from the thoughts slowly swirling around in my head. I wanted to claw Daddy's brains out. Yell and scream. And have one of my big fancy tantrums. Oooh, I felt a fit of vandalism coming on, ripping down curtains and smashing out light fixtures.

But I couldn't do it.

Not with Daddy. He was still Daddy to me. Still the man who had loved me all of my life. No matter how far he'd traveled in his day, he'd always made time for me—always calling, always e-mailing and texting, always bringing me back some delicious, shiny trinket and juicy tales of his most exotic adventures.

So how could I slap him upside the head with my purse? I gripped the handle of my handbag tighter as guilt swept through me for having had such unkind thoughts.

I had to remind myself that Daddy was the one who loved me most. Even when he was somewhere on the other side of the globe, he'd still felt more present in my life than my own mother. Kitty could be right here, in the same house with me, and still be so far, far, away.

Distant. Detached. Disinterested.

And yet Daddy brought life (no matter how jumbled) into an otherwise dead space. He knew how to fill an empty room with excitement. Even now, in all of his feebleness, he knew how to breathe life into a room.

I blinked Daddy back into view and tried to force a smile to spread over my face. But it was hard fake-smiling when all I saw was a shriveled shell of a man lying across a sofa in a pair of boxers and dress socks.

All I saw in my mind's eye was Daddy with a bunch of oozing bed—well, sofa—sores. *Ugh.*

Finally, after standing in the same spot for almost forever, I whisked over toward the sofa, then leaned in and kissed him on the forehead.

"Okay, Daddy. I gotta go. Please take your meds. Okay?"

He stared at me through confused, wrinkled eyes and said, "I think I know you."

My bottom lip quivered. "I think I know you, too," I whispered, before turning on my heel and moving swiftly toward the double doors.

And then the entire room moved. At first, I thought it was because the ground was shaking from an earthquake or that the floor was just dropping out from under my feet, but then I realized Daddy had leapt from the sofa and had grabbed me by the arm and swung me around to face him.

"Get me out of here, *Cleola.*"

"Tell me now. Who is she?"

I heard Kitty's breath hitch. Then she clucked her teeth. "Who is *who?*"

I paced the length of my wraparound balcony. "Oh, don't dilly-dally with me, lady. And don't play dumb, although you do it so well. Who is Cleola?"

"Oh, for the love of God, not this again. Heather and her wretched mother just stormed out of here, and now I need to—"

"Yes, Mother. *This* again. And you need to start flapping your gums," I said, placing a hand on my hip as I stalked up and down and around the length of my balcony. "I don't care about Heather or her cockamamie mother storming out of your goshdiggity-dang office. Daddy called me *her* name again. And I want to know *why.* Why does he keep talking about her? It's not making sense. I'm getting tired of him talking about this ole biddy, if she even is one. Maybe she's not some old slore; maybe she's his mistress."

"And maybe you should delete my numbers, Spencer," my mother said snidely. "I have more pressing matters to contend with, like destroying a career, like teaching little tramps a very valuable lesson about life and business. Now—"

"Oh, shut it, Mother! All I want to know is who in the heck this Cleola Mae is?"

Kitty huffed. "Spencer, darling, tell me why I ever gave birth to you? Why did I carry you for nine excruciating months, then suffer through twenty-three hours of labor to only push out a dimwit, huh? Please tell me, my darling child. Because clearly you calling me about the ramblings of some shriveled old man with more cobwebs in his brain than reality is beyond the scope of my intelligence.

"That man needs to be put down. He needs to be thrown out into the wilderness and left to be eaten by wild boars. He's useless. Can't you see that? Can't you see how scattered he is, huh, Spencer? The man spends his days picking his nose and trying to remember which day of the week it is, smelling like the inside of a zoo, and you have the audacity to call me about some imaginary woman named *Cleola?* You damn ditz-ball! How am I supposed to know? Maybe she's some dead woman, some ghost your father sees in that little pea-brain mind of his."

I blanched. Felt the blood from my face drain. Kitty's unexpected tirade felt like I'd been shot up with a vial of Novocain, and suddenly I felt numb. I felt my throat closing.

"Who is she?" I pushed out over a choke.

"Spencer, I'm warning you: Don't bother me with this nonsense. It's nothing but foolishness. Your father is sick. Demented. I don't even know why I ever married him in the first place. I should have married that Ahmed boy, the young Saudi Arabian prince I met in that scandalous sex club in Greenwich Village in New York, instead of getting hitched to some old mule. Wealth or not, I should have known something like this would soon happen.

"Take it from me, my darling Spencer, never marry an old man with money or you'll end up with an old coot whose man parts don't work and all he has is a mind full of mothballs. Now stop this madness, Spencer. There is no Cleola

Mae. She doesn't exist. She's some crazy figment of your father's overactive imagination. So let that man have his imaginary friends, and let me get back to teaching your junkie-whore friend and her mother the lesson of their miserable lives, before I forget you're my daughter and give you a tongue lashing that'll make your ears bleed and wish you were deaf."

"Oh, bring it on, Kitty!" I screamed into the phone. "You wanna rumble with me, huh, Kitty? You wanna get your edges pulled back? You, you, leech! You bloodsucking harlot! You don't want any of this fire I spit, lady! I will burn you down, Kitty! Set your entire life ablaze! You, you...!"

Silence.

"Hello? Hello? Kitty?"

The line was dead.

"Aaaaah!" I screamed, grabbing the crystal goblet I'd left on the small round table and throwing it over the side of the balcony.

9

Rich

I was at Lavender Lounge.

A small boutique bar in Beverly Hills.

Solo.

I should've been a duo with Spencer, though.

But I wasn't.

Why?

Well...let's see...there were only two other places Whorebie could be...

On her knees.

Or in the backseat of some MCM's car unlatching her jaw.

Needless to say, she was over an hour late, leaving me to violate my usual diet of clean eating with a platter of bacon-wrapped, barbeque-dipped hot wings and a pitcher of beer, straight from the tap. Olde English, to be exact. Or malt Community Service, as I liked to call it—my way of giving back.

You gotta do it for the people sometimes.

Can't be bourgeois all the time, which is exactly why I poured a li'l beer from my mug onto the bar.

"And exactly what are *you* doing, Miss Girl?" The bartender snapped, quickly wiping up my wet shrine.

All I could do was snort, 'cause obviously he wasn't ready. "*Bish*, please!" I looked him over from the red flip-flops on his feet to the jelled spikes in his black hair. "Now snap, snap, zap! Run along!"

He frowned, shook his dome, and walked away.

Ask me if I cared.

Not one raggedy damn. As long as he kept this beer flowin' and these hot wings greasy, his small thoughts were of no moment to me.

Chile, cheese.

Boo, please.

What. Ever.

Any. Way. Like I was sayin', Spencer or no Spencer, I was gon' sit at this pink glass bar, heels off, and toes stretched out, while I sucked barbeque juice off my fingertips, rocked my shoulders to the beat of the stage, and was entertained.

Rosita, a six-three man-queen, donned the small stage in a glittering kelly-green bodysuit, five-inch matching heels, and a layered honey-blond wig that swung from side to side. And this heifer sang not one, but was on her third give-me-life number! About sweet love, making love, giving up good love, and why you should never trust love. All of which touched my heart and set my blue-blooded soul on fire!

She sang to me, honey, *saaaaaaang!*

Rosita belted out, "Love shouldn't hurt/And if it's not sweet like 90's R&B, I don't want it..."

"Sang, *bish!*" I screamed, a barbeque-drippin' hot wing in one hand and the other testifying in the air. "If it's not sweet like 90's R&B, baby!" I said, then grooved into a hum.

Rosita sang, "I don't wanna say good-bye/But I gotta go/I gotta leave!"

"Preach!" I waved another hand to the heavens.

Rosita greeted my praise with a wink, while the bartender

wiped up the barbeque juice that dripped onto the bar with a groan.

Ig. Nore. He was invisible to me. All that mattered was Rosita as she sang my love story.

"You got tears pourin' from my eyes /And divas don't cry." Rosita interrupted my thoughts. And shut. The. Whole. Bar. *Down!*

The crowd went wild.

Tears filled my eyes, but I refused to cry. Like this heifer had said, "Divas don't cry! They give good love. And testify!"

Rosita had torn both ends of her boxin'-panties with me. All I could do was stand up and give a slow clap after every word I spoke. "You. Better. Have. Church. Up. In. Here. Tootsie Roll!"

I stomped my stocking-covered foot as Rosita continued on.

"You betta talk about it," I screamed, reaching for another hot wing as I retook my seat.

But.

Just as I stuffed a hot wing in my mouth, the music came to screeching halt, and Rosita said, "Wait, just wait." She blinked in disbelief, then walked to the edge of the stage and placed her hands over her eyes like a sun visor. "I knew I knew you, honey. Is that Miss Rich Montgomery? The. Rich. Montgomery?" She squinted. "Oh, my God, it is you. Well, clutchin' pearls! The queen of the Pampered Princesses is in the lounge tonight!"

I pulled a bone from my mouth and stopped mid-chew.

"*Yasss*, honey!" she squealed. "That *is* you! The diva of all divas, honey!"

I gave her a closed-mouth cheese, waved my barbeque-drowned fingertips in the air, and finished chewing my hot wing.

"I can't believe you're here! Clutching, pearls, chile, cheese!" She carried on, mocking me. I swallowed and smiled but didn't say a word as Rosita carried on, "Girl, we love you up in here! I know you over there tearing up them wings but, ummm, Miss Girl, you're the turn-up queen, and I need you up on stage with me!"

Stage?

My eyes scanned the room. All eyes and camera phones were on me.

Click, click.

Yasss, honey! Catch all this fabulousness!

Click, click.

Rosita continued. "Yesss, doll, yesss! We 'bout to really get it lit up in here! Come on, everybody, let's show Rich Montgomery some love!"

"You're my girl, Rich!" someone shouted out.

"We love you!" poured from the back of the room.

Oh.

My.

God.

This was all Spencer's fault. She was supposed to be here to help me eat and drink my pity away. But *noooooooooo...* she was somewhere in the lowlands collecting carpet burns. Meanwhile, I was being forced to get it crunked, as if I was in a constant state of turn-up.

It was levels to this.

But I wasn't in the mood. This man-tramp had to know me and Justice had broken up! So she had to know I was in mourning. Grieving the loss of the love of my life. I hadn't signed up for this. All I'd come to do was have me a few hot wings and a few pitchers of beer. Not do show tunes in the Lavender Lounge.

But the crowd kept chanting my name, and all I could think to do was, do it for the people. So I had to come through and do what I was put on this heavenly Earth to do. Be fabulous. And carry out what the goddess of all things great, juicy, and tender charged me with: to make those who were less fortunate feel good about themselves. So I had to give my Richazoids what they wanted!

What they needed!

What they lived for!

Me.

I wiped my hands until they were sauce-free, stepped back into my heels, and sashayed my way to the stage, told the DJ to play "Knuck if You Buck" and dropped the toughest boom-bop, make-it-hot twerk in the land!

Straight hit 'em over the head with it, baby!

Rosita rapped, "Clutchin' pearls! Pop-pop-boom-bop, get it-get it! Drop that judy-drag on 'em and bust 'em wit' it!"

I knew I was doin' the Goddess of All Things Extraordinary proud.

The people were out of their seats, some clapping feverishly; some snapped pics, others recorded, and the rest twerked along with me.

And then when the song ended, everyone clapped and cheered and stomped the floor. Made the windows rattle and all the tables shake!

"Go, Rich! Go, Rich! It's your birthday, *bish!*"

Rosita handed me the mic, and I said, "Thank y'all for the love!" I hesitated and looked over the sea of awed faces. "I know y'all Richazoids have read the blogs, and you see how they are spreading alternative facts, fake news, and dragging me."

"Eff 'em! We love you, Rich!" Rosita said into the mic, draping her big muscular arm around me and pulling me close, her big hand dangled over my shoulder.

I stepped out of her—uh, I mean his—musty embrace. Yuck. *Don't put your hands on me!* "I love y'all too, boo. But I'm here to tell you that sometimes when you're pretty, fly, rich, and er'body loves you, it's a blessing and a curse. Because there's always a bandwagon of haters out there tryna do you."

"Talk about it!" someone yelled across the room.

"You feel me," was my response. "But I'ma be all right. Why? 'Cause divas don't, *whaaat?*"

I pointed the mic to the crowd, and they shouted back, "Cry!"

I snapped my fingers. "That's riiiiiight! Divas don't cry, *bishes!* We dust our shoulders off." I flicked invisible dust from my left shoulder, then my right. "Put on some heels," I said as I tapped my feet. "Slide on some lipstick." I blew the audience a kiss. "And handle it!"

"Bam!" Rosita said, and the crowd clapped, with a few people yelling, "*Yaaaassss!*"

"I knew y'all would understand." I said. "And the blogs are out there dying to be all in my business. Talking about a source close to me told them this and told them that. Lies and deceit! I am very shy, quiet, and private. I don't tell nobody my business. I keep everything between me and my God. You feel me?"

"Amen!" somebody yelled.

"*Yasss.*" I stomped a foot, feeling good. "That's the only way to be. How the blogs gon' run a story saying me and my man, my JB-boo, was fighting in the street, when they weren't even there! First of all, we weren't fighting in the street. We were in his apartment. We didn't have a fight. We had a li'l love battle.

"A little pushin' here, a little shovin there. But he ain't never in his life full-on put his hands on me. That boy is trying to make black history, not be black history. I ain't that kind of ho. No. I'm an upstanding ho. You slap me, I'ma slap you back."

"I know that's right!" a lady with pink spiked hair yelled from the bar. "Tell 'em, sistah!"

"Me and my baby got a love thang goin' on. And that last quarrel we had that the press can't seem to let go of was not over his Facebook page per se. See, I'm gon' tell y'all what really happened because y'all my people and you deserve to know. The truth, the whole truth, and nothing but the holy truth! See. It started like this…"

"*'Give me my damn phone, yo!' Justice stormed out the bathroom, with nothing but a towel wrapped around his waist. He snatched his phone from me, but I ain't care. I'd already seen what I needed to see.*

"*I hopped out of the bed and wrapped the sheet around me. 'And who is White Chocolate-baby? And why are you liking all of her pics? And why is she loving all of yours? And why is she calling you boo on Snapchat and y'all following each other on Instagram?'*

"*'I can't believe you, yo! It's always some drama with you! Dumb-azz! You so effen insecure it's pathetic. Matter of fact, you're pathetic! Questioning me, yo. Are you out'cha mind? I knew lettin' you spend the night was a mistake!'*

"*'And the mistake I made was loving you! The only thing that is pathetic is your singing career. Ole wannabe Trey Songz! You need to change your name to No Songz! Tryna be Drake, but you a fake!'*

"*He jumped up in my face. 'Oh, word? That's how you doin' it, yo? That's how you comin' at me? Huh, Rich? Huh, fat girl? Hatin'-azz!'*

"*'Okay, I'm fat. Whatever you say, Justice. Mr. No Career! Mr. Never Gonna Be Nobody! I should have never let myself love you! All you are is a user!'*

"*He huffed. 'Use you? What I use you for huh, Rich? Sex? Hell, you was givin' that away. Easy drawz! Ya stupid-azz can't even spell! And the only thing you ever gonna be good for, Becky, is bobbin'…'*"

But instead of telling the crowd all that, all I told them was that he'd disrespected me, took my love for granted, and tried to play me and use me. He thought I was his meal ticket to stardom because I was Rich Montgomery. My name rang bells, and he thought I was gonna be ringing his.

Not.

I looked out at the crowd, who were clinging onto my every word, and finished off with, "So after he tried to bring it to me I reared my hand back and slapped the spit out of his mouth. After he tried to do me, he deserved that face slap. And so what if he grabbed me by the throat? That's how real love is. That's how it goes. But I'm over him. And it's over between us."

"Go on, black queen!" someone shouted.

"That's right, girl! You deserve better!"

"You're right I do," I agreed. "Still, you gotta be a soldier for love. And ready for the battlefield; otherwise, you playing. And I don't have time for games..."

"Ohmygod! Rich," an unwelcomed voice invaded my inspirational conversation. I batted my lashes. Dear God no! It was Spencer. "Sweetgodbabyjesus! What in the hot hellfire are you doing up there?" She arched one brow and dipped the other. "Get. Down."

I curled my upper lip to the right. "And who are you? Are you the same trick that was supposed to be here two hours ago, and now that I'm up here serving my Richazoids and giving the people what they want, and what they need, you wanna make like magic and appear. Chile, cheese."

"Boo, please!" the crowd yelled in unison.

"Snap, snap!" I said into the mic.

"Clutchin' pearls!" the crowd roared.

"Rich!" Spencer hissed like she had lost every ounce of her mind. "You need to get down right now! Why are you telling these people that that ole trick-daddy, that that thug-boy in Timbs puts his hands on you, when you told me he didn't?"

My eyes burned, and my jaw clenched. "*Beyaaaatch*. Lies and fabrications! Don't do me! That is *not* what I just gave to the people. I gave them a testimony of strength, of courage, of black love! Black love matters, ho! Not you tryna be all up in my crotch life! You need to worry about your own hot pocket! Me and my ex-man are just fine! He loves me! He'd never put his hands on me...

"We're happy, whore!"

"I thought you just said it was over," she questioned.

"Lady, bye! It *is* over! But that's none of your business! God, Spencer. You're so pathetic! So weak! We're still in love! Real love doesn't just die! It lives on inside of you for months before it finally withers away and leaves you! It takes time! Something you know nothing about, *Speeeencerrrr*, because no one loves you! Because no one will ever love you! When I needed you, you were somewhere baggin' tea...!"

Spencer's eyes widened as if she was in shock, but she should have known not to come for me while I was doing community service, while I was testifying to the people. I was tryna save lives, save love. Real love. Good love. Sweet love. Not fight with this slore.

I dusted my hands and simply glared at her. "Now good night, you mop head! You're dismissed. Now go sop up some boy's milk!" Then I turned to the DJ and said, "DJ, drop that 'Knuck if You Buck' one mo' time!"

10

London

Meeeeeeeeow!

Can we say catfight, my little kitties?

Looks like it was a war of words that turned ugly at Hollywood High yesterday. Sources who witnessed the café food brawl between hip hop's ratchet Rich Montgomery and runway train wreck London Phillips say that the melee erupted after tempers flared, and London gave Rich Montgomery a dirty piece of her mind...

I tossed the article to the floor, but not before I glanced at the hideous photo of me with cocktail sauce dripping from my face and eyelashes. They'd zoomed in on me! Caught me with half-bitten shrimp in my hair and chilled condiment in my face.

Ohmygod! I wanted to storm over to Rich's first thing this morning, drag her out of her house by her weave, and bang my fist into her oversized face. I wanted to beat her eye sockets in. But since I had no intentions of trespassing on her property, I reached for my smartphone and called my mother. I hadn't spoken to her in almost two days, and a part of me was still angry with her. I wanted to pick a fight.

"Why, Mother?" I snapped the moment she answered her phone.

"Why *what*, London?" she said, her tone sharp. The hairs on the back of my neck rose. She sounded irritated that I— her only child—had called her. Disrupted her carefree life over in Italy. The life she chose over her family, over...*me*.

But why was I not surprised that she'd flee the first chance she could?

Because being a mother had always come in second, maybe third or fourth—or *fifth*—to modeling and building her own fashion empire.

She'd told Daddy several weeks back that she was leaving him and that she was taking me with her. But he'd forbidden it. Told her *she* could leave if that's what she wanted, but taking me out of the country to live was out of the question.

"You aren't taking London with you..."

"I most certainly am. Try to stop me, Turner!"

Well. He stopped her. How, I don't know. But in the end, Daddy had won. And for once in my life, I'd been given the choice to go or stay. I chose to stay. Here, with Daddy.

"Why are you pretending like everything is okay?"

She huffed. "*Pretending?* What on heaven's earth are you talking about now, London? No one's pretending about anything."

I took a deep breath. One of the things I'd been working on in therapy was saying what was on my mind. Not holding things in, which is what led me to light into Rich at school yesterday. And now this call to my mother.

As Dr. Kickaloo said, "If it doesn't feel right, then it isn't right."

And so nothing about my mother living in another country—not keeping a watchful eye on her man, allowing him to roam wild and free with some other woman—felt right with me. Not one dang bit. Yes, my father was a cheater! A low-down, dirty...well, it wasn't his fault. It was my mother's.

Even I knew a woman was supposed to be there for her man. Stand by him. Love him. Keep him satisfied. Keep him happy. Keep him wanting her. Missing her. Needing her. *Not* push him into the arms of another man-hungry woman.

"Why are you *not* back here trying to fight for your marriage, for Daddy?" I snapped, feeling myself slowly becoming overwhelmed with emotion. I was angry with her for leaving him, and *me*. And I was mad with Daddy for rolling around in the sheets with some high-priced troll. Some, some re-formed men's locker room stalker.

God. Men, like boys, could be so stupid. Insensitive. Thoughtless. Oh, and did I say stupid?

My mother blew out what sounded like an aggravated breath. "You are kidding me, right? You've called me at this ungodly hour to ask me this nonsense? Really, London?"

I pushed out a breath, trying to bite back my temper. "Yes, Mother. I did. Early or not, I want—no, *need*—to know why you have given up on us. Me. Daddy."

There was a shocked silence.

"You don't know what you're talking about, London."

"I do so, Mother. I know all about Daddy and his mistress. *Mrs.*—"

"London, not another word."

"Can't you see, Mother...you're letting that groupie whore win?"

"Watch your mouth, London. And stop with this foolishness. No one has won *any*thing. And as far as your father goes, he made his choice long before I boarded my flight. So don't you dare—"

"*I want a divorce!*"

"*Fine! Go be with your mistress, Turner! London and I will move to Milan...*"

"I know everything, Mother. So stop."

"And what exactly, London, is it you *think* you know, huh?"

"About why you really left. About Daddy's cheating with—"

"London, you stop right there. Don't you *dare* say another word...I'm warning you."

"No, Mother, *you* stop. I overheard *every*thing. That night you and Daddy were down in his study arguing, the night I'd had my meltdown at Nobu's. I'd come downstairs to—"

"Shut your mouth, London," my mother warned again. "Or—"

"Or *what*, Mother? Are you going to cut off my allowance? Punish me? You walked out on *me*, so you don't get to give me any ultimatums," I said boldly.

My mother gasped. "London—"

"No, Mother. Tell me why you never *wanted* me."

"London. Just stop with this madness. You have no idea what you are talking about. I never said I didn't *want* you."

I huffed. "Well, you sure as heck didn't want to *carry* me, now did you?"

"Fine, London," she snapped. "Let's get it all out in the open and finally be done with it. Here's the truth: Your father wanted children. I didn't. Not right away, anyway. I was young, and my career was really taking off, and that was what I wanted more. I wanted children later in life. Not right then. But I loved your father, and I wanted to make him happy. So I gave him what he wanted most. A child. And, yes. I used a surrogate."

I felt my chest tighten. Hearing her admit this was, was... hurtful. And so, so very telling. That she'd never really wanted me.

"I couldn't stop doing what I loved. Modeling was everything to me..."

Mmmph. It still is...

"I was a rising star," she continued. "I'd become the fresh face of the runway, and I just didn't want to give that up. I didn't know how I would do both: be a mother and have a career. It was all too frightening. So a compromise was made. One that your father agreed to. So I paid to have someone else carry you, then give birth to you. I was there with your father to watch you come into this world. Do I regret it, London? Do I wish I could do things differently? Well, the answer is no, absolutely not. And I will not allow you or anyone else to try to make me feel any less of a woman for doing so. I loved your father. He'd been my first, my everything. And I wanted more than anything to be his wife..."

I took a deep breath.

"And I'm sorry, darling, that I couldn't be the type of mother you wanted. I was the best that I could be. Could I have been better? Yes. Could I have done better? Yes. Did I make some mistakes along the way? Of course I did. But I tried to instill in you the best morals and values I could so that you would flourish into a young beautiful woman."

I blinked. In my mind's eye, cameras flashed. The camera clicked and popped as the photographer moved around the floor capturing my image from different angles. *"Magnificent, darling. Yes, yes,"* my mother had called out to me. *"The camera loves you."* The photographer continued snapping photos of me until he had about thirty frames.

"You were born to be in front of the camera..."

I blinked again. I was suddenly transported to another place. I was eight.

"Back straight, London, darling. Now walk. One foot in front of the other."

And I did.

Walked.

The weight of a phone book balanced on the top of my head. One, two, three, four...three more steps and the phone book toppled from my head and hit the floor.

"No. No. No. You're walking like a slew-footed klutz, Lon-

*don. Poise. Grace. That is what I am trying to teach you.
Pick your feet up off the floor, darling. Do not drag yourself
like some baboon. Now again."*

Eight hours later, I was still walking. Over and over and
over, up and down the long hallway until my body ached,
until the back of my legs burned, until fire burned through
the soles of my feet.

That night, and every night thereafter, my mother painfully
taught me poise and grace. And in between catwalk training,
she'd taught me how to make friends with the camera. Mouth
slightly ajar, lips always pouty, and then...the pose. Thrusting both hips forward, shooting one hip out to the side,
while balancing my legs, one behind the other.

And then came the hours of standing in front of the ever-
present wind machine no matter how badly my eyes burned.

"No blinking, London," she'd warn. "No blurry eyes."

So, dry-eyed and all, there had been no blinking.

Ever.

And then came years of unnerving weigh-ins. My mother's
beloved digital scale, her leather-bound journal and exquisite ink pen, and all of her meticulous recordings of my weight
and measurements. Monitoring my caloric intake had been
her life's work to ensure I remained tall, thin...a human
hanger, wafty and slender.

"Diet is everything in this industry..."

But my weight wouldn't always cooperate. And my binge
eating couldn't always be controlled. And so my weight would
yo-yo up and down. And so my full breasts and rounded hips
became the enemy, the antithesis of the perfect body.

*"...at the rate you're going, you'll never make it on the
runway. You'll only be good enough to shake and bounce
for rap videos..."*

And at the cost of nearly stripping me down to protruding
bone, she'd succeeded—right up until that god-awful day in

Milan, the Fashion Week finale. The day I'd sliced into my arm and across my wrist with a razor, then collapsed as I made my way down—

I rubbed along my arm, my fingertips brushing over my scars. The marks I refused to have removed by plastic surgery. My reminder.

That I wasn't perfect.

That I'd never be perfect.

"Maybe I was too hard on you," my mother admitted, cutting deep into my reverie. "Maybe my delivery hasn't always been the best. But know this, London. I have loved you. I have always loved you, from the moment I held you in my arms. And I have only wanted nothing but the best for you."

Suddenly, I felt drained. I blinked back the beginning of fresh tears. I hadn't heard her say those words in so long, too long. *I love you.*

And for the first time in a long time, the words sounded, *felt* real. Not rehearsed, like every other time. I flopped down on my bed and choked back a sob. When I'd called her I hadn't expected...I mean, I wanted...I mean, I needed... answers, but I didn't, I hadn't—

"So are you and Daddy really over? Are you divorcing him?" I pushed out, reaching for a manila folder sitting on my nightstand. I walked over to my chaise and sat. I opened the folder and shuffled through its contents. Photos. My heart beat against my ribs.

I heard my mother take a long deep breath. Then she slowly exhaled. "Right now, London, your father and I are separated; that's all I can say for today. Until he and I work out the details of our separation and parenting, I will be flying back and forth to spend time with you at the estate when your father is doing business in his London office."

And he'll probably have his mistress sneaking off to be with him.

"So you're avoiding him?"

She sighed. "No, London. I'm spending time with my daughter. I'll see you in a week or so."

"Okay," I mumbled, before we said our good-byes.

I glanced over at the time. I had less than thirty minutes to get to school. I quickly finished dressing, grabbed my clutch and keys, and sauntered out the door.

11

Heather

The moment I snapped open my eyes, hot fire assaulted my chocolate orbs as sunshine flooded my room. *Ugh!*
I blinked.
My head pounded.
I felt like crap.
I blew out a hot breath and frowned. I cupped a hand over my mouth, then blew into it and almost threw up in the back of my mouth.
Oh…my…gaaawd! My breath smelled like an open grave.
Horrid!
God, I needed a quick swig of mouthwash and a pinch of goodness, just a little to kick-start my morning. That annoying half-French, half-Italian, half-a-man Philippe Pinelle would be storming through my room in any second with the camera crew, and I needed to be ready for him and his heavy makeup, which dripped like clay as he sweated like a pig.
Yes, yes, yes. I needed my medicine.
And a breath mint!
But that was beside the point. What I needed most was to

have my mind ready for all of Philippe's crazy antics. That goddang man was worse than a woman. A straight *beeeeey-otch!* All he did was nag, nag, nag! *Cuuuuuut*, this! *Cuuuu-uut*, that! Cut, cut, cut!

Ugggggh.

But he was the best reality-TV director in the business. Heck, in the world! And he was on his way to making me a bigger star than I already was. I was going to be hotter than Cookie Lyons. Be more talked about than all the Trickdashi-ans put together. Have more Twitter followers than Angelina Jolie. More YouTube views than Beyoncé's *Drunk in Love* video.

Yasss, honey, yasss! Philippe Pinelle was about to do the damn thing! And then I'd be able to tell Kitty, Camille, and all them corny, whack-azz pampered slores to go to H-E-L-L.

I was destined for greatness. Shoot. I already had iTunes on lock. Now all I had to do was, as Camille had stated, "follow the yellow brick road to success."

And Philippe was going to be directing all eyes on me. Still, when he was all up in my ear barking orders, telling me to stick to the script, I wished he'd cut out his vocal chords and shut the *eff* up!

I knew the lines to my script. Heck, I lived it every day. Everything I was. Rehearsed lines. Uncut lines. Missed lines. I was one big performance. This was what my life was. A scripted mess!

I just happened to be on set, living it out in front of the world. Still, I hated this reality-TV crap! But I needed the checks. I needed to keep a roof over my head and money in my vault to keep me laced in my designer one-of-a-kinds.

I took a deep breath, tightly shut my eyes, and said a little prayer.

Thank you, dear God, for not letting Camille destroy my career. I owe you one. Umm. Maybe two. Peace out and amen.

I pushed out another sigh. After the stunt Camille pulled in Kitty's office last week—slapping her and dragging her for the filth she was—I still needed to stay in her good graces and keep the peace.

I needed to do damage control, which is why I'd sent my publicist a text last night to have an apology bouquet of flowers and a card sent to her office.

Like her or not, Kitty was also the best in the business. She knew television and media the way that crazy Spencer knew her way around a boy's body parts. That skank!

Ooh, Camille, had called her out real good.

Permanent knee pads? A battery pack in her neck?

Bwahahahahahaha.

I reached for a pillow and covered my face as I screamed with laughter into it.

Camille *did*. *That.*

Yasss, God, honey!

Bwahahahahahaha.

And so far, there'd been no backlash from Kitty. *Mmmph.* Check her boo. Still, I needed to not sleep on her. Kitty was known to be ruthless in the industry. Vicious. So I knew I had to stay on my A-game. I had to keep the drama turned up on the set, and keep my ratings up.

Still, I couldn't lie. I was pissed at Camille for doing what she'd done. She could have handled things another way, I thought. And I told her so. But she'd blown my tirade off. Told me that Kitty wasn't crazy enough to retaliate. That Kitty would take her lumps and play nice for a while. That she had it all under control.

"Let me *handle, Kitty," she'd warned. "And you keep a handle on your pill snorting. The last thing I need is a damn junkie on the loose. And before you open your mouth, you need to stop acting like one! Stop acting like some thirsty trick! A gutter rat fiend!"*

"I'm not a gutter rat! And I'm not a fiend! Or some thirsty trick!" I protested.

She slung her drink in my face, then jabbed a finger in my face. "Shut your lies, Heather Suzanne! Just stop with the lies! You are what I say you are! And right now, from where I'm standing, everything about you screams pill-junkie fiend! Now not another lie about what you think you're not. Because, between you and me, sweetie . . . you suck at it!"

She was drunk.

"I'm Camille Cummings, goddammit!" She threw her glass at the wall. "An Academy-Award-winning actress! I've given up everything for you. Everything! And all I have to show for it is a child who can't seem to decide if she wants to be a man or a woman! All I have is a child who wants to end up facedown in some muddy river with a bunch of powdered pills shoved up her nose! Get out of my damn sight before I forget I gave birth to you and loved you even when I didn't feel like loving you or loving my-damn-self!"

Really?

I inhaled. Held my breath in for as long as I could, then slowly exhaled. I wiped more tears from my eyes, then shook my head.

I wished there was a way I could get a refund for having Camille as a mother. I loved her, but hated her more. I needed her, but wanted nothing more than to be free of her. She was my mother. I couldn't *not* love her. I didn't have it in me.

Clearly, there was something wrong with me.

And Kitty?

I shook my head again.

I wanted to hate her too. But I couldn't. She'd been the only one willing to pull me out of a sinking ship. That crazy woman had become my lifeline. I was stuck with her. And, sadly, I needed her.

I closed my eyes and bit back a scream as my reality bloomed in clear view.

Kitty Ellington was my master.

I was her slave.

And she owned me.

But if I was really, really honest with myself, she believed in me in her own sick, twisted way. She showed me tough love because she cared. She *knew* I was a star. And I knew she wanted to—

I jolted up in my king-size bed. Then listened.

Wait. Why was it so quiet?

I glanced over at the clock on my nightstand. It was nearly ten o'clock in the morning. Philippe and his loud mouth should have been here by now with his camera crew in tow. But they weren't.

Hmm. That's strange, I thought as I gazed across the room at my strewn clothes from the night before. I frowned. It was frickin' too quiet in here.

I slithered out of bed; my feet sank into the deep purple carpet as I reached in back of me and pulled the string of my thong from out of my heavenly lumps. I yanked out a pair of faded jean booty shorts from my dresser drawer and wriggled into them. I slid my feet into a pair of wedged heels.

Then headed out the room.

I marched my way into the kitchen. Quiet. Next the living room, then the great room, then all the bathrooms. Still quiet!

I stalked toward the front door, swinging it open and looking out. Nothing. No Philippe. No crew trucks. No cameramen. Nothing.

I slammed the door, then headed straight to Camille's room and barged right in.

I rolled my eyes. There she was. Mouth open, drooling, lying on her stomach, her nightgown hiked up over her hips.

"*Ca-*"—I quickly caught myself—"Mother?"

She didn't budge. And for a split second I didn't think she was breathing, until she passed gas. Ugh.

I shook her, but she just let out a loud snore and buried herself deeper into the bed. "Mom!" I shook her again.

"Whaaat?!" she yelled, swatting a hand at me. She peered up at me through her long, white-blond hair. "What is it, Heather? Don't you see me in here trying to get my beauty rest? Now what the hell do you want?"

I rolled my eyes and frowned. She reeked of booze. It was seeping through her pores. "Have you talked to Philippe? He's not here."

She grunted, swatting at me again. "Yeah, you idiot! I slept right through the conversation. You're so ridiculous, Heather. You wake me from my sleep for this? Take me from Idris to ask me about some fat tart? Are you kidding me?" She jumped up and reached for one of her king-size pillows and swung it at me. "I was about to straddle him, damn you, Heather! Get the hell out so I can catch him before he pulls his pants up."

I sucked my teeth. "Fine! I'll just call him."

"Well, that's what you should have done any-damn-way. You dream snatcher! You better hope he's still in my dreams when I shut these eyes or I'ma kick your—"

"Whatever," I mumbled under my breath as I slammed her door shut behind me.

"Bring me a drink!" she yelled.

I kept walking.

"Heather Suzanne? You hear me? Fix me a drink, so I can get my day started."

Ignoring her, I fished my phone from my bag, then called Philippe, as I walked back out to the living room. "The subscriber you've called has a number that is no longer in service..."

I frowned, staring at the phone screen. "That's odd," I said, redialing his number. I'd just spoken to him yesterday from this same number. Again, the automated voice said his number was no longer in service.

What the *fu*—

My phone rang. Unlisted number. I frowned again. Who would be calling *me* from an unlisted number? Then it dawned on me. It was probably Philippe or someone from his crew calling to let me know they were running late.

"Hello?"

"Heather, it's Charlotte Emmons."

I blinked. Charlotte Emmons was my new publicist. She'd been referred by Kitty and so far had been a godsend.

"Oh, hi. What's up?"

"We have a problem," she said, flatly.

My stomach lurched.

"A problem? What kind of problem? Did you send Kitty the flowers I asked you to?"

"Right now, Miss Cummings..." I blinked. *Miss Cummings?* Uh-oh. She was being formal. Not a good sign. "... flowers are the least of the problem."

I swallowed, hard. Then tried to act natural. "Oh. Then what's the problem?"

"You and your mother, Camille, have been officially banned from Kitty Productions. Neither of you are to step foot on or near the premises of any of the Kitty buildings or its affiliate enterprises."

Wham! My knees buckled. I felt like I'd been sucker-punched.

My hands shook. "Exc-c-cuse me? I think there's a bad connection."

"No, Miss Cummings. There's no bad connection. All ties with Kitty Productions have been severed, effective immediately. Your trailer has been cleared out of all of your belongings and will be sent to you by a driver."

Wham! Another blow to my gut.

"Wait. She's firing me...for *what?*"

"For your libidinous behaviors over the last several weeks. And the libelous behaviors displayed by your mother, Camille. Attacking Mrs. Ellington, slandering her name. You and your affiliation with your mother as your manager are not a good fit for the Kitty brand. Mrs. Ellington has opted to not file charges, but she has been advised by legal to cut ties."

Oh God, oh God, oh God! I'm being fired! Fired! Oh God! I can't be fired!

"God, no," I pleaded. "This has to be one big misunderstanding. If I can—"

My voice went. The tears escaped my eyes.

"No misunderstanding, Miss Cummings. Weak links break chains. So your time with Kitty Productions has come to an end. And with that being said, I will no longer be representing you as your publicist. Good day. And all the best to you."

She hung up.

I blinked. "Hello? Hello?"

And as if my world hadn't already been bulldozed enough, the doorbell rang.

I swung it open. *"Whaaaat?"*

"Heather Cummings?" a freckle-faced man with a mop of woolly red hair atop his head asked.

"Yeah," I said over a sneer. "Who's asking?"

"Here." The man thrust a cream-colored envelope at me. I stared at his hand for a beat, then snatched the envelope from him. "You've been served."

I blinked. *I've been what? Served?*

I glanced at the sender's return address at the top of the envelope: KITTY PRODUCTIONS.

And crumbled to the floor.

12

London

By the time I made it to my fifth-period AP English class the following day, I was pretty much done with being here—in class, in school. My mind was everywhere else except here, where it needed to be, especially since I had an exam coming up in my French class next period.

I closed my eyes and shook my head. I didn't want to think about it. This place. All I wanted to do was get through this period, then the next, and then get home.

I knew I'd be watching the clock and counting down the minutes until this day was officially over. So far, it *drrrrr*agged!

Luckily, I hadn't seen Rich but only three times today. Once at her locker; the second time, she was twerking along with Spencer in the middle of one of the hallways; and the third time, I'd nearly bumped into her as she'd come barreling out of one of the girls' lounges.

I didn't speak. And neither did she. Instead, she'd rudely brushed by me, sucking her teeth. The old me (the *me* before counseling) would have snatched her by the back of her weave and yanked her scalp back.

But I was really trying to be a different type of girl. Really. I was.

"Oh-my-*gaaawd!* No *way!*" I heard the girl sitting directly in back of me shriek. I couldn't remember her name. Something insignificant. But her voice was whiny and annoying, and she loved cladding her Pilates-toned body in black lace.

I shifted in my chair, brushing my bangs to the side, before rummaging through my bag to retrieve my books, notepad, and a pen, pretending to be disinterested in their mini preclass gossip session.

"Yes, girl," I overhead her bestie say. She was also someone with a name I could not recall. Another insignificant. "Heather's reality show has been canceled. No. Correction: She's been *fired*. It's all over the blogs."

Ohmygod, I thought, as I tried my best to scoot farther back in my seat so that I could listen discreetly without being obvious. Heather fired from her show? I had no idea. And though I wished Heather no ill fortune, she did need to be knocked down from off her high horse. She'd gotten too big for her own good. Cocky. She'd become real snotty—umm, or should I say, snottier than before.

Heather really thought she was all that.

"Aww, that's horrible news," Whiny Girl said. "I loved her reality show."

Her friend grunted. "Um. *Hated* it."

Whiny Girl giggled. "Oh, stop, Natasha. It was entertaining."

Oh, Natasha. Right.

"It was more like a train wreck, if you ask me," the Natasha girl stated with a *tsk*. "I don't know which was worse: hers or that horrid *Here Comes Honey Boo Boo* TV series."

Whiny Girl snickered again. "Oooh, I loved that show too. Honey Boo Boo was adorably..."

"*Fat,*" her friend stated rudely. She groaned. "The whole cast, a hot mess! Ohmygod! Another television show gone all the way wrong," she continued. "TLC should have been shut down for ever airing that piece of trash of a show."

"Well, that's your opinion. Still, I loved it. And I loved *Kickin' It with Heather*," Whiny Girl stated. "I thought the show was funny. And her mother is . . ."

"A *drunk*," the Natasha girl stage-whispered. "But *any-whooo* . . . I liked Heather better when she played Wu-Wu Tanner. At least I could *relate* to that girl."

"Of course you could," Whiny Girl commented, "since you have two perfectly wonderful parents and you've lived such a perfectly wonderful life, everything perfectly in place."

"*See*," the Natasha girl agreed. "Just like Wu-Wu."

Yeah, right. I rolled my eyes and bit back a grunt of my own. These L.A. hoes were so fake. They sadly didn't know fact from fiction.

"So when was her show canceled?" Whiny Girl wanted to know, her voice tinted with dismay.

"Like yesterday, I think. Read the blogs," the Natasha girl urged. "They're quite juicy."

"*Scandalous!*" Whiny Girl exclaimed. "I'm so distraught."

The Natasha girl laughed. "Are we talking the-first-time-you-had-your-period distraught, or are we talking the-time-you-were-in-the-boys'-bathroom-stall-with-Corey-Marshall-and-looked-up-and-saw-your-name-and-number-on-the-wall-sprawled-in-black-ink distraught?"

I frowned. Ohmygod! She'd been with Corey, too? What a man-whore that boy was. He'd sleep with anything wearing a skirt and a weave. He'd also been one of Rich's many boyfriends here at Hollywood High, and he'd cheated on her with Spencer.

Eww. See my point?

"Ooh, you *bish*," Whiny Girl hissed. "I told you that in confidence, you skank. But no. It's more like an I'm-bloated distraught."

The two bimbos broke out in laughter.

I couldn't believe what I'd heard about Heather. I quickly pulled out my cell and punched in my password, then pressed the tab for the Internet. I typed in Heather's name, and there they were—the captions.

Tons of them.

A hand flew up over my mouth in disbelief as I scrolled through a few of them.

IS THIS THE END FOR HEATHER CUMMINGS?
HEATHER CUMMINGS CANNED AGAIN!

Probably from her drugging, I thought as I continued to scroll. God knows her C-list acting skills wouldn't be the reason she was back on the unemployment line.

WILL IT BE BACK TO THE FLOPHOUSE FOR TEEN STAR
HEATHER CUMMINGS?
LIGHTS OUT! HEATHER CUMMINGS'S STAR HAS BEEN
SMASHED OUT.

The tabloids and gossip sites were dragging Heather for *filth*. Mostly reporting, assuming, speculating that she was back to her druggie ways and with one foot back into rehab.

Although I kind of felt bad for her, I was embarrassingly relieved that it was her being dragged by the media and not me.

The rudest headline caption thus far read:

FROM THE KITTY TRAIN TO THE DUMP TRUCK! HEATHER
CUMMINGS FIRED FROM THE KITTY NETWORK! TOSSED OUT
LIKE TRASH!

This was simply too much to take in. I mean, it wasn't, by far, the first time Heather had been fired from a television network. But, still, I had thought she would have learned her lesson from the last time. Her pill snorting and partying were what had gotten her contract as Wu-Wu Tanner terminated. Now this.

When was that girl going to finally learn?

Probably never, I mused, as Mr. Robinson whisked into the classroom.

"Okay, class. Let's get started..."

Blah blah blah. I wasn't even focused on anything Mr. Robinson was saying. And although I had more important things to obsess over, like what Daddy was doing in his free time over in London, Heather's demise was a disturbingly nice distraction.

Sadly, I almost felt sorry for her.

Almost.

"...I take it you are all prepared to discuss yesterday's reading assignment..."

I flipped open the book *Outliers*, by Malcolm Gladwell, trying to redirect my attention onto class. I knew Heather and I didn't like one another. And yet I found myself sitting here, in this hellhole, my thoughts fixated on her. Wanting to do something nice for the poor wretched girl.

Dear God.

What was happening to me?

13

Spencer

"**M**ove, move, *get out the way!*" I yelled out the window of my sports car at no one in particular. Goshdiggity-dangit! I was hotter than a jalapeño pepper. The traffic flow was horrific!

The Mercedes-to-Bentley traffic on Santa Monica Boulevard was *hell*alicious! Front bumpers were nearly kissing the backside of other luxury vehicles. And I wasn't in the mood for any of these trickeroos playing bumper tag with my car.

Deargodbabysweetjeeeeeeeeezus! Please don't let me end up with a hemorrhoid from sitting for almost forty-five minutes in all this traffic. Please and thank you.

Horns blared, so I pressed down on mine. Then I flipped some two-hundred-year-old-looking lady, with rocker-chick makeup plastered on her face, the bird for giving me the finger for trying to go around her. The old bat had the nerve to drive the speed limit!

Who did that?

"Sojourner Truth!" I yelled out of my window. "You don't want it with me, you roadkiller! We can pull over and take it to the streets!"

Woosah. Woosah. Woooooooosaaaaaaaah. I turned on
the stereo. I needed to calm my nerves before I rammed my
shiny new car into someone. *Wooooosaaaah.*

The second Rihanna's "Breakin' Dishes" poured from the
speakers, I started bouncing in my seat and singing along
until the music faded and a call rang through.

Rich.

*"Now good night, you mop head! You're dismissed. Now
go sop up some boy's milk...!"*

That trick was nothing but fictitious storytelling, and she
had another think coming if she *thought* I was about to chitty-
chitty, chat-chat with her after she disrespected me at that
man-lady club. Those big burly lady-boys were frightening.
No, no, no. Miss Trixie had the wrong number. She'd turned
her panty liner inside out with me.

And I was done with her!

Again!

I let her call roll right into voice mail. And then I reached
for my cell and texted: CALL ME AGAIN N I WILL BLOCK UR #!!!

Less than a second later, Rich texted back: BIH, I DARE U.

Then she boldly called again. I pressed IGNORE. Then
blocked her.

The music came back on, and I shimmied my shoulders.
By the time August Alsina's voice filled the cabin of the car—
six songs later—I was *still* stuck in traffic, but at least I was
bouncing my booty in my seat.

"Yesssss, yessss! I'm a young diva who just lives life! It's
hell on earth! Pull up to my bumper, boo-boo!" I sang out,
trying to turn this horrid moment into a sing-along. "Let me
slam on my brakes and let you get all up in my tank! Let me
break a dish upside your bubble head!"

I dug my nails into the steering wheel.

I was on the verge of a full-blown road rage attack. It was
a quarter to three, and I had only fifteen minutes to get to my

appointment. I was meeting with my dick. Heeheehee. I mean, my private eye.

I needed to get to the bottom of all this Cleola Mae foolery once and for all. And today was the day that I would finally claw out the meat and bones of this madness and get down to the nitty-gritty and expose this invisible woman Daddy apparently was so—

The music faded out again. The caller was from a 619 area code. I frowned.

"Spencer here," I said curtly. "State your business."

"You bone licking *tramp!* You hateful skank!"

Dear Lawd Jeezus...

"*Rich?*"

"Yeah, hooker! Thought you could run, huh? Run, Homer, run! But you can't hide! I will always hunt you down!"

I sucked my teeth. "Um, Ugly Betty. I'm not running. I'm riding. And it's Forrest."

"*Betty?* Clutching pearls! Do I sound like a Betty to you, huh, *Speeeeeencerrrr?* I'm from the loins of Shakeesha Gatling! Pop, pop! It's all Crenshaw over here! Get it right! Ain't no Bettys in the hood! And the only ugly one is you. Wait. Forrest? I'm not about to run through no forest, girl. You know I'm allergic to jungles. My name ain't Gretchen!"

I sighed. "It's Gretel, Rich. You know, from Hansel and Gretel."

"Trick! Don't play word games with me. I'm too old for the playground, li'l girl. Did you block my other number?"

I rolled my eyes around in my head. "Uh, duh. Yeah. I warned you that I would."

She snorted. "Ha! Shame on you! And you thought I was just two-one-three and three-one-zero..."

"No, Rich," I stated snidely. "I knew you were a ho with different area codes."

"*Yaaaassss*, honey, *yaaaaasssss!* I'm worldwide."

I clucked my teeth. "Mmm-hmm. A globe-trotting *thot*."

"Yes, yes, yes...wait! Are you tryna be low-key messy, *Speeeeeeeeencerrrrr?*"

"Rich, are you stalking me?" I demanded to know.

"*Stalking* you?" She scoffed. "Don't do me, slore! You are not stalker-worthy! I stalk three-legged men, honey. Not some nasty meat juice lover."

Not today, girlie! "The number you have reached," I began as I maneuvered around another slow-moving vehicle, "has been suddenly disconnected. Please do not call back again."

Click.

I turned off my phone as the music spilled out of the speakers again.

Lordjeezus! I had to focus. I was twenty minutes late. I pressed down on my horn, again, then quickly swerved out from between two cars that practically had me sandwiched in, nearly taking off the rear bumper of the hag in front of me.

By the time I finally arrived at my destination (nearly thirty minutes late!), I was close to hyperventilating. I quickly slid out the car, shouldering my distressed leather and ostrich bag, and slammed the door shut before smoothing a hand down the front of my pleated miniskirt. I paired it with a cute black T-shirt with a gigantic pair of glossy red glittery lips that exploded over my chest. And then I paired my ensemble with a pair of strappy crystal-studded heels.

No gaudy jewels. Just two diamond-encrusted bangles and a pair of diamond studs. Today it was all about the heels. Always, always kill them with a good heel! Heeheehee. My look was sassy, yet schoolgirl sophisticated. I tossed my hair, then stepped. My heels clicked with purpose as I strutted toward our arranged meeting spot.

Sweaty and annoyed, even though there was a cool breeze whisking around me, I narrowed my eyes and swept my gaze around the area. I didn't see him. I batted my lashes, then took another look around.

"He's not here!" I screamed in my head as I pushed my oversized Dior wraparounds up to the crown of my head and did another scan of the pier.

I'd been driving on a traffic-jammed highway for over an hour and fifteen minutes, and at the very least he could have waited for me!

Or—

Oh. My. God.

Purse now dangling in the crook of my arm, I plunged my hand into its depths, past brass knuckles, canisters of Mace, nunchuks, my wallet, Kleenex, wipes, a flyswatter, and binoculars. I pulled out my iPhone and quickly powered it up.

There were nine messages. Seven from Rich, who'd called me back to back seven times. One from RJ, who'd called just to let me know he was thinking of me (awww, he was so sweet!). And then came the very last voice mail—from my P.I.

"Spencer. Mike here. Um, listen. I need to reschedule our meeting. Had an unexpected emergency. My twelve-year-old daughter's bichon poodle has been kidnapped and is being held for ransom. I'll call you when the crisis is over."

I blinked. Blinked again. Then replayed the message. No, no, *noooooo!* This couldn't be right. I played the message a third time. My teeth started chattering from the anger rapidly swelling inside of me.

I'd been ditched for a dang poodle!

14

Heather

*D*_{*ing dong.*}
Ding dong.

I frowned, glancing over at the time. It was almost eight p.m. *Who in the heck is ringing the doorbell all heavy?* No one was expected. And I knew Miss Co-Co wasn't coming through since I'd only gotten off the phone with him less than a second ago. He wanted to go out prowling, instead of coming over to comfort a friend.

What a shady skank muffin!

So what if Camille couldn't stand him? So what if she called him crude names to his face? Or sneered at him every time he came around?

He was still supposed to be *my* friend.

The truth of the matter was that Co-Co was only good for a turn up. He was only really my friend as long as he was benefiting from said friendship. He was my ride or die as long as I kept him front and center—on the set, on stage, in front of the camera lens, in the studio, on the red carpets. As long as it was popping off, Co-Co was ready to *twerk*, *werk*, and *slay*.

He thought I was stupid. Thought I didn't peep his card.

But I knew better. He was using me, but I was using him too—for his get-right. As long as he kept my party bag lined with crushed treats, we were besties 'til the end.

Ding dong.

Ding dong.

I sighed. The only person who'd actually ever wanted me in their life without wanting something from me was... *Nikki.*

She'd cared about me. She'd treated me like a person who mattered. She'd made me feel wanted and special. And somehow I'd managed to screw that up, like I do everything else.

We'd gone from talking every day on the phone and Face-Timing to an occasional text with nothing more than one- or two-word replies back. *Hi. Thank you. You too. K.*

And if I were lucky enough, she'd grace me with an emoji.☺

Everything we'd shared—the long talks, the laughter, the secrets—in those very short months had become reduced to nothing more than a memory now, all because some stupid pap couldn't keep his camera lens from out of my personal life.

All because of that stupid photo captured of her and me outside of El Amor café, where we'd had our first ice cream date. Well, okay, maybe it wasn't a *real* date. But that's what the butterflies that had been beating in my chest had made it feel like. A date. With someone I really liked. And wanted to get to know more—a whole lot more. Nikki was someone who I was so, so happy being around and sharing my world with.

We weren't friends. We were special friends, with a special connection. She'd made my heart smile, and made me want to take her hand and skip through the streets and dare any-one to say something.

Nikki had made me want to be bold and daring. Carefree. She had me giving thought to the future, the possibility of going to college (Lord knows how much I despise school!). She had me dreaming of being not only her secret boo, but pledging her sorority, AZT, and becoming one of her sorority sisters as well so we'd always be connected.

"You're kind, funny, sweet, pretty, and I like you."

I sighed inwardly, dabbing a tissue under my eyes as the tears fell. "I know you really cared about me, Nikki," I whispered as I stood before the mirror and stared at myself. "Maybe one day we can be special friends again."

I lifted a finger to my lips and closed my eyes, remembering our first kiss. But the heated memory was replaced with that photo of Nikki and me and its nightmarish caption:

TEEN STAR HEATHER CUMMINGS CAUGHT MAKING OUT WITH
COLLEGE CUTIE NICOLE ASHFORD OF SAN DIEGO STATE, BOTH
PICTURED BELOW.

All it had been was a kiss on the cheek. A take-care-see-you-real-soon-had-a-great-time kiss that had felt filled with promise. And the paparazzi took that innocent moment and tried to turn it into something dirty and scandalous. And then Kitty with her meddling-azz! Had she not sent the camera crew down to Nikki's campus trying to monopolize on my personal life, none of this would have happened. And Nikki would still be in my life.

My life? Ugh. I hated it!

What a royal fuckup...

Your one shot at happiness, and you couldn't even get that right.

You're so worthless, Heather! So damn pathetic!

I swallowed, hard, struggling to keep the tears that threatened to erupt from my eyes at bay. God, I didn't need this crap—not right now. I turned from the gilded vanity mirror to walk away but turned back and stared at my reflection again. My aqua-blue contact lenses made my eyes look almost catlike. "Meow," I heard myself say, trying to perk myself up to no avail. *Psst.* If only I felt as frisky as one.

I continued staring at my reflection. *Get yourself a pinch, Heather. Stop denying yourself. You know you want it.*

I shook my head. "No. I'm not a junkie. I don't need it."

Girl, bye. You're nothing without it. All you need is a little pinch. Two sniffs and boom-bam-wham! You'll be good as new. Your super powers back! You know you're always at your best when you've had a line or two of goodness.

No! Shut up! Get the hell out of my head!

I didn't want a pinch of goodness. I just wanted to feel good about myself. I wanted to be able to look in the mirror—any mirror—and see something beautiful staring back at me. All I wanted to do was to see what Nikki had once seen in me.

I had to keep it together. I couldn't afford to fall apart. Not now. I had to keep these bills paid. I couldn't give the haters, including Camille, reasons to drag me any more than they'd already been doing lately.

No, no, no. I couldn't end up back in some seedy motel room with all of my belongings stuffed in garbage bags and cardboard boxes. No. Not again.

I had to keep slaying it.

But with what money?

My coins were slowly evaporating. Between the six-thousand-dollar-a-month rent payments, the twenty-five-hundred-dollar light and water and cable bills—add that up with keeping my chef on salary along with my driver (although I really could drive myself, but that was so, so not cute—driving yourself around *allll* the time) and my personal stylist on speed dial, then times that with keeping Camille's liquor cabinet stocked with three- to five-hundred-dollar bottles of scotch and maintaining my one-of-a-kind creations. Add it all up, and I had more money going out than I had coming in.

What was I to do?

I'd just spent a hundred grand on a new wardrobe. I needed to slay. I couldn't be caught slipping, so I had my Korean designers hook me up with some sequined catsuits and several fitted bejeweled jumpers, along with several one-of-a-kind handbags.

The doorbell rang again.

"Heather Suzanne," Camille called out, "who the hell is out there ringing my damn bell like that at this time of night? You know I don't like my cocktail hour being disrupted. Now go get the damn door and tell whoever it is to get the hell on!"

I sucked my teeth. Lady, bye. Every hour is a cocktail hour!

"Heather *Suzanne!*" Camille screamed at the top of her lungs. "If I have to get up and get ugly up in here, it isn't going to end pretty. Now go tell whoever is outside to get the hell off my doorbell!"

Lady, bye. *You answer the damn door!* I wasn't moving from the confines of my room. Whoever it was would eventually get the hint. Nobody's home!

I glanced around my bedroom. Clothes were strewn all over. My bed was unmade. And there were dirty dishes everywhere. I couldn't afford to keep the maid, so we had to fire her. I stared over at my bag lying across the chaise, then stalked over to it, yanking it open and dumping out all of its contents until I came across what I was looking for—my little black velvet pouch, my party bag.

Just a pinch.

I pulled open the drawstring, then peered inside. *Just a pinch.* Yes, yes, to help me deal with Camille. One nostril, two . . . I closed my eyes, then sniffed. My veins slowly heated. I inhaled. *Yes, girl, yes. You did that! See. That's all you needed. A pinch.*

I shook my shoulders, then pulled the drawstring closed, and—

Bam!

My bedroom door flew open, slamming back into the

wall, causing me to jump. And then came a heel whirling in the air toward my head.

"Heather Suzanne! Didn't I tell you to answer that damn door?"

I blinked. Camille had kicked my door in, and there she stood in her featured attire—the sheer nightgown, with sheer coat to match, a tumbler of scotch in one hand, and a Virginia Slim dangling from the corner of her thin lips, glaring at me.

"I told you if I had to get ugly," she continued ranting, "that it wasn't going to be goddamn pretty! Now you've gone and made me break one of my heels off in the door." I frowned. There in the center of the door was one spiked kitten heel poking out from the wood.

"Get out!" I yelled, quickly slipping my pouch into my back pocket. "*You* go answer the door! Can't you see I'm busy?" I was so sick of her. "And when you're done doing that, how about you go find a job. Oh, wait..." I snapped my fingers. "No one will hire a drunk! It's *my* money keeping you with a roof over your straggly-azz head, so you should be on your knees kissing the soles of my feet," I said nastily. "Not giving me—"

Before I could finish my sentence, Camille had managed to leap in the air like Batwoman (or maybe my mind was playing tricks on me!) and catch me by the throat with her free hand. Scotch splashed over the rim of her glass—which she gripped in her other hand—like a tidal wave and washed over her fingers.

Ding dong.

Ding dong.

"Don't have me send you to the morgue stuffed in a suitcase, Heather," my mother said through clenched teeth. "Because I will. Now answer the door!"

She let go of my throat, but not before flicking her fingers at me, droplets of her devil juice splashing in my eyes.

"I can't stand you!" I snapped, nearly elbowing her in her gut. On purpose!

"Well, I can't stand you either! But you don't hear me complaining about it," she yelled in back of me. "No. I suck it up. I suffer through it. I drown my pain. And I pray for the day you turn eighteen so I can..."

Blah blah blah.

"Ole drunk," I mumbled, stomping toward the door in my teeny-weeny pink boy shorts that were wedged up in between my booty cheeks and a pink wrap shirt that had my boobs practically spilling out of it.

"Who the *fu*...?" I tugged open the heavy oak door. And there stood a bobblehead peeking around the side of a humongous basket, her diamonds sparkling under the porch lights, looking like she'd just stepped off the cover of another fashion magazine.

London!

God, I despised this girl. What the heck was *she* doing here?

"Hey, Heather," she said so sweetly that I almost wanted to puke from a sugar rush.

I frowned, blocking the doorway with my body. "Can I help you?"

"Um, I just wanted to drop this off." She thrust the huge basket toward me. "Here. I heard about—"

"Girl, bye," I snapped, slamming the door in her face.

"Who was that?" Camille asked, walking up in back of me.

I huffed. "Nobody."

Ding dong.

Ding dong.

"Then why the hell is *nobody* still ringing my door?" She pushed me out of the way and swung open the door. "Yes?"

"Um. Hi, Mrs. Cummings," I heard London say.

"It's *Miss*. Now how can I help you this evening? Who you with, the church missionaries?"

"Um, no."

Camille grunted. "*Mmmph*. Then why you dressed like some holy-sanctified church lady?"

I was too pissed at Camille to snicker.

"Listen, ma'am. I only wanted to drop this off to Heather…"

"Oh, really?" Camille said, snapping her neck over her shoulder and glaring at me before giving that amazon her attention again. "And you are?"

"London."

Camille widened the door. "Oh, *you're* London. Come in."

I cringed.

"Heather, why didn't you let London in, huh, Pookie? You know I raised you better." She stepped back. "C'mon in from that night air, sugah. It's about time you made your ole fancy-self known. And why you wearing them old-lady pearls? You're too young to be looking so matronly," she said, snatching the basket from out of London's hand. "And what is this we have here?"

I sucked my teeth.

"Oh, just some goodies." London looked over at me, and I rolled my eyes at her.

"Well, we don't need your so-called goodies," I snapped. "So take your li'l raggedy basket and scat!"

"Heather! Stop! Don't be rude!" Camille snapped, giving me a deadly look.

I was pissed. But I wasn't stupid enough to give Camille reason to turn up in front of this fake-azz trick.

Camille sauntered over toward one of the white sofas and set the basket down. And then she began tearing open the purple cellophane wrapping, pulling out wheels of expensive cheeses, an assortment of gourmet olives, rolls of smoked sausages and salami, boxes of artisan crackers…

"Oh, no. You shouldn't have," Camille said, plucking out two bottles of very expensive wine. "Heather, sweetie. Why didn't you tell me London was so sweet? She's nothing like what you told me. I don't know why you go around calling her Bobblehead."

London frowned. And I shrugged.

"No. You really shouldn't have," Camille said again, as she pulled a box of chocolate truffles from the basket. "But I'm glad you did." Camille gave London another thorough once-over. "London, you're cuter than I imagined. It's a shame you're so unstable, though."

"Oh," London said, her eyes widening, her hand on the door handle.

"And your head isn't as big as it looks in all your photos," Camille added, before giving the basket her attention again. "Heather, dear, show your friend to the door."

I almost balled over in laughter. Ooh, the shade. Camille was being messy.

But before I could move my feet, London was already out the door, and it was shutting behind her. *Trick.*

"Oooh, lookie here, Snookems," she said to me, "wine."

I rolled my eyes up in my head. That troll knew Camille had a drinking problem, so why would she bring over *wines?*

To be messy, that's why!

"Pooh," Camille said sweetly as she pulled out a sleeve of sesame crackers, then peeled open a wheel of cheese. "Fix Mommy a drink to go with this cheese and crackers."

15

Rich

Dear Diary,

It's been two weeks.

Four days.

And too many tear-stained nights to count since I've spoken to my man, my baby-boo, the mister to my missus, my Justice.

I wish I could pick up the phone and say, "Wassup, boo!" without him hanging up on me.

Show up at his door and be welcomed in, without being called a stalker. Or having his fat, triple-chin, six-hundred-pound life neighbor call the cops on me, when all I wanna do is see my man in peace.

So what if we argue, scream, bust out a right hook or a backhand, or yank each other's collar every now and then? Everybody knows that's foreplay!

Besides, anything worth having is worth fighting for. And maybe if double gut stopped snacking long enough to roll out of my love life and into her own she would know that...but nooooo, she wanna be a mad cow, call five-oh, and have 'em troll me.

I don't know how much longer I can be without my man, though. Every day that drips by, this sinking knot in my stomach gets bigger and tighter, and twists more.

Some days I can't breathe.

I just wanna lay my head midway on my baby's chest and feel the ripples of his six-pack beneath my cheek.

Soak in the heat of his brown skin.

Rise and fall to the beat of his belly.

Have all my pop, drop, and make it hot come alive as he explores the inches of my curves, channels through my Mother Earth, and blasts my sea with a twinkling of forever.

I wanna scream out, "Daddy!" while he whispers, "Bae."

I'ma keep hope alive, though, 'cause one thing I know, and I put this on everything I love, like my collection of pink diamonds and my vintage Chanel bags—oh, and my designer shoes—the next time me and my baby-boo are in the midst of cuffing season and the Goddess of All Things Petty orders me to go through his phone, I'ma do it . . .

But I'm not gon' get caught.

"Well, well, well, if it's not 'Miss Teen Socialite, Pop Off on the School Steps in a Watts Minute' Rich Gabrielle Montgomery."

Oh.

My.

God!

Clutchin' pearls!

I didn't even have to look up to know that standing there, all uninvited, was none other than the original groupie gone wild, the one and only bourgeois hood rat herself, better known as my mother, Logan Montgomery.

Immediately, I stopped writing, slammed my diary shut, and dropped my gold Tiffany pen onto the bed.

Then I twisted my full lips to the side and pushed out a puff of air.

All I could do was shake my head. Here I was minding my black goddess business, taking a moment before school to collect myself, and up pops she-devil comin' for me.

I swear, I can't do nothing around here in peace.

Mmmph!

I promise you this, though: she can come for me if she wants to.

But.

It ain't gon' end pretty.

It took everything in me not to suck my teeth or roll my eyes, as I finally sat up in bed, leaned against my headboard, and shot my mother a look that clearly said, "What do you want?"

She blinked, then took two more steps into my room. "You better fix your face."

I fixed it, but only because I wasn't in the mood for her drama. Then I said, "May I help you?"

She batted her extended lashes. "Help me?" she chuckled. "You don't have any money or skills to help me."

Breathe, queen, breathe.

She continued, "The question is what do I need to do to help you understand how tired I am of you dragging your father's good name down the media drain!"

Oh, no, she didn't!

Oh.

No.

She.

Didn't.

What in the tick-tick-boom was this?

I snapped, "Excuse you! Let me help you? Your husband and his bastard kids have dragged the Montgomery name down the media drain on their own! Check the seven-year-old, the nine-year-old, oh, and the latest claim to M.C. Wickedness's loose loins, Heather Cummings—excuse me, I mean Montgomery?"

Silence.

Dead. Silence.

Obviously, my mother wasn't ready for me because she stood there blinking all wild like her lashes were coming undone and her thoughts were all jumbled up.

I continued on, and this time I went in for the kill. "And let's not forget about your super son, RJ, and his help in dragging the Montgomery name! You and Daddy talkin' about he's home on summer break! Psst, please. Last I checked, it was September, which is the winter, thank you." I paused, giving her a minute to take that in.

I continued, "So what did your golden offspring Richard the Second do? Wait. Don' tell me. Is he back to bedding all the French white girls from England? Or was he suspended from his British Ivy League school for being a Dominican weed broker, or is he the Irish CFO of a meth lab?"

Still no response, so I capped off what I had to say with, "Always blaming something on me! If anything, I'm keeping the Montgomery name clean!" I tossed the covers off of me, and just as I stood up, my mother rushed over to my bed, gathered my pajama top's collar in her hands, and pushed her pissed-off face into mine.

She blacked, "I don't know who *the hell* you think you're talking to, but don't make me haul off and slap the shit out of you, because I will, and you know it! For the life of me, I don't know why you insist on trying me. Do you want me to toss you over that balcony!"

Clutchin' pearls! She is so freakin' dramatic! "Really, Ma? Really? Why are you always gunnin' for me?! Meanwhile, RJ gets away with everything! But whatever, I'm used to being treated like nothing around here! So would you just let me go?! I have to get ready for school!"

She batted her lashes wildly again and screamed, "Get ready for school! I don't know what for! You're not learning a damn thing! And don't think I'm cutting Westwick another check for your grades this year! You wanna be grown, you wanna buck up at me, then you can be stupid on your own! We try and give you the world, and instead of acting like you have some freakin' decency and manners, you're out here droppin' your panties all over the concrete, acting like a used coochie sex fiend!"

Used coochie?

I spat, "I resent that! I haven't used my coochie in years, and I have never dropped my panties on the concrete. They have always hit the floor!" I paused, because I also wanted to tell her, *I don't have sex! I make love!* But judging by the blood that rushed to her eyes, I changed my mind and instead said, "Now can you let me go? Like I said, I have to get ready for school, and it's important that I be on time!"

"Important?" she said. "Little girl, bye. The only thing important to you is whatever can be shoved between your legs or comes by way of a shopping bag!"

I don't believe she said that! "Well, it must run in the family, because the only thing important to your son is dumping his seed between some chick's cheeks!"

"Rich, you better shut the hell up. I'm warning you I have dropped li'l loudmouth, no-hand bishes like you before. Don't do me!"

"Oh, real classy, now you wanna let loose the Crip on your own daughter!" I was tired of her having me hemmed up, so I boldly flung her hands from my collar and stepped to the side.

Just when I thought I was free, my mother took her right arm and forcefully pinned my left arm behind my back, then swiftly took the crook of her left arm and snatched me into a headlock.

"Ouch!" I managed to scream. "You're hurting me! Mommy, let me go!"

My mother pushed her lips against my ears and said, "Oh, now I'm Mommy? You thought this was a game? When I tell you to shut the hell up, I mean it! 'Cause I'm not that bum-azz smoky lounge singer, wannabe YouTube sensation you out here trickin' for and trippin over! And you will not disrespect me! You wanna be a woman so bad, but can't even handle your damn man! Out here chasing him around like he's the prize. Don't you know your man is a direct reflection of you, so if he ain't worth a damn, neither are you! I'm ashamed to even call you my child! Here I tried to teach you the game, yet your thirst level is on an all-time high! I will not—"

Bzz...Bzz...

Thank God, my mother's cell phone rang; she lightly loosened her grip, but not much, as she focused in on her ringtone.

Bzz...Bzz...

Without warning, she shoved me away and dusted her hands. "Let me tell you something, sweetie, the next time you even think about coming for me you better step your hand level up, 'cause I will end you. Understand?"

I didn't say a word.

She stepped out of her heels. "I asked you a question."

Still no words.

She took a step forward. "Is that a no?"

"Umm-hmm." I mumbled, "Yeah, I understand."

"Thought so." She stepped back into her shoes, smoothed the invisible wrinkles from her cream-colored blouse, and walked toward the door. "And another thing." She stopped in the doorway and tossed over her shoulder, "I don't know what's going on with your body, but you better make a doctor's appointment and have him figure it out, and quick. Now get yourself together. Your brother's home, it's breakfast time, and the chef needs to know if you want one strawberry crepe or two."

16

Spencer

Yessss, goshdiggitydangit. I felt my booty shaking—to the left, to the right. It was jiggling, baby. Swinging. Bouncing. Clapping as my heels clicked against the gleaming marble floor.

It was Wednesday. Humpty-hump day! And I had been humping all last night and into the wee hours of the morning. Oooh, sookie-sookie. Yes, yes, yess! I felt good. I might have been wearing a stylish wrap dress, with a pair of six-inch red bottoms, but beneath the silky fabric I was bare. Commando.

I was being naughty, feeling naked as a beaver in heat.

And I felt liberated.

Felt real *loosey-goosey*.

And I was *loving* it.

Heeheehee.

Why hadn't I thought about bearing it raw—I mean bare—before?

I shook what my momma gave me. Enticed all the boys to stomp the yard and lick up my double decker, but I wasn't paying any of them nasty horndogs any mind. So they could catcall and whistle until the cows drowned. This milkshake wasn't on the dessert menu. And there was no way any of these dirty toads were going to be lapping at my milk bowl.

I paused and scanned the crowded hallway, catching the eye of Corey, that ole nasty polygamist. Cheater. Liar. Dirty horndog. He was one of Rich's many ex-boos and one of my side thing-a-lings.

Yes, he'd cheated on *her* with *me*, then swore he was leaving *her* to be with *me*. But then he turned around and chose smutty Rich over me. Then dumped *her*, for the next trick. Anywhoo...

There was a video of the two of us—me on my padded knees, my face pressed into his—

Ugh.

He licked his lips and grinned at me.

I felt like pulling out my flyswatter and running up on him and swatting his handsome face up. I still couldn't believe I'd wasted all of my good tongue tricks on that heathenish boy. Ooh, he was lucky I was still drunk on a whole carton of man nectar from the night before; otherwise, I would have turned this hallway inside out.

I sneered at him, then spotted Rich at her locker. I rolled my eyes. I wasn't speaking to that, that hood roach. She was so unappreciative of my good-good friendship, so dang ungrateful of my loving and kind ways. And I was downright sick of her foolery.

Godjeezus! She looked so stank-a-dank in them tight pants. I guessed she was going for the skinny-jeans look, but it was an epic fail. It looked more like a big girl trying to stuff herself into a three sizes too small.

Ugh!

I swear. Sometimes Rich could be so dang trifling. All her life she'd been known to turn to hot wings, beer, and boys to fix her life—when she was down, or bored, or lonely, or simply being trampy. All she knew was eating, drinking, and bouncing on bedsprings. First name *Hook*, last name *Er*. She was a pimp's delight.

I turned my nose up. I could smell the stench of her nasty ways from where I was standing, and I felt the bile rising in my throat. It was a messy job, but I supposed who better to be piggish and whorish than her. So I wasn't going to judge her. Not today.

I ran my fingers through my hair, then sauntered over toward my locker—all coy and cute. I was too dang blessed with good jewels, good heels, and a juicy meat-basket to get home to, to be stressed by the likes of Queen Petty.

Heeheehee. *Ooh, I wonder what Rich would do if she knew RJ was still tucked tightly beneath my sheets, half-naked and snoring.* RJ flew in from London last night and greeted me at the door of my bedroom suite with a wide smile and a pet rock that couldn't wait to be played with.

Mmmph. I felt my body shaking from the inside out as I punched in the code to my combination, then opened my locker, making Rich invisible.

Several long moments later, she slammed her locker shut. "Don't do me, skank-breath. You dumb blonde. I know you *see* me. Or are you that damn blind?"

I peered from around my locker door. "Oh, hey, Piggy-Wiggy," I said, gazing down at her diamond-stiletto-clad feet. "Cute hoofs."

Her perfectly lined eyes widened as she shouldered her bag. "*Piggy? Hoofs?* Trick! Whore! How dare you disrespect me! I ain't no damn piggy. They're fat and nasty, and those ugly pink things stink. I'm cute like a bichon poodle."

I blinked, then said, "Ooh, yes. I see the resemblance." I blinked again. "Yes, you definitely have the face of a dog."

"You got that right, tramp. And a cute one, too." She frowned. "Wait." She placed a hand up to her chest. "*Clutch-*

ing pearls! Are you calling me dog-faced?" She stamped her
heeled foot. "I know you're not tryna call me ugly, *Speeencer!*"

I smirked. "Oh, no, Rich. I would never call you that. You're
a cute poodle, remember?"

She narrowed her eyes. "Don't make me slice you with my
fingernails, trick. You make me so sick, Spencer. I mean,
God! Don't you know I have feelings too? Do you even give a
damn about what happened to me this morning...?"

I shrugged. "No. Not necessarily."

"Mr. Westwick tried to do me in front of the press," she
said, disregarding me. "That old nasty tea bagger tried to embarrass me on the red carpet. And then, to make matters
worse, that damn globe head London tried to set it off too."

"Ma'am, stop," I said. "That's so two weeks ago."

Rich scoffed. "Well, it feels like it just happened. I'm still
grieving, Spencer. Every time I walk up the stairs and don't
see the red carpet, I have a panic attack. And where the heck
were you, huh?" She jabbed a finger in the air. "I'll tell you
where you were, *Speeeencer.* You were somewhere on your
knees trolling back alleys!"

I stuffed my physics book inside my bag, then slammed
my locker shut. "Rich, shut it. Worry about that waterbed
hanging over the waistband of them tiny pants you have on.
Now good day, lady."

I spun on my heels and started shaking what my momma
gave me down the hall. But Rich caught up to me, walking in
step. "Oh, so you think you can run off, huh, *Speeencer?* You
think you can dismiss me? Well, you can't. I'm not dis*miss*-
able. And I will *not* be ignored. I'm all over you, *Speeeencer*.
You damn troll. You, you bobblehead."

I tossed my hair, ignoring her haranguing. I felt her gaze
burning into the side of my face. I saw her from my peripheral, eyeing me up and down. And then I didn't see her anymore. She stopped.

I glanced over my shoulder.

"Oh, my!" she exclaimed, one hand on her hip, the other pointing at my salt shaker.

Then she hurriedly caught up to me. "Why are your booty cheeks clapping all over the place? Are you wearing a thong, tramp?"

"Bye, Harriet Tubman," I said, ignoring her question.

"*Harriet Tubman!*" Rich said indignantly. "Didn't she play in that Madea movie? I am not that old lady who was driving that train. Isn't she Jane Pittman's sister or first cousin or something?"

Lawdjeezus. And I'm the dumb blonde?

I shot her an incredulous look. "No, Miss Celie. They were mother and daughter," I said sarcastically.

"Oh, right. I knew they looked alike."

I nodded my head, smirking. "Unh-huh. And you were the Underground Railroad, letting everyone trample through you."

"And I was a damn good railroad, too, *bish!* My tracks are real wide, and greasy, honey. I keep it lubricated, honey."

"Choo-choo," I sang out, pumping my arm in the air, like a conductor. "*All aboard!*"

"Yasss, honey, yasss," Rich said, excitedly. "Hop up on the Midnight Express."

"Yes, boo," I egged on. "The good-time party ride, non-stop. Hop on, hop off."

"Yasss, girl, yasss. I'm the last stop to goodness."

I rolled my eyes. But laughed along. "Unh-huh. You're a one-stop train ride to the clinic."

"Yasssss, honey, yasssss." She frowned. "Wait. What are you trying to say, *Speeeeencer?* Don't do me. I haven't been to a clinic in months."

I clapped my hands together, my diamond bangles clinking as we rounded the corner toward homeroom. "Hip-hip-hooray! You should be so proud of yourself, Rich. What a major accomplishment."

"Girl, it is," Rich said, sounding pleased with herself. She lowered her voice. "I was so sick of wearing them damn ugly disguises. Those hideous wigs gave me nightmares and a bad case of acne across my forehead."

I smirked. "Well, at least you're not smelling like Swiss cheese anymore."

"*Whaaaat?* Clutching pearls! I don't do *Swiss* cheese, tramp. If it ain't Brie, it ain't right! Don't do me."

"Oh, I won't," I said, immediately spotting Mr. Sanchez Velasquez, one of the permanent substitute teachers. And one of Rich's one-night stands. And she'd had many—too many to keep count of. I'd lost count around fifty-one, fifty-two—and that was like in eighth grade.

God, this girl had a lot of miles on her cootie-cat.

And Mr. Fine Man Sanchez Velasquez might have taught physics, but that night when Rich dragged him up to her hotel suite, after several drinks and platters of hot wings, she'd taught him about the laws of being a ho.

"Oh, but I know who *would* do you," I said snidely.

"Who?"

"Oh, don't play coy, Rich," I said in a hushed tone. "You know who I'm talking about. You see him standing there in them nicely fitted khaki pants."

Rich sucked in a breath, then snorted. "Lies! And fabrications! I would never do an old man like him. No matter how fine and sexy and kissable he was—I mean is. I have standards. And I don't do teachers. Ever."

I gave her a look. She was a ding-dang liar. Oh, how she just randomly forgot that she'd already confessed to me her dirty transgressions. She'd told me all about how she twerked it up and down his love pole.

But, okay, whatever; she could stay stuck in her delusions.

"And after a round of drinks," I stated flatly, "you, your panties, and your standards drop real low."

"*Bish*, lies and deceit," she hissed. "Don't do me! I keep my panties up over these curvy hips."

"Rich, you exhaust me," I said, feigning a yawn.

"Heeey, Mr. Sanchez," she cooed, giving him a little finger wave as we approached him.

"It's Velasquez," I corrected.

She sucked her teeth. "Same difference."

Mr. Velasquez flashed a gleaming smile. "It's cool," he said coolly. "Either one is fine." He glanced at his watch. "You both might want to get a move on it before you're late for homeroom." He flashed another smile, then shifted his weight from one foot to the other.

Of course, I didn't say a word, just stood there eyeing Rich as she batted her eyelashes, sucked in her belly fat, and poked out her double Ds.

I almost spit up a little in the back of my mouth. Rich was truly walking in the valley of whoredom. So I did what any classy woman would do. I left her standing there just as the bell rang, all doe-eyed and slutty, walking into homeroom as Mr. Westwick rounded the corner.

17

Heather

"*At the end of the day—when you find yourself tossed out of your dressing room with your nameplate thrown in your face, all of your belongings stuffed in some raggedy box, and that little twinkling silver star gets yanked out of your hands, do you really think anyone is going to care about who you used to be in Hollywood...?*"

Kitty's voice haunted me, her words taunting me.

Lady, bye! I was still about to get this money up. Yeah, okay, maybe I got a bit sidetracked, slid back a little to my old ways, but homeless I would never be. I belonged on top, and that was exactly where I planned to be. Period, point blank!

"*...what you better do is figure out who Heather Cummings is. Because right now, from where I'm sitting, Heather Cummings is broke! Heather Cummings is irrelevant...!*"

But I wasn't irrelevant!

Was I?

No. Hell no. I was Heather Cummings. Famed star. Actress. Singer.

"*...you want fame? Then be smart about it! Amass you a fortune! Because fame without fortune doesn't mean a* *thing when you're sleeping in a tent under a bridge, which is where you're going to find yourself, little girl—smelling and looking like the inside of a third-world sewer, if you don't stay focused..."*

I felt myself get light-headed. I felt like the walls were closing in on me. I felt like I was being attacked from all sides. The enemy was everywhere. Everyone was trying to do me, to see me fail.

Kitty. Camille. And these frickin' tabloids.

I gripped the magazine I was holding in my hand and read the latest dirt being tossed on me by the media.

This time *Gutz & Glam* was coming for me.

It'd been almost three weeks since my so-called termination from the Kitty Network. And I wasn't gonna lie, the news had shaken me a bit. But I quickly bounced back. I was a star, baby! More than some overnight sensation! And the last place I'd ever end up was in some damn sewer or under some bridge. There were levels to my success, to my hotness. And I had enough fans to keep me relevant, so screw Kitty!

And screw that filthy gossip rag!

Still, I gripped the pages of the magazine and read the story:

> Well, shut down the airwaves, my hungry gossip hounds! Old news is sometimes still juicy news. Looks like the good-time party girl, Heather Cummings, has gotten a swift kick in that ten-thousand-dollar artificial rump shaker of hers by none other than Kitty Ellington herself.
>
> An anonymous source close to the Kitty camp states that the media mogul and queen of all things good and dirty has snapped shut the purse strings and pulled the plug on that horrid reality-TV show *Kickin' It with Heather*.

Womp, womp, womp!
Hated it!

That show was about as dry as the bottom of Heather's wide feet, so we can all rest assured there'll be no award nominations with her name on them. and the only Oscar Heather will ever touch is the one her mother won over a hundred years ago. So it's safe to say it looks like there's another washed-up actress in the Cummings household.

If you ask me, my sweet cherubs, Kitty Ellington did the world a favor by pulling the plug. Hand clap to Mrs. Ellington for trying to resuscitate Heather's lifeless career, but not even Jesus Christ himself could resurrect her. The teen star's acting was mediocre at best. And her defunct Wu-Wu Tanner show was—uh, can we say—overrated. That woolly-haired girl couldn't act her way out of a trash bag. But a source states that if she doesn't get a handle on all of her frivolous spending, she'll be picking through more Hefty bags than she can count, trying to find her next meal ticket.

Catch it, my sweet chickadees.

The pop-locking, dropping-it-like-it's-hot iTunes hit maker is near broke!

Yes, my loves. You read it here first.

Don't be surprised if in the coming months we don't spot the blunt-wielding hooch selling her tramp-stamp fashions to the locals and tourists down at Venice Beach. Gasp!

Or in the words of her arch nemesis—oops, or is that half sister?—Rich Montgomery, "Clutching pearls!"

I felt myself swoon. Those stinking *beeeeeeyotches* stayed coming for me when I didn't call for them. I felt myself shaking from the inside out. They didn't know a damn thing about me, and yet all they wanted to do was talk about me. Try to drag me for filth!

Kitty hadn't shut *ish* down! So what if I wasn't on her *wack*-azz television network, anymore. I didn't need her or her measly handouts! I was still on top! I wasn't broke! My coin purse was still heavy. Dollars in the bank still had multiple zeros behind them.

So that effen hater (all of them!) could go choke on a—

"Yo, Ma!" a voice boomed through the intercom system. "You wasting my time, yo! *Dafuq!* Are we laying tracks or watching you daydream?"

I blinked and caught the eye of the thick-muscled, dark-skinned producer who everyone called Black, as he glared at me through the glass partition.

Co-Co and I had come to Thug Hitz to lay down the tracks for my fourth single, "Catch Me If You Can." But so far the only thing I'd done was stare at this stupid magazine, reading and rereading the slander printed about me.

Mediocre?

Me?

Washed up?

Never that.

They had me all kinds of twisted. There was *nothing* mediocre about my acting skills. I wasn't some second-rate actor. I was a phenomenon, a world-class act.

I swallowed, then glanced down at the crumpled issue of *Gutz & Glam* in my hand.

"Heather Suzanne, you can't get anything right, can you?"

"I don't need another junkie on the loose…"

I shook my mother's voice from my head.

Get your mind right! I mentally scolded myself. *Don't let them hoes get to you. You're the hottest thing poppin'! You wanna keep the haters talking, so let 'em talk! And let 'em keep hatin'!*

But she called me washed up! Broke!

You're not washed up! You're not broke! Four million dollars in the bank is not broke!

But I would have to skim back my spending.

Oh, God, *no-no-no-no!*

I had to let nothing get in the way of my hustle and flow. Not Kitty. Not Camille. And not the hating-azz media.

Where the hell is Co-Co? That shady ho is never around when I need him.

Mmmph. He was probably somewhere in some bathroom stall treating some rapper to some wet sunshine. I didn't know who was worse, him or Spencer.

But anyway...I had to get this money. Prove them all wrong. All I needed was a pinch of goodness so I could get my mind right.

I slammed the magazine down. "Give me a second," I finally muttered, grabbing my clutch and scrambling toward the door that led to a private bathroom.

Once inside, I locked the door, then quickly rummaged inside my clutch, retrieving my black velvet get-right pouch.

One line, two at the most...that was it. I wasn't addicted. I had it under control.

I got this, I thought as I wiped my nose, tossed my pouch back inside my back, then slid a fresh coat of cotton-candy-pink lip gloss over my lips.

I slung open the door. Stepped back into the booth. Grabbed the microphone, then said, "Let's lay these tracks."

"It's about damn time," Black snapped, giving me a disgusted look. "This trick-azz," I heard him mutter just as he hit the switch.

18

London

It was mid-afternoon, bright skies and sunshine. Everyone else was in school—or should have been—and I wasn't. I had fled the West Coast and decided to spend the day on Fifth Avenue in New York, doing a little retail therapy, followed by a light lunch. Yes. Once again, I'd decided to ditch Hollywood High for a bit more excitement than being around a bunch of evil, hateful girls. I needed a moment of peace.

I needed an escape from . . . *them*.

Lately, I'd been toying with the idea of being home-schooled. Just making an appearance on campus was slowly becoming a daunting experience. I was slowly beginning to feel like I had no real purpose there. I knew I needed, *wanted* my education. I just didn't know if I wanted to continue it at Hollywood High. All I knew was, I wished I could click my heels and fast-forward my life, my total existence.

I desperately needed a do-over.

With all the tension swirling around Rich and me like a thick fog, I truly didn't feel like I fit in there anymore. I was a misfit. An outcast. Or at least that was how I'd been feeling of late—ever since I'd come back from Milan, ever since my suicide attempt. I felt like a leper. And the painful truth was, I didn't feel understood, or wanted, at Hollywood High. And even though I pretended it didn't matter, I didn't have any friends there.

Real friends.

Rich wasn't ever that, yet we'd been friendly. And had had some good times. But I wasn't naïve to the fact that she hadn't been capable of ever being genuine.

And neither had I.

I'd been using her. She'd been using me. Our friendship was based solely on what we thought one could do for the other. Quid pro quo. Same thing with Heather and Spencer, although I didn't necessarily fool with either one of those trolls; they were also users of each other. And somehow—in some disturbing way, we all benefited from—

A taxi screeched to a nasty halt, ripping me from my reverie, its horn blaring angrily at me, the driver yelling and cursing at me. My heart jumped in my chest.

"Hey, dumbass! Watch where you're going!" the driver screamed. "Frickin' moron!"

God. I needed to pay attention.

Anywho...

I was in Manhattan. Away from all the West Coast drama, and all I wanted to do was enjoy the day. I looked up, my gaze taking in the buildings reaching into the sky. New York, New York, big city of dreams. Something was always going on in the city. The people, the traffic, the noise...God, there was so much life here.

Orchestrated chaos. And I loved it.

I inhaled. Breathed in the New York air, stale and hot and full of excitement. I hadn't been on the East Coast in like forever, since moving out to L.A., so the hustle and bustle of the city that never slept was a welcome breath of fresh air. It filled my lungs with energy and temptation. And gave me my life back.

I felt immediately alive.

Excited.

And free.

It'd been weeks since I'd run up my credit card—well, Daddy's black card, the one he allowed me to use *sparingly* as he always warned—and I was long overdue for some reckless shopping.

Yes. I felt like being rebellious.

I wasn't depressed. I wasn't sad. But I wasn't miserably happy either.

I was just *blah*.

My therapist thought I was addicted to fame, that I was withdrawing from the attention that came with it, that I missed the adrenaline rush that came with the thrust of cameras and recorders and microphones in my face.

Lies. And more lies.

I wasn't like Rich or Heather. Attention whores. Starved for the spotlight, hungry for the flash of cameras. No. I shied away from being the focus of everyone's interest.

I preferred my privacy rather than public scrutiny.

Spencer had been right. I was a nonfactor these days. No one was really talking about me. And, honestly, I didn't know what to do about it. Or didn't know how I should feel about it. I mean, I liked the fact that no one cared enough to want to know what it was I was doing most days. I wasn't being dragged in the media or on the blogs the way Heather and Rich were catching it. So I was relieved about that.

Heck, the fewer busybodies in my business the better. But on the other hand, being called things like a *bore...a flop... depressing...pathetic...*weren't exactly self-esteem boosters either. And neither was being ignored, or being made...*invisible*.

On the early-morning flight over here, I'd been browsing Instagram under my alias account—the one I'd created after Rich had blocked me from all of her social media pages—when I saw photos of her at some R&B lounge with Spencer. The caption beneath the photo read:

YASSSS, BIHS, YASSSS! ON TURN UP WITH MY GIRL SPENCER!

They were both mudslingers. Talking trash about the other. And yet Spencer had the nerve to call *me* two-faced. *Mmmph*. Those two slores deserved each other.

Another photo was of Rich standing on stage while Justice held a microphone, obviously singing to her. The caption read:

SANG, DADDY, SAAAANG!

She had numerous selfies with the caption:

SEE. WAIT FOR IT! BIHS WISH THEY COULD BE ME!!

Sickened by it all, I clicked onto some of my official pages, and read some of the comments by people who I'd once thought idol—I meant, *liked*—me.

Twitter:
@LONDONTHEGODDESS *u used to be a dime now u half a penny.*
@LONDONTHEGODDESS *when u gonna let me paint ya lips wit dis eggplant sauce?*
@LONDONTHEGODDESS *u wack AF these days yo! Step ya game up!*
@LONDONTHEGODDESS *I c u still got that phatty. Let me beat it up 4 ya.*

@LONDONTHEGODDESS *u used 2 b that chick. WTF happened?*
Get yo life, boo!

Facebook wall:
That bish gotta big head!
Bobblehead!
Oooh, hahahahaha. London still cute tho.
That ho stuck up.
She crazy.
Hide your knives, hide your razors.
Hahahaha. Ikr...crazy trick!

I winced. Disgusted, I'd closed out of each browser, seriously considering shutting down all my pages. God, social media could be so, so heartless. Cruel.
Click.
Click.
Click.
Click.
Stunned, I blinked at the succession of four quick flashes. Someone—unwanted, uninvited—had just taken my picture.
"Ohmygod! I told you that was her, Mommy," one blond-haired, blue-eyed passerby commented, nudging a middle-aged woman, a mini version of herself.
"It is *you*. That teen supermodel?" the woman shouted, drawing the attention of others. "My daughter loves you. Please, one picture?" she pleaded, thrusting her daughter toward me.
I looked at the young girl and, with a slight shrug, acquiesced.
"Ohmygod, I'm so excited," the girl squealed. "You're my idol. One day, I wanna be a model just like you," she said over a wide, toothy grin.
I cringed inwardly. I was so flawed, so imperfect. I'd never considered myself anyone's idol; never gave thought to any-

one, especially a young girl, looking up to me. I'd done nothing spectacular. And yet someone more innocent than I would ever be had told me that one day she wanted to be like me.

I kneeled, pressing my cheek to hers. "No, sweetie," I said in almost a whisper. "Don't be like me. Be better than I could ever be."

Her kind words had touched a part of me, and I choked back a sob. My life as a model was over. But I wasn't. I was alive. And still had my whole life ahead of me to get it right. To finally figure it all out.

Or not...

Several pictures and autographs later, several passersby stared at the tears sliding down my cheeks but said nothing. And just as I was about to step off the curb, a bus approached, nearly hitting me.

Nerves shaken, I jumped back onto the sidewalk, and there, staring back at me, was a poster that ran the length of the bus of a girl I barely recognized—posing, milk chocolate shoulders shimmering from the glow of lights, a five-carat pink diamond necklace hanging from her elongated neck, her lips sumptuously glowing in hot pink.

She wore a slinky pink dress. Flawlessly captured through the lens of the renowned Italian photographer Luke Luppalozzi.

A model.

An illusion.

There I stood. Nose to nose with the ad for the fragrance Pink Heat.

There I stood. Staring into the eyes of...

Me.

19

Spencer

"I'm asking you one more time, Mother," I urged, sitting at the table across from her. Out of all the rooms in this palatial estate, the kitchen seemed to be where Kitty preferred to keep her rump-shaker parked.

She peeled her eyes away from whatever article she was reading and peered at me from over the edge of her magazine. She sighed.

"You're asking me *what*, Spencer?" A hint of agitation coated her tone. "How utterly ridiculous you look with that clove of garlic hanging from your neck? How angry I am at my uterus for carrying you for nine months? How insulting it is to be associated with you as your mother? Is that what you'd like to hear, Spencer, huh?"

I bit into my bottom lip. And instead of leaping up from my seat and doing the Superman on her face, I simply tilted my head and then smiled at her for effect. "Your spirit is evil, Kitty," I said calmly. "But that's nothing new. And it's nothing that can't be fixed by exorcism." I tilted my head to the other side. "This clove is keeping me safe from your evilness. But don't fall asleep tonight. The boogeyman is coming to get you."

I stared her down, then raised an eyebrow.

She huffed. "Spencer, get out of my face before I have you committed."

I laughed, tossing my head back in dramatic fashion so she could see the back of my sparkling white thirty-twos. Then, after several seconds of staged laughter, I abruptly stopped and clasped my hands together like I was praying. "Let me see you try it. But know this: If I get wrapped up in a mummy suit, so do you. So don't test me."

She slammed a hand down on the table. "Spencer, don't try me, dammit! Now what the hell do you want from me?"

"Your *life*," I said curtly. "But for now, I'll take the truth. You do know what *that* is, don't you?"

"Oh, for the love of God, Spencer! The truth about what?"

So she wanted to play duck-duck-goose with me, huh?

I took a deep breath, then sat on my hands to keep myself from reaching over and knocking her coffee cup over.

"About this Cleola Mae," I said. "So before I go digging up people's graveyards, cracking open caskets, and snatching out skeletons, I'm going to ask you one more time, Mother. Who is she?"

She opened her mouth to speak, but I placed a hand up to stop her.

"No, no, no. Unh-uh-uh. Don't do it."

"Oh, for the love of God, Spencer," she spat again. "Don't do *what?*"

"Tell another one of your lies." I narrowed my eyes at her. "And don't you dare give me that cockamamie bull about Daddy being delusional—even though he is a little cuckoo these days—because he's *not* delusional. A little forgetful, yes. But do not play him—or *me*—for crazy. Now who the heck is *Cleola?*"

She let out an exasperated sigh. "Oh, all right, Spencer. You want to know who Cleola is?"

I gave her a blank stare. "Um, that is what I've been asking, right? So let's follow the yellow brick road, Dorothy."

Kitty glared at me. "Don't push me, Spencer. You want the truth? Then shut your filthy piehole for once in your despicable life, and let me speak. Now do you want to know who she was or not?"

I batted my lashes. Pursed my lips. Then stared at her. Kitty was testing my gangster. She knew I was a classy diva. And—*lawdgawdjeezus*—I didn't want to bring out the ratchet, but if I had to get hood-ish I would. And I'd do it real quick.

I nodded my head. "Proceed."

"Well then," Kitty said, "she was some ole country bumpkin your father was once infatuated with..."

I grimaced. "Why was Daddy making goo-goo eyes over some country bumpkin?" I asked, half-believing her. "Some ragamuffin like *that*? She sounds hideous."

Kitty shrugged. "Back then, Ellington—your father—had a thing for wayward girls. He liked them wild and unruly and barely legal."

I frowned. "That doesn't make any sense to me. Daddy was a renowned author, a professor, and a world traveler, so why would he need to pick through trash for some lady-girl with an ugly name like Cleola?"

I eyed her as she lifted her ceramic mug to her lips, purposefully blew into its steamy depths, then took two slow sips. "Because your father was an old perv, Spencer. A predator. An old nasty goat that man was." She shook her head, and grunted. "Ellington always had a thing for young, vulnerable girls."

I blinked. Um. Let's see. Daddy was now eighty-eight. Kitty was forty-two.

Now let me calculate in my head.

Daddy was forty-six years her senior. He'd found Kitty hanging upside down from some disco pole when she was eighteen. Then, a year later, he'd married her.

I blinked again. It was the first time that I'd done the math.

He was sixty-five years old when he'd married Kitty. Ugh. *Yuck.*

I stared at Kitty.

So she was also one of those poor trashy wayward girls she was referring to.

Ugh.

I shook my head in disgust. Suddenly, I felt my yogurt curdling in my stomach from this nasty realization.

"But why?"

She shrugged again. "I guess you'll have to ask Ellington. Who knows why that man did half the things he did back then. He was carefree."

I never knew why my mother called Daddy by his last name, but she did. Always. And I never really cared to ask her why. "Well, Mother," I said, trying to bite back my temper, "if Daddy's brain wasn't scrambled, don't you *think* I would be upstairs having this talk with him? Don't you *think* I haven't asked him this already? And all I get is some jumbled mess. Now, stop farting around with me, lady, and tell me what I want to know so I can put this mess to bed. I have more pressing things to contend with than snooping inside the panty drawer of one of Daddy's ole trashy ho-bags."

Kitty calmly took another sip of her tea. Oh, she was so composed. Almost too composed. And I didn't like it one bit. Why wasn't she trying to serve me up a dish of her nasty attitude? Why was she all of a sudden acting all cute and calm?

It wasn't adding up.

I tilted my head back to the other side. "Then why does he call *you* Cleola Mae?"

Kitty scoffed. "Think, Spencer, think! Why else would he? The same reason he calls *you* her. Your father's Alzheimer's has him hallucinating."

Hmmm. She has a point. He does call me her *too.*

Kitty pushed back from the table and stood, then whisked over toward the sink. "I know you don't want to face it, Spencer darling, mostly because you are about as empty-headed as your father is. But Ellington needs to be put down. He's no good to anyone." She set her mug into the sink, then ran the water. "Not even to himself." She walked back over toward the table. "But you're too selfish and inconsiderate to see that keeping him around is doing nothing more than making you look and act as crazy as he is."

I swallowed, hard.

She placed a hand on my shoulder, then squeezed. "Send him back out into the wild, Spencer. And let that man live out the rest of his days like the wild beast he is."

I flung her hand off me. "Don't touch me," I warned.

"Fine. Be like that, Spencer." She grunted. "The one time I try to comfort you and you push me away."

Comfort me? Oh, please.

Lady, bye!

I stared out to the mountains through the ceiling-to-floor windows and held my tongue. I fought the urge to roll my eyes. But I also fought the urge to bawl my eyes out. I was conflicted about Daddy and his condition. But I was sick of Kitty trying to play me for a dingdanggity fool more. Even a blind man could see that there was something more to that cloak-and-dagger foolery she tried to feed me.

I knew Kitty was holding out on a juicy secret. That secret had another secret. And I planned to drop down low, dig it up, and sink my teeth down into the meat of it.

"Oh, and Mother," I said as she prepared to saunter out the kitchen, "one more thing."

She let out an exasperated sigh. "Now what, Spencer?"

Back straight, face forward. "You had better sleep with both eyes open," I warned. I slowly turned my head toward her and narrowed my hazel eyes at her, holding the clove of garlic up. "I'm coming for you."

20

London

"You will learn to love him…"
Those were the words floating around in my head that had me suddenly clicking my heels out of Bryant Park, foregoing my plan to sit on a bench and people watch, or sit at one of the small tables and sip my avocado smoothie until it was time to head back to L.A.

Anderson.

Thoughts of him were suddenly taking up lots of space in my head. I couldn't stop thinking about him. Anderson Ford. God, why now?

I hadn't spoken to him in weeks. Since the day he'd rudely ended my call with him. And now here I was, boldly crossing the pristine lobby of his family's New York office building on Madison Avenue, walking up to the oval receptionist's desk.

Though the Fords' main headquarters and operations for their multibillion-dollar oil company was in Texas, I knew from my incessant perusing of news articles and browsing the company's website that Anderson was now working here in their New York offices. How else was I supposed to keep up with the happenings in Anderson's life?

After all, he'd cut me out of his life. Told me he no longer wanted anything to do with me.

Still...

My pulse raced as I parted my lips and said, "Um. Hi. London Phillips for Anderson Ford, please."

The snooty girl with the neat granny bun looked up from her computer screen and peered at me over the rim of her Gucci eyewear. No *hello*. No *hi*. Nothing. Stank trick.

"Is he expecting you?" is all she said as she eyed me.

"Um. No," I replied, glancing over at the see-through elevators as they zoomed up and down, transporting bodies to and from. I caught myself admiring the glass staircases leading to a second floor. And on that floor were another set of glass elevators leading up to the remaining twenty floors.

"I'm sorry. Mr. Ford doesn't take walk-ups," she said snottily, bringing my attention back to her. "Would you like to set up an appointment?" She slid her fingers over the face of an iPad. "He's free on the twenty-eighth at two p.m.," she offered.

"The *twenty-eighth?*" I shrieked. "That's almost three weeks from today."

"Yes. Shall I *pencil* you in?"

I felt the marble and granite floor beneath my feet slowly spread open.

"No, ma'am, you may not," I snapped. "I will wait. Please call him to let him know that London Phillips is here to see him."

"Then you might as well get comfortable over there"—she pointed over toward a bank of white leather and chrome sofas—"because that's where you'll be sitting *and* waiting." She shooed me away.

All I could do was thank God for my therapy sessions. I was a changed girl. I simply rolled my eyes and marched over toward the sofas and plopped down on one of them, sinking into its plushness.

Huddled in my seat, I waited and waited and waited, shifting from side to side.

"Anderson is a good man..."

"I know, Mother," I muttered as I fumbled with my phone, then opened my Facebook page while I waited. Without much thought, I clicked onto Anderson's page and saw that he'd changed his status from SINGLE to IT'S COMPLICATED, and I twisted in my seat, staring at the status as I wondered what had become complicated in his life. Was he still with that Russian model chick? Was he out man-whoring with multiple girls?

After ten minutes of scouring his feeds, I clicked out of his social media, then clicked back in. This time I landed on his Instagram page.

I scanned a few pictures.

Him with some of his fraternity brothers. Him leaning up against his Bentley. Him posing on some red-carpet event. Him with...I blinked...Daddy. On a golf course! His eyes were shielded behind a pair of designer aviators. He looked so...*good.*

Why hadn't Daddy mentioned that he and Anderson kept in touch? Didn't he know I *needed* to know stuff like this? This was pertinent information he'd been withholding from me. Why hadn't he shared it with me?

In my hand, on my phone screen, I stared at Anderson, his smile wide as he and Daddy looked into the lens of the camera. And then I had to catch myself from fantasizing about a life with him. Married with two—maybe three—kids. Wait. No, no. Absolutely not! Two kids at the most.

We'd be so—

God, this is ridiculous, I chastised myself, quickly logging out of Facebook. *Anderson's status or what he does in his private life is none of your business.*

I know, I know...

"Miss Phillips," another receptionist called out as she approached me, forty-seven minutes later, "Mr. Anderson will see you now."

Slowly I rose to my feet. A sigh of relief, then trepidation, escaped my lips. I was handed a visitor's badge, then directed to take the second-floor elevators to the top floor.

I did as instructed. Rode the elevators up, holding my breath, my nerves a jumbled knot of mess, until the elevator finally dinged. I stepped out. And there was another receptionist's desk.

"Hi. I'm here to see Anderson Ford," I said, straining to keep my nerves in check.

The receptionist stood to her feet, and came around from her station. "Yes. Right this way."

And there he was. Anderson. In his glass office. Behind a handsomely sleek desk. In a crisp designer suit and starched shirt and a purple pinstriped tie.

Looking professional and all grown up.

"You have five minutes," the receptionist stated, deflating any hopes of having lunch or any early dinner with him, as she led me to his office.

My heart sank. How on earth would I be able to say everything I needed to say to him in five minutes? It was utterly impossible.

God. I'd almost forgotten what he looked like, smelled like, in the flesh. I took in a deep breath and tried to breathe him in through my nostrils.

"What's up, London?" Anderson said coolly, seemingly unexcited to see me. Not even a little. "Why are you here? In New York?" He narrowed his eyes at me. "Why aren't you in school? You *are* still in school, aren't you?"

I nodded. "Yes. I just took a therapy day."

"Oh, right. Therapy." He sat back in his chair. Then glanced at his watch. "How's that going for you? Therapy?"

I blinked, wondering why he hadn't offered me a seat in one of the chairs situated in front of his desk. I already knew the answer. I wasn't welcome here.

I shifted my weight from one foot to the other. "It's fine. No. Actually, great," I stated honestly. "It's the best thing that could have happened for me."

Anderson studied me. Then nodded. "Good. That's what's up." He glanced at his watch again, and my heart sped up.

In back of him was an open view of New York City, but Anderson was the only view I was interested in looking at. Too bad the energy in the room wasn't mutual.

"Well, I won't hold you," I said lamely. "I was in the neighborhood and thought I'd stop in to say hi, since we haven't spoken in a while."

"You could have called," he stated flatly. "Oh, wait. I changed my number."

I cringed. "I know. But I wanted to see you anyway."

He gave me a quizzical look. "Why? For what?"

I swallowed. "To say—"

His cell rang. He ignored it.

"To see how you were doing."

Finally, he stood to his feet. "Well, as you can see, I'm well. Making moves. Living life."

My lips quivered as I smiled. "I see. I'm happy for you."

My knees shook as we stared at one another.

"Why did you come here, London?" Anderson asked, his eyes burning into every part of me, making it nearly impossible for me to think, to speak.

"I-I..." I stammered. "I...well..." I swallowed back the ball of cotton that had somehow managed to invade the inside of my mouth. I suddenly needed water—no, a martini. Dirty. Real dirty.

"Well," he urged, impatience coloring his tone. He glanced at his watch a third time. "The clock is ticking. So, like, can you wrap it all up in a neat red bow? I don't have all day."

Oh, God. Why did I come? I knew showing up here was a bad idea.

I swallowed again. Felt myself shrinking. Then all of a sudden, I felt jet-lagged. And then I felt overwhelmingly sick to my stomach. Staring at me with what appeared to be a look of amusement, Anderson walked around his desk.

"Well..."

I swallowed. "I wanted to see you. That's all."

"And?"

I nervously bit into the left side of my bottom lip. "And I was thinking of you."

He snorted. "Oh, word? All of a sudden you were *thinking* of me? Why?"

"I was hoping we could be..." I paused, shifting my nervous energy from one foot to the other.

"You were hoping we could be *what*, London?" He snorted. "*Friends?*"

"Yes. If we could."

"Nah, homie. You know you ain't about that life," he said, mockingly. "You don't know how to be a friend, home slice. Just like you didn't know how to let me into your life and be *your* man."

"I made a big mistake," I admitted. "I was stupid. But I—"

"Nah, *son*," Anderson said sarcastically. "You didn't want a good man, London, remember? You wanted a thug-daddy, a projects dude who disrespected you, a bum-dude with four baby mamas. I told you that boy was nothing but trouble. Told you he would do nothing but bring you down. Every time that bum hurt you, every time he made you cry, or left you high and dry, who was there to pick up the pieces? Who was there to save the day?"

I inhaled deeply. "You were."

"Say it again?" he urged. "I didn't hear you, homegirl."

I pushed out a shaky breath. "I said *you* were."

"*Exactly*. Captain Save a Dumb Ho."

I cringed.

"I was the one," he said, pointing a finger at his chest, "who kept your secrets. I was the one who played your confidante. I was the one you turned to time and time again every time that clown abandoned you. I was only good enough for you, yo, when it was convenient for you. And still I was the one there for you. And what did you do, London?" He paused, pinning me with a hard stare. "You still chose *him* over me, remember...?"

I winced as I nodded ever so slowly and somberly.

Silence. And suddenly I didn't know what to say. Because he was right. I did do that. All of it. And yet...

"I was wrong." God, I sounded pathetic. Was that the best I could offer? "You didn't deserve that. And I'm so sorry for how I treated you, Anderson. I feel horrible."

He grunted. Then puffed out his chest, straightening his tie. "Well, you should. You could have had a good thing with me. We could have been good together, London. But—" He stopped and stared at the wall of glass behind me, seemingly deep in thought. I craned my neck to look behind me to see what had caught his eye.

Ohmygod!

Ivina.

The Russian model chick he'd been spotted with on numerous occasions at numerous social events—all hugged up, all lovey-dovey. God, she was so freaking beautiful! And one of the hottest teen models in the international fashion world. And I was jealous!

Jealous that *she* was with Anderson.

And I wasn't.

Surprise registered on her face when she noticed me, and then a smile spread across her face as she gave me a cute finger wave.

I forced myself to smile and wave back, then tore my eyes

from hers, catching Anderson's gaze as he held a finger up, signaling for her to give him a second. He would soon be dismissing me. My stomach churned at that knowing.

He cleared his throat, then pushed out, "Look, London. I'm not gonna say I am the best you could have had, but I'm damn near close to it. But you won't ever know that now, will you?"

I choked back a sob. "I really screwed up," was all I could muster up to say. How fricking lame!

Anderson leaned back against his desk and folded his arms across his chest.

And stared.

I wanted so desperately to tell him that I missed him like nobody's business. That I wanted to be with him. That I was ready to be the girlfriend he deserved. That all the things I thought I hadn't wanted, I wanted—with him. That *he* was all that I wanted.

I even considered mentioning how I stalked his Twitter and Facebook feeds three, four times a day because I cared about him, cared about how he was, as if that news was worthy of him forgiving me for being such a shitty *pretend* girlfriend because pretending was all I had done. And I had sadly failed miserably at that.

I wanted to fall to my knees and beg Anderson to give me another chance, this time not for pretend. No, this time I wanted to be his for keeps. But my pride wouldn't allow it. And all I could see in my mind's eye was Anderson . . . with *her*.

Ivina.

I chewed on my bottom lip. "Are the two of you serious?"

He frowned. "Who?"

I swallowed. "You and Ivina?"

He glowered at me. "Why do you care?"

I felt all the air around me go thin, and then I felt lightheaded.

"I-I—" I fought back a snivel. I refused to shed a tear, in front of him or over him. But still. I had to know. "Do you still love me?"

He scowled a little, eyeing me. As the seconds ticked into minutes of him just standing here, staring at me, I realized Anderson wasn't just *staring* at me. He was peering into my soul.

"It no longer matters," he finally said, easing his arms back into his crisp gray jacket. "I'll have my secretary show you out."

I felt my heart tightening as if a fist was squeezing every beat out of it as he brushed by me toward the door. The door opened, and I was quickly ushered out while Ivina stood to the side and waited her turn...with *him*.

Before walking toward the elevators, I glanced back and caught the two of them locked in an embrace.

Oh God, oh God, oh God. What had I been thinking showing up here?

Anderson was right. I was delusional. What had I been hoping for? That he'd sweep me up in his arms and smother me with his chocolate kisses? That he'd fall down on one knee and profess his undying love to me?

Wrong.

Anderson didn't want me. He'd moved on.

21

Heather

"**M**iss Girl," Co-Co said with two snaps of his fingers as I stepped out of my car and handed the key to valet. "You are serving me catfish realness, *hunnnnty*."

I tooted my lips and popped my hips. My porn star body was on *fleek*. Small waist, *pow!* Plump boobs and bouncy booty, *pow-pow!*

Co-Co and I had done a few pinches of goodness—(Co-Co called it "Miss Honey," and it was a combo of crushed Percocet, bath salts, and a pinch of cocaine)—before stepping out of the car, and now I was gliding on a white puffy cloud.

My skin tingled.

Warm honey flowed through my veins.

I felt good all over.

My fire-engine-red catsuit had a high neck with diamond cutouts on the sides and one in the back that dipped extra low, almost to my crack. Sans panties, my booty was swishing every which way.

My eyelids were shadowed a smoky shade of bronze.

I had my hair out, giving them Lion King fever with my

long ponytail. My face was beat for the *gaaaawds*. Wait. Did this make-believe geisha girl liken me to a *catfish?*

Weren't they like scavengers of the sea? Bottom feeders? Dirty?

Or was this man-tramp trying to say I was pretending to be someone I wasn't? That I was cat*fishing*, like was he tryna call me fake?

I cut my eye over at him. *Mmm. Look at him in his short silk kimono.*

His long black wig had red streaks and two buns on each side of his head. On his feet, he wore Japanese wooden sandal clogs, and he carried an Asian purse.

I rolled my eyes. "I know you not even tryna call me some..." My voice trailed off as I spotted a cluster of paparazzi photographers huddled outside the velvet rope near the front entrance.

God, I couldn't go anywhere without paparazzi lurking somewhere nearby, waiting to drag me anyway they could in the press. I didn't need this. Not right now.

Co-Co and I were about to step inside Nobu Malibu—a swanky Japanese restaurant overlooking the Pacific Ocean—for a meeting with Kitty.

Yes. She still had a restraining order against me coming anywhere near her buildings, but she would see me out in public. Mmmph. I'd been summoned by her earlier in the day to meet her here. "Six p.m. Dinner on me. To discuss what's left of your career," she'd said. "And don't be late. Oh. One more thing: Leave your wretched mother home." Then she'd hung up before I could refuse.

So here I was, with Co-Co in tow, feeling easy and breezy and carefree. So I didn't need drama. Thankfully, the paps had their backs to us, their attention facing the front entrance, perking up whenever the door opened with their cameras on the ready for their next big mark.

God. Sometimes I wished I wasn't famous. That I wasn't

Heather Cummings the TV star. Heather Cummings the iTunes megastar. Heather Cummings the Twerk Queen. Heather Cummings the daughter of a blackballed actress. Heather Cummings the alleged daughter of a hip-hop mogul who had yet to claim me as part of his gene pool. Heather Cummings, the mixed-breed girl who struggled to fit in.

Sometimes. I hated my life. Okay, okay...*most* times.

Still, I couldn't imagine being anyone else. *Ever.* Truthfully, I wouldn't *know* how to be anyone else. I was who I was. And it was all I knew to be, even if I sometimes felt like a glorified extra starring in my own life.

Yet. At this moment, I was Heather Cummings, the fly girl. Heather Cummings, the boss *bish!* I was Heather Cummings. Pretend or not.

Floating like a butterfly...

"Tryna call you *what?*" Co-Co asked, pulling me from my reverie. He stopped in his tracks.

I glared at him, slinging my ponytail over my shoulder. "Tryna call me fake?"

"Miss Girl, I *saaaaaid* you was *giving* catfish realness—catsuit and all fish, minus the fishy smell. Get it? So don't go getting in your feelings, boo. I'm so not in the mood for your low-rent antics."

Low-rent? I frowned. "Whatever, Co-Co. You stay throwing shade."

"No shade. Miss Co-Co never throws shade." He snapped open his oriental fan and fanned himself. "I just throw a little breeze."

"Save the lies," I hissed as we neared the entrance. "Just do me a favor. Let's ease by those pap dogs before they spot us. Do you think you can do that for me?"

"I got you." He smacked his lips together. "Miss Co-Co always delivers, *hunnnnty*. We'll slip right on by, like phantoms in the night. *Swoosh*."

Mmm-hmm.

But the moment we neared the entrance, Co-Co called out, "Heather Cummings and Miss Co-Co Ming in the house, giving porn star realness!" And then he spun around and grabbed me, striking a pose, pulling back the opening of his kimono, showing thigh and a hint of his flat booty cheek.

The camera shutters clacked in response, leaving me standing smack in front of the photogs, trapped like a deer in headlights.

"Heather, over here!" called out a voice.

"Please, Heather, just one over here!"

"Are you and the Pampered Princesses no longer friends?" one of the paps barked.

"Puhleeeze. We were never friends," I snapped back. "They're all insignificant, pampered trolls."

"Heather, what about you and Rich Montgomery?"

I scowled. "What about us?"

"Will the two of you ever be close?"

I slung my ponytail. "Never. She's fat trash."

"Heather, baby, what will you do now that you've been fired from the Kitty Network...?"

"Check your facts, boo," I cooed. "I was never fired. I'm on break. I told them"—I turned to the side, and Co-Co slapped my rump—"to eat the cakes!"

"Please, Heather, just one over here!"

Co-Co stood in front of me and pulled open his kimono. "Who wants a pickle?" he said, striking another pose.

Everyone gasped. And then there were a few chuckles. But no cameras flashed, and Co-Co huffed, tying his sash back and then tugging me by the hand. "Enough," he snapped. "Me and my client have dragons to slay."

As I was being dragged inside, I turned, blew a kiss, and offered a finger wave to the reporters. More flashes went off, and then suddenly I was yanked inside.

"Co-Co Ming here for Kitty Ellington," Co-Co announced, snapping open his fan and waving it over his face. The hostess, dressed in all black, ignored him and stared at me instead.

Her eyes widened. "Ohmygod! *Heather?* Heather Cummings? I know you! I loved you in *Kickin' It with Heather!* Ohmygod!"

I smiled. "Thank you."

"Ohmygod. Do you think I can take a selfie with you?" The hostess whipped out her cell phone and thrust it at me.

I shrugged. "Sure. I guess."

As the girl positioned her camera to capture us together, Co-Co tried to photo-bomb us, but the girl was not having it. She shot him a nasty look. "No. Not with *you* in it." She pushed him back, then snapped her photo with just the two of us.

"You oversized giraffe! You and your family are officially banned from any of the sixteen Ming buffets," Co-Co snapped. "I will have your atrocious face plastered everywhere, *biiiish!* I will ruin your chances of ever getting a hot buffet the rest of your pathetic life."

She snubbed him. "Right this way, Miss Heather."

I rolled my eyes at Co-Co. "No one cares," I said as we followed the girl to a private dining area where Kitty was sitting. Kitty set her wineglass down and peered at us as we made our way over to her. And then she frowned.

"Why did you bring *that* with you? I thought I told you to come alone, Heather."

I shrugged. "You said not to bring my mother." I pulled a chair out and slid into the padded seat.

"I'm Heather's new manager," Co-Co stated.

Kitty scoffed. "And *what* exactly are you managing, huh? Her trips to the welfare office? Because that's exactly where she'll be, digging clothes out of Goodwill bins and eating day-old bread, if she doesn't get her mind right."

"Ooh, the shade," Co-Co said, sitting as well.

Kitty glanced down at her diamond watch and *tsked* me.

"And you're late. Time is money, little girl. And you've just wasted several thousands of it by being late."

"I'm sorry," I muttered.

Co-Co reached over and popped a complimentary piece of tuna roll in his mouth. "See. I told you to be on time," he said between bites of the savory, spicy treat. "Miss Kitty, girl, I tried to get her here, but she said you could wait."

Kitty shot me a scathing look. "Listen here, you little Pop Tart. You are here because you have potential, Heather." She placed her wrists on the table and steepled her fingertips. "That's the only reason I would be caught dead out in public with you in that hideous whore suit."

I shifted in my chair.

"You look like you just rolled out of some cheap, sleazy movie." She shook her head, and I felt myself shrinking in my seat. "You're too pretty of a girl, Heather, to be coming out in the streets looking like an Xtube clip of *Sluts Gone Wild.*"

Co-Co giggled. "Ooh, the shade is real."

I sucked my teeth, ignoring him. "What's wrong with my outfit?" I asked, defensively.

Kitty gave me a blank stare. "And the fact that you can't see what's wrong with it is problem *numero uno.*" She sighed. "Do you know why I fired you, Heather?"

I shrugged. "Because you don't like me."

"Ooh, the lies, *hunnnnty.*" Co-Co reached over for another piece of tuna roll. "You told me she fired you because she was a jealous whore."

Kitty snarled. "Co-Co, isn't there a toilet bowl you can go lick clean while Heather and I talk? Another word from you, Tinker Bell, and I will have you thrown out of here."

He tooted his lips and snapped open his fan again. "Well, then I guess I'll just sit back and catch the breeze."

"Heather," Kitty continued, staring at me, "I fired you because of your lackadaisical attitude, because of your poor work ethic, and your addict behaviors. The world could be yours if you learned how to cut off"—she glanced over at Co-Co—"the trash. And put down the drugs."

I shifted in my chair. "Miss Kitty, I don't do drugs."

Co-Co snickered.

"Shut it, Heather," Kitty hissed. "Your mouth reeks of filthy lies. But I have a way for you to redeem yourself, for you to get your life and your career back on track."

I sat up in my chair. Tilted my head. *Oh.*

"I'm going to help you save your life—*and* your career. I'm sending you to rehab for three months. All expenses paid. In Coral Springs, Florida."

I blinked. Oh, she had me all the way *effed* up. I didn't need treatment. And I definitely didn't need three months in some corny Florida. *Waaaaay* across the ocean! I was not about to sign up for that. No. Hell no! I didn't have a problem.

"And then when you return," Kitty continued, "you will continue your studies at Hollywood High, graduate, and remain drug-free. Then—and only then—if you have successfully passed drug screenings and have gotten your diploma, I will roll out the red carpet for you and give you the career of a lifetime in television and film. The world of entertainment could be yours, Heather, dear. But you'll need to choose. Live your life as a junkie. Or live it as one of the world's most coveted actresses. Which is it?"

My mouth watered. Ohmygod. Did she just say movies? Could it be true? Was Kitty offering me stardom?

"Well?" Kitty drummed her nails on the crisp white linen. "What will it be?"

"I-I..."

"Ooh, Miss Heather," Co-Co cooed, pointing at my face. "What's that caked up around your nose?" A nervous laugh escaped my mouth before I could swallow it down. Co-Co played too much. He stayed being messy.

Kitty narrowed her eyes as I quickly reached inside my bag and pulled out my zebra-print leather compact. I flipped it open. My eyes rapidly blinked, like that of flashing lights.

Oh. My. God!

There was a layer of white powder caked around one nostril. Why the hell hadn't Co-Co said something while we were in the car, cackling?

Kitty tilted her head and stared, her eyes flicking with a hint of disgust as I quickly dabbed the corner of my napkin in the glass of water, then wiped my nose, glaring over at Co-Co.

Kitty cleared her throat, reaching for her wineglass. "This meeting is over. Get clean, Heather, before it's too late." She snapped her fingers, and then out of nowhere four buffed men in black appeared. "Please show Miss Cummings and her teacup pooch out."

"Ooh. *Yasssss*," Co-Co said. "Who needs drugs with all this fine chocolate?" He grabbed two more pieces of tuna roll and stood to his feet. "Cuff me. Show me the way to ecstasy," he said around a mouthful of tuna roll.

He flicked his gaze over at me and pursed his thin, glossed lips in a way that felt messy, and I knew then...

Trust no one.

22

Rich

1:43 a.m.

That was the time that glowed back at me in burnt orange lights on the dashboard of my Hennessey Spyder. I'd traded in last month's version for another customized upgrade. And it was *evvv. Errrrry. Thang!*

The world was mine, honey. And the only thing that could have made my already fabulous world more fabulous was Justice. But noooo!

Jussssssstice was not answering his damn door. The door I'd been banging on for the last forty minutes, up until that nosey ole biddy across the hall from him came out with her cell in one hand and a baseball bat in the other, threatening to break my kneecaps, then call the cops on me—*again!*

Old snitch! She was lucky I didn't believe in violence and I'd given up my collection of switchblades and razors or I would have given her a face full of stitches for her snitching. My alias-ego, Shakeesha Gatling (my mother's birth name before she transformed her groupie-self into Logan Montgomery), didn't play those kinds of games.

Any*whoooo*. Screw that prune-faced trick!

Jussssssstice was ignoring me. *Jussssssstice* was still sending my calls to voice mail. *Jussssssstice* was ripping my heart out from my chest. And *Jussssssstice* didn't give a damn!

He was spiteful.

He was trying to hurt me purposefully. He was trying to have me lose all of my fabulous edges missing him.

Not!

Who did that?

King Petty Justice, that's who!

He was so frickin' childish!

Ugh!

I banged my fist on the steering wheel. "Damn, you *Jussssssstice!*" I screamed. "You bassssss*tard!* You no good mother*fu—*!"

My phone buzzed. I quickly grabbed it from the passenger seat and stared at the screen, thinking that just maybe my man had come to his senses and called back.

Urgh. It was Spencer. Hating troll!

WHERE R U, RICH? HOPE YOU'RE NOT SOMEWHERE FLOODING YOUR THROAT WITH BOOZE.

I frowned. This slore was out of order! Who texted someone at this time of the night? She was selfish. She was inconsiderate. She had no regard for my emotional turmoil. No respect for my love jones.

I replied back: DON'T DO ME, MEAT GOBBLER! WORRY ABOUT YOUR OWN THROAT N WAT U KEEP IT FLOODED WITH!

The nerve of her!

Coming at me like I was some drunk. Girl, bye!

A second later, she responded back.

U HEATHEN! U NEED BABY BLACK JESUS! MY PRAYERS CAN'T SAVE U, TRAMP! GOOD DAY!

I don't need your damn prayers! I need my man! He was my salvation! My road to joy! My love and light to the Promised Land! To the land of milk and honey!

Justice was what sweet dreams were made of. He was homebred goodness. My boo, my present and future, my always and forever, my chocolate knight in the hood, Justice was every part of me. My body ached for him. My skin burned for his touch. My lips craved his butter-soft kisses. It'd been days since me and my man had torn up the sheets and cried out like wild cats, and I was starting to get the shakes.

"Justice, baby," I whispered sweetly into my cell. "I'm out in the parking lot, waiting for you to get your mind right. Don't you miss this sweet cookie? She misses you. I'll sit out here all night, if you want me to. You want me to be a fool for you, is that it, boo? Well, fine. I'll be your fool. Just answer my call, *please*."

I ended the call.

This boy wanted to play games. Wanted to play me like a violin. Wanted to stomp all over my good loving.

I redialed his number again. Then left another message. "*Jussssssstice*, this is it! I'm not gonna keep calling you, not gonna keep sweating you. I'm not even about to be no damn fool for you, boy! If you don't want me, just be a man about it. Come outside and tell me to my face. Just be a damn man about it..."

And then I broke out into my own version of Toni Braxton's "Just Be a Man About It." "Justice, stop your bullshit/Just be a man about it/oooooh-oooooh, yeah, yeah/If you can't give me what I need/If I'm not what you're looking for/then let me go/if I'm too much woman for you...just be one hunnid with it/stop playing games with my heart, baby/don't have me slashing tires tonight/don't have me busting windows out tonight/pick up your phone/oooooh-oooooh..."

I sang the chorus a few times, then ended the call.

I wasn't gonna cry. Nope. I was too fabulous for tears. I didn't have any more to shed any-damn-way. These tear ducts were dried up. I had nothing left to give.

I reached for my forty ounce of St. Ides tucked between my legs and took a sip.

"*Jussssssstice!*" I screamed inside the cabin of my car.

I loved that boy. But he was making me hate him, hate everything he stood for, when all I'd ever been to him was G-U-D. *Good.*

I was a good woman. Period.

I didn't lie. Ever. I kept it one-*hunnid* with him, always.

I belched. Then frowned, fanning a hand over my nose. I belched again. Everything about this beer I was drinking was rotten. But it was soooo good. So hood. It quenched my thirst. And gave me the buzz I needed for the night.

I belched again. Then cracked the windows.

Why couldn't Justice appreciate me? Why couldn't that boy love me? Why was he tryna play me for a fool?

I didn't play games. I played for keeps.

I'd been nothing but faithful to him. I was a good, faithful woman. A born-again virgin. Wait. That one night of sin I'd had down at the Pink Lounge several months back with that Latino cutie-boo didn't count, did it? I mean. That sexy butter-pecan Puerto Rican had been ripe and ready and *(whew!)* I'd plucked him every which way through Sunday and still had time to make it to church to get my praise dance on.

Amen?

Amen.

And so what if I'd let him melt all over me. He wasn't the love of my life; he had been a love for the night. Besides, I'd told him my name was Sasha Fierce. So no—*hell* no! I hadn't cheated.

Not Rich Montgomery.

That was all tequila talking that night. It was *not* me!

It was the devil in disguise.

Jose Cuervo.

3:39 a.m.

That was the time glowing back at me. I blinked. Two forty ounces and another bladder full of urine later, and I was still sitting outside Justice's condominium complex.

I'd already been reduced to using the bathroom outside twice. I wasn't gonna do it again. I was done!

"You know what, *Jussssssstice!* I'm done with you!" I yelled into my cell. "You win! I've been out here *allllll* frickin' night, burning *allllll* my good gas, waiting for you to open your damn door! I don't know what *beeeyotch* you have up in there with you, but I know she can't drop it low like I can! But whatever! Now you can throw her up against a wall! I hope she's worth it! But don't let me catch that whore, because I'm gonna punch her eye sockets out, then stomp her face in! I promise you, *Jussssssstice!* I'm gonna—"

The call dropped.

"Aaaaah!" I screamed as I called back.

"Yo, you know what to do. Lick the tip. Leave a message." *Beep-beep.* Then came the dreaded recording, "I'm sorry, but the mailbox is full."

I tossed my phone over onto the passenger seat, slid my Chanels back on my face, then sped out of the parking lot, like a bat on fire. I swung out into the street, did a U-turn, and raced through a stop sign.

I needed to get to a bathroom. *Quick!*

I zoomed down every shortcut and secret alley, practically taking corners on two wheels. My legs shook as I floored the gas. I saw the light ahead of me. But then I blinked, and it was now a yellow blur, then red.

I said four quick Hail Marys and flew right through. This was an emergency, dammit! I would purge my soul and ask for forgiveness later.

For now—

Whoop, whoop!

My gaze slid up to my rearview mirror, and I couldn't believe my eyes.

I blinked.

A police car was behind me. *Me!*

I cursed. The police stayed tryna do me. All I ever did was mind my own fabulous business, and all these hating-azz cops wanted to do was see a beautiful woman go down. They really wanted to see me wading in muddy waters.

My whole body started to overheat as my bladder stretched to full capacity. Lord Jesus! I was gonna burst if I didn't get to a restroom.

I pulled over, my whole body practically convulsing.

Surely, the cop in back of me would understand.

I eyed him through my side-view mirror as he walked up to my window.

My window slid down. "Hi," I said calmly. "Can you make this quick, kind sir? I'm having a bladder emergency."

"License, registration, insurance," he said rudely.

"Clutching pearls! Is there a reason why you're stopping me?"

"License, registration, and insurance?" he repeated more forcefully. Ole prick!

"What seems to be the problem, officer?"

"I said license, registration, and insurance. Don't have me ask again." And then came blinding lights—his flashlight all up in my personal space. "Have you been drinking?"

I hiccupped, squeezing my legs shut and bouncing in my seat. "No, not tonight."

I belched again.

"Can you please lower your flashlight? You're violating my civil rights," I sputtered. Then I belched again. "This is racial profiling. This is illegal stop and seizure! I will have your badge for this!"

"Step out of the vehicle" was the last thing I heard him say before I felt the golden flow of warm fluid seeping out of me.

23

London

"**O**h, there you are, my darling…"

I cringed as my mother whisked into my bathroom and stood behind me as I sat at my vanity. I fastened a diamond stud into my left ear and then gazed up and looked at her through the mirror.

It was nearly seven in the morning, and there she was, ever the epitome of poise and grace, looking like a bronzed goddess, her hair pulled up into an elegant chignon, her jewels sparkling beneath the recessed lighting.

"You look wonderful," she said, nearly beaming.

"Good morning, Mother," I replied around a smile of my own as I slipped the other diamond into my right earlobe. I was surprised to see her. "When did you get here?"

"My flight landed at two in the morning."

"Oh." I reached for a tube of cherry-red lip gloss and spackled my lips. "And how long will you be staying?" I inquired.

"For a few weeks, at least," she stated.

I raised a questioning brow. "With Daddy *here*?" He wasn't here now. He was away on business in London—how convenient—managing his clients there. But he'd eventually be returning. And I couldn't fathom what it'd be like with the two of them under the same roof again. It felt like forever since I'd had both of my parents... *home*.

With me.

"Your father and I have spoken about it. And he's fine with the idea. In fact, he suggested it."

I gave her a surprised look.

"The estate is big enough for the both of us," she quickly replied. "And my extended visit gives you and me time to catch up."

Oh.

It sounded good. But I wanted to know if her staying longer meant she had come to her senses and was planning to fight for her man, if she thought her marriage to Daddy was worth saving. But instead I held my questions in.

"I see you're almost ready to head off to school."

I shrugged. "I guess."

God, the thought alone made my stomach churn. The constant tension between Rich and me was at an all-time high. I was sick of trying to be nice to that girl. And yet Dr. Kickaloo continued to encourage me to either extend the proverbial olive branch or cut Rich off for good, once and for all.

"And how are things on campus? Have you and those horrid so-called Pampered Princesses made peace?"

I sighed. "No. They're still who they are. Miserable wenches. But whatever... I'm so over them."

"Good for you, my darling," she said, running a hand through her perfectly coiffed mane. "They were always beneath your station in life, anyway, especially that wild child, Rich. That girl has never had any respect for anyone. Not even herself. But that's to be expected. Look who her parents are."

My mother's dislike for the Montgomerys did not go unnoticed, but I pretended to not catch it. Still, hearing Rich's name and the mention of her parents made the hairs on the back of my neck rise, especially the image of her trampy mother with her thirsty paws on Daddy.

Ugh. I didn't want to start my morning with thoughts of her and her whoring ways. It was bad enough I'd have to see her slutty daughter at school.

I slid on my diamond-encrusted bangle. "Let's not talk about them," I said, changing the subject. "It's too early in the morning for that. I need to start my day with positivity."

"You're right, my darling. How about I fix us a light breakfast?"

I blinked. *"You?* Cook?"

She chuckled. "I do know where to locate the pots and pans, my darling daughter."

"Umm. Okay. But do you know how to *use* them?" I'd never known my mother to cook. Ever.

"Well, I was thinking I'd whip up a fresh fruit salad with cottage..." She saw the blank expression on my face. "Okay, how about I have..."

"No. That's fine, Mother. I'll have what you're having."

She smiled. "Then I'll get to it."

"Okay," I said, reaching for my hairbrush.

"It's good to be here. With you," she said before turning to leave.

"Honestly, I didn't think you were really coming."

My mother stopped and turned back to me. "Of course I was coming, my darling. Why would you think otherwise? I've been so looking forward to having some quality mother-daughter time with you."

Hmmm. Since when?

She walked back over to me, removing the hairbrush from my hand. She began brushing my hair, the way she would when she thought the world she was creating for me was perfect and right.

"You've done nothing but put your modeling career before me, our daughter, and this marriage!"

I shook my father's haunting words—words I'd overheard him spew at her during an argument they were having—from my head as I gave my mother a curious, yet suspicious glance.

"Oh, don't look so surprised, London darling." She brushed my hair several more strokes, then set the brush down on the vanity as she leaned in and kissed my cheek. "Have you no idea how much being away from you weighs heavy on my heart?"

But you left anyway...

My stare locked onto her questioning gaze. Growing up, my mother's absence, her extended travels to and from Paris, were regular occurrences that had become a part of my existence. Her being gone was more normal than not. Her absence soon became more wanted than not, for having her home brought along more grief than gratitude.

The constant badgering, the berating, the browbeating—about my fluctuating weight, about my looks, about what was expected of me—at the hands of my mother was most times more than I could bear.

Her approval mattered to me. And yet no matter how hard I'd try, it was still never enough for her. I couldn't be the perfect daughter with the perfect life plan. I didn't want to always color within the lines she'd drawn. Sometimes I wanted to draw outside the neatly constructed box she created for me. Sometimes I wanted sketch my own lines. And simply color my life the way I wanted to. I wanted my life to be mine. Not hers.

It was all too much for me. Her expectations.

They'd once drained me. Consumed me. Confused me. Controlled me. And I'd felt like my voice, my thoughts, my feelings, my desires weren't my own.

A long moment slipped by before I finally answered. "I didn't think you really cared."

"Why on earth would you think such a thing?"

I inhaled. Then pushed out in one breath, "Because I didn't think I was good enough. I know I've been nothing but a disappointment to you." There. I'd said it.

"Oh, my darling London!" she exclaimed, placing a hand to her chest. As I eyed her through the vanity mirror, I couldn't tell if she was feigning insult or if she was genuinely hurt by my words. "Nonsense. You have not been a disappointment..."

I shot her a "yeah, right" look.

She smiled. "Okay, okay, my darling. I've been displeased, yes. Have you been a challenge? Yes—at times. Have some of your choices been disappointing? Yes. But that doesn't mean I've ever loved you any less. If anything, I've loved you more."

She leaned in and pressed her cheek to mine. "Look at you, my darling child. You're beautiful. And you were born out of love. And though I haven't always, admittedly, been the best mother, my intentions have always been good. All I've ever wanted was to bring out the very best in you."

I stared at her. I loved her, but I disliked her too. Disliked her for the way she'd treated me. Disliked her for not fighting for Daddy. Disliked her for not being a better mother. But I was working on forgiving her. I didn't want to *not* like her. She was my mother, for Christ's sake. And I was in many ways just like her.

Counseling was helping me to see that in myself.

And it frightened me. I didn't want to be her. But I didn't know exactly how to be me, either. Because every time I looked at myself in a mirror, the only reflection I ever saw staring back at me...was *her.*

I smiled at her, shifting in my seat before standing to face her.

Heather's mother, then Spencer's, then Rich's all came into view. Mine was controlling, but at least she expected the best from me; she pushed me to be better, to be brighter, to not settle.

I guess life under her roof could have been unhappier. I

could have been raised by one of the other girls' mothers and turned out worse than I already was.

I could have turned out to be an addict, a psycho, or a delusional, man-stealing smut.

I sighed inwardly, thankful for my blessings.

"I know, Mother," I finally said in almost a whisper, before leaning in to give her a cheeky air-kiss. "You've done your best."

24

Spencer

Reckless driving.
Running red lights.
Underage drinking.
Resisting arrest.
Bwahahahahahahahahaha!

Moo-Moo the Cow was out of control. She was lucky I was feeling charitable and accepted her collect call when she called me from the police station because I didn't usually do crooks. Ole criminal. Lush. Repeat offender.

Rich would never learn. She was hardheaded. Obviously, she hadn't learned a goshdiggity thing from her last arrest. I was starting to think she liked being in the back of police cars. Liked being handcuffed. That she enjoyed being caged.

Mmmph. The cluckers always came back to the henhouse to roost. And Rich was one big ole clucking bird. She'd forgotten how she'd texted me all nasty-like late last night—well, early this morning—and yet I was the first person Man-Eater called.

Mmmph. Her dear ole daddy, ole Mr. Dirty Dozen, Mr. Rolling Stone, was out of the country sowing through cornfields, plowing out his next love child, I was sure. And her ex-gangbanging mother, the queen of gunfire, was in London for the weekend, probably at some whips-and-chains bikers' rally.

Either way, Rich had no one else but me and her publicist—who'd signed for her to be released—to have her back. And, once again, Momma Spencer had to swoop in to save the day. Whew! I was exhausted chasing behind these hookas. My job was never—

"Ooh, oooh, lookie-lookie," I said, getting hyped, clapping my hands as I spotted Rich half-walking, half-running out of the precinct, stepping out into the morning light. I clapped my hands. "Here she comes. Yeah, you little troll doll, come to Momma." She looked a hot, wrinkled mess. "Yes, yes, yesssss! Run-walk the hall of shame, you drunken streetwalker! You, you, stank-mouth cooter! You sidewalk lush!"

Bwahahahahahahaha . . .

"Not a word, *bissssh*," Rich hissed the second she quickly slid into the passenger seat of my McLaren. "Now drive!"

I sped off before she could get the door closed.

I made a face.

I sniffed.

Sniffed again.

Then snuck a peek at Richzilla from the corner of my eye. She looked like one of those skid row toilets. And she smelled like one too.

I frowned, turning my attention to her. "Um, Rich, why do you smell like horse piss?"

"Clutching pearls, you selfish slore!" she snapped, her voice rising an octave. "I've been in hell for hours! I had to fight six half-girls, half-aliens off of me! Had to sleep with both eyes open to keep Big Bertha and Bam-Bam from eating my cookie, and all you can ask is, 'Why do I smell like horse piss?'! No hello. No so glad to see you. Tramp, your breath smells like horse piss!

"God, Spencer! I can't stand you. I swear I can't. I don't need your judgment. I need you—for once in your atrocious life—to be a damn friend!"

I pressed a button and let all the windows down, then pressed on the air-conditioner. This girl stank worse than roadkill.

I stuck my head out the window as I drove and took a deep breath of fresh air. The hum of the engine purred out against the wind. I smiled as the wheels spun and gripped the road and hugged a curve.

"Aaah!" Rich screamed, yanking my arm. "*Tramp!* Get back inside this car and stop tryna kill me! You lunatic! You deranged skank!"

I gulped in as much air as I could, then jerked my head back inside the car.

"Oh, shut it, you wild dog," I hissed as I glanced over at her, "before I dial nine-one-one and have you arrested. No! Have you shackled and dragged through the streets."

She shot me a hot glare. "God, you're so ugly, Spencer! How do you do it?"

I let out the air I'd held in my lungs and then made a face. "Do what?"

"Live your life in ugliness? Just once, don't you wish you could wake up and be as fabulous as me?"

I blinked. Oh, she'd guessed my dirty little secret. That I'd aspired to be her—the cuckoo jailbird! Yes, yes, yes...my secret was out the cat bag.

"Oh, how'd you guess, Rich?" I said sarcastically. "That's my life mission, to be you."

"It's all in your eyes, Spencer. Envy. I almost feel sorry for you. If I could hand you a bag of pretty, I would. But my humanitarian duties don't stretch that far."

"But your legs do," I said, snidely.

"*Yasss*, girl. Don't hate. Handstands and Jamaican splits."

I gawked at her. "They're Russian, Rich."

"*Whaaat?* Clutching pearls! Jamaicans are from Russia? Girl, since when?"

Oh, what a Dumbo! I had to bite my lip to keep from laughing.

"No, the splits," I finally said.

"What, your split ends?"

I shook my head, rolling my eyes up in my head. It was useless. She was a lost cause. Hopeless.

"God, my heart aches for you, Spencer. I'm going to give you the name of my plastic surgeon. He'd do wonders for that face."

"Ooh, nice. And I could look just like you. All I'd need for the finishing touches is a fat suit, and we'd be twins."

"Clutching pearls! Lies! Nice try though, boo-boo. But no matter how hard you'd try, you'd never have these fabulous hips and this bubblicious booty. You'd still be an imitation. A knockoff. Just some ugly troll in a fat suit. You're not in my league, sweetie. My fabulousness is waaaaay over your..."

Caaa-caw, caaa-caw...

The crows cawed in my head as she spoke. This girl was wild and crazy.

I leveled a ferocious glare her way, then smiled ever so sweetly. "Rich, it must be so hard being you."

"It really is," she said, flipping down the sun visor, then sliding open the lighted mirror. "Dear God, Father of Shakeeta and Raheem! I need a touch-up. And a facial."

I smirked. "And you need your skin peeled back and soaked in buttermilk. You smell like a skunk."

Rich slammed up the visor. "And you need your tonsils knocked out, you damn apple bobber."

I giggled. "Mm-*hmm*. I love my apples. Big, round Granny Smiths."

"*Yassss*, honey, *yasss!*" Rich sang out, shimmying her shoulders. "Sweet and sour."

"Crunch, crunch," I rang out.

"You the new Becky Appleseed!" Rich exclaimed.

I laughed as I whizzed down Sunset Boulevard. "Yes, girl, yes! Wet mouth. Juices all down my chin."

"Omygod, tramp! I can't with you. You're so disgusting! Hurry up and get me home. I can't be seen out in these streets with you."

I reached for the stereo and pressed it on. Rihanna belted out through the speakers, singing about feeling like a brand-new person. I sang along.

Then came Rich.

Next thing I knew we were both singing along to every song on Rihanna's *Anti* album. When "Love on the Brain" started playing, Rich nastily demanded I shut up.

"I don't need you tearing up my song," she jeered. "Just sit back and let a pro handle this." And then she broke out in song, singing hard and heavy and loud, outsinging the song. She clutched her chest, then held her head. Then ran her fingers through her knotted hair. Then shook her fists. Then slid her hands, her nails lightly grazing, down her ashy, unwashed face.

God, her breath stank.

I held my breath and threw a hand up in the air and waved it, my foot heavy on the gas pedal.

Rich was taking us to church. And I didn't have the heart to shut down her praise worship, so I let her sing while I drove. By the time we sang through the album a second time, we were way up in the Santa Monica Mountains.

I stuck my head out the window again and gulped in a mouthful of fresh air, then stuck my head back inside the car's cabin when the album reached the end for the second time. I lowered the volume and looked over at Rich.

"You miss him?"

Rich frowned. "Who?"

"Justice?"

She sighed, dramatically. "Yes, girl. I can't shake him, Spencer. God knows I try. But every time he throws me up against a wall, he kisses me and lovingly puts me back together again. Girl, I'm a fool for his sweet love. He takes me higher than any boy has ever taken me."

The car swerved. Horns blared. I just missed sideswiping a SUV.

"*Whaaaat?* That boy threw you up against a wall? When?"

"Ohmygod, Spencer! What are you tryna do? *Kill* me? Eyes on the road, *bissssh!*"

"Oh, shut it, Rich! Now tell me. And don't"—I deliberately swerved again—"lie or I will take us over the cliff."

"Aaaah!" she screamed. "You crazy whore! Yes! Yes! Okay, yes! Now slow down, you damn psycho!"

I swerved again. "Yes, what?"

"Justice threw me up against a wall!" Rich gasped, trying to catch her breath. She clutched her chest. "There I said it! Happy?"

I let my foot up off the gas. "No. I'm not happy. Why'd you let him do that to you? Throw you into a wall? That sounds like abuse to me."

She waved me on. "Girl, it was nothing. Just a few love taps; that's how we make love."

My eyes bulged open. "Lawdgawdsweetheavenlylambchops! Rich, are you frickin' kidding me?! Are you *craaaaazy?* Why are you willing to play a fool for him?"

Rich sighed, giving me a dismissive flick of her hand. "Spencer, stop being so dramatic. Like I said, it's nothing." She shook her head, holding a hand up. "Anyway, girl. Rihanna said it best: 'What's love without tragedy'?"

My lashes batted rapidly as I screeched to a halt on the side of the road. Dust and gravel kicked up around us.

"What is going on?" Rich wanted to know, looking around. "Why are you stopping?"

Right in front of us, up on the mountaintop—near the cliffs, was a 180-degree view of Los Angeles stretching out to gleaming blue water, the Pacific Ocean.

"Because, you stinking slore," I said through gritted teeth, "this is where you get out and jump!"

25

London

For the last two weeks, I've done nothing but obsess over the idea, even the likelihood, of my parents getting back together. And for a fleeting moment, I actually thought that the possibility would bloom into a reality.

They'd been getting along. Laughing and even talking more, something I'd hadn't seen from the two of them in like forever. So in that possibility came hope. Hope that we'd be a family again. Hope that I would have Daddy all to myself again. That things would somehow work their way back to the way everything used to be.

Not perfect. But perfect enough, if that made any sense.

But this morning, my mother and father managed to snatch away any wishful, hopeful, thinking that I might have had or held onto.

"Now that Mother is back home," I said to Daddy over morning breakfast, "and the two of you are getting along..."

"Oh, no, darling," my mother said, removing her linen napkin from her lap and dabbing the corners of her mouth. "I'm leaving to go back to Milan..."

I blinked. "You're what? *When?*"

"In about another week or so," she stated in a matter-of-fact tone.

My heart sank.

"And when exactly were you planning on telling *me* this?"

"Today, actually. I thought it would be nice if you and I spent the day at the spa, then did a little shopping together."

I sucked my teeth. "I don't want a *spa* day. And I don't want to go *shopping*. I can do that anytime, Mother. What I *want* is to know why you have to leave? *Again*."

"Oh, London, darling. You make it sound like I'm abandoning you?"

I gave her a look but said nothing. She really had no clue. And she never would. So what was the point? I mean, really? Why try to get her to see that she was abandoning me? That she'd abandoned me in some way most of my life?

"I need to fly back to handle some business," she said, missing the opportunity to assure me that I wasn't being forsaken. "But I'll be back before you know it."

I scoffed. "And you can't handle it from *here?* Isn't that what assistants are for? To handle matters when you can't?"

Mother shook her head, reaching over to grab my hand. "It's not that simple, darling. I have a business to run. And commitments to tend to."

"But what about your commitment to *me*, huh?"

"Your mother and I are very committed to you, sweetheart."

I stared at my father. "Just like you're so committed to chasing some other man's wife!"

Daddy scowled. "Excuse me? What was that?"

I boldly repeated myself. Then added, "Yes. I know all about you screwing Rich's mother! Of all the whores in the world, why did you have to pick my enemy's mother?"

My mother gasped; the blood from her face drained. "London, stop this. Don't disrespect your father. You're out of line."

I slammed my spoon down. "No, Mother," I hissed, fighting back tears, "Daddy's out of line." I swiped a lone tear before it slid down my face. I'd been holding this in for far too long. I had to let it out. Dr. Kickaloo had told me that holding in my resentments was like swallowing poison. That it would slowly kill my spirit.

"Don't either of you care about how this crap is hurting me? Do either of you even care about me and my feelings?"

"Of course, we do," Daddy stated calmly. "Your mother and I love you."

I gave him a blank stare. "Oh, really?" I tilted my head and waited for his response.

"London, don't," my mother warned.

"No, Jade," Daddy said. "She's entitled to know. We owe her that much."

I let out a breath I didn't even know I was holding in, swiping another tear.

"Your mother and I love you very much, sweetheart. Period. And there's nothing either of us wouldn't do for you to make sure you have the very best of everything."

"Then why can't the two of you stay together?"

Daddy looked over at my mother, and she held his gaze for a moment, before averting her eyes. "Because, honestly sweetheart," Daddy said as gently as he could, "your mother and I are no longer in love with each other. We care deeply for one another, but not in a way that would work in a happy marriage. She doesn't want to pretend anymore, and neither do I."

I swallowed, hard.

"I haven't been happy in a very long time."

My lip quivered. "Then go to marriage counseling."

Daddy sighed. "Everything isn't so cut-and-dried," he said in a way that sounded almost lawyer-*ish*. "I wish it could be, but it's not. Not always. Still, for the last two years, we've tried to hold on—your mother and I—to stay in our marriage, for your sake. But…"

"But?" I prompted.

"But it was making your father and me more miserable," my mother interjected.

Daddy looked over at my mother and smiled wearily. "I love your mother, London. And I always will. I'm just not *in* love with her. And neither is she with me."

"Your father and I want what's best not only for each other, but for you as well. You will always be our priority."

Yeah, right. Blah, blah, blah.

Since when?

I scoffed. "And how is a divorce what's best for *me*, huh, Mother? How is that a priority for me? How am *I* the one benefiting from *that?* Sounds to me that the only ones benefiting are you and Daddy."

More tears fell. And this time I let them fall unchecked.

Daddy cleared his throat, shifting in his seat. "Sweetheart, you have a right to be upset by this. And I wish your mother and I had had this conversation with you sooner."

I looked at him through tear-drenched eyes. "Then why didn't you?"

He shrugged. "There's really no answer to that. We—"

"We thought it best that you only know as much as you needed to know," my mother cut in.

I grabbed my linen napkin and dabbed at my eyes. "And neither of you have yet to tell me how I benefit from any of this?"

"Well, sweetheart," Daddy said, "you have the benefit of knowing that you have two parents who love each other enough to not want to keep hurting the other."

I sighed, looking over at my mother. "What do I need to do to keep the two of you together, huh?" Then I glanced over at Daddy. "What do I have to do to keep you away from that married *whore*? Cut myself again?"

My mother gasped. "Ohmygod, no, darling. Please don't talk like that. And don't speak ill of another adult. We didn't raise you to be disrespectful."

"Well, that's what you called her, Mother. A *whore*. Daddy's *slut!* I overheard, remember?"

"London," Daddy warned, his voice never rising. "Don't let me hear you call her out again. Ever."

I saw my mother cringe, but she kept her composure.

I huffed. "Oh, great. Defend *her*. Your side piece! Oh, wait. Since I guess you and Mother are still divorcing, that would now make her your *main* piece, right? But wait. How does that work since she's *also* married? Does Mr. Montgomery know?"

"London!" my mother snapped. "This is not like you. Are you still on your meds?"

I frowned. "Seriously, Mother? Is that the best you can do? I'm trying to understand why Daddy is out there cheating on you with that ghetto-acting *tram*...woman...and all you can think to do is ask me if I'm on my *meds?*"

I shook my head, throwing my napkin onto my plate. "Yes, I'm taking them, Mother. Every day. Even on days when I don't want to."

"Then why are you speaking like that? Talking about..." She couldn't finish the sentence. She simply placed her hand up over the diamond pendant hanging around her neck.

"What, Mother? Cutting myself?"

"Sweetheart," Daddy said, "maybe we should call your thera—"

I cut him off. "I don't need to see her. I'm not in crisis, Daddy. In fact, I'm probably the only one around here with sense, since neither of you had the sense or the decency, before now, to be adult enough to talk to me about what is going on with the two of you, instead of tiptoeing around me, ignoring the big pink elephant in the room."

I shot my mother a hot glare. Then burned my gaze over at Daddy.

"You're right, sweetheart," my father said. "Your mother and I are still getting a divorce. Nothing has been finalized as of yet. But, for now, we have agreed to a separation. This is still your mother's home, so she will come and go as freely as she chooses. We will both parent you until you turn eighteen. And then we will allow you to decide where you wish to live. Here or in Italy. That choice will be up to you. But until such time, you will remain here in L.A. And your mother and I will co-parent."

"Finally," I said sarcastically. "Some clarity."

Daddy sighed. "I apologize for not having this talk with you sooner. Your mother and I really thought the less you knew, the better. But we were wrong. You did have a right to know something."

I didn't know how to respond to all that had been said, or how to feel about it. I felt my heart sinking in a way that I couldn't describe. And I blamed it all on his mistress.

I pushed back from the table and stood, knocking the chair over.

"This is so fucking ridiculous! Why do you get to go off and screw some other woman? Why do I have to be the one to suffer because you can't keep your man parts to yourself?"

"London!" my mother snapped.

"No!" I yelled back, sobbing as I stabbed a finger in the air at Daddy. "I hate you for being a cheater!" Then I stabbed a finger over at my mother. "And I hate you for not fighting to keep your husband! I hate that I'm living in a broken home!

And I hate Logan Montgomery for being a man-stealing *biiii-itch!*"

My parents sat, wide-eyed and slack-jawed. My vehemence clearly shocked them both. It was so out of character. But necessary, I felt. And I didn't care about what the consequences might be for my outburst.

All I knew in my head was this: I was sick of this bullshit!

26

Rich

"So we still beefin'?"

*Clearrrrrrrr*ly this mothersucker had the wrong one. Arms folded tightly across my chest. I blinked. Stared long and hard into the face of no one other than Justice! My man! My boobie! My chocolate thug daddy! My Mr. MIA!

He didn't even have the decency to accept my collect calls after I'd been arrested over a week ago. But he was here. *Now!* Looking like a chocolate God.

I'd always said Justice was an exquisite piece of black art. Sculpted goodness.

And, yeah, Justice was fly.

And a great kisser.

And he had the hands of passion.

Geezus…

Justice was everything that made a good girl like me sin. He was everything that made me forget my morals and values and good-natured manners. I was wholesome and pure, and all this boy did was pull me down into the sweaty sheets with him.

I bit into my bottom lip, taking in his muscular arms that

were folded neatly across his chest. He licked his lips, watching me, as I stalked closer to him.

My mind flashed back to the first time I'd seen him perform at the Kit-Kat Lounge in Santa Barbara—right in the middle of his set, our eyes had locked. And instantly there were sparks shooting out from every one of my pores. Then he'd invited me up on stage to perform an Erick Roberson piece with him.

He'd stood behind me and wrapped his arms around me as I grooved my boom-bop up on his crotch. It was love at first touch. And when the song ended, he leaned into me and sank his luscious lips onto mine, and then I had to throw a hand up to the Love Goddess and wave it in the air as our unexpected kiss filled me with an explosion of heat.

I knew then. I was in love.

And he was here! On campus! Waiting for *me!*

Ooh, he was so fine!

My mouth watered at the sight of him, leaning against the driver-side door of my car, in his River Wash Robin's jeans and a fitted Billionaire Boys Club tee.

I blinked. Wait. Wait. *Waaaaaaaaait!*

He wasn't my man anymore! Right? We were broken up! Right?

Right. Right. Right.

So I had to let him go. It was for the best. He was too much drama. And I didn't do drama. *Ever.* He played too many games. And I didn't have time for the playground.

I was too fabulous for his childish ways.

Psst. Please. Divas didn't get dumped. They didn't get treated like some world-class trash! No. A diva got even. A diva gave the boy who made her heart skip three beats in a row her whole ass to kiss!

"Can I help you?" I said nastily the moment I approached him. I stepped back out of arms' reach. And then I sneered. "Are *you* lost?"

"Nah, I'm right where I need to be," he said over a smirk as his gaze dropped down to the plunging neckline of my Chanel blouse, where it stayed locked onto my bubbling cleavage.

Damn him...

Hand on one curvaceous hip, head tilted, I gave him a deadly stare. "Oh, really? Well, where the hell were you last night, Justice? Or the night before that, and the night before that and the seventeen other nights I'd been trying to get in touch with you, huh, Justice?"

"C'mere," he said sexily.

"No, Justice! I'm not coming anywhere until you tell me. Why didn't you return any of my calls or text messages? You had me looking like some thirsty thot begging you, sweating you, banging on your door all hours of the day and night, stalking your parking lot. I don't sweat no boy. I don't stalk anyone. Ever! But all you did was make a fool out of me!"

"Because you love me," he said, reaching out for my arm. "Because love makes us do crazy *ish* sometimes. It makes us wanna fight hard and love harder. That's what love makes us do, baby. You and I were built for this kinda love, baby."

Lord, have mercy on me.

I moved my arm from his grasp and glanced down at his Pierre Balmain high-top sneakers, before slowly sliding my eyes back up over his body and locking onto his gaze.

"You and I are love, baby. We're the real deal, yo. Real love. Isn't that what you've told me? Me 'n' you against the clowns of the world."

Yes...

I mean, hell no!

He reached for me again. And this time, I allowed him to pull me into him, and then he tried to kiss me. But before I could get lost in his sweet kisses, I jerked my head away, and his lips caught the side of my mouth.

I pushed back from him. "No, Justice. You don't get to

show up here looking all fine and sexy and smelling all delectable, tryna seduce me, tryna get me to forget I'm not wearing any—never mind, my cookie covering is no longer any of your concern."

He smirked again. "Oh, word? That's how we doin' it now?"

I rolled my eyes, and crossed my arms over my chest. "Yup. That's how you wanted it. So that's how it is."

"Yeah, a'ight, yo. You got it effed up, yo. Everything about you *is* my concern. You mine, baby."

Ooh, my man is so sweet.

"I'm *yours?!*" I shrieked, giving him an incredulous look. "Boy, bye! Lies! I wasn't yours all these weeks of you ignoring me. I'm nothing to you!" I said, fighting back tears. "And I don't appreciate you coming here acting like you never threw me out of your apartment or ignored my calls or blocked me from your Twitter and IG and Facebook pages! Who does that?"

"You were buggin', yo," he stated calmly. "Spazzin' out on my posts, inboxin' broads who liked or posted on my posts."

Well...okay. Maybe I had threatened a few of them. Maybe I had showed up at a nightclub or two and cornered two or three of his little fan club bimbos.

So what?

Those tricks needed to know I was watching their every move.

But he didn't have to *block* me.

"You know I'm out here tryna get this bread, yo. And instead of you bein' my ride or die, instead of you trustin' in ya man, you be on some flip mode ish, goin' through my phone, callin' potential clients 'n' poppin' off at the mouth, messin' wit' my money, yo. I'm not feelin' that. I tryna eat too. I'm not lookin' for no handouts, yo. I'm out here on my grind, baby. Grindin' for us."

Well...them hoes had to know to stay in their lanes, or

catch it with these hands and feet. I was a lady, but I wasn't allergic to a good street brawl.

I pursed my lips. "Well, I didn't want any of them skanks in your face."

He shook his head. "I wasn't even checkin' for any of them effen broads, yo. I'm all about this paper, yo. And you should know that."

I grunted, giving him a doubtful glare. "*Mmmph*. Yeah, right. I know you, Justice. And I know you've been humping some tramp's bones because you surely haven't been humping"—I slid my hands over the sides of my body—"all of this goodness. And I'm glad you haven't had that chiseled, sexy body all over mine because you're so not worthy of all of my tricks 'n' treats."

He smirked, and his biceps pumped as his muscles flexed. "Oh, so you've been givin' out my treats to some other mofo?"

I huffed. "Boy, bye! Why you care? I'm not your girl. Remember? You tossed me out, remember? Blocked me out of your life, remember?"

"Yo, relax," he said. "I only blocked you from my social media. You being my girl never stopped. You're still my baby, yo. Always will be." He reached for me again.

I slapped his hand away.

"Boy, bye! Do I look slow to you? Do I look like I'm cheap 'n' easy to you? I'm a good woman, Justice! I've never cheated on you, lied to you, or mistreated you. But what do I get for being an honorable woman, huh, Justice? Nothing but games and lies! I'm done with your bullshit, Justice. And I'm..."

My voice trailed off the moment I caught sight of London. *Yeah, tramp. I see you watching me. Way over here, I see the envy in your eyes, boo. Yes, bish, I see the jealousy all over your face.*

I smirked. She wanted my life. Wanted what I had.

But she could never be me! Or have what I have. And I wasn't ever gonna make it easy for her to try to imitate me.

So I did what any fabulous diva would do.

I forgot all about how Justice had been treating me and pulled him into me, then stepped up on my tippy-toes and slid my tongue into his mouth.

27

Spencer

"Oooh, yes, RJ. Right there," I said over a giggle. I was in bed, with my plush blankets pulled up to my chin, staring at him—well, *most* of him (heeheehee)—on my phone screen. We were having our nightly ritual of late-night FaceTiming, something we did until we were able to claw each other's clothes off again.

Right now, RJ was showing me what was in store for our next meet and greet.

"Mmm. Stop," I cooed. My cheeks bloomed with fresh heat. "You're going to make me have the pilot fuel up the jet and whisk me across the Atlantic to get to you, boy."

He laughed. "C'mon. I dare you."

I stuck my tongue out at him.

And then he said something too private and too cute for me to repeat, but I grinned wider. "Mmm-hmm. You know it, boo." And then I meowed.

"I miss you, baby," he said, bringing his chocolately face back into clear view. "I can't wait to spend the rest of my life with you. We're forever, Spencer, baby."

Aww. My man was too cute. "I miss you, too," I whined,

poking my bottom lip out. "When are you coming back to pet my—"

My phone beeped. A 619 area code flashed across my screen.

I narrowed my eyes at the screen, trying to figure out whose number it was. But I couldn't. Probably some solicitor, trying to get my good coins on some makeshift invention, I thought as I sat up in bed and adjusted the straps to my sheer teddy.

Finally, I had a man who appreciated all my good panty-sets, a man who deserved all of my tricks and treats. But sometimes RJ couldn't keep up. Sometimes he ran out of gas and left my engine revving.

But I was loving and kind. And always thoughtful, so I never threw him out or disconnected our calls when his choo-choo train sputtered, then stopped, while I was still ready for another ride.

RJ was a good man. He was my man. And, for once, I didn't have to worry about my mother trying to sample his goodies, like she'd done with Curtis and Joey (my two other boyfriends) in the past, and like she had tried with Ander—

Wait. He didn't count. All Anderson was, was a tease, a quick fling, a light appetizer with no finger samplers on the platter. He was a waste of my good panty-sets. That man-boy was too busy pining over London back then, mooning and cooning for a sniff of her bathwater. But all that hobbit wanted at that time was that ghetto-boy, that thug-daddy in Timbs—Rich's now boo.

Ha. You see the mess in that?

Anyway. So, nope—scratch Anderson off the list.

Still, Kitty had tried to crawl her way into his boxers too. She was shameless. But I will never forget her words to me: *"Do you actually think Anderson is going to be with a girl like you? Ha! You're too unstable, dear. A man like Anderson needs a strong, powerful woman who knows how to fol-*

low rules and play the game the way it's supposed to be played, then alters the rules when he least expects it. Not some dizzy little tart who gets her panties all up in a knot every time she gets knocked off base. Learn how to play your position, darling. And you won't ever have to worry about someone else coming along and taking your spot..."

That's what she'd said to me when I'd threatened to claw her eyes out for looking at Anderson. Ha! What did I know? He was never really interested in me like *that*.

All he wanted me to be was his sideshow piece. But Kitty's words stayed tucked in the back of my head. Anderson may not have wanted me, but RJ did. And Kitty knew better than to even think about trying to seduce my man. I'd sic his guard dog on her real fast. Logan would leap on Kitty, then bite out her jugular, if she even tried it.

I bit back a snicker at the visual.

"I'ma be back home in a few more weeks, baby. Maybe sooner," RJ said real low and husky, pulling me out of my thoughts.

"Ohhhhh, okay," I said, feeling a tinge of disappointment wash over me.

"But you can always come here," he said, waggling his eyebrows. "Me and your *friend* would love to have you." He winked.

I giggled. "Oooh, I know the two of you would. But I can't play hooky from school, and my weekends are—"

My phone beeped again. The same 619 number popped up on the screen. Seconds later, my phone buzzed, alerting me that a text had been sent.

I rolled my eyes up in my head. Then slid the straps of my negligee off my shoulders again. "Are you ready for round three?" I said to RJ all flirty-like.

He yawned. "Damn, bae. You're killing me." He yawned again. "Sorry, babe. I'm worn out. Ready to knock out."

I blinked. "You're *tired?*" I frowned at the absurdity. How could he be tired—already—when I was just getting started? "Are you serious?"

"Sorry, bae. I really need to get some sleep."

My eyebrows dipped low. "You have got to be kidding me," I murmured.

RJ apologized again, cursing under his breath, then blowing me a kiss. "I'll make it up to you tomorrow night. Promise. Okay?"

Now, I'll admit, I was hotter than a Texan heat wave. I had more fire than an inferno blazing through me, but I wasn't going to go all Shotgun Suzie on my boo.

No, no. I was loving and kind—remember?

I nodded. "Okay. I guess I can keep a lid on all this goodness until then."

RJ smiled, and my heart melted. "Yeah, that's my girl. Give Daddy a kiss."

I rolled my eyes. "Boy, you know I don't play them daddy games. I already have one of those, even though he's halfway out of his mind."

"Stop, bae. You know I'm only playing with you."

I smacked my lips together. "Well, you better learn how to play with something else."

He laughed. "I got you, bae. Give me a kiss."

I pursed my lips. "Oh, all right. I guess you deserve a few wet kisses," I said in between heated breaths. And then I started making kissy-sounds, kissing the front of my phone screen. He kissed me back, then gave me one last man show for the road, before saying good night.

I leaned my head back against my headboard. Then closed my eyes and tried to savor the memory of our heated phone time. But my eyes popped right back open as I remembered the text someone had sent.

I grabbed my phone. The text was from the same 619 number.

HEY SWEET MUFFIN. ITZ ME. YA BOY MIDNIGHT. I CAN'T STOP THINKN BOUT U. LIL BIT VIOLATED PAROLE, SO SHE BACK UP THE RIVER 4 THE NEXT 3 TO 4 YEARS. I MISS U. AND I MISS THEM SWEET CAKES WIT ALL DAT SWEET CREAMY FROSTING . . .

I frowned. That man-dog had lost his mind if he thought I was going to hop back on his meat wagon. He and that humpback prison whale he'd chosen over me could go eat rocks.

I deleted the text. Blocked his number. Then snuggled into the comforts of my warm fluffy bed, with loving thoughts of RJ.

I was a changed woman.

28

London

I stood in front of the open doors of the Sub-Zero, leering desperately into its icy depths. Seeing Justice and Rich in the parking lot of Hollywood High yesterday, all lovey-dovey, had brought up so, so many memories and feelings.

Hurt and betrayal clawed at my heart the worst of them all. I was over *him*. But I wasn't over what used to be my so-called friendship with *her*. That snake, that skank, had really hurt me. She'd turned her back on me. Didn't even have the decency to accept my apology and try to *act* like she wanted to be friends again. Time and time again, I'd offered her an olive branch. And she couldn't even be woman enough to know how to be civil. But what did I expect? Rich was a barbarian.

I knew it was bound to happen. Running into Rich with Justice. But I hadn't expected it to be on campus. And then Rich—*mmmph*. The nerve of that messy *tramp* to grab all over Justice, her hands gliding all over his body and then... and then...lifting up on her tippy-toes and pressing a kiss to his lips. Being all territorial and clingy, marking *her* claim to her man. *Girl, bye.* If what she had with Justice was all that, she wouldn't have had to put on a borderline burlesque show for my benefit.

Now would she?

Mmmph.

"*Goddammit*," I hissed. "Where are you?"

God, no, no, no! I knew I'd hidden it. But where in the heck was it?

Frantically, I searched for my secret stash. Ah, yes. There it was. Hidden beneath slabs of ribs and a beef brisket.

Ice cream.

A carton of butterscotch pecan, it was exactly what I needed to throw myself into an immediate sugar rush. My mouth watered in anticipation.

I knew I didn't need it. Ice cream was the enemy. I had a love/hate relationship with it. It loved my hips and booty. And I hated its power over me. And yet I needed *it*, its cool, creamy sweetness. Something to soothe me, to ease my rattling nerves.

It was just a matter of time before Rich and Justice would most likely land on the cover of some filthy gossip rag with a full-page spread. Calling them the face of young love, the hottest young couple in Hollywood.

God, gag me. Please and thank you!

Ugh.

I reached for the carton of ice cream and then slammed the freezer's door. I grabbed a large spoon out of the utensil drawer, then sat at the breakfast nook. Licking my lips, I pried off the tub's lid, then gazed lovingly down at the rich swirls of butterscotch. Spoon poised over the tub, I hesitated.

If I eat this, I will suffer later.

Girl, go for it. You know you want it. Yolo, boo! Eat it and be merry.

I groaned inwardly.

The thought of being plagued by cramps and bloating, crawling to the bathroom, and clutching the sides of the porcelain bowl in the middle of the night should have been motivation enough for me to toss the twenty-five-dollar pint of heavy cream and sugar down the drain.

Ha. It wasn't. My inner greedy girl won over everything else. One teenie little bite wouldn't hurt me, now would it? Sneakily, I glanced around the palatial kitchen to make sure no one was looking over my shoulder, although I knew Daddy wasn't here and my mother was at some charity fashion show event. So, aside from the housekeeper, I was home alone.

Finally came the moment I'd been craving for. The moment—

"Oooh, goodie! Just in time to stop you from a sugar binge!"

I jumped, dropping my spoon.

It was Spencer, in all of her nuttiness, standing in the archway of the kitchen, her lithe dancer's body sheathed in a silk multi-print bodysuit—all crazy swirls of color—with a white wrap skirt that wrapped softly around her hips. Red strappy sandals adorned her feet, and her full, pouty lips were set aglow with fire-red lipstick.

Ohmygod, what is she doing here? And how the heck did she get in?

I blinked, taking in her flawless skin as she stalked her way toward me, her six-inch heels clicking against the tile.

"No need to go all Adele on me with the hellos. I won't be staying long." She tossed her oversized Hermès bag atop the counter. "I see you didn't try to run off with the grim reaper again. Whew." Tossing her hair, she added, "God, I hate you, London. You're so dang selfish."

I took a deep breath. "Spencer, who let you in?"

"Why weren't you in school today?" she asked, dismissing my question, head tilted, both hands positioned on one hip.

I frowned. "That's none of your business. So why do you care?"

"Actually, I don't. I just don't want you doing anything stupid either. And we both know how pathetically impulsively dumb you can be. Godjeezus, London. You're almost as dumb as Rich, and that's a real stretch. But at least she pays someone to make her look smart. So what's your excuse?"

I heard Dr. Kickaloo's voice in my head, telling me to stay calm, stay focused, to stay centered. And so I took another deep breath.

"Spencer, see yourself out the way you came in. *Please* and thank you."

Ignoring me, Spencer boldly leaned over and stuck a manicured finger right into the tub and scooped out a dollop of ice cream. She stuck her finger into her mouth, then moaned.

"Mmm, yes. I go wild for caramel." She used the same finger and swiped another dollop out, sucking her finger back into her mouth. "Ooh, yes, goshdiggitydanggit. This is what will have you rolling around in a wheelbarrow. Yes, you Lorax. Get your fat girl on, London. Moo-Moo the Cow is depending on you. It's what you're destined to be. A big wide Mack truck. I mean, look at you. You're already a fifty-foot tree. So you might as well be—"

I gave her an incredulous look. "Are you *frick*ing kidding me? Get out, Spencer! You will not come up into my home and insult me. *Ever.*"

"Oh, shut it, London, you ole street urchin. It's your parents' home. Not yours." She flicked imaginary dirt from beneath her fingernail. "You're simply the house pet. Wait, your mother does still live here, *doesn't* she? I'd heard she'd made the great escape a few weeks ago. Fled the scene."

"Spencer, get the hell out," I said through clenched teeth.

"I'm so sick of you and your mean girl act. You don't like me, fine. Then stay the heck out of my life. I don't need your approval or your friendship."

She clapped. "Yes, yes! Encore! Encore! Give it to me, baby! Now listen up, chipmunk. I'm not here offering you friendship. And your approval rating is already down in the poop chute. Have you *not* seen your Twitter feed lately? Crickets, chickie. *Cric…kets.* Chirp, chirp. No one's talking about you, London. *Hash-tag*-hot-mess-dot-com; you're insignificant. A nonfactor to the world." She ran her tongue over her teeth. "Mmm, that caramel is still clinging to my gums, so yummy and sweet. Decadent. Mmm. Reminds me of when my ex-boo, Midnight, marinated his sausage in honey, then let me nibble on it all night."

Spencer's shoulders shook.

I cringed. This girl was so vulgar. "I don't care what people are saying or *not* saying about me, you freakazoid. *Next.*"

She waved me off dismissively. "Oh, London. Liar, liar, pants on fire. You know you care. It hurts you knowing you're a flop. A catastrophic mess. A national disaster."

I rolled my eyes. "Whatever. And why exactly are you here again, Spencer? You were not invited here, so take your insults and go hop back on your broomstick and fly yourself off the nearest cliff."

Spencer snorted with laughter. "Clap. Clap. Oh, London. Stop with the dramatics. You're such a wild little pussycat. I didn't insult you. All I did was state a fact. Obviously, you haven't looked at yourself in the mirror lately. But let's not quibble over details of how atrocious you are. Oh, wait. Did you know there's a video of you on Facebook, picking your nose at a stoplight?"

Mortified, my stomach flipped over. "*Whaaaat?*" I shrieked, reaching for my cell. "Ohmigod! *When?* I don't recall picking my nose out in public. *Ever.*"

I began scrolling through my newsfeed.

form was simply trying to be nice in a messy, underhanded way. And that knowing made me shift uncomfortably in my seat.

This whole scene had become eerily awkward.

She gathered her bag, allowing its straps to drop into the crook of her arm. "Well. My charity work for the day is done here." She tossed her hair over her shoulder. "Play hooky tomorrow, London, and I will hunt you down. Harpoon you right in them big ole whale humps you call a booty."

I frowned. "Get out, Spencer."

"With pleasure, chickie. This trap house has given me nothing but gas."

She spun on her heel, then sashayed out the same way she'd come in, her honey-colored curls bouncing and her booty shaking every which way.

And there I sat.

Flustered.

Staring down into a tub of melting ice cream.

29

Spencer

RJ.

RJ.

RJ . . .

Mmmph. Mmmph. Mmmph.

Hot like butter. Smooth like silk. Sweetest man I've ever milked. I mean, known.

Heeheehee.

My boo was finally home. Oooh, yes. Mm-mm-*mmmph*. He was smack your bald-headed Grandmama finger-licking good! And he was all mine. Yessss, goshdiggitydanggit. Pull up to my bumper, *baaaa*—

RJ put his hand on mine, and electric sparks shot through me. My whole body shook. I swore right then that God had swept down from the moonlit sky and blessed me with one of his most heavenly gifts.

Ooh, he made my Duncan Hines all moist and gooey.

RJ was the light to my fire.

Yes, yes! Come on, Daddy, light my fire, goshdanggit!

Ooh wee. Yes, yes!

He was the wave to my rippling sea.

Oh, say can you see...by the size of my boo's hands?

Yes, honey, yes!

He was my twinkling star.

Twinkle, twinkle...turn out the lights, goshdiggitydanggit!

My, my, my...*mmm*...

My body shivered just at the recollection of our earlier daytime romp.

RJ was the heat to my sun. Blazing hot and bright.

He was a sudden burst of fireworks. Boom. Crackle. Pop.

He was red tulips on a snow-capped mountain.

He was like riding all the fast water rides at an amusement park, especially the ones that soaked you. Sweet heavens. I loved the way he splashed me and wet me up. Yes, yes, yes! Splish-splash, splish-splash. I was taking a hot bubble bath!

Anywho...

I forced myself back to the moment, back to RJ, back to my boom-shaka-laka, my chocolate warrior with the long, pointed spear. RJ had spent most of the morning snacking on my sweet rolls, while I marinated his meat basket in all of my special sauces. Heeheehee. And then we'd spent the rest of the afternoon lounging by the pool house under the dazzling sunshine. Then by dusk we'd nibbled on lobster salad and sipped fresh mint and cucumber water (you know to keep us hydrated and refreshed—heeheehee) before feasting on dessert.

Each other.

And now gaslight torches illuminated the perimeter as RJ and I sat side by side in two of the many cerulean chaise lounges that dotted the deck. Ours were situated at the edge of the infinity pool.

RJ looked at me, and his dark eyes flashed. "You're so sexy, Spence, baby."

I tooted my lips. Batted my lashes. Then blew him a kiss. "And you're so...mmm. Delicious." I started licking my fingertips. "Finger-licking good."

He laughed. Then he leaned over and kissed me on the lips. We were still in our swimwear, still wet from our most recent romp in the heated pink Himalayan salt water.

He looked at me, then waggled his brows. "Wanna go again?"

I giggled. "Oooh, you greedy hound. Have you no shame?" I licked my lips. "Come to Momma."

He laughed. "You're a beast, bae. But I meant as in *swim*."

Oh.

Heeheehee.

Standing, I reached for my goggles and put them over my eyes. RJ did the same. And then I reached up and pulled out the diamond hair clip that kept my still-damp hair up in a bun, letting my mane fall freely to my shoulders.

RJ stood, smoothing down his trunks, then reached for my hand.

We both jumped in. And I giggled.

RJ dove down. And so did I.

Like two dolphins, we swam down, down, down until we were almost at the bottom of the pool. Pulling with my arms and kicking with my feet, I shot back up for air. And a beat later, so did RJ, popping up beside me.

My sweet daddy-boo's skin glistened like melted chocolate, as tiny droplets clung to his lashes. Lawdgawdsweetbabyjeezus. I had to bite the inside of my cheek to keep from licking his face.

He grinned at me. And just as he leaned in to kiss me, I ducked back under the water and swam away.

"Oh, real cute, bae," he said over a laugh. "I'm gonna get you."

I giggled to myself as I flipped and flopped like a mermaid. And *ha!* I beat him to the ledge, grabbing hold and wriggling myself out. Instantly, the night air turned on my headlights, and I shivered. Beep, beep...who had the keys to the Jeep? Turn out the lights!

I reached for my towel and wrapped it tightly around me as I watched RJ climb out of the pool and move toward me. "You got that, bae. And now I got you." He grabbed me and pulled me into his arms and kissed me, and all I could do was back it up on him and let it jiggle, baby.

"I'm crazy about you, Spence," he said, all low and sexy-like.

I turned to face him, and he looked down at me and grinned. I grinned back and felt myself go all hot and tingly.

Kissmekissmekissme. Ohpleasegiveittomegoodohpleasegiveittomegood—

And then, before I could jump his bones and dial up my ho-girl meter for another round of boo-loving, he snatched away my almond joy.

"I gotta get back."

"*I gotta get back?*" I echoed, giving him an incredulous look. I was seriously taken aback. Where in the heck did he have to get *back* to? Everything he needed was right here—with *me*. And last I knew, he wasn't going back to Oxford until the end of the week.

"I'm sorry, babe," he said apologetically as he pulled me into him. "I have to meet with my pops over at the label." He glanced at his watch. "He wants me to sit in on some meeting."

And he was just now telling me this? Really?

Blank-goshdang-stare.

This boy must have thought I was about to fall for the whoopty-wham. *Ha!* He had another think coming.

"Then I'll see you later tonight, no?"

He grabbed me and stole a warm, juicy kiss, then slowly pulled away. "I wish, bae. But I gotta chill with the family."

I blinked. "Then what about tomorrow?"

"I'm not sure, bae. Maybe for an hour or two, but I can't say for sure. My moms seems to have my whole day planned. She wants me to show up for Rich's court hearing tomorrow."

I rolled my eyes. Oh, so, Moo-Moo the Drunken Cow had court? Mmmph.

"Why does she have court?" I asked, feigning ignorance. Something I did so well.

"You know, for her DUIs." He shook his head. "Rich stays doing BS."

That's because she's dumb and nearly brain dead. But I bit the inside of my cheek to keep from spilling that from my lips. "You know, boo," I said sweetly. "Your sister could be halfway good and decent if her heart wasn't soaked in embalming fluid."

RJ chuckled, shaking his head. "You're so cute, babe. I love your way with words."

I twirled a lock of hair around a finger and popped my lips. "And I love your way with *me*. But don't sidetrack me, RJ, or have me get it crunked out here. Now tell me. Why do you have to babysit Rich in court?"

He laughed. "It's my mom. She wants me there for support." He shook his head and let out a chuckle. "And you know there's no saying *no* to her when she summons you."

I raised my brow. Oh, joy! What a momma's boy! I bit my tongue, though. There was no need for me to drag his ole hoodrat mother or his drunkard sister. Well, not to his face, anyway.

"Then what about afterward?" I asked.

"I might be able to sneak off for a bit. I'll have to let you know," he said. "My moms called a family meeting, and then I'm catching the jet back to Oxford. I have to be back on campus."

"Whaaaat? You have to be back on campus?" I repeated, not caring to mask my disappointment. "Oh, really?" Skepticism coated my tone. I tried to stay cute and coy and cool as a cucumber dip, but my insides were churning butter at the thought of him running off to be with some British strumpet, some, some yuck-mouth crusty dragon. And since when did the Montgomerys start holding family meetings?

Mmmph.

RJ was another lying horndog. Another man-boy with loose loins who ran through girls' cute little panty-sets, then tossed them aside, taking all of their silky goodness along with him, like Joey and Curtis and Corey and—

Wait.

Anderson?

Scratch him. He didn't count. He wore panty-sets too. Or maybe he didn't. I didn't know for sure. And I'd only had the word of a junkie-skank—Heather—that Anderson was secretly dating her lady-boy friend, Co-Co. But who knew how true that was. I was still waiting for the Rainbow Coalition to expose Anderson, to turn his boxer briefs inside out for all to see if his man tank was full of sugar or hot cream.

RJ frowned. "Damn, bae. Why you say it like that?"

I returned my attention to him. "Like what?"

"Like you don't believe me or something," RJ said.

I stared at him, taking in all of his milk chocolate goodness, his defined chest and chiseled abs—a rippled eight-pack of never-ending muscles, his dripping-wet swim trunks, his, his, his—

He was not about to clown me. No, no, no. I was not going to be his Becky stuck on his stick, his dumb, goofy bobblehead. He had me all kinds of cuckoo-cray-cray. I was not the one, two, or the goshdang three!

I narrowed my eyes. "Tell me now, RJ. What English tea whore are you over in England making it rain on, huh, RJ? And don't lie, or I swear on every precious heel and handbag I own that I will slice open your meatballs and fry them on an open fire." I tilted my head. "I will claw your gizzards out, RJ. Now try. *Me.*"

RJ shuddered. "Ouch, bae." He cupped his family treasures. "Why you gotta go for the jewels?"

Hand on hip, I shot daggers through him. "Because if you think I'm going to stand for you letting some lollipop-licking trollop, some little British cockroach, wear any of your pearl necklaces you have another think coming. I will shut the jewel shop down."

RJ shook his head, then a slow, lazy grin eased over his handsome face. And all I wanted to do was leap in his arms and bite his one dimpled cheek out.

How dare he stand here and try to use his trickery on me! I was not to be fooled or toyed with.

"Listen to me, bae." He reached for me, his arms encircling my waist. "You have no reason to be jealous, babe. It's you and me."

I pulled away from him, before I got too caught up in the feel of his hands on my skin and forget I was trying to be mad at him.

I gave him an incredulous stare. *"Jealous?* Boy, bye. You had better do a Google search on me. Check my stats, boo. Check my credentials. Check my YouTube pages. I have nothing to be *jealous* about."

He smiled, pulling on his T-shirt. "You definitely don't, bae. Not when I'm all yours. You're all I think about, Spence. Them other girls don't have nothing on you, baby. You got this on lock."

"Oh, do I?" I asked, unsure. I pressed my lips together and waited for him to respond.

"Yeah." He licked his lips. "No doubt, bae. You're the only one who holds the key."

"Oh, really?" I reached for the waistband of his swim trunks, then yanked them down. I looked up at him and said, "Then prove it."

30

London

Hmmpf! Finally. The tabloids and the bloggers were right for once. Anderson *was* back in Tinseltown. I knew he was due to travel to the West Coast, but his social media pages hadn't really given much of a hint as to exactly when. *Soon* was all that had been posted.

Something about that news of him being here made my heart skip several excited beats. Seeing him in New York a few weeks back hadn't quite gone the way I'd envisioned it in my head. But I realized my visit had gone awry because I hadn't thought it through. I'd gone to see him impulsively.

Seeing him, and his standoffish demeanor toward me, had disarmed me. Had unexpectedly jumbled my thoughts and given me a bad case of the babbles. But with him back in L.A., with him close enough to touch (oh, how I wanted to run my fingertips over his skin!) I had a chance to redeem myself. All I needed now was a way to run into him.

Still, bloggers and tabloid rats couldn't be trusted to print the truth, mostly never. They lied and stretched truths to spin salacious tales all the time. Like how I was a snob and thought I was better than everyone else, which was so far from the frickin' truth. Like how I had a rare form of alopecia, which was why my hair was now short. Some messy bloggers had even gone as far as to say that hair scalpers had held me down and hacksawed my hair out to sell to weave shops.

God, how frickin' awful was that?

Had they had their facts straight, they would have known that I'd been left no choice but to cut my luscious hair off *after* Spencer had come into my home and attacked me with a handful of hair remover. Clumps of my hair had fallen out. Hence the now stylishly short hair.

Now.

Back to my new, very pressing, very important dilemma.

Anderson.

I reached for my iPad. Powered it up. Then slid my finger over the screen and began surfing the Net and clicking through all his newly tagged pictures. Ugh. There were a few photos of him with a group of AKAs at some pink and green affair, some photos of him on his yacht, *Buff Daddy*, with bikini-clad girls. There were other photos of him with girls in tiny shorts and no bras in wet T-shirts.

Ugh.

Sluts.

And pictures of him with Ivina, his new boo—or whatever she was to him. *Skank.*

Seeing him with her bothered me, but there was nothing I could do about it.

For now, I reasoned in my head as I stared at all his photos, dissecting them as I scrolled through each one. And each photo led me right back to one person.

Anderson.

Where are you staying?

I quickly scanned his Twitter feed:

@ANDERSONFORD DID U REALLY REPLACE LONDON PHILLIPS WITH THAT SKINNYBISH? #IHOPENOT #PLEASESAYITAINTSO.

@ANDERSONFORD HEY BOO! WHEN U READY 2 DROP WHITE CHOCOLATE COME C ABOUT ME! #IGOTTHATGOODGOOD.

@ANDERSONFORD U SO FINE! I WANNA CALL U BUFF DADDY N SCREAM UR NAME.

@ANDERSONFORD AKA BUFF DADDY CAN I GET A TASTE?#THISHEADGAMEONPOINT.

@ANDERSONFORD I LIKED U BETTTER W/THAT LONDON CHICK #SORRYNOTSORRY.

@ANDERSONFORD @MIDNIGHT WATZ GUD FRAT? PARTY NEXT SAT NITE@CLUB66? MAD BIDDIES GONNA B UP IN THAT JAWN. U WIT IT?

I found myself aching a little. This wasn't the Anderson I knew. *Since when did all these thirsty tricks start throwing their panties at him?*

Urgh. I tossed my iPad. I'd seen enough for one sitting. Groaning, I sat in the center of my huge bed and pulled my pink Betty Boop T-shirt over my knees and wrapped my arms around my legs; then I buried my face there.

God.

I used to think I had it all. Money. Beauty. Heels. Handbags. Fabulous jewels. A boyfriend (Justice) who loved me—or so I thought. I thought the world was mine. That everything I wanted was at my fingertips. At least everything *used* to be. But now I knew that everything that I thought mattered, that I thought I needed, was everything that I was still missing.

Anderson.

God. I was so frickin' stupid, blinded by fake love and the likes of Justice, for not seeing Anderson for who he was. My mother saw it. My father saw it. And all I saw at the time was an arrogant, egotistical cornball. A boy too educated. Too driven. Too proper. Too gentlemanly.

All I saw was a boy not rugged enough. Not rough enough.

Not street enough. All I saw was a boy who wasn't Justice. And look where that had gotten me.

Nowhere.

Well, no. Wait. It'd gotten me an extended stay at Heartbreak Hotel.

I'd kept Anderson dangling on a string. Even after he'd professed his love for me. And still, I shunned him. Pushed him away.

For what?

Sleepless nights. Betrayal. Tears. That was my reward, my prize, all that I'd gotten for choosing Justice over Anderson.

God. What an *effen* bitchy snotball I'd been to him. I had to make it up to him. Somehow, some way, I had to get him to see that I wasn't the same confused girl he remembered. That I had grown. Matured. That I was ready to be everything he needed, wanted. I needed him to know that I was ready to open my heart to him and give him every part of me.

I ran a finger over a picture of him—a selfie—my fingertip lightly caressing the screen as I traced over his features. God. His mouth, his lips...

I reached over and shut off my lamp, sinking my body into the warmth of my comforter. A smile eased over my lips as I closed my eyes.

I knew what I wanted. Knew what I needed.

I *wanted* Anderson. I *needed* Anderson.

And I knew what I had—no, *needed*—to do to win him back.

First, I needed to get him away from that Russian whore!

Slowly, I drifted off to sleep.

31

Spencer

Before I even rolled out of bed good, at six a.m., this morning, I found myself looking at my cell to see if there had been any text messages or missed calls from RJ.

But there hadn't been. *Nothing.*

However, he did—hours later, *after* I'd texted him like over ten times—so graciously take a moment to send me a goshdang smiley face. A *smiley* face!

Really?

Yes. Really.

Oh, and a text. *Thinking of u, bae.*

Mmmph.

I didn't know what kind of cat-in-the-bag trickery RJ had going on, but I did not appreciate it. Anyway. I didn't even like cats. *Ugh.* Then he had the audacity to send me an emoji with red hearts popping out from its eyeballs, like that was supposed to make up for him not coming back to the estate last night after his so-called meeting with his father—if he even had a daggone meeting. He didn't even think to creep back over early this morning for a little heated romp before I had to get ready for school and before he had to hold Rich's hand at court today.

Court?

I glanced down at my timepiece. 7:47 a.m. Pretty soon RJ and the rest of the Montgomery clan would be rolling out in the family car headed to the courthouse in one long, sad processional to Rich's doomsday.

Maybe she'd get fifty years of probation. Maybe house arrest until her thirtieth birthday to keep her off the streets. *Mmmph.*

I scratched those *maybes* for something a bit more entertaining. Ha! Rich in a black-and-white jumper, legs and feet shackled, her head wrapped Aunt Jemima style, looking like that real old lady comedian Daddy loved watching in those old black-and-white videos of his—Moms something or another. Mobley? Mobey?

No, no. That wasn't it. Mabley?

Yeah, that was it—Mabley! Moms Mabley.

I giggled.

"I've been working on the chain gang," I sang out as I bounced on my heels down the long hall. The halls were full of talking and laughter and clanging lockers, but that didn't stop me from having my own little party in my head. "Cliché, cliché...Ow, *yasssssss!*"

With my YSL handbag dangling in the crook of my arm, I snapped my fingers to the tune, then dipped my knees just a bit, my head moving from side to side, my hair swinging back and forth. Then I stopped and twirled my hips. *"Yasssssssssss!* Whips and chains on deck. Diamonds around my neck! She's been working on the chain gang..."

I made my own personal soul train line down the hallway toward my locker, sliding and gliding in my heels, bumping into whoever stood in my way.

Some kids chanted, "Go, Spencer! Go, Spencer...!"

Some stood and clapped in sync to my moves.

Others stood in my dang way. Haters!

"Move, move…get out my way before I stick you for your paper! *Yassss*." My fingers popped. "Before I blind you by the…"

My voice trailed off as I stopped in my tracks. There was Heather. *Heather!* She was at her locker, bent over, digging in the bottom of it, searching for something. She had her hair pulled back in a shiny long ponytail, which suddenly made me want to start singing the theme song to *My Little Pony*.

But Heather didn't know the first thing about friendship. She didn't have a beautiful heart. She wasn't faithful and strong! And she knew nothing about sharing kindness. And there was nothing magic about looking at the center of her crack, both booty cheeks on nasty display.

Oooh, that filthy rug rat!

I hadn't seen or spoken to that, that pill-popping-hooka-in-heels in weeks. She'd been avoiding me. Sending my calls to voice mail. Ignoring my texts. And ducking me in school—whenever she decided to show up, that was.

My nostrils flared at the thought of her stomping on my friendship, spitting on my kindness. I'd been good to that imitation Nicki Minaj. And all she wanted to do was talk gritty about me, trash me on the blogs, tear down my good loving name to anyone who'd listen to her. And I'd done nothing but be a supportive friend.

I was the one who'd rescued her like the stray wolf she was. I was there for her when she was counting roaches and eating paint chips off the walls of that slum-motel she and her mother had been living in. I was the one who'd watched her rummaging through Dumpsters and walking the ho-stroll. Oh, how it broke my heart. Seeing Heather so, so downtrodden. But I'd been there to save the day. In my red-customized cape and diamond-tipped stilettos, I swooped in to rescue a wretch like her.

Look at her. I frowned. *All bent over with her wide*

booty—that I paid for—spread on display in that nasty cat-suit.

Mmmph.

I should give it to her real good…

I eased up on her and slid my hand down into my hand-bag, pulling out my jeweled flyswatter.

Whap!

Whap!

Two swift whacks to her plump cakes!

"Aaah!" she yelped, jerking upright. "What the *fu*—!" She banged her head. "*Ow!*"

A few people laughed as camera phones caught the action live. I didn't care, though. Go live or go home, that was my new motto!

"Spencer!" she snarled, rubbing the top of her head. She yanked off her headphones. "You stupid bitch."

"Where you been, Heather, huh?" I asked nicely. I tilted my head, ignoring her nasty glare. "And don't lie or I will light your eye sockets on fire," I warned.

She slammed her locker shut, shoving her headphones down inside her bag. "You crazy trick! Do I *know* you? Are we *friends?* Do we *talk?*" She hoisted her bag up over her shoul-der. "*Hellllllll* to the naw! So don't worry about where I've been. I've been minding my business. Making hits. Stacking coins. And tryna stay far away from whores like you! Now get out of my way."

She tried to barge her way around me, but I blocked her, staring her in the eye.

"Oh, no. Not so fast," I said. "Tell me now, gutter rat. Did your mother put her hands on my mother?"

Heather smirked. "And what if she did? That's their busi-ness. Not mine. And if your mother did catch it by Camille, it's probably because her messy-azz was tryna bring it and got handled. So your *point?*" She slung her ponytail over her shoulder, then slung it back.

I blinked. Then narrowed my eyes. There was something different about Heather. Strange almost. She had a crazed, glassy, wide-eyed look.

She looked, um, uh...

"Ohmygod! Sweetlawdjeezus! Say it ain't so," I crowed. Then with a barely audible *tsk-tsk*, I shook my head. "How could you?"

"Bye, *bish*. I'm not here for you," Heather sneered, pushing me out the way. But I was ready for her. My name wasn't Bonnie, and she wasn't Clyde, but I was ready to click-clack and push her wig back!

"Are you high?" I stage-whispered, trying not to bring any more attention than we already had our way.

Heather frowned, a look of disgust coloring her face. "*High?* Don't come for me, DumbKeesha! I don't get high. I get right. So get it right, SlowRita."

"Lies!" I snapped. "You *are* high. So don't even try to lie to me, Heather. I know high when I see high. And right now, you are higher than a bird, a plane! You're higher than a spaceship. Higher than Jeezus!"

"Stay outta my life, you eggplant-eater!" Heather scoffed. "I don't worry about how many times a day you're on your knees, so don't worry about me. And for once and for all, I *don't* get high. I'm *not* on drugs. I'm not an addict or some junkie! I'm doing me. So if I *look* high to you, it's because I'm high on life." She shifted her bag farther up her shoulder. "Now beat it, before I bring it to your face with my fist."

I saw several people elbowing and shoulder nudging each other, whispering and pointing over at us. Then more cell phones went up in the air in our direction.

Oh, so they wanted a show—hmmm?

"Oh no, oh no, girlie," I said, putting an arm up. I was ready to give her an old-fashioned Mother Goose beat-down out here in these halls. She needed me to stamp my hands on her face. "You better pay the piper before you get your pickled peppers picked."

"Girl, bye. I don't owe you *shh*—"

Whap!

Before she could finish her rant, I swatted her across her mouth.

Stunned, Heather dropped her bag and then gave me a shove, cursing and screaming. But unlike her, I didn't use filthy talk. I used fists and feet and flyswatters.

And by the time security finally made it over to pull us apart, I was swinging Heather's thirty-two-inch ponytail piece in the air like a lasso.

Giddy up...

32

Rich

"I've already checked us in," my very tall, very brunette, very high-priced attorney said as she shifted her Italian leather briefcase from one hand to the other. Michelle Mac-Andrew was one of the top criminal attorneys in California. But why Logan Montgomery felt the need to hire this white woman was beyond me.

It was a waste of good coins, and a waste of my damn time. I wasn't a criminal. I hadn't broken any *real* laws. Hadn't committed any *real* crimes. All I was ever guilty of was being fabulous. The only crime I'd ever committed was making a boy forget his momma's name and rocking him to sleep.

And maybe I was guilty of having that threesome with those sexy twin brothers, Jason and Jonathan. And, okay, okay, maybe I was guilty of getting Mr. Velasquez, the substitute teacher, drunk, then taking him up to my suite at that cute little boutique bar I'd run into him at. How was I supposed to know he taught physics at Hollywood High?

I didn't do physics. I did religion. And I worshipped in

the house of Keep Your Legs Shut at All Times Except on Mondays, Tuesdays, Saturdays, and Sundays.

So I was *not* the whore the media stayed trying to make me out to be. I was far from that. I was a lady. Classy. And, truth be told, I was basically half a virgin. I was almost a nun. My cherry pie was half-bitten, not all the way eaten, so *eff* the media! The boys might have come to the yard for all this thickalicious goodness, but I only let 'em sip on this shake. Only gave 'em a li'l taste.

And I was definitely not a *drunk*.

So, moving along.

I huffed, glancing at my diamond Cartier. "What time are we going in? I have things to do." I smoothed a hand over my glorious hip and planted it there.

My whole morning was being disrupted. And I didn't appreciate being inconvenienced. Being dragged into court like I was some crook, some thief!

Ugh! If I had the chance to lay hands on Spencer I would. I would beat the skin off her face. This whole mess was *allllll* that hooker's fault. Calling the cops on me because I didn't want to stay the night at her shack after we'd drunk three bottles of champagne. Jealous trick! Telling me I should stay the night. That I shouldn't drink and drive. *Bisssssssh*, bye!

I'd left her trap house because I was grown. I didn't need her to babysit my mouth. That effen broad didn't know when or how to mind her own business. Being all up in my breath, monitoring my alcohol intake, like she was my personal Breathalyzer.

I couldn't stand that annoying slore. Always tryna look down in my throat. I wasn't a drunk. I was a social drinker. I only drank on occasion, or when I wanted to get out and let my hair down. What was wrong with having a few cocktails after a hard day at school?

"When we're called in to see the judge..." my attorney stated, forcing me to take her in. *Cute heels*, I thought as I glanced down at her feet. Girlfriend definitely was serving them lovely, honey, in her signature navy-blue pantsuit. "... I'll speak on your behalf."

My gaze flickered to the diamond studs popping out from her ears.

Bling, bling...she was killing it.

"This shouldn't take long," my attorney said. "The judge will read off your charges. Most likely give you a lecture. Then you'll more than likely be ordered to..."

Blah, blah, blah. I pressed my lips and tapped my foot against the floor, taking a deep breath. I was so over this ish. Why the hell was everyone making such a big damn deal out of nothing? Most times, all I drank was a pitcher or two—but never, ever, more than three pitchers—of beer. Ever.

Snap, snap!

And there went my mother's fingers all up in my face, causing me to jerk my head back. "Are you listening, Rich? Are you hearing anything your lawyer is saying to you? Huh?"

Blink, blink, blink. I rapidly batted my lashes. Oh, this lady had lost her whole mind trying to do me. Right here. Right now. *Allllll* in front of this white lady! She was about to have me bring it to her. Chop her right in the throat.

I stared at her.

Deep breath...

Inhale. Exhale.

"Don't try me, Rich." She stared at me, daring me with her eyes to give her a reason, to say something slick, so she could turn up. "I asked you a question. Now, speak."

I silently rolled my eyes up in my head. This woman was so extra.

"Yeah," I said dryly, "I heard her. Now can you move your fingers from my face? *Please.*"

She glared at me, giving me a scathing look, one that said she would bring it to my flawless face if I even thought about serving her up in here.

"Rich. Don't try me," my mother warned. "If you knew when to slide off from the damn barstool, we wouldn't be here in the first place. And I wouldn't be spending my morning in some damn courthouse. But *noooo*. I have a lush for a daughter, who likes to drink, then get behind the wheel of a car and drive her drunk azz to God knows where. Haven't I taught you anything, huh, Rich? Do your dirt behind closed doors. Not out in public. You wanna drink, drink. But drink responsibly. Not get behind the wheel of a car, all liquored up." She shook her head. "I'm so sick of—"

Logan's mouth was really off the hook this morning, but I wasn't going to bring it to her. Not today. I was going to let her live. She could thank me later.

The attorney cleared her throat, gently touching my mother's arm. "Now, now, Mrs. Montgomery. Not here. This is a family matter that should be discussed, um...perhaps in *private*."

My mother narrowed her eyes. Stared me down, hard. Then shifted her eyes to the attorney. "You're right. We'll finish this later when we get home."

Oh, no the hell we won't! You will not be beating me in the head with your holier-than-thou Don't Get Drunk *speeches. I was gonna be laid up with my man.*

And besides...like I'd already said once before, I didn't get drunk. I got nice.

Period.

So she could—

"Hey, Ma..."

Blink.

Oh no, oh no, oh no!

"What is *he* doing here?" I snapped, staring into the face of my father's twin, my brother, RJ.

"Love you too, sis," he said smugly, before wrapping an arm around Logan's shoulder and kissing her on the cheek.

She beamed. *Ugh.* "Your brother's here as a show of support," she said over gritted teeth. "So not another word." She tilted her head. "You hear me?"

Deep breath.

God, I hated him! Mr. Goody Two-shoes! Mr. Cornball! Mr. Nerd! Mr. Doofy! He did no wrong in the eyes of my parents. Smoke weed? He got a talking to. Crash a car? He got a new one. Sleep around? And he got an award for spraying his fertilizer.

But me?

All I ever got was a hard way to go. Stress. And headaches. Everyone loved RJ—everyone except *me*.

"Well, hello," the attorney said over a smile as she extended her hand to shake his. Her straight white teeth sparkled against her smooth porcelain skin. "You must be RJ, Rich's brother."

God help me. I felt sick watching this pasty-faced lady make googly-eyes at him, like he was royalty.

Perfect Prince RJ. *Ugh!*

I huffed. "I don't have a brother," I said just as we were called into court. "He's nobody to me."

33

London

Ten a.m. . . .

I quickly slid out of my seat and tiptoed out of my advanced Latin class, towing my ginormous purse with me, to answer my buzzing phone.

The caller was from overseas—and judging by the country code, Italy, to be exact. But I wasn't familiar with the number.

"Hello?" I whispered into the phone as I rounded the corner away from the classroom door.

"London, darling?"

I blinked. "Yes?"

"It's Gisella, my darling. Gisella Grace, with . . ."

"Yes, yes, I know who you are," I quickly said, surprised to be hearing from her, especially after my Fashion Week fiasco. "You're with Grace Modeling Agency."

"Absolutely, darling."

"Hi," I said meekly.

"What have you been up to, my diamond in the rough, since I last saw you? Mending well, I hope."

I swallowed. "Yes. I've been doing exactly that. Mending."

"So glad to hear. Did you get the cards and flowers we sent?"

"Yes. I did. Thank you. I apologize for not sending out any thank-you cards."

"Nonsense, my darling. No apology needed. Healing is what's most important. We were all here praying for you."

I felt my eyes welling, but I fought back the urge to cry.

"But, listen darling. I have great news...!"

Oh?

I gripped my cell.

"I've got a casting coming up in a few months, and I would love for you to be there. You, my darling, will be..."

I blinked. My stomach lurched as, in my mind, I saw images of me standing in wait for my turn down the runway in that beautiful snow-white, one-shoulder shift dress with the sheer train and matching satin heels and ankle cuffs. My face covered in a veil.

I'd never felt more beautiful than I did that day. I momentarily closed my eyes and cringed inwardly as I relived the bite of the razor's blade as it sliced open my flesh, along my arm, then across my wrist.

I could almost still feel the heat flashing through me as I stepped into the flashing lights and owned the runway as my arm burst into fire and bled.

"London, darling? Are you there?"

My lids fluttered open as I shook loose the memory.

"Yes." I swallowed back the thick lump forming in the back of my throat. "I'm here."

"Well, darling...what do you say? Are you in?"

I pulled up my sleeve and took in the sight of the scars left behind, reminders of what my life had been. Empty. Sad. Lonely. Lost. Scars that reminded me that I never wanted to ever go back there, to be that hurt girl again.

"I'm sorry, Gisella. I appreciate the offer, but I can't. Not after what happened the last—"

"London, darling," Gisella exclaimed. "What happened the last time—though tragic—had everyone in the industry talking. Quite frankly, they're still talking, darling. About you!"

I cringed.

"You, darling, touched the hearts of everyone here in the fashion world. Because of you and your Pink Heat ad, sales for the coveted perfume have been through the roof. Darling, you now have designers from all over Europe clamoring to have you saunter their collection down the runway. So what do you say? Shall I book you? I'll handle everything, darling. And, of course, I'll be more than happy to speak to Jade—um, your mother. I know she'll be thrilled."

I couldn't believe what I was hearing. This was all simply too much to take in. Modeling had never been my dream; it was my mother's. She'd thrust me into her world without me having a say. But now, I had a voice. I had a say.

I didn't think I belonged, not in my mother's world.

"I'm sorry, Gisella. I can't. But thank—"

"Wait, darling. Don't be hasty in your decision. Before you say *no*, think about it. And remember this: from the moment I laid eyes on you, I told you that you were the next *it* girl. And you still are, London, darling, my precious jewel. Come back and finish what you started! And let's take the fashion world by storm." She finally took a breath. "Oh, darling. I have another call coming in. Although I plan on holding a spot for you, because my instinct says you want this as bad as *I* want you to want it, I'll give you a few weeks to mull it all over..."

"I-I've already—"

"Kisses, darling."

And then she was gone.

I blinked, then leaned up against the wall, still stunned and reeling from Gisella's phone call. She wanted *me*. She said designers from everywhere in Europe were seeking me. How could that be?

Hadn't they seen what I'd done? Sliced myself? I'd tried to commit suicide. Hadn't they been there to witness it? Hadn't any of them seen the pool of blood? Hadn't any of them seen the butterflies covering me and slowly lifting me?

I know I hadn't imagined any of that. I had the scars as proof. I saw the scars every day, refusing to have them removed. I needed them to keep me grounded.

I needed them to keep me humble and thankful for still being...*alive.*

Still gripping my cell, I rummaged through my bag for a handful of tissues and dabbed the inside corners of my eyes. They weren't tears of sadness, but of joy.

I was simply so happy to be living and breathing.

And—

A sarcastic voice broke my reverie. I cringed.

"Well, well, well," Mr. Westwick said, tapping his Birkenstock-clad foot. "Lookie-lookie-Lou. What do we have here? Miss Drop Top London leaning up against the wall, holding a cell phone."

I swallowed.

"I—"

"I was, *what?*" he said, rudely cutting me off. "Waiting for your pimp? Your dealer? Or were you waiting for the next train to suspension?"

I blinked. God, I despised this man. "I had a call I needed to take."

He tilted his head. "Do tell. From?"

I frowned. "No disrespect, but I don't think that's any of your business."

"Oh, but it is, little Miss Debbie Cakes." He held out his pudgy hand. "And what is our school's policy on cell phones?"

I huffed, handing over my cell. "No cell phone use during classroom hours."

"Exactly." He slid my phone into the front pocket of his suit jacket. "Have your demerit payment on my desk by the end of the day, or you won't ever see your precious phone again. Now get back to class before I have you dragged off my campus!"

I sucked my teeth and headed back down the hall just as the bell rang.

Frickin' Westwick!

34

Rich

"All rise!" the buffed bailiff bellowed out as he opened the back courtroom door. He might have been *waaaay* too old—like granddaddy old, but from the neck down he was built like uh, um...

I dug into my pink Balenciaga purse, pulled out my compact, and quickly made sure I still had my fabulousness on fleek. I did, so I snapped my compact shut.

In walked the judge, looking like royalty, like she'd been dipped in African clay. Her rich, dark skin glowed. And the bling in her ears was giving me my whole life!

The courtroom fell silent as the judge made her way toward the bench, her black robe swooshing behind her as she climbed up the stairs to the bench and sat.

Yassss, honey, *yassss!*

Dark and lovely!

Girlfriend slayed!

"Court is now in session!" the bailiff barked. I tooted my lips. I knew I had this on lock. "The Honorable Danielle Viola Preston presiding. All electronic devices are to be turned off now. Please be seated."

I took my seat, like the lady I was, crossing my legs at the ankles and folding my hands up on the wooden desk. The judge swept her gaze around the courtroom. "Good morning." She glanced down at something—a file I thought—then looked back up. "Counselor, please identify yourself for the record."

My attorney stood. "Michelle MacAndrew for the defendant."

The judge nodded. Then glanced back down at a file. "We are here on the matter of the juvenile Rich Montgomery. Docket number..."

Juvenile? Oh no she didn't! She tried it. I was not *juvenile.* I was a grown woman. "Um, excuse me," I said, waving my pointer finger in the air to get her attention.

My attorney leaned in and whispered, "Rich, not now. Let her finish."

I shot her a dirty look. Chile, cheese. Lady, please.

The judge cleared her throat. "Counselor, is there a problem?"

My attorney stood. "Um, no, Your Honor."

"Um, yes, your highness, I do have a problem." My attorney reached for my arm, but I yanked it away.

The judge eyed me, hard. "And your problem can wait until I'm finished speaking. Understood?"

Oh, she tried it. "Clutching pearls," I muttered, placing a hand up to my chocolate and pink diamond choker.

The judge glared at me. "I heard that, young lady. And for the record, you will check your mouth and your attitude in my courtroom, before I *check* you. You will have a chance to speak when I am done. Do you understand?"

I batted my lashes in disbelief. How dare this ole ugly, bald-headed trick try to come for me! I grunted. Then nodded.

"You are to open your mouth and speak when I speak to you. A head nod does not suffice. Do I make myself clear?"

"Yeah," I said, folding my arms tightly across my chest.

The judge darted her eyes over at my attorney. "Counselor, I warn you to advise your client that she had better mind her p's and q's in my courtroom. Otherwise, she'll be clutching more than her pearls."

"Yes, Your Honor," my attorney said. I rolled my eyes as she leaned over and whispered, "Rich, this is not the time for your antics. Please."

I made a face. "*Antics?* I don't do antics. I do semantics. And I speak several languages."

I pressed my lips together. I was ready to hop up and boom-bop-drop-it on her. But my religion kept me grounded in my faith. Not to lay these hands on her.

"On the matter of docket CC-3176-A," the judge continued, "Rich Montgomery, said juvenile, has been charged with two counts of underage drinking, two counts of reckless driving, one count of resisting arrest, three counts of possession of alcohol, and four counts of driving while under the influence." The judge looked up from her folder. "Counselor, does your client understand the nature of her offenses?"

The attorney stood. "Yes, Your Honor. She does."

"Good." The judge shuffled through her folder, then narrowed her eyes at me. "Young lady, it appears you have had no regard for the law, or for rules. Even after numerous chances given to you by the local police, you have been pulled over for underage drinking and driving while under the influence at least six times this year, which, frankly, I find appalling and consider a blatant disregard for the law."

I blinked. "Lies and fabrications, your highness! I'm a law-abiding citizen. I've had my citizenship since I was born. The only laws I've ever broken have been driving while being black and beautiful. And rules are my..."

"Your Honor," my attorney interjected, quickly standing to her feet, "if I may address the court. My client tends to be a bit, um, how can I say...?"

"Let me help you out, counselor," the judge said pointedly. "Rude? Obnoxious?"

I hopped to my feet. "Order in the court, your highness. I am nothing but loving and kind, and taken advantage of. And I don't think I should be dragged into your courtroom for one moment of weakness, your highness. I'm human. I might be fabulous, but I make a few mistakes here and there. I'm trying to get it right. But it's hard out there in the streets for a young single woman—I mean, girl—like me. I wouldn't even be in this mess if it hadn't been for my ex-ex-ex-BFF being hateful and messy. She has always hated on me…"

My attorney tried to jump in, minding my business, but the judge shut her down. "No, counselor. Let her finish." The judge clasped her hands together. "This should be quite entertaining. Continue, young lady. So everyone hates on you, is that so?"

I heard RJ mumble something in back of me. Something slick, I was for certain, because he was another hater. "Yes, your royal highness. It's hard being fabulous. The spotlight is always on you, and you have to always watch your back. There are haters everywhere, lurking, waiting to do me, even in my own family." I shot a look over at RJ. "Haters will stop at nothing to try and destroy me.

"But I am here to testify to the holy truth and nothing but the holy truth. Yes, I had a few cocktails. *And?* I wasn't intoxicated. So I think that should be struck from the record. Like I said, the only thing I'm guilty of is being beautiful. Everything else is all hearsay. You know, superficial evidence."

I heard a grunt and "for the love of God" in back of me. Then I heard, "She's stupid as hell, Ma."

"Oh, shut up, RJ," I snapped, jerking my head to the left and glaring over my shoulder at him. "See, your highness. Haters."

"Order!" the judge barked as she banged her gavel. "Order

in my courtroom, I said! Counselor, do you need a moment to counsel your client?"

My attorney nodded. "Yes, Your Honor. If we could have a five-minute recess."

"I'll give you ten," she said tersely. "And when we return I expect your client to have her mind right."

"My mind is right," I snapped. "And I don't need a recess. And I don't need counseling from this sellout attorney. What I need to do is pay this fine and be on my way. There's no need in hogging up your precious time with this foolery, your highness. I ran those red lights because I had to use the bathroom. And that time I swerved off the road was because I saw something lying in the middle of the street, a rat or pos-sum or something. All I know is, it was big and hairy. It might have even been this beast girl I know—London Phillips. Whatever it was, I didn't wanna run it over. That's the only reason why I was swerving."

"And going *seventy* in a twenty-five-mile-an-hour speed zone," the judge interrupted, all snotty-like. "And another time you were doing eighty..."

"Oh, yeah. About that part," I said. "It's all a big misunder-standing, that's all. And, for the record, I want the court to know that I'm *not* juvenile. I'm very mature for my age. Al-most grown." I took my seat. "That is all, your highness," I ended, folding my hands again. I heard my mother grumble in back of me, but I didn't give a damn. I needed to let this dog-faced lady in a robe know.

She scowled at me. "It's Your *Honor*," she snapped. "And you are skating on very thin ice, young lady."

"Oh, yes. I am truly honored," I replied, running a hand through my hair. "And pleased to make your acquaintance, but I haven't skated in years."

The judge let out a grunt and shook her head. "Oh, this one here"—she glanced over at the bailiff—"is a real smart one." He shook his head, smirking. "Seems to me she needs a swift lesson in courtroom etiquette." She glared at me, catching my frown.

"Your Honor," my attorney said as she stood, "if I can interject for a brief moment..."

"Make it quick, counselor."

"Mrs. Montgomery is here, and she is very concerned about her daughter's behavior. If the court is prepared to dispose of this matter, then the family is more than willing to address my client's drinking. The family is planning an intervention."

An intervention? Chile, cheese. Lady, please! What I needed was a snack and a nap. I was getting hungry and tired, and this whole ordeal was starting to make me queasy. I felt like I had a hundred bats flapping around inside my stomach, just a moving every which way.

"Is this so, Mrs. Montgomery?"

My mother stood. "Yes, Your Honor. My husband and I, along with her older brother, are very concerned with Rich's behaviors."

I rolled my eyes up in my head.

"And so you should be," the judge stated, before zipping her gaze over to me. "Thank you. You may be seated. Young lady, what do you have to say for yourself?"

"Well, your honorable highness," I said, standing, "I'm not sure what behaviors that lady is back there talking about. But I'm not surprised one bit that she'd stand up in this courtroom and drop dime on me, dry snitching, tryna spill tea. She's only telling you that bold-faced ugly lie because her precious golden child is here. Mr. Smoke Weed and Squirt Baby Batter All Day."

The judge stared at me. "Oh, is that so? So let me get this right. Your mother, who loves you and has—as I am sure—given you the best of everything, is standing in my courtroom making up stories about you. Is that what you are telling me?"

I nod. "Yes."

"Oh, for the love of God," my mother said. "Rich, stop."

The judge tilted her head. "Okay, so your mother is a liar. I'll make a note of that. Now how are you doing in school?"

"Fabulous," I quickly stated. "The school loves me."

The judge gave me an incredulous look. "Well, that's odd." She looked down at that stupid folder again. "I have a letter from a Mr. Westwick—the headmaster at the very private, very expensive school that your parents pay for you to attend—and he seems to tell a different story. Stand up, young lady."

Take a deep breath. Breathe. Breathe. Breathe. Don't go off.

"Yes, yes, yes. Don't forget to breathe," I told myself as I stood to my feet.

"Mr. Westwick states you are failing all of your classes. And he describes you in his letter to the court as belligerent, aggressive, disrespectful, self-righteous, and entitled..."

I gasped. "Clutching pearls! That man is a confused liar! I did fabulous last marking period. I got two C's, four D's, and one F. I am nothing but loving and kind and thoughtful in school. I keep the school fabulous, and Mr. Westwick hates that I get more attention than he—"

The judge twisted her lips. "Okay, enough!" the judge snapped, cutting me off. "Young lady, I've heard enough of your delusions. Young lady, you are heading down a path of destruction. You're caught up in your own lies. You think you can do and say whatever you want, whenever you want, because you're privileged. And you think because of your social status that you are above the rules and laws that apply to everyone else your age. Well, guess what, young lady. You're not. What you are is a spoiled, rotten brat..."

I opened my mouth to shut her down, but she held a hand up and stopped me before I could get a word out.

"I warn you," she said, stone-faced. "Not one word. You are in *my* courtroom. And I have heard enough from you. And what's most disturbing to me is the fact that you are a role model to hundreds of thousands of young, impressionable girls who want to emulate being you. They look up to you. And yet you show no regard for how your reckless behaviors might impact them.

"Instead, you'd rather be in lounge clubs, wielding your fake IDs and tossing around your father's name as if it were a black card with unlimited privileges. You'd rather run around with every little boy willing to show you attention, all loose and easy. You want the spotlight? You think everyone is out to get you, to *do* you—as you say? Well, newsflash, sweetie: the only person *doing* you is *you*."

My extra lush lashes batted.

"You have no true sense of self. And because of this, Rich Montgomery, I hereby order you to pay a fine in the amount of three thousand and fifty dollars. I'm ordering eighteen months' loss of license on two counts of driving while under the influence. In addition to loss of license, you are to complete five hundred hours of community service down at one of the nearby homeless shelters and thirteen weeks of anger management."

My knees buckled. "Don't do me, your highness. Don't. Do—!"

"No, young lady. You did yourself," the judge said nastily. "And your mother—or *that* lady, as you referred to her—can't help you, either."

I felt myself shrinking as the judge stared at me long and hard. My hands shook. I broke out in a sweat. And then out of the corner of my eye I spotted two officers coming toward me.

"In addition to the imposed stipulations, Rich Montgomery,

you are hereby sentenced to ten days in the Lorna P. Johnson Youth Detention Center, where you can clutch your pearls and be fabulous."

I crumbled to the floor. "*Nooooooo!*"

The judge banged her gavel down.

"Sheriffs, get her out of here. Next case..."

35

Heather

Kee-kee-kee...

Oh, God, what was that awful cackling sound?

My head pounded.

Kee-kee-kee...

Someone was laughing.

"Ooh, yasssss, hunnnty. Look at that stank bish. Dead to the world..."

Hunh?

Was I dreaming?

Yes, yes. I had to be.

Damn it. Why did Camille have the AC up so high?

I inhaled. My nose scrunched. Something smelled foul, like rancid meat and Swiss cheese. *Ugh. Disgusting.*

"Damn, though. That *phatty* right," I thought I heard someone say.

But, nah...that couldn't be. I was dreaming, right?

My lids fluttered a bit, but they refused to open.

I heard someone *tsk*. "Boo, please, that thing's fake..."

Wait. Was that Co-Co?

"Anyways, why you looking at that? She's all plastic, all sil-*iconed* out. I'm the real deal, ready, willing, and able..."

"Yeah, but you a dude, brah. I don't roll that way."

Kee-kee-kee...

"Well, close your eyes, and let's pretend..."

"Nah, B. I'm good on that."

I heard someone's lip smack, or teeth suck, or something.

"Oh, well. Your loss. You'll be missing out on all of this duck sauce."

I sniffed again. *Ew*, I thought, grimacing. It smelled like a funk factory in here.

Did Camille forget to take out the trash?

Kee-kee-kee...

"Mmmph. Look at her," I heard.

It definitely sounded like Co-Co. But Co-Co wouldn't be in my room. Camille would rather shoot him between the eyes than welcome him inside.

Kee-kee-kee...

My head throbbed. It felt like someone was banging cymbals inside my skull.

Lord, I wish they'd shut up all that cackling. Yeah, this was definitely a dream. No, a nightmare. Yet there were no images of anything or anyone swirling around in my head.

I was so, so tired. I tried to snuggle deeper into my—

Wait. Why was my mattress so hard?

Eyes still shut tight, I stretched my arm out and patted my mat—

Ohmygod! I wasn't on a mattress. I was on a wood floor. No sheets, no blankets.

One eye snapped open, then fluttered back shut. It was so damn bright in here. I blinked a more few times and tried to lift my head, but it was lead-heavy.

Finally, I was able to force my eyelids open long enough to peer through my long purple lace front wig. In a haze, I strained to focus my view. Head still pressed to the floor, I blinked, then managed to lift an arm to swipe hair from out of my face.

My eyes batted several more times.

The room finally came into view. And there stood two sets of feet. A long pair of smoky gray Timbs and a pair of dainty feet stuffed into silver peep-toe pumps.

And then I felt it.

The draft. A chill swept over my body, and I shivered.

"Well, look who has finally been resurrected," a voice said.

My other eye opened, and then they both widened as I shot up from the floor and met the gaze of Co-Co and some tall, husky dude with lots of big clunky gold chains dangling around his neck from, from...

Last night.

"*Aaah!*" I screamed, realizing I was in nothing but my red thong. Where were my clothes? I threw my arms over my boobs, trying to cover myself. "What the hell happened here last night? Where are my clothes?"

"Girrrrrrrrrrl, you slayed," Co-Co said, throwing me some quilted blanket. "No need to play coy now. We've all seen everything you're made of." He giggled. "You're new name is Pole Rider, hunty."

I cringed, wrapping the questionable blanket around me, stomping around the sparsely decorated loft until I reached my clothes, which were somehow strewn in a pile over in a corner on the other side of the large space.

We were at a party last night. I'd done a walk-through at Club Tantrum and had towed Co-Co along. And then from there we'd gone to a new spot called Sweet Sensations. I made my coins, then we—wait. What did we do after that?

I groaned as my memory suddenly became clearer. But I still didn't recall coming here.

"How'd I get here?" I questioned, slipping into my purple jumper. I shoved my feet into my crystal-studded heels.

I remembered drinking (yes, there had been lots of drinking!) and lines of goodness and lots of dancing. God, no! It was all coming back to me. I'd been up on a table and then on a stage, getting caught up in the hype.

"Oh," Co-Co said. "You remember Dope Boy, don't you?"

I blinked, then shook my head and frowned. "No."

He grinned, showing a row of gold fronts. "What's good, ma? You sure know how'ta party."

"Is this your place?" I asked, ignoring his lecherous leer.

He nodded. "Yeah. It can be yours, too, if you want it to be." He licked his lips, and I rolled my eyes.

"How did I get here?"

"Miss Hunty," Co-Co said, snapping his fingers and thrusting his pelvis, "we rode the limo and got *allllll* the way lit, boo. We had that one-fifty-one, that sizzurp, Ciroc, endless bottles of Cristal, and goodie bags of White Mink."

I groaned. White Mink was another brand of Co-Co's powdered goodness, which—as he told it—was a crushed mixture of Ritalin, NoDoz, Dramamine, and cocaine.

I tried to swallow, but it hurt like heck. My mouth felt like it was stuffed with cotton balls. My fingers tingled. I shook my hands out, trying to get my circulation flowing again.

I looked around for my purse. "What time was the party over?"

Gold Fronts and Co-Co glanced over at each other.

"*Girrrrrrl*, the party was two nights ago."

36

London

Saturday night was finally here.

The night of reckoning, I thought, as I glanced out the window of my limo. I reached for a bottle of champagne, then set it back on the bar, deciding against it. I didn't want to be sloshed. But I needed something for my nerves. I reached into my purse and pulled out my pill case, opening it and taking another one of my anxiety pills.

I swallowed it dry.

I'd been stalking Anderson's social media pages all day to make sure his plans to party with his frat brothers were still on. They were. God, I felt so desperate. Heck. I *was* desperate. But what else could I do? I didn't have any other choice. Without taking drastic measures, how else would I get Anderson to notice me?

And I needed him to see me. *Tonight.* All. Of. Me.

The thick glass partition slid down. "We're here, Miss London," my driver said as we pulled up in front of Club Sixty-Six Paradise in Santa Monica.

Under normal circumstances, this wasn't a place I'd be

caught dead at. But there wasn't anything normal about any of this. I was on a mission to reclaim what was rightfully mine—my place back on Anderson's arm.

The limo stopped. And then, seconds later, the driver was opening my door, helping me out. My stomach lurched. I'd never gone to a nightclub by myself.

Let alone one like *this*.

I hadn't been here but one other time…with Rich. I shook the images of her running up on her ex-boyfriend Corey, who'd she'd learned had been cheating on her with multiple girls, and attacking him.

"Shall I wait for you?" my driver asked, shutting the door behind me.

I nodded. "Yes. No. I mean, you can come back if you'd like. I should be no more than an hour."

"Very well," he said. He stood outside and waited for me to open the doors of the club. I frowned. Where were the doormen? Where were the red carpet and velvet rope? I glanced back at my driver, then waved, then stepped inside, the heavy double doors closing behind me.

Missy Elliott's "I'm Better" blasted through speakers. The whole club was bathed in the glow of red lights. The place was packed. People were everywhere. Wannabe rappers. Wannabe models. Wannabe actors. College students. And then there were a slew of trust-fund babies tossing bottles and bouncing to the beat.

When the DJ slid Chris Brown's "Party" on, the crowd went wild, moving and bouncing in mock Chris Brown fashion. I heard catcalls and girls doing their sorority calls. And then I heard barking.

I squinted, trying to adjust my eyes to the strobe lights and fog to catch a better look. But all I could see was a sea of bodies jumping up and down. I didn't know where to look or when to stop staring.

Clutching my purse to my chest, I stood on my tiptoes, straining to get a better look. But all I saw were people dancing, not just on the floor, but on tabletops as well.

"*Daaaaamn*, baby," someone said in back of me, leaning in my ear, "you hotter than a bowl of pepper sauce. Can I get a lick?"

I froze. My heart stopped.

I craned my neck over my shoulder and came face-to-face with a gap-toothed guy wearing dark designer shades and a do-rag. He flicked his tongue at me, and I almost screamed.

"You fine, baby. Wanna dance? I wanna give you my babies on the dance floor."

Ew. Yuck. I frowned. If I were anything like Rich, I would have knocked him in the head with my purse or offered him a breath mint. But I wasn't Rich, so I simply moved away from him, nearly running toward the other side of the club.

I positioned myself near the bar and looked out over the dance floor.

"You know, if you stand on one of the tables, you'll get a better view, and you'll give us all a better view of *you*," a brown-skinned guy said, bending down to shout in my ear, a flirty grin on his face.

In back of him were a group of guys all gawking at me, grinning.

Suddenly, I felt severely overdressed (and yet very naked at the same time) in my five-inch gold metallic open-toe T-strapped Giuseppe Zanotti sandals and slinky off-the-shoulder black way-too-form-fitting dress that outlined every curve and dip of my body.

A dress I would have never dared to wear if it hadn't been for the fact that I was on a mission.

I blinked. "No. I'm good. Thank you." And then I was ignoring him leering at me. I stood on my tiptoes again, letting out a sigh of relief when I finally spotted a group of fraternity guys in the center of the dance floor, all wearing purple and gold.

Oh. My. *Gaaawd*. Was that Anderson lifting some girl up in the air and spinning her around, while his boys barked and did rhythmic steps?

The guy spun his dance partner around several times, then let her down, and she slid between his legs before grabbing him by the waist and grinding on his butt.

I frowned.

Someone handed the guy a bottle, and I watched as he shook it—a magnum of champagne—and then started spraying two girls wearing pink T-shirts and white booty shorts and what looked to be six-inch heels.

I blinked.

It *was* him…Anderson!

Now what was I to do? Stalk over to him and demand he put her down? Or did I play it casual and shimmy my way over to him and pretend I didn't notice him?

Ugh. I didn't shimmy. And I didn't I have the guts to simply storm over there and tap him on the shoulder. But it was now or never. What was a girl to do…?

"Wanna dance?" a voice asked over the music.

I sized the guy up. He was nondescript, almost nerdy, and seemingly harmless enough. Still, I wasn't interested.

"No. No thank you."

He looked disappointed. "Well, let me buy you a drink, please." He waggled his brows. He saw the look on my face. Then added, "No strings attached. You just look like you could use something to relax you."

"Um…"

Wait. What was I thinking? I wouldn't get to the man of my heart's desire by playing wallflower. No. I had to play the game and make my way to the dance floor.

I forced a smile. "Sure." One drink couldn't hurt. Could it?

* * *

Three finished drinks later, heels stuffed in my purse, apprehensions gone, caution tossed to the wind, the goody-goody girl persona tucked away, I was on the dance floor singing along to Nicki Minaj's "I Am Your Leader."

I'd left my fourth drink half-empty on one of the cordoned-off tables. I couldn't remember the guy's name I was dancing with, but he wasn't the guy who had been buying me drinks. He said he was a rapper, on Grand Records.

Grand Records?

Wait. Isn't that?

God, what's his name?

Born Sun, or Born Allah, or something like that.

"Baby, me and my mans wanna take you home," he said, leaning into my ear. His warm, Hennessy-soaked breath tickled my earlobe.

I giggled over the music. "Oh, I already have a driver," I said, my words coming out in one big slur.

God, my head was spinning.

Bright lights flashed.

Another shower of champagne rained down on everyone's head, and I giggled again as I twirled under the flashing, multicolored lights, throwing my hands up and letting myself get wet.

And then...and then Born-something-the rapper was pulling me into him, his pelvis pressed into me, his hands sliding up the sides of my dress. I closed my eyes and tried to concentrate on the music, but his hand crept up just below the edge of my panties.

I pushed his hands down and spun out of his grasp. God, I hadn't come for this. To be pawed on. All I wanted was my man. Where was my man?

I want my Anderson. Anderson, baby. I'm here. Blurry-eyed, I glanced around the fog-induced dance floor. Where had Anderson gone?

Mr. Nasty Rap Boy was right back in back of me, one arm gripping around my waist, while his free arm grabbed my boob. No, no, no...

I spun out of his grasp and tried to walk off the floor. But he yanked my arm and pulled me back into him. "Yo, don't walk away from me, you li'l tease. I'm not done with ya trick-azz." He nipped at my ear. "You know you want this wood." He slammed his pelvis into me. "You feel that?"

God, no, no, no...

The throbbing in my head wouldn't stop. The dance floor spun, and more fizzy liquid sprayed over us.

"Get your filthy hands off me, you *asshole!*" I screamed, slapping him. I pushed him in the chest, and he stumbled back. His eyes narrowed as fury washed over his face and as he drew his hand back. And I saw his fist coming.

Ohmygod. He was going to hit—

To my complete bewilderment, a huge beefy hand caught Rapper Boy's fist as if it were a baseball landing in a mitt.

"Nah, brah. Not here," a big burly man wearing a black suit and a headset said over a Mozzy rap song, squeezing the rapper's hand, causing him to drop to his knees and scream. Cameras flashed as the bouncer roughed the rapper up, dragging him off the dance floor.

I backed hastily away, wanting to get out of this rattrap as fast as I could before the rapper boy's posse caught sight of their friend being hauled out of the nightclub and it turned into a melee.

I would have run if my legs hadn't been wobbling. So I quickly turned and bumped right into—

Anderson.

I blinked. He was holding an icy bottle of Cristal and had a scowl on his face.

"London? What the hell are you doing here?"

"Oh, Anderson," I squeaked. And though my mind was in a haze, I remembered leaping up and throwing myself on him, wrapping my arms around his neck, and kissing all over him. "Mmm. Mmm. I miss you so much. I love you, Anderson."

I heard my words slurring.

"Whoa," I heard Anderson say. His voice droned in and out over the music. "Are you...*drunk?*" He pried me off of him, sliding me back to my feet.

And then suddenly I didn't feel so good. I felt woozy. Everything blurred. My purse dropped. And the last thing I heard was a loud *thump* as I fell to the floor.

37

Spencer

I always knew Low Money was from the kingdom of holland.

Bwahahahahahaha...

LONDON PHILLIPS CAUGHT SAUCED, SLURRING HER WORDS AND DROOLING OVER THE VERY RICH AND VERY BEEFY ANDERSON FORD AT A SANTA MONICA NIGHTCLUB...

At the bottom of the caption were two black-and-white photos of ole Miss Puritan. One was of her hugging onto Anderson, her legs wrapped around his waist, her dress hiked up over her hips, while her arms dangled haphazardly around her neck. And she was planting what appeared to be either kisses all over (or licking on) his face (eye roll). And the other photo was of her sprawled out on the dance floor, her dress barely covering her amazonian assets.

Heeheehee.

I balled over in a fit of laughter before I continued reading the article.

Rumor has it London desperately wants her once-upon-a-time parent-approved beau back. Partygoers watched as a very inebriated (um, code word for sloppy drunk) London practically offered the young billionaire her ovaries on a champagne-soaked dance floor. Um, no shade, but doesn't Anderson Ford have his sights—and perhaps his hands and other body parts—on a very hot Russian who shall be nameless? Hint, hint—she's a famous teen supermodel...

I sucked my teeth. London was so thirsty. Desperate. And apparently she was a lush too. I took another glance at the two photos, and this time I shook my head.

What a tragic mess!

I moved onto the next headline.

POPPING BOTTLES WASN'T THE ONLY THING LONDON PHILLIPS WAS CAUGHT DOING SATURDAY NIGHT. LOOKS LIKE THE TEEN SOCIALITE WAS POPPING THE OOCHIE-WALLY TRYING TO GIVE MONEY SHOTS AS SHE BACKED THAT *THANG* ALL THE WAY UP ON UP-AND-COMING-RAPPER, BORN SUN-ALLAH, WHO'S KNOWN BY THE STREETS FOR HIS GRAPHIC LYRICS AND THUG PERSONA...

Beneath the caption, there was another picture of London with said rapper, who had his big body folded over her back with his man basket pressed up into her cookie jar and his hands up the sides of her short dress.

"YO, SON," THE YOUNG RAPPER STATED IN AN EXCLUSIVE, "IT WAS LIT THAT NIGHT. THAT BROAD IS A TEASE, YO. SHE KNOW SHE WANTED IT; FEEL ME?"

Ugh.

I scoffed at the thought of London letting all that good, strong rapper-meat go to waste. Mmmph. How disrespectful. She couldn't even get her T-H-O-T life right.

Beneath the caption was a link for a video to capture London's nightclub shenanigans. I clicked onto it and then watched in wide-eyed amazement. I didn't even bat an eyelash or move an eye muscle at the sight of London being half-dragged and half-carried out the club. Then she was captured outside the nightclub, crouched by the gutter—where she belonged—puking her guts up.

I frowned. *Mmmph. These little-grown girls can't even hold their liquor. Ole lightweight hookas.*

Someone's camera zoomed in on London as she slurred, "Anderson, b-b-b-baby. D-d-don't leave m-m-me t-t-this w-waaaay. Don't y-y-you understand I c-c-can't survive without you?" She grabbed him and tried to pull him into her. "K-k-kiss m-m-meeeeee. D-d-do me right here."

"London, chill," Anderson said, trying to shield her face from the cameras. "You're drunk."

"N-no, I-I-I'm not." She belched. "Oopsie." And then she giggled.

Ugh.

"I-I-I'm drunk in l-l-love with you, Anderson. Let me love y-y-you."

"Hey, get those cameras outta here!" Anderson yelled at someone as he lifted London and shielded her from the camera's view. Then the video went dead.

Bwahahahahahaha...

I struggled to catch my breath from laughing so hard.

Deargodsweetbabyjeezus! Hang me upside down and have your way with me. Right here, right now! London had really reached an all-time low offering that man-boy her crumbled cookie. Even he didn't want them soppy crumbs.

I shook my head. Having seen enough of London's pissy-face drunkenness (she was an embarrassment!), I clicked out

of my browser, then slapped shut my laptop, just as my landline rang.

I glanced at the caller ID. *L.A. County.*

I rolled my eyes up in my head. Oh no, oh no,
ohhhhhhh no!

The second I answered and spoke into the phone, I was
greeted with an automated recording: "You have a collect
call from... *Rich* ... at the Lorna P. Johnson Youth Detention
Center. To accept this call..."

Click.

I hung up. That little dirty jail-birdie was not about to run
my bill up with her lies and jailhouse tales. Served her right.
Mmmph. Trying to use me for my good phone service. Not!

Rich had another think coming. I was done with her. Again.
No, really. This time I was emphatically done. Finished.

My cordless rang again.

I clicked TALK, then END.

Rich was suddenly becoming worse than a pesky fly. Annoying. As far as I was concerned, she and I had nothing to
talk about. And, besides, the last time I tried to be loving and
kind to an inmate, the junkie-troll turned around and stabbed
me in the back, talked bad about me, and disrespected my
good nature after I'd given her money to get back on her feet
and out of that filthy rat-motel she stayed in with her mother,
given her a new car to ride around in so she could rest the
bottom of her brick-hard feet, and then paid for her to get
that big, bubblicious booty she now happily bounced and
dropped every chance she got.

I was the one who helped little Miss Flatty Patty retire
them nasty booty pads she religiously wore to fluff up her flat
back. But *hmmph*—whatever! I wasn't ever messy, so I wasn't
going to mention any names.

The landline rang for a third time.

"*Whaaaat?*" I snapped into the receiver. The recording

started again. I drummed my fingers and patted my cottony-soft foot on the rug, then started gripping fibers with my painted toes.

I pressed ONE.

"*Spppppeeeeencer!* Were you hanging up on *me?* Tramp! Trick! How dare you try to do me! You know I'm on lock-down. You know I'm in here doing hard time. I've been in here fighting for my life. Fighting to keep my virginity intact. Fighting to keep my edges from falling out. Fighting to stay fabulous. And all you wanna do is play me! Take advantage of my love and light. Girl, these broke-down, bald-headed trolls stole my weave tracks! Anywho, Slowkeeta, I need for you to order me two trays of hot wings—extra blue cheese—and smuggle them up in here on visits. My stomach can't handle this slop they serve us. It gives me gas. I think I have an ulcer..."

Yawn. It was too late in the evening for this dumbness.

"Ohmygod! I almost forgot," Rich continued, unfazed by the fact that I hadn't said a word since I'd accepted her call. "I need for you to send a money order—no, wait. Go online and transfer two thousand dollars into Knuckles—no, wait. That's her street name because she has big hands and fights like a man. Her government is Unique Asia Mercedes Shay-Shay Jackson..."

I blinked.

"We were playing spades and I lost. You know I don't gamble, and I don't play cards. But when in jail you do what the Romans do. Play spades. You do what you gotta do to survive with the Spaniards. Girl, I'm petrified. Long story short, I gotta get that he-man her money by noon tomorrow, or she said she was gonna shank me, poke holes into my liver. *Speeeencer!* Are you hearing me, tramp? I'm too fabulous and too cute to be walking around with bullet holes in my kidneys..."

I slid my tongue over my teeth.

"*Speeeeeeencerrrrr?* Hello? *Hello?* Are you there?"

"I'm sorry," I said in mock recording, "but the person you are trying to reach has a number that has been disconnected..."

Click.

38

Heather

Wednesday.
Eight a.m.
If only...he knew me...
I wonder if my name would've been Heather.
I bet it would've started with the letter R too...
And I would've been called Reese...
Or Renee...
Or Richelle...
Or Rikelle...
Or Ri...ch...
Rich...
And maybe...just maybe...the sun would've shone my way, God would've made up Her mind to be kind, and Richard Montgomery would've loved me too.
And I would've been daddy's little girl.
His heartbeat's sweetness.
His heartstring's weakness.
The one he wanted.
Then he would see that I was just like him.

Strong.

Solid.

Bold.

Took no shorts.

Was a rose in the middle of the concrete.

Then maybe...in a long string of maybes...he would agree to love me, and I could rein as teen queen again.

Get my Wu-Wu back.

Get Luda Tuda on track.

Get on wax and not just iTunes.

Be my own black beauty...

Stop feeling like Hollywood slop.

Stop trying to outrun my own shadow. And be strong enough to shove the weight that I should've been a creamy stream of blankness that ran down my daddy's leg, instead of being bred into Camille, off of my shoulders.

And maybe...just maybe...I would know what it was like to simply take a breath.

But I didn't.

'Cause mistake-babies like me didn't breathe. We just held it all in and contended with the fact that we were what happened to a thot when a player hit it and quit it.

I sat Indian-style in my bed, reached into my mirrored nightstand drawer, and took out my ball of foiled goodness, better known as One-Eight-Seven—Co-Co's newest powered recipe of crushed Adderall and Xanax sprinkled with a li'l molly (*pixie dust*, as he called it).

I sucked in a long string of air through my nose and blew it out of my mouth, then flicked my nostrils for good measure. I had to be sure they were clean, clear, and ready for my next mission: to be lifted up where I belonged, before I hit the steps of Hollywood High and was forced to deal with those pampered and bourgeois hood rats.

* * *

10:45 a.m.

Whap!

"*Heather Suzanne!*"

What was that?

I felt a stinging sensation blaze across my cheek as my eyes popped open wide. The place was a blur...but I knew I was in some kind of room...

Is that a bed?

Wait, am I sitting on a bed?

Is that a TV?

I smiled.

I should be on that TV.

Whose room am I in?

Is this my room?

Nah.

I don't think this is my room. Where am I?

And how did I get here?

Did I fly here?

Can I fly?

Yooooo, I think I got wings!

I cracked up, and just as a smile bloomed onto my face, I was met with another blaze across my left cheek, this one fierier than before, one that forced my neck to the right and left it stuck there.

I reached my hand up toward my cheek, but someone snatched my face, cupped my chin, pressed their fingertips into my jaw, and said, "Heather Suzanne, look at me!"

I blinked.

Blinked again.

First my vision was hazy...then whoever had set my face on fire was clear to me.

I would know that look of disgust anywhere.

Camille.

And she had just blown every ounce of the best high I'd
had in a long time.

Damn!

I should hop up and drag her.

No.

Let the drunkard live.

I shoved Camille's hand away from my face and said,
"What the hell is wrong with you, lady?!"

Camille leaned into me, her white gown hung loosely
around her neck and shoulders, giving gross peeks of her
lemon-shaped breasts and pink inverted nipples. I was two
seconds from throwing up in my mouth. She snatched my
face again and spat, "I'm so tired of being the mother to
some li'l shameless junkie. I know you were in here sniffing
some powdered Clorox mixed with cow dung and hog piss!"
She narrowed her eyes. "Of all the nuts and bolts that
Richard Montgomery had, why did I have to get the screw?!"

Camille's words stung, but the last thing I was gonna do
was let her know she'd gotten to me. I closed my eyes, seconds away from putting this old bird into a headlock. Then
slowly I opened them again and stared at her.

"What do you want Camille?"

She snorted, then spat, "What do I *want?* Little girl, I want
my career back! I want to walk the streets of Beverly Hills and
shop until my heels hurt and my toes ache. I want Chocolate
Thunder from the Cheetahs strip club to grip my waist and
rock my backside in the Champagne Room for free, because
I'm tired of paying him to do it! I want you to stop being
some low-level crackhead, in here snorting up donkey shit
and killing what's left of my gene pool! But you can't give me
any of that, can you? Therefore, at this moment, what I want
is for you to get up and go to school!"

School?

School!

Oh, my God!

I looked over at the clock: 10:49 a.m.

I was late.

Mad late.

But I had to go to school anyway. I hadn't been in two weeks, and yesterday Westwick called here, in the middle of Camille's afternoon cocktail, and threatened that if I didn't come today I'd be expelled.

The last thing I needed was to be expelled. Although Kitty had ruined me, she did say that if I got clean and did well in school, she would take another look at me.

Though I could drink loads of water and eat herbs to re-birth my piss, I couldn't control Westwick. And if I got kicked out, I knew for sure Kitty wouldn't touch me with somebody else's stick. And even though I hated Kitty with a passion, I needed her.

I pushed past Camille, hopped out of bed, and took a quick shower. I didn't even have enough time to match my heels to my catsuit, so I pulled out a pair of pleather-neon yellow shorts, a short-sleeve zebra print pullover sweater, and a pair of five-inch Timberland stilettos.

I let my own sandy brown coils of thick hair hang wild, as I zipped out the front door, and into my red '57 Chevy, cranked it up, and took off for the wood—Hollywood.

Noon.

And who was the first face I saw:

West. *Wick.*

I rolled my eyes toward the marble ceiling. I swear I couldn't stand this mothersucker! Why was he at the front door, standing guard, his chub-club-Judy body blocking me from taking another step into the school? Didn't he have something else to do?

Ugh!

I blew out a hard breath and shoved both hands up on my hips. My pleather, neon-yellow hobo bag, from my exclusive Ching-Chow Korean collection, slid down my right arm and hung around my wrist.

Instead of waiting for Westwick to piss me off by spewing some unreasonable and expensive request, I said, "I don't have time for the ying-yang. You called and said I needed to be at school today, so here I am. Now if you'll excuse me, it's time for my math class."

He clucked his tongue. "As if your bottom scrape, low money behind can even add beyond the price of a nickel bag." He smacked his lips. And I could tell by the dumb look in his beady eyes, the smirk on his tight mouth, and the way he held his head down, forcing his double chin to slap into his fat neck, that he was amused with himself.

Sucker.

Westwick carried on, "In. My. Office, Gator."

Gator? As in some ancient and old crackhead?

Ohhhhhhh, I'm 'bout to cuss this fool all the way out!

Deep breath in.

Deep breath out.

Just go into his office.

Let him run his mouth.

Write him a bad check, and then head to class.

Don't nobody have time for Westwick!

I walked past the team of receptionists in the main office and into Westwick's dungeon. He took a seat, slapped his feet onto his desk, pointed to his credit card machine, and said, "You know the routine. You want in? Well, you have to pay. Now, credit card, please."

I didn't have any credit cards. Actually, I didn't have any credit.

Before I could tell him he better take a check and shut up, he spat, "And don't even think about writing me a check. Everyone knows all the banks have shut you down."

Blood rushed to my face, and the fine hairs on the back of my neck stood up. I blew out a hard and heavy breath, then snapped my fingers in a Z-motion and said, "Lady, bye. Who you think got time for this?" I paused and looked him over, from his shiny bald head to the black red-bottoms on his feet.

I continued, "This is a school, and you're supposed to be the headmaster! Not up in here money laundering, tryna snatch my wig off and take food out of my mouth. So peep this: I ain't giving you crap! Not one dime, not even a penny. As a matter of fact, I wouldn't give you an ounce of spit if you were on fire and needed something wet.

"I'm tired of you coming for me. And what you not gonna do is try and choke me for another moment. Now, like I said, I'm going to class."

Westwick blinked. Cleared his throat. Blinked again. Then stood up and clapped.

That's right, that queen stood up and clapped. Like I'd just given him the performance of a lifetime. "Bravo! Bravo! Splendid! Now are you finished? Or is there more to that ratchet sonnet?"

I hesitated, and instead of him letting me get my comeback together, he carried on. "Looka here, Lady Confusion. Hear me and hear me well. If you think you're going to come up in here, run me, and stroll through Hollywood High anyway you choose to, you're high and mistaken. Little lost girl, this is my world, and I run this universe anyway I please. No one told you to be out there in the streets, steps away from being Miss Two-dollar-drop-to-her-knees. That was your decision. You had the whole world at your feet. A number one television show, a chance to be a Disney princess. Holly-

wood's doll. But you wanted to be a wild child, the new millennium Lindsey Lohan and Britney Spears. A follower."

He paused, like he dared me to say something. But for
some reason, what with the massive verbal kicks he'd just
landed in my gut, I couldn't quite get my words together.

He continued, "And now you wish to come for me, like I
owe you something. I don't owe you a thing, sweet cheeks.
Not even a second chance. Now, had you come in here humble, perhaps with some ownership of your unhinged and
jungle behavior, along with a li'l gift card, a fruit basket, or
something, I may have allowed you a payment plan. But
nooooooo, you came up in here with those broad shoulders
squared and that plastic behind wagging like a horse, trying
to check me.

"Well, *tsk, tsk, tsk*, that's not how this works, darling. Now
either you hand over your credit card or you are expelled.
And don't think Ms. Kitty hasn't informed me what expelling
you will do for your cancer-stricken career."

My heart raced, and my chest heaved. I was beyond pissed,
hurt, and embarrassed. I couldn't believe this had happened
to me. I felt like Westwick had sliced open my throat and
ripped my mouth out.

I felt dizzy.

Out of control.

My palms were sweaty, and all I saw was Westwick standing
there, judging me, looking down on me, like I was nothing.

Without thinking twice, I reared a hand back, brought it
down, and swung it straight across Westwick's desk. His family photos crashed to the floor; causing shards of glass to
shatter and glassy pricks to pop into the air. His fresh yellow
roses went everywhere, and the water from the vase ran all
over his desk, drenching his stacks of important papers and
school files. And that stupid credit card machine hit the wall,
then fell onto the floor and smashed into broken pieces!

Westwick's mouth flew open, and now he was frozen and speechless.

I shoved my bag up on my shoulder, straightened the hem of my sweater, fluffed my curls, and said, "You can't expel me because I quit! Out. Of. Here!"

Then I wagged my behind, just like the horse he accused me of being, storming out of his office. And a few moments later I was in my ride. I cranked my hydraulics, dropped my top, and took off toward the sun, leaving Hollywood High and Westwick's shitty face in a cloud of dust.

39

London

I couldn't believe it. Heather had quit school. Rich was in jail. And I had managed to make a complete and utter fool of myself for the whole world to see.

I stared at the recently written article written in *Teen Enquirer*:

FROM PAMPERED PRINCESSES TO BRATTY PAUPERS

Tinseltown's darlings, Rich Montgomery, Heather Cummings, and London Phillips, have proven to the world that money can't buy class, and it definitely doesn't guarantee a happily-ever-after. From jail cells to crack dens and drunken meltdowns, these three socialites have managed to shame the devil himself with their disturbingly entertaining, yet self-destructive antics. Rich Montgomery was seen going through one courtroom door, then being dragged out from another in what looked to be handcuffs, while reality-star Heather Cummings was spotted coming out of what sources call a traveling "get-right" lounge hosted by her closest friend, Co-Co Ming. And London Phillips? Well, we've seen the recent videos. Right? She looks like she's ready for a long stay in a padded room. Now, as we sit back and watch the rest of their lives unravel, the only link missing in this chain of craziness is Spencer Ellington. The world waits with bated breath to see what she does to trump her three frenemies. Or shall we say her nemeses? Stay tuned...

I slung the magazine across the room. This was a hot mess. We were a hot mess. All three of us! And we were all being dragged in one gossip rag or another. Every one of us except for Spencer! Somehow, she'd managed to duck and dodge pap bullets, while the rest of us stood in the spotlight and allowed ourselves to be target practice as the media aimed and shot fire.

A video of me drunk-crying and hugging on Anderson had gone viral.

Oh, my God!

What had I done?

Online bloggers and gossip hags had been hounding Anderson for a response, but so far, the only thing he'd been kind enough to say was, "No comment," or he kindly ignored them all together, the way he'd been doing me.

I couldn't begin to imagine what was going through his mind now. *He must hate me!* He just had to because I hated myself. And, even after all of that, I still hadn't gotten a chance to say anything I'd wanted to say to him.

Or had I?

Parts of that night were blank. There was a block of time I couldn't account for. The only thing that I had as an ugly reminder of that night, aside from the videos and blog bashing, was a nasty knot on the side of my head from where I'd fallen and hit it.

I croaked back a scream.

Nothing I'd hoped to achieve that night going to Club Sixty-Six had gone as planned.

LONDON PHILLIPS DRUNK IN LOVE read one caption.

LONDON PHILLIPS DIRTY DANCING WITH RAPPER BORN SUN-ALLAH read another caption.

LONDON PHILLIPS LEAVES HER PANTIES ON THE DANCE FLOOR! exclaimed another blogger.

Lies. Lies. And more lies!

I was too embarrassed to read any of the articles attached to the headlines about that horrid night. The bloggers had me painted as some love-obsessed alkie. My God! How could they?

That was furthest from the truth. Was I obsessed? Um. Maybe. A little.

But was I an alcoholic? No. That was Rich.

The only thing I was guilty of was wanting Anderson back. And I hadn't even managed to do that right.

And Anderson's fan club haters were dragging me the worst.

Twitter:

HELL NO @ANDERSONFORD THAT BEYOTCH DOESN'T DESERVE U!!

@ANDERSONFORD DON'T DO IT BOO!! I BEG U!

@ANDERSONFORD LONDON IS A THIRSTY THOT! U CAN DO WAY BETTER!

@ANDERSONFORD TELL THAT BIHH TO GO KICK ROCKS! SHE HAD HER CHANCE!

SHE CUTE @ANDERSONFORD BUT SHE CRAY-CRAY!

I'm not crazy! Those whores don't know me, I thought, as I stared at a picture someone had taken of me that night. I had to blink several times before I recognized who the girl staring back at me was. I had never looked so carefree, like I was having the time of my life.

Too bad I couldn't remember if I had or not.

I clicked onto Anderson's Instagram page, but then thought about sending him a DM on Twitter or inboxing him on Facebook instead to please call me.

But I'd already done that. Ten messages later on each page! And *still* no replies back. I had no way of contacting Anderson unless I called his New York office, something I really didn't want to do. Again. But what other choice did I have?

The last six times I'd called for him, all I got in return was what felt like a prompted script: "I'm sorry, Mr. Ford is not in his office today."

I was so desperate to talk to Anderson that whatever cardinal rules there might have been about seeming thirsty for a boy were forgotten. And, honestly, those rules didn't matter to me.

I reached for my cell, typed in my password, and then scrolled through my call log for Anderson's office number.

"Hello?" I said the moment I heard one of his assistants' voices. "May I please speak to Ander... uh, Mr. Ford?"

I thought I heard a sigh. "Is this London Phillips *again?*"

I frowned. "London Phillips?" I repeated, feigning indignation. "Who in the heck is that? No. This is Mrs. Foster from the Make a Wish Foundation."

"Oh. I'm sorry, Mrs. Foster. For a moment there, you sounded like someone else. Mr. Ford will be out of the office for the next few weeks, but all of his messages are being forwarded to him. Would you like to leave one?"

"Um. Is he on the West or East Coast?"

"I'm sorry, ma'am. I'm not at liberty to say. Would you like to leave a message?"

I ended the call. Then I went onto his Facebook page.

Stalked through his photos. But then my attention locked onto his status. He'd changed it.

Oh, my God!

My eyes widened, then started watering.

Oh God. Oh God, oh God, oh God. *Oh God*.

He'd actually changed it. *In a relationship*, it said, and I nearly died. A stray tear slid slowly down my cheek. My heart pulsed, then stopped, as I yelled the words in my head. *In a relationship!*

With who?

I already knew the answer: with that Russian whore! Another tear slid down my face. The world tilted a little. And then suddenly I flat-lined. All I needed was a silk-lined coffin to flop myself into, then slam the top shut.

Those three tiny words—*in a relationship*—had killed me.

40

Rich

"Hallelujah!" I wanted to shout to the Goddess of Freedom and Liberty Bells. I'd been finally set free! And I was all the way ready to ride up to the mountaintop and ring bells and shout for joy!

But this right here.

This moment.

This minute.

This pause in time was some straight bullshit.

The highest level of disrespect!

It was all I could do not to clutch my pearls and break 'em!

It had only been an hour since I was released and restored to my throne. And was no longer the property of Los Angeles County, item number 5678963, where I'd spent two weeks practically tied down and forced to be on a chain gang by day. Afternoons spent fighting off man-girls wanting to shank me into being their bride. And nights locked away in a cage. And instead of being greeted with a welcome home party, a glass of bubbly, strawberry crepes, and a masseuse, I walked into an intervention sponsored by the get-along gang from hell.

My mother—Empress Ghetto; my father—MC Wicked Slut-Rat; their son—li'l British crack-dealer-meth-slayer; and some self-appointed Jesus wannabe—Reverend Doctor Shirley Byrd—all tryna perform some psycho baptism on me.

All four of 'em tryna do me! Talk to me about my behavior, how it needed to change, and how I needed to get right with the Lord.

Psst, please.

Chile, cheese.

I was already saved. And I worshipped in the House of Fabulousness. I laid my collection plate down every night. So they couldn't preach me no sermon. Not up in here. First of all, I needed my weave done. Why? 'Cause some horrid creature-woman in a correction officer's uniform had been hatin' on me and had forced me to cut out and leave my ten-thousand-dollar tracks on some wet concrete.

Second of all, I needed a pedicure. My toenails were a mess! Why? 'Cause for the last two weeks, I'd been forced to walk the yard in some rubber-cheddar-cheese-colored slides from Jail-Mart.

You see where I'm goin' with this?

I didn't need the stress.

Plus.

I had a headache.

"Rich," Dr. Byrd called my name, like she'd been granted permission to get me together. "Welcome home," she said. "We'd like to discuss the reasons why you've been acting in the ways that you have and come up with some alternative solutions to expressing yourself in public."

Oh.

No.

She.

Didn't.

Is she steppin' to me? Tryna chin-check me? Me? Rich Montgomery?

This old bish got a set of steel balls!

"...*Alternative ways to expressing yourself...*" Is this skank tryna say I'm an embarrassment?

Should I just reach out and slap her now, or let her live, especially since she practically said I'm out here being a pigeon in these streets!

I paused. Took in this high-yellow heifer, from the white wingback chair she sat in, her black Easy Spirit pumps, to the pinned-up, sandy-brown dreads on her head.

Dr. Byrd continued, "What are your thoughts on that?"

I sucked my teeth, then said, "Oh, now you wanna know what I think? I think you can stop the press and hold the mess. 'Cause I'm not about to sit up here and be spoken to like I'm some li'l musty thot twerkin' on the concrete, because I'm not. I'm high steppin'-classy, *babeeeee!* And the only places I twerk are in boutique bars and five-star clubs. Thank. You. Now, if you'll excuse me."

I inched to the edge of my seat, but before I could stand up, my mother said, "Rich Gabrielle Montgomery." The mere fact that she'd called me by entire government said that she'd already practiced some whack speech she'd written to impress her husband and come for me.

Don't say nothing, queen. Stay silent because you already know anything you say can and will be used against you.

You know this. So just let Lo-ho pop her bra strap and show off.

My mother carried on: "Rich, we have had enough of your nonsense, and you being sentenced to detention was the last straw! You're doing terrible in school—"

I had to cut her off and said, "Excuse you? Not today, ma'am." I zigzagged my index finger in the air. "You're the one who stopped paying for my grades. Do you think Westwick is just going to give me A's? Umm. How about *no!* So don't blame me. From what I can see, me not doing well in school is your fault, not mine."

Instead of agreeing with me, Logan, leader of the ratchets, jumped out of her seat, stalked over toward me, and hogged up my personal space. She bent down and leaned into my face. "You better shut up before I shut you up!"

I shook my head. It never failed; she always wanted to fight me.

I let her carry on, her hot breath burning my nostrils. "You think this is a game? You think we're playing with you? Well, we're not! We are tired of giving you everything, and all you do is whore with this boy and that boy—"

"Not true. It's one boy at a time, so you can take the word *and* out!"

I could tell that threw her for a loop. She hesitated, then said, "Didn't I tell you to shut your crazy behind up?"

I didn't even respond to that, the last thing I was...was crazy.

She continued, "I'm soooo sick of you!"

That makes two of us!

"I guess we have something in common," I said snidely.

My mother threw up her hands in disgust. "You know what? I'm done. Every time I turn around, you are in some blog or on the cover of some rag for being the world's biggest drama queen. If you're not hemmed up in some bar brawl or fighting with one of your friends, you're running behind some low-budget, low-level boy or getting arrested for drinking—"

I cut her off. "How you gon' say anything about *my* man, huh? You don't know him. You don't know what he's been through. He's no lower budget than you were before you managed to trick your way into the backseat of your husband's limo. So I resent you for saying that! There's nothing low budget about Justice. He can't help it if he has to live on a budget until he can get his name out there. Furthermore, the only low-budget one in this room is your li'l prince over there." I pointed to RJ.

My mother gripped me by the collar, her eyes flashing fire, rearing her hand back to slap me. For the first time, ever, I didn't flinch. I just stared her down.

"Mrs. Montgomery." Dr. Byrd called for my mother's attention.

Lo-rat quickly let me go, then said, "Little girl, you had better thank Dr. Byrd for saving your life." She retook her seat, closed her eyes, and blew out short reps of air, I guess practicing the anger-management techniques Dr. Jesus taught her before I walked in here. But whatever! I was only going to take but so much.

"Rich, damn. You need to learn to shut up!" RJ snapped, I guess coming to his mother's rescue. "You're so stupid with all of your drunk theatrics. All in court trying to tell the judge off, instead of listening to Ma and shutting up!"

I sucked my teeth and flicked my wrist, "Bye, boy. Don't you have a plane to catch? Maybe, if my prayers are answered, it'll drop down into the Pacific Ocean and you'll go missing."

"Rich!" my mother snapped. "Don't have me bust you in your mouth. Don't you *ever* wish something like that on your brother! Ever. Have you lost your damn mind?"

"Nah. It's cool, Ma. Rich is ignorant."

"And you're a piece of shit," I snapped back. "I can't stand you! Mr. Perfect. Boy, bye! Now what you can do is get outta my sight and take Dr. Jesus with you."

I looked over at Dr. Byrd—ole Shirley Caesar wannabe, who I could tell struggled to control the indifferent look on her face.

"Rich, that's enough!" my mother warned, taking up for her crown prince. "You will *not* say another word about your brother. And I mean that! Nor will you be disrespectful to Dr. Byrd. She isn't going anywhere. And this has nothing to do with your brother. This is about *you.* We are all here to help you, because we care. And because we love you!"

"Help me?! *Psst.* Because you care? Because you love me? Lies! Puhlease, I don't need any help. I'm good on that. And I don't need y'all tryna serve me when all I do is go to school, hang out with my friends, and live my life. But what do I get in return? Sent to jail. And then I come home to the Get-Right Gang trying to perform an exorcism on me! Chile, cheese. You got me messed up!"

I scanned each of their faces, stopping at my father's, and he clearly had an attitude. Hopefully he was pissed off with himself, 'cause obviously he hadn't spent enough time with his wife, who'd been watching too much reality TV. And was now trying to shove some bad-acting Lifetime bull crap down our throats, like we were a house full of white folks.

Seeing as though no one else said a word, I added, "I'm done here." I pointed to RJ. "Use Dr. Byrd to handle Mr. International Incident. Now good day." I stood up and took a step toward the door.

"Rich," my father said, his voice two octaves deeper than usual. "Sit your ass down. *Now.*"

I started not to listen. But I turned around, and judging by the look on his face, I knew I needed to retake my seat, at least for a moment.

"Richard," my mother said, "don't get your blood pressure up, baby. Let me handle it."

"Handle what?" he snapped. "I've been letting you handle it for seventeen years, and now we have an easy-lay-down-with-anything-with-a-penis disaster on our hands! I've had enough of letting you handle it. You said bring Dr. Byrd here and things will be fine, but from what I can see, I'm about to pay Dr. Byrd three hundred dollars an hour for a wild, little girl with a disrespectful mouth who clearly needed her behind kicked a long time ago. So *no*, Logan, I'm not gon' let you handle it another moment. I got it from here."

He turned to me. "Let me help you. From this moment

forward, you gon' do what I tell you to do, or I'ma bust yo' ass. Simple. Fair exchange. No robberies. 'Cause you will not slut it up another moment on my dime or be labeled a drunk in every other headline. And if you're not tearin' up some bar, you and your mother are around here whispering about you being pregnant, again, planning secret flights to Nowhere, Arizona, because you can't keep your legs shut. You think I don't know what they call you out there in the streets, huh?"

I rolled my eyes and shifted in my seat. "Yeah. Fabulous," I said, staring him dead in his face. "They say I'm a lady in the streets—discreet and classy. Period."

He shook his head. "Rich, shut your dumb-ass up. I would laugh if you didn't sound so damn pathetic. Here I have made every effort to give you everything, and instead of making something of yourself, you wanna whore in the streets! Nothing about you is a lady. Nothing about you is discreet. Everything you stand for is cheap, greasy, and lowlife."

I swallowed, hard. Richard Montgomery had *never* spoken to me like that. How dare he disrespect me and try to drag my good name!

I was done! And I was a split second from telling them all to kiss my—

He continued, "Now your mother might play games with you, but I ain't the one. So this is your life from here on out: in the house by nine thirty on school nights and ten o'clock on the weekends. No more drinking. No driving. No bar hopping. No endless shopping sprees. No carte blanche access to credit cards or cash. No sluttin' it up. And if I hear another whisper about you being pregnant, then both you and your mother are gettin' tossed out of here. Do I make myself clear?"

I couldn't believe this was happening to me. All I wanted to do was relax and get my snap back, return to being my fabulous self. Yet here I was in the middle of the Wild-Wild West.

Unreasonable orders being barked at me. Accused of being a failing student, a drama queen, a drunk, and some cheap and easy lay!

Like, seriously, this was insane, and yes, I was a lot of things, but I was none of the things he'd called me! And there was *nothing* dumb about me. Nothing!

I was intella... intella... is it intellazent? Well, I wasn't dumb.

Therefore and forever more, the last thing I was about to do was let this played-out crew try me for another moment.

No sir and no ma'am!

So I stood up and let them see the arch in my back twitch and my behind switch as I walked out of the living room, clicked my heels up the stairs, grabbed my Louis Vuitton suitcase, and tossed in my diary, some clothes, and my favorite heels.

Then I asked Chef Jacque to have the house manager help him quickly pack up the rest of my wears. When they were done, I called for three Ubers: one for me, two for my things.

And, no, I didn't know where I was going, but I knew I was getting out of here. I tucked my Chloé clutch under my arm, held my suitcase in my hand, and with Chef Jacque and the house manager behind me, I stormed downstairs, walked by my parents, RJ, and Dr. Byrd, and clicked my heels to the front door.

And just as I slammed it behind me, I heard my father saying, "She's cut off."

41

Spencer

"*Rich.* What in the world are you doing here?"

"Thank God!" she exclaimed, pushing her way into the foyer. She gripped a YSL duffel bag in one hand and had her clutch tucked tightly under her other arm. "You're home."

I blinked. "Of course I'm home. Where else would I be? This is where I live. Now again, what are you doing here? Why did you just barge your way in here? And why is your hair all wild and crazy-looking? Did you escape from jail?"

It looked like she'd taken her whole head and mopped a floor with it.

She gave me a dismissive wave. "Spencer, don't do me right now. I'm stressed *allllll* the way out. And, no, I didn't escape, tramp! I just got paroled..."

"Paroled?"

"Yes, honey! Paroled. I've been out of prison for less than two hours..."

"Rich, you were in juvie jail. Not prison."

She huffed. "Trixie! It was prison. And it was hell. I served ten days of hard time, girl. You don't know hard times until you've been stuffed into a black-and-white jumper and locked in a cell with four other women—well, two of them looked like women." She shook her head. "That other one, I'm not so sure what that was. But anywho...you don't know anything about life unless you've been surrounded by concrete and barbed wire."

I rolled my eyes. "Rich, the jumpers were orange. Not black and white."

She dropped her duffel bag to the floor. "*Trick!* Were you there? Did you have to squat over a steel toilet? God, I missed my bidet. That toilet paper they gave us was hella rough on my lady parts! I haven't had a good wipe and rinse in weeks..."

I sighed. "Rich, tell me *now* why you're here, so I can throw you out."

"Ohmygod! You're such a hater! You don't give a damn about anyone except yourself."

"Yes, that is true. Now why are you here?"

She huffed. "RJ and my parents ganged up on me, Spencer. They tried to do me right in front of some wannabe voodoo priestess. Who does that? I had to flee for my life!"

My eyes widened. "They did what?"

"Pay attention, *Speeeeennnncerrrrr!* I *saaaid* the Montgomerys tried to jump me. Straight outta Compton me! And Logan pulled a razor out on me and threatened my whole entire life! What kind of mother does that?"

I gasped, slapping a hand up over my mouth.

"Yes, girl. I barely made it out of there alive. And then RJ tried to put me in a headlock to keep me from leaving, but I punched him in the gut and broke all four of his ribs..."

I gasped. "Ohmygod, no! RJ?"

She nodded. "Yes. RJ. Mr. British American!"

I frowned. "*Wait.* RJ wouldn't do that to you. And how did you break *all* four of his ribs, when humans have twenty-four? Twelve on each side."

She stomped a heeled foot. "*Bish*. There you go taking up for that troll hunter! Did I ask you for a history lesson on RJ's bones? No. You don't know him like I do. That boy was born with only four ribs. He's defective. And he's—"

I cut her off. "Man-eater, stop! I don't wanna hear any more of your lies about RJ. Now tell me why you're here. And don't lie."

Rich placed the back of her hand up to her forehead, then grabbed onto the side of the large entryway table. She paused for a moment, then placed a hand to her chest. "Spencer, I'm so tired, girl. Everywhere I turn, someone is tryna do me. My parents. RJ. The judge. The police. COs. So-called friends. The bloggers." She dug inside her purse and pulled out a mini pack of tissues. Although I couldn't see a tear in sight, she dabbed under both eyes.

I pursed my lips. Tilted my head. "Mmm-hmm. Go on."

"Spencer, I know you don't know anything about being fabulous, but it's hard being me. It's like everywhere I go someone is watching me, talking about me, writing lies about me..."

My head tilted to the other side. "You're a loudmouth attention whore, Rich. You love to be seen. And heard."

"Clutching pearls! Lies and deceit! I resent that, Spencer."

"Okay. Now how can I help you?"

"I need a place to stay—only for a few days," she quickly said, "until I can get my mind right."

I blinked. "A place to stay? Why?"

Rich narrowed her eyes. "You damn slore! Haven't you heard a word I said? I've been thrown out onto the streets, Spencer! I'm seeking asylum. My own family turned on me. I'm not safe, Spencer. And I have nowhere else to go. I need refuge."

My shoulders slumped. "Rich, sorry. I wish I could. But I

don't have enough room here for you. My home is not big enough to accommodate you, your ego, and all your drama."

"Clutching pearls! Lies, girl! All this house"—she spread open her arms and spun around the foyer—"and you can't open up one of your wings for a good-good friend? We've known each other for almost forever, Spencer."

"Yeah, you're right," I agreed. "Since buckteeth and barrettes."

"*Yasss, yassss!*" Rich clapped her hands. "Since roller skates and dodgeball. We were thick as thieves on the playground. Couldn't anyone touch us in double Dutch."

I chuckled. "Uh-huh. But you would always be out of breath after a minute or so. And I would have to bring us to victory."

"Girl. That's because I would forget to carry my inhaler with me."

Oh. Okay.

Rich was still telling lies.

"God, Spencer. Those were the good ole days. We were like sisters."

Mmm-hmm. Until you turned on me . . .

"Spencer, you always had my back."

"Yup. I always took up for you, Rich. Even when girls would tease you and chase you through the school yard because of that big mouth of yours. I was right there ready to fight for you."

"You never let me down, Spencer. Like I said, we go way back."

I pursed my lips. "Mmm-hmm. Way back when you wore those thick glasses and had that big round body."

"Oh, my God, *girrrrrl*. No. Don't go there. You tryna do me. Thank God for Jenny Craig and my plastic surgeon."

My gaze dropped to Rich's hips. They were spread out like

a wide, curved road with lots of miles on it. "Looks like you need Jenny back in your life," I said.

"Screw Jenny. All that trick did was keep me hungry."

A horn blew outside.

"Who is that?"

"Oh. Uber," Rich calmly stated.

I gave her a look.

"Long story. That hatin-azz judge took my license from me, and now I can't drive."

"Oh."

"Anyway, Spencer. Can I stay for a few days, *plllease!* You know I don't beg, girl."

"No."

"Whaaaat? Clutching pearls! You hateful whore! You couldn't even take my collect calls while I was away at war. Didn't even have the decency to visit me or write me. And now I have that postal disorder, so the least you can do is—"

"Who's down here clutching pearls and clucking like some ole wounded hen?" Daddy snapped as he hobbled down the stairs and into the foyer. He waved his cane in the air. "I can't find my shotgun. I know one of you thieving hyenas stole..." His voice trailed off as his eyes landed over at Rich.

"Daddy, you remember Rich—Rich Montgomery, don't you?"

"Hi, Mr. Ellington," Rich said, all sweet and sugary, trying to pretend to be nice.

Daddy squinted at her. "You a thick one, huh? You're one big biscuit. I bet you like to eat, don't you, gal?"

Rich blinked.

"Are you a stripper, 'cause you look like you know your way around a pole?"

Dear Lawd Jeezus...

"Daddy, nooo. Play nice. Rich, give me a second," I said, looking over at her. I hurriedly took Daddy by the arm and ushered him toward the stairs before he said something hurt-ful. "C'mon, Daddy, let's go get you back up to your suite so you can pack the crazy away. Rich, I'll be right back," I said over my shoulder.

"Girl, no worries. Take your time."

"Better yet, Rich," I said, "on second thought, you can see yourself out. I'll call you later."

Rich gasped. "Clutching pearls! Spencer, don't do me, girl..."

"Why is that gal always clutching pearls?" Daddy stage-whispered.

"It's a figure of speech, Daddy."

He grunted. "If she wants something to clutch, I—"

"Daddy! Don't have me get a Brillo pad and scrub your filthy mouth out!"

He chuckled. "You a feisty one. Back in my day, I woulda put a strap to your behind. Tanned it red."

I sighed.

"Now, why is that gal here again?"

"Oh. She needs a place to stay," I told him.

He shook his head. "Don't do it, Punkin. She smells like trouble. Send that gal down to the nearest street corner, and let her get out there and earn her keep."

I bit back a giggle. "Daddy, stop. That's not nice."

Once I got him back up to his suite, I yelled at his atten-dants for not doing a better job of keeping him under lock and key; then I quickly dashed back down the stairs to lock my—

"Aaah!" I screamed. "What is all this?"

The foyer was flooded with Louie trunks, garment bags, and suitcases.

"Oh, this?" Rich said nonchalantly. "Just a few things until I can figure out my next move." I blinked. "Relax, Spencer. I promise. It's only for a few days. You won't even know I'm here. I swear, girl." She headed toward the stairs. "Now show me to my wing."

A horn blared again.

Rich stopped mid-step and looked over her shoulder at me. "Oh. I need for you to pay those three Uber drivers. My credit card was declined."

And then she was gone, leaving all her belongings in the middle of the floor and three loud horns blowing.

42

London

Someone knocked on my bedroom door, but I was too distraught to respond or to get up and answer it. I'd spent the last several days in my room, cutting myself off from the world. I hadn't gone to school or therapy. And hadn't known my therapist to do house calls until she'd shown up here yesterday.

Daddy had called her. "Worried," she'd said. Trying to roll my eyes made my head hurt. But I had to admit: Although my world still felt bleak, talking to Dr. Kickaloo had made me feel a little better.

Before our session ended, she had taken me by the hands and reminded me that I was loved. That I had two parents who loved me, and that my light shone brighter now than ever, that all I needed to do was get out of my own way. And then she'd said that I needed to forgive my parents and let them navigate through their own mess (my words, not hers, but that's how I heard it).

But I couldn't see any light. And I didn't know how to get out of my own way. And it hurt too much to try to forgive anyone. All I was surrounded by was darkness. Because my parents were really getting a divorce, and the one person that I wanted to love me didn't love me back.

But guess what?

I knew I couldn't make my parents stay together, and I knew I couldn't make Anderson feel something he didn't anymore. And that was what hurt the most.

Still, I didn't want (wasn't ready) to accept that it was really over between my parents and that Anderson had really moved on with someone other than *me*. That he'd found something (or saw something) in that Ivina bitch that he couldn't find or see in *me*.

Yet, in my head, I'd still clung onto the fantasy of he and I spending the summer in Milan—him riding a sleek motor scooter with me on the back, clinging to his waist, as he whizzed through the narrow, cobblestoned streets, where we'd make our way up into the sun-drenched hills and make sweet love.

God! How stupid of me. Fantasies didn't come true. And fairy tales didn't exist in my world, only horror tales with sordid endings. And, yet, I still stalked Anderson's social media as if I'd find some hidden clue to his heart. It might have been over—well, okay, okay, it hadn't ever gotten started—between Anderson and me, but I still found a way to somehow delude myself into thinking that I still had one last fighting chance.

And I was going to take it, before I threw in the towel.

There were rumblings in Twitterland and on some blogs that Anderson was hosting a "Who's Who" party on his yacht, *Buff Daddy*, next month. I had to be there. I had to walk up on that boat focused and ready to show Anderson once and for all what kind of girl I was really made of. Even if I had to wrap myself in ribbons and tie myself to buoys.

Anderson Ford was going to *see* me.

Still...

It hurt too much knowing that he'd really chosen that, that...goddess. It hurt just trying to—

There was another knock.

"London?"

"Go away," I said over a sob as I shut my iPad, then slid it under my pillow.

Knock, knock, knock...

The double doors opened, and Daddy peered inside.

"Sweetheart," he said in that gentle fatherly tone I'd forgotten how much I missed, "what's wrong?"

"N-n-nothing," I managed to say over another sob. "Please leave. I'm fine."

I turned my head away from the door to avoid his gaze, burying my face into one of the pillows.

Go be with your whore.

Daddy perched awkwardly on the edge of my bed.

"Talk to me, sweetheart," he said. "You know you can talk to me about whatever is bothering you."

I wailed. "No, I can't! I used to. But now I can't! So please. Just go away. Leave me alone."

"Don't talk like that. I'm not going anywhere. It hurts me to see you like this."

I cried harder. Daddy had always been my knight in shining armor. He'd been the kind of man I always imagined myself one day marrying—kind and thoughtful and loving; just l-l-l-like Ander...son!

I felt his hand on my shoulder, and my body stiffened, then slowly I began to relax as he spoke to me. "No matter what's going on between your mother and me, I love you, sweetheart. And no matter what, I'm going to always love you..."

I wanted to cover my ears and scream. I'd heard those words countless times—*I love you*—and now more than ever, they felt emptier than I could have ever imagined.

"And I am going to always be here for you, sweetheart," Daddy continued. "Always."

My sobbing erupted into wailing and then hiccupping coupled with snot and spit and swollen eyes. My chest hurt. Everything I'd ever thought about Daddy had been a lie.

All he was, all he'd ever be to me now...was a *cheater!*

How could I ever trust anything he ever said to me?

I couldn't.

"London, sit up, sweetheart. Please."

I couldn't stand to look at him, and yet I missed him. And my heart ached because I had lost the two most important men in my life—Daddy and Anderson.

I'd lost Daddy to Rich's mother and Anderson to that pretty Russian trick. And so I did what my heart wanted me to do, even if my body didn't.

I sat up in bed and cried into my father's chest as he rocked me side to side, smearing snot and tears all over his custom-tailored dress shirt.

When my sobbing eventually subsided to sniffles, Daddy lifted my chin and wiped my eyes with a handkerchief I hadn't seen him pull out.

"Here," he said, handing me his monogrammed hanky. "Blow your nose."

I did. And when I tried to hand it back to him, he looked at all the snot I had blown inside it and said, "Umm, that's okay, sweetheart. You hold onto that." He smiled, then said, "Now talk to me. However you need to talk. I'm listening."

I gave him a wet-eyed stare and a raised brow.

"I promise. Curse, scream...do whatever you need to do; just let it out. I won't try to talk you out of your feelings. Okay?"

I nodded, then sighed deeply. I felt unable to talk to him about how I was really feeling without crying or getting angry. I felt so paralyzed with hurt that I was afraid I would choke on the truth. Yet he had to hear it.

"I'm so angry at you. I don't want to be, but I am. I don't want to hate you, but I do. I don't know how not to. You running around with that *bit* (I caught myself)...Rich's mother. You cheated on Mother with that...*her*. And yet you tiptoe around here like everything is okay. It's not okay, Daddy! You broke up our family to shack up with some other woman. I can't even look at you without seeing *her*. Rich's mother." I bit back another sob. "Men like *you* don't cheat. Men like *you* stay with their families. They don't abandon their daughters and wives to dump their worries on some other woman's sheets."

I placed my face into my hands and sobbed again. And then, when I was able to pull myself together, I continued, "All I want to do is turn back time and make things right again. I want a do-over, that's it. I want my father back—not just pieces of him; all you are to me now is a shell of who my father used to be. Ever since I left for Milan and cut myself, you're here but not here. It's like your mind is somewhere else, like on *her*."

Daddy said nothing at first. He just looked at me. Silent. Pained. And torn. I could see it in his eyes.

"I can't imagine what all this is doing to you, sweetheart," Daddy said finally. He looked stricken. "I'm so sorry. I can't imagine how hard any of this must be for you." He held his head down, then pulled in a deep breath. "Or for your mother," he added after a moment. "I'm flawed, sweetheart. All men are. But that doesn't make us all bad either. Many of us are still loving fathers and husbands; we just sometimes fall short. We screw up. And then we have to look into our wives' and daughters' eyes and see the pain we've caused them and try to figure out ways to make it right."

Daddy pinched the insides of his eyes, trying to hold back his own tears.

"I apologize for shattering your images of me," he said. "I never wanted to hurt you or your mother." Now he seemed to struggle to look at me. "But I see now how badly I did. And it's eating me up inside."

I swallowed. "Do you love *her?*" I blurted out. Stunned that I asked the question. But I wanted to know. I had a right to know.

Daddy took me in for a moment, then reached over and brushed my hair from out of my face. He held the side of my face in his large hand. It was warm. And I felt myself on the verge of crying again.

"It's complicated," he offered. There went that word again. *Complicated.* I wanted to scream. What was so complicated with giving a yes or no answer? He either did or he didn't.

More tears fell from my eyes. Unchecked.

"Is she leaving Mr. Montgomery?"

Daddy's body seemed to stiffen at the sound of the name of one of his biggest clients.

"Probably not," he said solemnly. "That's not something we've talked about. And it's not something you need to concern yourself with."

I stared at him. "I see." I shifted my body on the bed. "Well, Mother might be okay with your cheating ways," I said, pushing myself farther away from him. "And she may not have any fight left in her." I climbed off the bed. "But I do."

Daddy frowned, giving me a confused look.

I looked him square in the eyes. "You *don't* get to keep both of us in your life. You don't get to be my father and keep *her* as your slut. Sorry."

I stomped toward my bathroom.

"London, don't—"

I cut him off, putting a hand up. "No, Daddy. Either she goes or I'm moving to Milan with Mother and never speaking to you again!"

I slammed the door, leaving Daddy sitting on my bed.

He had a choice to make. And so did I.

I pressed my back to the door and slid down it, sobbing.

43

Spencer

Do this, do that; take me here, drop me off there; clutching pearls this, clutching pearls that...

Rich was slowly getting on my last-mothersuckin'-flim-flammin' nerve!

A few days had suddenly turned into one hellish week. My eyeballs ached from seeing her big wide face and that spreading nose of hers every darn day! All she did was eat and sleep and complain. Oh, and run off to be with that Justice boy every chance she could. Then try to wobble back in the wee hours of the night.

She was trying to turn my loving home into a flophouse. A one-woman brothel!

Twice already, Kitty demanded I keep her locked out and not open the entrance gates to let her back in. But I couldn't. Kitty was evil. But my loving heart wouldn't allow me to leave Rich out on the curb, like trash. Even though she was trashy.

Still, I refused to let her inside the main house—if she couldn't get back from her boxer-and-panty play before the bewitching hour, then she wouldn't get inside my home! Instead, I would show her the way to the pool house. However, a few times, Rich simply hopped back inside Justice's car and returned to his rumpled bed sheets.

Jeezuslawdfather...

I was getting sick of her. And I didn't know how much more of her I could take before I lost my mind and acted a fool out here in these streets. Rich was taking me all out of my Zen, just sucking every ounce of my positive light and energy out from my bone marrow.

And I didn't like it one ding-daggity bit!

But I was trying desperately hard to stay kind and patient with this trickeroo.

"*No!*" Rich shrieked when I flicked my blinker on to swing into a parking space. "Not there. Don't park there. It's too far. You know this horrid heat will melt all this sweet sugar."

I scoffed, swerving away from the parking spot.

"Okay, how about this one," I said, pointing to a space a few cars down. I was straining to keep my temper from flaring up.

"Clutching pearls! Don't do me! That's *too* close, girl. I can't have them seeing me getting out of *this* with *you*. Ew. Not. My reputation would be ruined."

I blinked. "Rich, your reputation was ruined the day you were born. So get over yourself. Next."

"Clutching pearls, skank! Lies and deceit! Don't have me slay you out here. My rep is on *fleek*, honey! But that doesn't mean I wanna be seen riding in...*this*. I mean...unh...don' get me wrong; this li'l car is *cute* and all, if you want a li'l knock-around car. But—*psst*, please—it's not something I'd ever be caught driving."

"*Bish*, shut it," I hissed. The nerve of her! "You won't be caught driving anything for the next eighteen months, so be grateful someone is willing to give you a ride. Otherwise, you and those Barney Rubble feet of yours can get to stepping."

She sucked her teeth. "Play nice, Spencer. I can't help if

my feet are swollen. It's from all this stress I'm under, being cramped up in a li'l room does a lot to a girl's body. I'm not used to living in a cottage, girl. You know my home is hu-mongous compared to yours; that's all I'm trying to say. No shade."

I glared at her. "Well, at least I have a home. Last I checked, you were tossed out on the street, remember?"

Rich waved me on. "Them haters. It was all a big misun-derstanding. Once Logan and Richard get their minds right, they'll be begging me back. Watch."

"Ooooh, yippee," I said sarcastically as I clapped. "I can't wait."

"Ah!" Rich screamed. "Hands on the wheel! Hands on the wheel!"

I rolled my eyes as I sped around the school's enormous parking lot, nearly sideswiping a Maserati, then pulled up in front of the school's entrance and slammed on the brakes, barreling over valet cones and nearly running down one of the valets.

The freckle-faced fool scrambled away mere seconds from becoming roadkill.

I quickly reached inside my purse and threw him a fifty for his troubles. "Sorry," I said apologetically. Then I glared over at Rich. "Get out, freeloader! Miss I Can't Drive Myself to School Because I'm Too Stupid Not to Drink and Drive!"

"Eww. Clutching pearls! That was so inappropriate, Spencer. Just hateful."

I rolled my eyes. "Rich, your whole life is inappropriate. Now get out of my car before I forget my manners and knock your front implants out!"

"Tramp-whore!" she snapped. "You will not abuse me or disrespect me. I don't need to ride in this ole cheap tin can! I can walk!"

"Then walk," I snapped, furiously pointing toward the

sparkling glass doors. "Go bounce right up those stairs and roll your roly-poly butt into class."

Rich flipped down the mirror and checked her lip gloss, then blew herself a kiss.

"Ugh. You're still ugly as ever, Rich. Now good day, ma'am!"

"Don't *ma'am* me, slore," Rich crabbed. "It's never a good day when I have to share air space with a troll like you!"

She swung open the passenger-side door, then slid out of the car and slammed her door so hard that my windows rattled and the whole car shook.

I threw my gears into DRIVE.

"Wait," Rich called out before I could take off. "I need money for lunch, girl. You got me? And we're still going out for hot wings after school, right? You know I need my beer and my bacon."

"Lady, bye," I said, flipping her the bird.

Rich gave the finger back. "Love you, too," she said and then stomped off in her bejeweled Valentino flats, yanking down her blazer, trying to cover the butt-crack she'd managed to stuff inside her Dassault Apparel jeans.

Ugh. Ole flat-footed heathen!

All I could do was take a deep breath and sigh, and pray for a miracle.

44

Spencer

Two weeks later...

"Spencer," Kitty sneered, "when is that gremlin upstairs going home? I'm sick of seeing her. I don't know what's worse. Your father picking inside his diaper and humming old Negro spirituals or having that little double-chinned barbarian girl here."

I rolled my eyes up in my head, brushing by her. "Rich doesn't have a home, Mother. And stop talking bad about Daddy. I won't have it."

She grabbed me by the arm, and spun me around to face her. "And you *won't* have your face in a minute, little girl, if you don't show Orphan Annie to the door. I'm not running a runaway shelter here."

I threw my head back and laughed, then said as I snatched my arm from her grasp, "You silly duck. You quack! Rich didn't run away. She was thrown out on the streets."

Kitty scoffed. "Spencer, shut it. As *hood*licious as that Logan Montgomery is, that gold-digging woman would never throw one of her meal tickets out. You can believe the lies Rich has told you if you want. But that little troll doll upstairs walked out. Why? Because, one, she thinks she's grown and doesn't want to follow her parents' rules. Two, she'd rather spend her life spread eagle than studying for the SATs. Three, because she's loud, obnoxious, and utterly rude. Four, because she drinks like a fish..."

I sucked my teeth. "All right, Mother. I get it. It's no secret. Rich is troubled. And loose. And she loves to drink. Still, I can't put my good-good—"

"That girl is not good for anything except a romp in the sack," Kitty snapped.

"That's not nice," I said. "You're being messy. Rich can't help herself."

"No, Spencer. Messy is that trap queen upstairs. I want that beast girl out of here, Spencer."

I blinked. "No," I said as I shook my head. "I won't put Rich out. Letting her stay with us until she can land back on her hoofs is the charitable thing to do, Mother. How humanitarian of me would it be to put Rich out? To turn my back on someone less fortunate?"

Kitty tilted her head and gave me a deadly stare. And then she balled her fist. "I should punch you into the next millennium. I want that girl gone, Spencer. Three weeks is enough. She's overstayed her welcome. *Mmmph*." Kitty swiped hair from out of her eye. "Flouncing around here like she has a free stay at the Four Seasons. No, dearie. We are *not* here to accommodate her. That sneaky trick is wandering all through here at wee hours of the night. I can't even bring my boy toys home or have a late-night romp down here on the kitchen table without her walking in on me. I can't—I *won't*—live like this, Spencer. I refuse to live in fear that some little hot pocket might try to offer up her little nasty self to one of my stud muffins."

"And the Mother of the Year Award goes to—drumroll, please—*you*, Mother." I sighed sarcastically and then shook my head. She was so disgusting.

"Save the mockery, Spencer. That pygmy girl upstairs is cutting into my late-night playtime."

I grunted. "Well, maybe you should get a room somewhere else instead of whoring in *my* home. Or, better yet, how about you conduct your slutty tricks in your bedroom. No, no. Better yet, how about you find yourself someone *your* own age instead of stalking college campuses."

She roughly grabbed my face, digging her nails into my cheeks, nearly breaking skin. "As long as they're over eighteen, my darling Spencer, they're fair game. And it's legal. But don't you dare try to make this about me, little girl. I'm the adult. And, like it or not, until you turn eighteen, I *still* have the say as to what does or doesn't go on in this house. Period."

She let go of my face. Oooh. She was so, so, lucky Rich was upstairs; otherwise, this whole downstairs would have instantly turned into a battlefield. Kitty and I were due for another mother-daughter brawl. But...

Not today.

"Now, like I was saying," she continued, narrowing her eyes, "I want that girl gone. I'm sick of seeing her wide back and that floppy behind of hers walking up out of this kitchen with a plate, like this is some all-you-can-eat buffet."

I huffed. "Oh, shut it. Rich can't help it if all she does all day is eat. She's a moose. She grazes, Kitty. That's what mammals like Rich do! Graze."

Kitty sneered. "Well, then, you had better find said moose a zoo or farm to send her to, because the one thing I won't tolerate is you trying to operate a refugee camp up in here. It's bad enough to have your father here, like this is some rehabilitative nursing home."

I opened my mouth to speak, but Kitty shut me down before I could get a word out.

"I mean it, Spencer." She stomped her foot. "You tell that girl she has three days to either go back home where she belongs or to find herself a nearby flophouse."

I bit my tongue. Kitty was right, though. This situation with Rich was slowly becoming a bit much. She was sloppy—*lawdjeezus*—and lazy. She didn't make her bed. She kept clothes strewn about the mini-suite I'd so graciously set her up in, even leaving her panties dropped in the middle of her private bathroom floor a few times.

Like, *ugh*...who did that?

Where were they teaching that level of nastiness?

Apparently at the Montgomery estate!

Rich really thought she had live-in maids at her beck and call. Not here, *punkin*. Not here. Oh, no. Our housekeeper was for the rest of the estate, not for Rich's personal use. I mean, as loving and kind as I was, Rich was taking advantage of my generous ways. She was disrespecting my positive energy and light with her uncouthness.

Consequently, I was struggling to stay classy and humble. Rich was homeless. I had to keep reminding myself of that. And nearly destitute—well, okay...she was broke. Flat broke! Her parents had cut off all of her credit cards and access to her three bank accounts, so mooching off me was the only thing she could do.

And I had to keep reminding myself of *that* too. Miss Mouthy, Miss Piggy-Wiggy was *broke!* And yet she didn't know when to shut her trap and show a little gratitude for having a warm, clean place to lay her head and a kind, loving friend to always save the day. Ole ungrateful slob.

Even though Rich had streetwalker tendencies, it was dangerous on those streets. And I couldn't see her on some corner holding up an empty coffee can, panhandling for her next shopping spree. Now what type of good-good friend would I have been putting her out on the ho-stroll, even if that was what she was most good at?

I wasn't heartless. I would never drag her name or put her out. Well...uh, um...unless she tested my gangster or totally violated my kind and loving ways. Then I didn't know what I'd do to her. I could be like a wild alley cat when crossed.

Until that time, I would simply shut off—no, no (I wasn't *that* cruel)—I'd put a timer on the water system on her side of the wing so she couldn't run the shower all hours of the day and night. It would cut her off after fifteen minutes. Next, I'd seal up the cabinets and put dead bolts on the refrigerator and freezer. She'd only be allowed three meals and two snacks. And her last feeding would be at seven in the evening.

And, finally, to keep her from prowling around here, I'd lock her in her suite from the other side of her double door and set the alarms on her windows and balcony door after eleven p.m.

There. Problem solved.

Still, Kitty had no goshdang right trying to stomp her heels at me and give me deadlines. Rich was *my* GGFEBF— my good-good-future-*ex*-bestie. And she needed me. So who would I have been to turn my back on her?

"Wait one ding dangdiggity minute," I said, pointing a finger in her face. "You do not run this household. And you do *not* run me. Rich stays until—"

Kitty grabbed my finger and bent it all the way back. "Ow, ow, owww," I yelped, trying to pry her hand from my finger.

"You wanna rumble, Spencer, huh? You wanna get down and dirty, huh, you little twit? Then try me, little girl. I will chop you in your throat and break your whole hand off if you *ever* point a finger in my face again. Do you understand me?"

She bent my finger back more, and fire shot through my whole hand. Tears sprang to my eyes. "Aah, aah...*yesss!* I heard *youuuuu*. Now let m-m-my finger go."

After several long moments of staring me down, Kitty reluctantly let go of my finger, and I immediately grabbed it and held it in my other hand, pressing it to my chest, thankful she hadn't broken it.

Her nostrils flared. "Now get upstairs and do what I told you to do, or *you* and *your* little pet project will be out on the street together."

45

Rich

Picture it:
Saturday afternoon.
3:32 to be exact.
I was laid across a white mink chaise lounge.
Feet up.
Head held back.
Face covered in an Egyptian mud and lotus-petal facial mask. Cucumbers concealed my eyes. My juicy birthday suit was draped in a crisp, white terry-cloth Chanel robe, and I was talking to the goddess on high. Asking her highness to swing down low and come see about a queen. Then, suddenly, out of nowhere, I was attacked!

Yes, attacked!

Straight-up dragged by she who shall remain nameless—Miss Spencer, honey.

You heard right, *Spencerrrrr!*

That skank snatched my pearls and scattered them all over the place!

I know it's hard to believe, but that's the cheese! That

thing lost her entire li'l mind and straight gunned for me Wild-Wild-West, low-down-dirty bish-style!

I'd been her houseguest for three weeks, and *allllll* of a sudden she wanted to look down her nose at me, as if she was better than me.

Like, *hellooooo*, excuse me, but I'm Rich Montgomery! I run these Hollywood streets. Believe that! 'Cause it ain't a ho out here who hasn't weighed her life against mine and asked God why she wasn't born blue-blooded chocolate. So the mere fact that Spencer—who was nothing more than a deep-throat-label ho, who looked just like her played-out, big ole tea-drinking donkey of a mother—

And considering the mere fact that Spencer-the-dumb-dispenser had simply forgotten all of who I was and what I stood for, when I was her leader, is what I called an intolerable hot-ass mess!

Annnnywaaaay, back to me relaxing in my mask and calling on the spirits...Soooo, I was attending to my own black business, when Spencer's daddy flung open my bedroom door and called me "Cleola Mae!"

Who. The. Hell. Is. Cleola Mae?

OMG!

I could see if he'd called me Queen.

Or Chocolate Bunny.

Or Hot-stuff.

Or Boom-boom.

But to straight dog out my pedigree by calling me some low-down, clay-dirt, backwoods-country Cleola Mae was straight comin' for my entire gene pool. And I was not gon' lie there and let that fossil try and do me for generations.

So I took the cucumbers off of my eyes and nicely corrected him. "My name. Is Rich."

And do you know what that ready-for-the-grave man said to *me?* He snickered and said, "Rich? Ha! Ain't that a hoot."

So I sat up and snapped, "First of all, you need to turn your hearing aid on and get the giggles outcha throat, because I didn't just tell a joke."

Then I stood up and said, "And second of all, *like I said*, my name is *Rich*. R-I-C-H."

And yes, I said *all of that* with a li'l bass in my throat. I was still respectful though; after all, that pissy thing *was* Spencer's father...or so her mama made her think. But you get the point: Spencer claimed him. So out of respect for our bestie-ship, I let him live.

Spencer, who I guess was eavesdropping, stormed into the room and said, "You had better watch your flytrap, girlie. Don't get smart with my daddy!"

So I blinked because I was tryna figure out who she was talking to, but before I could check her, Dr. Dead jumped in my face and said, "Look, Chubs, if I were you, I'd stop going around calling myself Rich. 'Cause from where I stand you *look* broke, and from what I hear, ya mama and daddy have thrown you out.

"And you showed up at our door begging and pleading for somewhere to stay, seconds away from being a streetwalker. Now you're in here living off my money and eating up all of my food. That's not *rich* to me! That's a broke-down leech. A wannabe. Your name is Broke-Down. Brokey-Brokey for short."

I felt like that old trick-daddy had taken his rusty foot and kicked me in the gut with it. And just as I went to lay Moses all the way down, Spencer said, "Come on, Daddy, it's time for your nap." She ushered him out of the room, and a few seconds later she came back and said to me, "Listen, you little ratchet dragon, don't *ever* talk nasty to my daddy, or you will find yourself rolling out of here on your head! Now, consider this a warning: Do. Not. Let. It. Happen. Again. Or. You and your li'l train of irreplaceables shall be caboosed out of here!"

I blinked.

Blinked again.

And blinked again.

Like, say what?

Clutchin' pearls!

Stop the press and hold the mess!

I spat, "Excuse me, *trick*. But I will never stand here and let no walking grave talk to me crazy! And since your balls are on supersonic today, let's get to the real problem here, because it isn't me. It's you and your mama!"

"*What?!*" she said, shocked.

I continued, "You heard me. I didn't st-st-stutter, *tramp*. You and your mama are the problem, and both of you need to stop being so selfish and give your daddy back to God! Anybody looking at him knows that his number has been called. Twice!"

Spencer gasped, and then said, "You're lucky I don't mace your face off!" she growled. "You had better learn to count, girlie! Because your days here are numbered! And if I were you, hot drawers, I wouldn't close my eyes tonight."

Then she raised one brow and walked backward out of that ole musty bedroom/utility closet with a li'l queen-size bed, a chaise, and some garbage bags she'd stuffed me in, and left me there.

That's when I decided that although I'd hit rock bottom, I wasn't gon' stay here and take death threats.

Not me.

Hell, no!

I'm too kind.

Giving.

Considerate.

Too gentle to be mishandled.

And too loving to be mistreated.

So I made up my mind to carry a few of my fine wears:

Five pairs of Stewart Weitzman heels.

Four Chanel trunks.

Three Louis Vuitton duffel bags.

Two of Spencer's Hermès carry-ons and her diamond en-crusted Dior belt that she never used and had lying around and wasting away—like her soul—and I was going to take all of it to Second Time's a Charm, a consignment shop that I usually donated my gently-worn-once things to.

But nothing would be given away today.

Why?

'Cause I needed *coins.*

Besides, charity began at home, and considering I only owned the best, I knew I could walk into Second Time's a Charm and walk out with at least three hundred thousand grips.

Enough to hire me a new stylist.

A new chef.

Custom-order some new Louie V luggage.

Buy my own condo.

And then be able to properly tell Spencer which side of my behind she could kiss!

Mmmph. I was outta this shit hole. Today!

I washed the mask off of my face.

Pulled my hair back into a ponytail, then twisted the pony-tail into a bun.

Slid on a pair of my Secret Circus jeans.

A fitted black T-shirt with a queen bubble-bee on the front of it.

A pair of sequined black Uggs.

A beekeeper's hat.

And then speed-dialed Uber.

46

Heather

My accountant was stealing from *me!* That was the only thing that made sense to me. That was the only explanation as to why my bank accounts were almost on empty, and why the lights at home had been shut off.

Camille and I were sitting over there in that mini-mansion with no damn lights! Thanks to my incompetent accountant, I was now living my life by candlelight until I could pay the five-thousand-dollar bill. And because there wasn't enough money to pay my chef for the last two months, he'd quit on me.

Quit! Packed his apron and his cutlery and bounced. King Petty even walked out with the seasonings and whatnots that he'd bought! Even my driver left. Abandoned me! And took his limo with him!

Jeezus. Everything was unraveling quicker than Co-Co's lace fronts. Not to mention, the landlord had nailed an eviction notice to the front door a few days ago, being messy! Why hadn't my accountant paid the bills? Because that trick-whore had been robbing me blind! Squirreling my hard-earned coins into her damn pockets, instead of making sure all my bills were getting, and *staying*, paid.

Who did that?

Thieving hoes did!

That was exactly what was going on. And all the while, she was telling me to curb my spending, to stop blowing money on frivolous things. Really? There was nothing *frivolous* about this ten-thousand-dollar Korean eel-skin hobo bag. There was nothing *frivolous* about all of my one-of-a-kind catsuits. And there was *nothing*—as that whore called it—*frivolous* about this thousand-dollar wet and wavy, thirty-two-inch weave either. Or these seven-inch gladiator heels—with the encrusted diamonds—I had on my feet.

Psst. Puhleeeeze! Another hating *bish* tryna ruin the queen bee. Come again. *I think not.* That light-fingered troll had me all types of *effed* up! Tryna steal my life!

Sticky-fingered *mitch!*

Ooh, just the thought had me *hawt!* And I swear, if I weren't afraid of going back to jail, I would have run up in her office and cracked her in the throat. And stupid Camille, *psst.* She had the nerve to blame *me* for this mess. I've done everything for that ungrateful woman, and still...it was never enough.

How did *me* being almost broke all of a sudden become *my* fault? Yeah. That's right. Use me as the scapegoat. Blame me. But whatever. I was about to get these coins. And do me. I had a party to host tomorrow night, and Miss Co-Co and I were gonna *slay.*

I started to renege at the last minute, but that twenty grand to do a walk-through and shake my luscious booty was sounding too good to give up. So it was gonna be lit. Yes, gawd!

Oooh, I can't wait.

I pulled out my little velvet satchel and glanced up into the rearview mirror of my red '57 Chevy convertible. Unlike my customized couture and my jewelry, this car was all mine.

Paid for. Owned. Free and clear. It was the one thing I didn't have to worry about anyone trying to take from me.

I pulled my giant sunglasses down over my eyes and slid my tongue over my teeth as I held my pouch of get-right in my hand, contemplating if I wanted another pinch. I'd already had two. Wait. Three. But who was counting? All I knew was, a fourth pinch of goodness would have me floating like a butterfly, light on my feet like a ballerina.

No, no. I didn't need it just yet.

Relax, girl. You still nice! Don't get greedy. The last thing you need to be doing is out here tweaking like some fiend. Save it for the turn up tonight.

You right.

I tossed the pouch back into my bag, then slid out of my car, pulling the fabric of my jumper from out of my cheeks. *Damn thong.* I shook my hips around to the back of the car and popped the trunk and gathered up two bags of clothes and purses.

I made the eleven-mile drive out to Pasadena, away from prying eyes and messy blog hounds, to make some quick purse change until my next iTunes royalty payment hit the bank. Word on the street was that the shop owner was real snooty, but Second Time's a Charm consignment boutique paid good coins for designer wears.

So here I was. Here to collect my coins.

I slammed the trunk shut, then swung my hips toward the brick-faced shop, nestled between a shoe repair shop and an all-night dry cleaner.

There were people walking tiny dogs and couples holding hands, most likely pretending to be happy and in love. But that wasn't my problem, or my lie to live.

Bells chimed as I entered the shop.

"Be right with you," a blond woman said from behind the counter, giving me a quick glance, before going back to help-

ing some chick with a humongous butt. She wore a big wide
hat with a black drawstring veil, like she was a beekeeper or
some lady in mourning.

There were an assortment of items lying flat on one side
of the long glass counter, and then she had a pile of clothes clut-
tering the other side; on the floor next to the chickie with all that
big-nasty stuffed in jeans were several sets of very expensive-
looking luggage, along with a Hermès duffel bag.

I blinked.

That big horse booty could only belong to . . . wait. Nah. It
couldn't be. No, no. Not the queen of fabulousness. Not Miss
High and Mighty.

No, no. Of course not!

"So are these bags *real* or knockoffs?" Blondie asked the
chick in front of me while sliding her hand along the inside
of what appeared to be a Louie bag. "As I was saying a few
moments ago, Miss Gatling. I run a reputable establishment.
Nothing but authentic goods are sold here."

Gatling? Oh, okay. Guess I was mistaken.

"*Whaaaaaat?*" the girl shrieked. I blinked. "*Clutching*
pearls! Heifer, there is nothing fake here. You better check
those fake eyelashes, boo! Don't do me! Now I need at least
five grand in my hand for that bag. It's a limited edition."

Oh.

My.

God.

It *was* Rich!

Ooh. Scandalous.

Bwahahahaha!

"Well, Miss Gatling. That may be true. But since I can't
seem to locate a serial number—and you don't have the papers or a receipt with you—I can't be sure on this one, so I
can't give you a quote on it just yet."

Rich huffed, shifting all her weight from one puffy foot to
another. "*Mmmph.* You Europeans stay tryna do a *sis*taaah.

You steal our men. Steal our babies. Steal our communities. Then you wanna try'n keep a good queen down when she's already down."

Lord...

Could it be true? Had the almighty Rich fallen from grace?

"I'm sorry you feel that way, Miss Gatling," Blondie said. "Would you rather take your business elsewhere?"

"Tramp dog! No! I would rather you hurry up so I can get outta here. And I'd like to leave out through the back entrance if I could. I'll have my driver meet me there."

Blondie gave her what looked like an amused look. "Who are you, a rapper? Wait. I know who you are," she said, snapping her fingers. "You were on *Dancing with the Stars*. That season with Lil' Kim, weren't you?"

"*Yass*, honey, *yass!* And I slayed the Stanky-leg, boo."

Bwahahahaha! No, no, no. This had to be a joke. My eyes and ears had to be playing tricks on me! I knew my get-right was top-notch. That too much of it could have you hallucinating for hours, but a few pinches here and there didn't have that effect.

I blinked again.

No. My eyes were seeing clearly, and my hearing was on point.

It *was* Rich.

"And this bag right here," Rich said, picking up a Chanel purse, "was donated by my good-good ex-friend, so I need you to give me at least ten grand for it. It's a fifteen-thousand-dollar bag."

Ooooooh, this was too damn juicy, I thought, stepping back a bit, positioning myself behind the nearest clothes rack and pulling out my phone. I took a photo. Then another. I quickly sent two text messages out.

SECOND TIME'S A CHARM! RICH MONTGOMERY IS HERE PEDDLING!

HOT OFF THE PRESS, BOO! RICH MONTGOMERY IN PASADENA BARTERING CLOTHES!

Then I angled my phone just so, catching all the *tea!*

I pressed RECORD.

"Uh-huh," Blondie said. "Keep hope alive."

"You got that right," Rich snapped. "Hope is all we have. Without hope, we're lost souls, honey. Ooh. See. You about to make me go to church up in here! Hope is what keeps me from boom-bop-dropping it up in here! I'm saved now. Happily reformed. But back in my ratchet days, back when I was spitting out razor blades and wearing brass knuckles as finger rings, Shakeesha Gatling was well known out there in them streets. Pop, pop! You better google me. Compton up!"

"Oh." Blondie blinked. "Should I call security?"

"*Whaaaat?* Clutching pearls! What, you think every black girl steals? Lady, bye! Honey, I'm a jewel thief! I steal hearts. I steal grown boys from little girls. I don't steal clothes! Now, can you please hurry this along? I need to get back to my ex-ex-BFF's trap house before her ole smelly, senile father tries to run through my makeup case and steal all of my eye shadow."

Blondie held up a thick leather belt. Its buckle sparkled under the lights. I zoomed my camera in on it. *Oh. My. God!*

"Um, who is Spencer?" Blondie asked.

I blinked.

Rich huffed. "Oh. This nobody. My ex-ex-ex-ex-BFF. She gave me that belt."

"Oh. Well. It's gorgeous, Miss Gatling. But unfortunately—Dior or not—name-plated belts don't sell here."

"*Whaaaat?*" Rich shrieked again. "Well, then pluck out the diamonds. There are about a hundred grand worth of gems in that thing!"

Blondie shrugged. "This is a consignment shop, not a jewelry exchange." She opened another handbag and slid her hand inside, then pulled it open and peered inside. "This is a cute bag," she said. "Okay. I'll take this one, and this one, and this one," she said, piling purses up on a cart.

Then she gathered up an armful of clothes. "And I'll take all of these."

"Girl, finally. Now we're talking," Rich said, planting a hand on one of her very wide hips. God, she was built like an African mule. Big. Stocky. Solid. All she needed were another set of hoofs and she'd be ready to plow fields.

Blondie pulled out a calculator and her fingers quickly moved, tallying up Rich's items. "Okay. The most I can give you for all these items," she said, looking up from her calculator, "is fifteen hundred…"

"Fifteen *hundred?* As in fifteen hundred thousand dollars?" Rich asked.

I blinked. What a goofball Rich was.

"No, Miss Gatling. As in fifteen hundred dollars, which equates to one thousand and five hundred dollars."

"Lady, don't do me! I can count! I have all A's in using a calculator! But I need you to add a few more zeros on the back of that fifteen hundred. *Please.*"

"I'm sorry, Miss Gatling…"

"Lady, don't do me! Don't have me begging up in here. Please God, no. My grandmother, LuLu, is an amputee, and someone stole her artificial legs and arms. Now I gotta buy her a whole new set. Now I'm tryna stay a classy lady up in here, but don't do me. Add a few more zeroes on that amount. Please."

"Oh, Miss Gatling. Sorry to hear about your grandmother. But, uh, let's see. I guess I could go up to two thousand. Now to finalize the transaction, I will need your ID."

"*ID?* Clutching pearls! Where they doing that at? I thought this was an anonymous shop."

"Sorry, Miss Gatling, but no ID, no money. We must be able to identify all of our sellers. Now please make a decision. You're holding up my other customers."

Rich slammed her hand down on the counter. "You racist

tramp! I'm discreet. Everything I do is on the down low. I get my creep on without showing my ID!"

"Well then, perhaps you should take your business elsewhere," Blondie said, placing all the handbags and clothes back on the counter. "But here at Second Time's a Charm, you show your ID or get shown the door. Now good-bye. And thanks for stopping by."

Rich snatched up all of her things, stuffing them back into suitcases and duffel bags, cursing all the while. And then she started knocking over mannequins and display cases.

"You trick! I didn't need your money anyway! I'm Rich, honey! And you can kiss my big wide fabulous azz!"

Rich stormed through the store, dragging her things with her, bumping into tables and knocking things over. The last thing I saw before she swung open the front door and stepped out onto the sidewalk was her getting swept up in a sea of paparazzi.

47

Heather

Eleven p.m. . . .

"Co-Co, turn that bass up. All the way up," I said as I nodded my head to the thundering beat. We were at Co-Co's hideaway, an abandoned building in West Hollywood where he'd squatted for the last month. He'd hooked up the first-floor studio apartment with dragon-shaped paper lanterns that dangled from the ceiling, two purple leather couches, metal folding chairs everywhere, a platform bed, a makeshift recording booth, and some engineering equipment for his new venture—Basement Records.

For the moment, this was the chill spot, where we partied with a few of Co-Co's strays: straight, gay, trans, tall, short, fat, white, black, Mexican, and a vampire. Better known as hangers, or the background hype crew, who only wanted to be around when you were famous, yet were gone the moment the lights weren't on.

But whatever.

This wasn't about forever.

This was about now. And right now, we were all twerkin',

drankin', and snortin' powdered clouds of what Co-Co called Purgatory: black beauty, Xanax, and a pinch of meth.

Er'body was lit and waiting for the clock to lead us to one a.m. That's when I was due to be thirty grips richer: ten stacks to walk through Club Tantrum. And twenty stacks to drop a pop-up concert at the grand opening of Queer Zone, a new club in K'town.

"Who shotcha, baby!" Co-Co screamed, as he spun around in the middle of the aged black marbled floor and went down into a split. He snaked back up, tossed his hands in the air, and shouted, "Wu-Wu!"

I tossed back a shot of tequila, then said, "Waddup, fool?!"

Co-Co rocked his shoulders to the beat. "Come on, bean flicker, and drop a free style."

Bean flicker?

The hangers laughed, then egged me on to perform.

I sucked my teeth, peered through the tweekin' crowd, and looked Co-Co over—from his plastic see-through vest, the taco meat on his bony chest, his denim booty shorts, to his six-inch red pencil heels, and said, "*Bean flicker?* Just what are you trying to say, Mr. Bottom?"

"Bottom today, sandwich tomorrow," he snorted, then chuckled. "Now stop being so sensitive and hit us with a free style, so we can upload it to iTunes. Bust 'em over the head with a lemonade surprise!"

The hangers cheered and chanted, "Free style! Free style!"

I was irked and tired of Co-Co coming at me sideways.

But.

The beat bustin' in the background was fire, and the thought of dropping another iTunes hit was sweet. Super sweet.

My eyes scanned the hangers, and seeing how hyped they were forced me to swallow the urge to drag this queen for filth. I smacked my glossy lips and said, "Hit the record button, nephew."

Co-Co smiled as I walked into the booth and slid the headphones on. I made a hand motion for him to turn up the beat —which was a mix between Prince's signature and high-pitched psychedelic guitar and a computerized keyboard.

I closed my eyes and went for broke, "Raindrops, drop tops, make it hot, why not?/Ain't nothin' else to choose, unless you wanna drown in Camille's booze. But why lose when you can be Richard Montgomery?/He stays winnin', and rollin' in the dough./Goin' from ho to ho/Droppin' babies like snow./Then sayin' no-no, you gotta go-go/Already got two I'm gonna show-show/Never lookin' back/Leavin' you feelin' whack/Heart all jacked, tears always in your eyes, but you refuse to cry./You'd rather sip some sizurpt./Pour it down your throat like a wizard, and blow up like blizzard!"

"Rich Montgomery, who shotcha!" Co-Co shouted unexpectedly across my rhyme.

And I followed up with, "Now he wanna know who shotcha, and I'm just like hell I gotcha!"

Co-Co cut off the music, jumped up and down and everybody went wild!

"Yooooooo, that ish was fiya!" said the vampire, who was still groovin' to the beat in his head.

"Yasssss, bish, yaasssss!" A few of the hangers congratulated me.

Co-Co screamed, ran over, yanked me out the booth, and into a hug, "OMG! You merked that, baby. Yes. You. Did. That. Shit! Whaaaat?! You know what this means, right?"

Before I could answer, he carried on, "This means you gotta hit this special treat before we head out the door." Co-Co pulled out a velvet tiger pouch from his back pocket and emptied two small plastic packs of brown powder onto a small card table. "Heather, the first line is yours."

My mouth watered, and I could feel my nose about to drip. "What is it?"

"China Doll, baby—OxyContin, coke, and a sprinkle of potpourri. Miss Girl, this buzz is gon' make you torch the stage! Trust, Black Beauty was the appetizer, but this right here is the entrée!"

The following day...

2 p.m.
Where.
The.
Hell.
Am.
I?

And why does my head feel like it's been hit with a ton of bricks?

I wiped what felt like dried milk from my mouth and stale bread crumbs from the corners of my eyes, and took the room in.

The bright afternoon sun shone through the curtainless and streaked glass windows, spotlighting the purple leather couches, the dragon lanterns that swung from the ceiling, and metal folding chairs. There were empty bottles of tequila, beer, and cherry-flavored Robitussin strewn across the kitchen counter and littered on the floor.

There was a vampire sparkling in the sun; his pasty white makeup was crackled and sank into the creases of his face. And next to him were two trans-boys, spooning.

I was still at Co-Co's.

But there was no Co-Co. And why was I still here?

Last I remembered, we snorted a line on our way out the door to collect my coins.

Wait.

The walk-through!

The pop-up concert!

My coins!

Where are my coins?!

I snatched my purse, which lay open on the table next to me and rummaged through it. Car keys—check.

Phone—no phone!

Where is my phone?

Wallet—empty!

Where the hell is my money?

Panicked, I hopped out of the platform bed, which I didn't remember lying down on, let alone sleeping in.

"Eww, what's wrong with you?" said some oversized Goth girl, with raccoon eyes and black lips.

"I'm looking for...for my..." I paused and zoomed in on her hand. "Gimme my damn phone!" I snatched it from her grip. "What the hell? And where is my money?! Did you steal my money?" I snatched her by the collar.

She pushed me back by my shoulders, forcing my hands to fall. "Don't be a douche! I make two of you, and I really would hate to beat you to a pulp. And I don't know what money you're talking about!"

"You stole my money!" I shoved her.

She hopped up and shoved me back. "What money? I was only using your phone to call my ride so I can get out of here!"

"Trick, you stole my money!" I lifted my hand to cop her across the face, but she caught my fist.

"What money?!" she screamed.

"The money I made from the clubs last night!" I wrestled my fist from her grip.

"You didn't even make it to the clubs! You snorted one line, went in the bathroom, and passed out! Me and Co-Co had to drag you out of there and put you in the bed!"

The bottom of my stomach dropped, and my heart fell to my feet. "What do you mean, I passed out and I never made it to the club? Lies! Trick! You stole my money! You thief! Where is Co-Co?"

"I don't know!" she said, before turning toward the door. She took off running.

I tried to run after her, but my head felt too heavy for me to keep up, so by the time I made it outside, she had turned the corner and left me in the dust.

I went back inside and did my best to get my thoughts in order. Did I really miss my walk-through? My concert? My coins? I needed those coins. I had bills, and I didn't have any money!

This is wrong, all wrong! Why can't I remember what I did for the rest of the night? And where the hell was Co-Co?! He had some explaining to do!

My phone's battery was on three percent, and I didn't have my charger.

I dialed Co-Co's number anyway, only to get his voice mail. I left a message. "Co-Co, what the hell happened here last night? Somebody stole my money, and you are nowhere in sight?!"

I hung up and called again.

Voice mail. "Co-Co, did you steal my coins? Ho, you know I need my money! I'm not playing with you, Co-Co! I gotta pay my rent! Where are you? And why did you leave me here with these freaks!"

I hung up and called again. This time the recording announced that his voice mail was full.

Tears beat against the backs of my eyes and streamed down my face. I felt like I was drowning in space.

Had this really happened?

Did I dream it?

Yeah, that was it.

I dreamed it.

I pinched my wrist, and pain shot through my arm. I wasn't dreaming. This was real.

Beep-beep.

I looked down at my phone. I had a text message . . . from

Co-Co. It read: I C U KEEP B/U MY PHONE. NOBODY COULD WAKE U LAST NITE SO U AIN'T MAKE NO $$, BEAN FLICKER. ANYWHO I'LL HIT YOU LATER.

WTF?

My head ached. My body ached. I wanted to scream, but I couldn't get the sound to come out!

I jabbed my fingers into my phone, but as I attempted to type my reply, my phone died. And for a moment, a split second in time, as I leaned against the wall and slid to the floor, I felt like I had died too.

48

Rich

Dear Diary,

Love is good.

Love is kind.

Love is important.

And sugar is sweet, but not like this.

Trust.

I wake up every morning, roll over, look at my chocolate Adonis, and know that true love does exist. Unlike a lot of these thirst-bucket squirrels—like London and Spencer. I would include Heather, but Heather wouldn't know love unless it was sold in a five-dollar rock. But those other two pampered thots have tasted the sweetness of love makin', and they both envy my panty drop. But little do they know that the hatred in their hearts is the reason they're single and I'm not.

And yeah, Justice, well, we live in a section-8-like sweat box. But so what? As far as me and my man are concerned, it's a love palace by day and a sex dungeon by night!

Okay!

Snap-snap!

Hot damn!

Give it to me one time, diary! Yaaaas, bish, yaaaas!

Er'body was soooo busy sleeping on me. Er'body
thought that Rich Montgomery was gon' fold and run
back home to ole granny-drawls-wearin' Logan. Psych!

And speakin' of Lo-rat. She's been calling my
phone, leaving voice mail after voice mail, and sending text message after text message. Ev. Ver. Ry. Day.
Begging me to come home.

Chile, cheese!

Boo, please!

Talkin' 'bout, "Mommy misses you, Richie-Poo.
We're a family, and we can work this out. We can make
it through anything."

Girl, please!

All Lo-zilla can do for me is reopen my credit cards.
Deposit my ten-thousand-dollar monthly allowance,
with interest. And step off.

And all she can get from me is a middle finger
emoji. She should've thought about how much she
loved and would miss me when she had her scrotum-
swingin' husband and his mini-me of a son, RJ, attack
me, and in front of that white woman in a black body!
Gon' accuse me of all sorts of things! And I'm just supposed to forget or pretend that drag-fest ever
happened? Never! Now Logan wants me to care that
she's feeling guilty?

I wish I would.

But I don't.

And I'm not gon' raise one ounce of my blue blood
pressure being worried about it. She made her bed of
shade, now she gon' have to snuggle on it.

Anywho, next!

Now, diary, brace yourself. A few weeks ago, I was almost murdered. Yes. Murdered! The media tried to kill me. Let me explain. Being the giving person that I am, I went to a consignment shop...to visit...well... to check out the scenery, sort of. And perhaps even see how I could make some extra money, maybe sell them a few things, you know, since Logan and her family tried to do me and shut my funds down.

Of course, the cashier and the manager were both in there hatin' on me and accused me of trying to sell them knock-offs! As if I would ever carry something that wasn't real! I break out in hives when I get next to something fake, so I know my designer wears were one thousand percent authentic. Well, you know, I turned it out. Cussed, screamed, and threatin' to have their heads.

Still.

They had no right to sic the paparazzi on me!

I'm talking TMZ, *Trashy Teen Trend Travesty*, *People* magazine, *E! News*, and *Ni-Ni Girlz*.

Yes, honey, they tried it.

I texted Justice a nine-one-one emergency and the address where I was. A few minutes later, my black man stepped up in the spot, wearing an invisible red cape, and saved the day! Yes. He. Did.

He looked into the cameras and yelled, "Get out of her face!" Then he gripped me by the forearm and practically carried me through the crowd. He said that he would've picked me up, but since I'd gained about forty pounds, he had to train to lift that much weight.

It's all good, though, because with all of this good lovin' we've been makin', I'm sure I've burned off at least ten pounds of bacon-wrapped hot wings and beer. And in no time, I'll be back to being a dime; as for right now, I'll have to settle with being a fifty-cent piece.

But you get the point. Me and my baby are everything brown sugar love is made of.

He takes me bowling. To play pool. Roller skating. Cooks for me and gives me money to shop. This boy loves me like a fat kid loves cake.

There's only one thing he expects me to do: get a job.

But I'm not.

I am the job. You have to work to take care of me. I see I'm going to have to slow-walk him to understanding that any man with me has the ultimate trophy, but all of this can change if Justice puts another unrealistic demand on me or doesn't come up with more money.

But other than that, we are stellar over here.

Anyway, diary, I need to bid you good day. It's nine a.m., which means it's time for me to turn over and wake my bae with some knee-buckling kisses.

Ciao!

49

London

"Happy birthday, my darling London," my mother nearly sang out, barreling through my suite's doors without knocking. I frowned, making a note to myself:

Lock door.

Yeah. Happy birthday to me! Yippee! Oh, joy!

Mmmph. *Not.*

There were no candles to blow out. No cake to slice. No elaborate party to look forward to. No guests to thank. It was *just* another day.

I was seventeen now, but I felt old. Older. Like I was a twenty-seven-year-old woman watching my life clock aimlessly spin. I shook the image, my mind settling on the idea of having a rich, decadent slice of cake. No, scratch that—the *whole* cake.

God, I would *kill* to have a huge piece of cake. With dark chocolate frosting. And raspberry mousse filling. With a delicious ganache topping. That used to be (no, it still is!) one of my favorite desserts. But I couldn't have any of that—birthday or not. Just like I couldn't have a box (because one pack would never be enough) of Drake's Devil Dogs—chilled, please—or Little Debbie Swiss Rolls or them scrumptious little round oatmeal cakes.

None of that I could have for fear of relapsing right back to binge eating. Still, my mouth started watering. Stop, London. Enough. Dr. Kickaloo had been working very hard with me on managing and respecting my urges to overindulge. I simply did not have the willpower to enjoy all the fatty, sugary, carb-loaded treats without gorging on them, without eating myself into a coma—so, no to sweets.

No to temptation!

And hell no to gas and bloating!

"Your father thought it would be a great idea if we..."

I blinked, bringing myself back to the present. Here, looking at my mother.

Suddenly, my chaise was covered in shopping bags—Chanel, Louis Vuitton, Hermès, Gucci—and the room filled with the scent of Tahitian vanilla; her nearly nine-hundred-dollar bottle of Clive Christian's No. 1 was one of her signature perfumes.

"I didn't expect you back so soon," I mumbled, turning my iPad mini facedown (I was on Rich's mother's Instagram page) and glancing over at all the designer bags. Had this been another time, I would have leapt in the air and begun tearing open each bag. But I had too much going on to give thought to what was in those coveted bags.

Like what the heck Logan Montgomery was up to. Who else's man was that trick scheming on? So seeing my mother surprised me. I wasn't sure if it was unwanted, but it was definitely unexpected. She had only been gone for a week, which was *so* unlike her. Usually she stayed weeks at a time.

"It's your birthday, darling. Of course, I'd be here for that."

I gave her a *why* look. But said nothing. "Besides, your father's been worried about you..."

Mmmph.

"He said the last week you've not been yourself," she continued. "What's going on, my darling? And why were you not returning any of my calls?"

I shrugged. "Sorry. I didn't feel like talking."

She let out an exasperated breath. "London, darling, I'm your mother."

"I know," was all I could muster.

"Well, I hope you are feeling better. I bought you some wonderful gifts." She lifted the Chanel bag. "Here, darling. Open it."

"Not now, Mother," I said, getting up and walking over to kiss her on the cheek. "You really didn't have to go shopping for me. But thank you."

She returned the gesture with a cheeky air-kiss of her own and then a quick hug. "Nonsense, dear. It's not every day you have a birthday."

I shrugged. "It's no big deal."

She scoffed. "It *is* a big deal and cause for celebration. Where would you like to go this evening?"

Umm. Let's see. To find Anderson, then follow Rich's mother around.

"Nowhere, Mother. I'd rather stay in."

"Darling, no." She looked disappointed. "We must get out to celebrate. Your father's made dinner reservations…"

Why? To pretend like we're some happy damn family?

I sat on the other chaise. "No, Mother. Really. I'm simply not in the mood for a family dinner. Not tonight." God, it felt good saying no. I no longer wanted her or Daddy planning *my* life.

"Okay, darling. I will let your father know. Maybe you'll be up for something this weekend."

I shrugged. "Maybe."

"Now tell me, darling. Why didn't you mention that Gisella

Grace had reached out to you a few weeks back? Imagine how I felt running into her at a charity event and she tells me this."

I knew it. It was always about *her*. I rolled my eyes and shrugged. "I can't imagine. There was nothing to tell," I stated nonchalantly. "And there still isn't. Gisella offered me a spot in her next casting. And I declined. End of story."

"London!" she exclaimed. "What do you mean there was nothing to tell?" She clapped her hands together. "This is fabulous news. Why would you decline?"

"Because I'm not interested," I said firmly.

And now it all made sense to me. Mother hadn't returned to L.A. for any other reason than to try to convince me to take Gisella up on her offer—hence all the unexpected shopping bags. Well, maybe that wasn't completely true, but it was partly true, and it made sense in my head.

"After the way you nearly disgraced..." She stopped herself from continuing her sentence. "I'm sorry, darling. It's just that after all that you've been through, the fact that Gisella wants to represent you..."

"She won't be representing me, Mother," I said calmly. "I'm not interested."

"London, why would you throw away an opportunity of a lifetime? Don't you see, my darling. This is what we've always dreamed of."

I sighed. "No, Mother. This is what *you've* always dreamed of."

My mother huffed. "Oh, London, stop with this nonsense. It's a blessing that designers are still vying for you after that tragic mishap."

I blinked. "Mother, it wasn't a *mishap*, as you call it. That *tragic* moment—although I regret it dearly—was neatly planned and thought out."

"However, darling, it's a blessing to *still* have the eye of some of the world's top designers wanting you to showcase their designs."

"Mother, please." I shook my head, feeling myself becoming annoyed. She wanted nothing more than to have me caught back up in the trappings of glamour. "Do not pressure me about this. It is my life, and my choice. Please."

"Fine, darling," she acquiesced, a little too easily. "I don't want to bicker. But have you even considered what you might do after Hollywood High?"

Yes. I know exactly what I am going to do. Become Mrs. Anderson Ford. Duh. What else? I gave her a dumb look, as if she should have already known this.

"It's not like you have suitors beating down the doors to marry you. At least when you were modeling you were more appealing."

I huffed, defiantly crossing my arms. "Gee, thanks, Mother. You talk as if I'm defective or something."

"No, darling. That's not what I mean."

I gave her a blank look. "Then *what* exactly do you mean, huh, Mother?"

She sighed. "London, a modeling career is good for you. You can potentially write your own ticket, darling. But I fear the longer you stay off the runway, the easier it'll be for you to get, well, you know...*chunky*, like your father's side of the family." She shook her head. "Right now, you look fabulous, darling, maybe five, ten pounds overweight. But it looks good on you. I just don't want you getting big and burly like your aunts. Modeling will keep you focused. Disciplined."

My eyes widened. I couldn't believe this. And here I'd managed to trick myself into believing she'd changed. Wrong.

"Mother, are you *fricking* kidding me?" I snapped. "How dare you! Modeling does nothing but keep me sickly looking and stressed—*you* keep me stressed—the heck out!"

"Now, now, darling. Let's not turn this into an ugly screaming match..."

"Um. Who's screaming? I'm simply making a statement. You made my life hell, Mother, with your scales, weighing me, weighing my food. It was all too much. So please. *Stop*."

"I'm sorry, darling. Really I am. I only want the best for you, darling."

I rolled my eyes again. "Mmmph. Well, right now, Mother. That's not what I'm feeling."

She started messing with another shopping bag. "Why don't I show you all the things I've bought you," she suggested. "I don't want you to be angry. All I was trying to say is, modeling is more of your world than you think. One day you will see exactly how much you miss the spotlight. But you will need to realize that in your own time, darling. Just as you will come to realize what an awful mistake you made letting Anderson go."

My body tensed; hearing his name hurt.

"Had you done what I'd told you to do—learn to love Anderson—you'd probably already be engaged," my mother insisted. "But instead, you pushed him straight into the arms of another girl."

I scoffed. "Like you've done with Daddy, huh, Mother?"

She blinked. "I did *no* such thing." Indignation coated her tone. "I never pushed your father away. He simply left. But this isn't about your father or me. This is about you and your future, darling. Anderson *was* a good catch..."

Was?

Last I checked, he was still single, still on the market, and still...

"That young man would have been on his way to becoming my son-in-law had you done what I'd instructed you to do..."

"I know Mother. I know. I should have listened."

She shook her head. "You know your father and I adored him."

My heart ached. "Again, Mother. No reminder needed, please. I know I was stupid. Dumb little London! Why don't you just announce it to the world? Confused London! Throwing away her entire life on some Brooklyn thug who ended up dumping *her* anyway, nearly destroying her."

"Street trash is beneath your station, darling. You simply snuck around with that boy to try to hurt your father and me. That Justice boy was nothing but trouble for you. And yet you defied my every rule where that hellacious boy was concerned. I'm glad he hurt you..."

I blinked, stunned.

"Face it, darling. It was bound to happen. It's better you learned that very painful lesson sooner rather than later, before he ended up swindling you out of your entire inheritance."

I had no words.

"Oh, dear," she said, oblivious to my shocked silence. "I almost forgot." She reached into her purse and pulled out a neatly rolled tabloid-sized magazine. "Here's a little motivation to hopefully help you decide your future, especially now that you're a year older. And, hopefully, wiser." She flipped to a specific page, and then handed it to me.

HEIR TO OIL EMPIRE SPOTTED WALKING OUT OF TIFFANY & CO. SPLURGES ON A 1.5 MILLION-DOLLAR BAUBLE FLOODED WITH EXQUISITE DIAMONDS read the bold headline. Underneath was a half-page photo of Anderson, walking out of the store flanked by security. And Ivina.

My heart sank.

"Mother, please go," I said, dropping the magazine to the floor. How was seeing *that* motivation? How was anything that she'd said to me, thus far, since walking into my bedroom, robbing me of my peace, celebratory?

I breathed in a deep breath, then pushed it back out into a swoop of agitated air as I schlepped to my bathroom and popped a couple of Advil, wishing like hell I had a bottle of vodka to chase them down with, to numb the early beginnings of a full-fledged heart attack.

In a matter of minutes, my mother had ruined a birthday that I didn't give one hot damn about in the first place.

Yeah.

Happy birthday to me...!

50

Rich

Dear Diary,

Logan called me today.

And I answered.

She asked me to please meet her for lunch at some li'l café called Sweet Teas in downtown L.A.

I started to tell her no.

But I was desperate.

I needed some money, and after the way she let her family drag me, she owed me. So I told her I would be there, but that she had to leave her goons at home, and her dogging my man was off limits.

Surprisingly, she agreed. *And* she offered to send a car for me. I accepted.

I just hoped she kept her word and didn't mention Justice. After all, there was no way I could admit to Logan that although black love was still sweet, chocolate still tickled my panties, and I still loved my sugar daddy...

Well, scratch that.

Justice really couldn't afford to give me no sugar.

He was more like ah...ah...a Splenda daddy.

He looked good, tasted good, but it wasn't the same.

Why?

'Cause my baby-boo had only one dime, and that he spent on rent.

Simply put: There was no way I could confess to Logan that she was right and that I really didn't know how bad Justice's pocket situation was until I moved in here. Then I got to see firsthand how the low-grade lived.

Now I understood why Logan called him a smoky-lounge, YouTube singer. A downgrade. Because he is.

I love him, though.

And the only person I would trade him for is a richer version of himself.

But.

That's not possible.

'Cause he's broke. And he comes from the bottom-scraping loins of a janitor and an LPN, better known as a street sweeper and home health aide. So he can't even borrow any money from his parents.

And yeah, Justice can sing, but he's no Drake, Bruno Mars, or even Chris Breezy. He's more like... like...Mario. A one-hit wonder, who by the time anyone has really heard of him, he's played out, or a homeless beach bum singing for quarters.

But that's it.

And that's all he gon' ever be.

Which would explain why all of these clubs and sets that he does amount to no more than a bunch of time-consuming...nothing.

And being the loving and kind, compassionate woman that I am, I tried to be his ride or die.

But.

The ride has no more gas. And I don't wanna die; it's not my time.

Straight up, I'm not built for this. I'm used to a château and an English garden. This place was Bates Motel with a personal parking space. And the furniture up in here, dear God, I think it came in a box shipped from Jail-Mart.

Chile, cheese!

Boo, please!

Honey, I need my luxurations back! I craved my three-feet-high, with handcrafted mahogany steps, four-poster, king-size bed.

I needed to roll around on my twenty-two-karat, 2,000 thread-count Italian linen. Take steamy showers beneath my gold rainspout without worrying the hot water would run out.

And my chef! Dear God, I missed my chef! I was dying for a taste of strawberry crepes, goose eggs with Gouda, and my diamond-studded pimpette cup filled with beer-mosas in the mornings!

Dear diary, I just needed to click my heels and bounce.

I loved Justice, but there was no justice in this relationship. Clearly, I was the prize, and he was winning, but where did that leave me?

I was upstanding.

Classy.

Elegant.

Graceful.

A lady.

Meant to be taken special care of.

Not some ratchet thot born to live in the hood-swamp with Dr. Welfare. Which was why I didn't know how long I could do this. And usually I wouldn't dump one boy until I had another to take his place.

But desperate times called for desperate measures, and in a minute, I was gon' send out a social media SOS and change my relationship status from "Booed-Up" to "Need to be freed from bondage."

"Baby," poured from behind me.

My heart thumped. I jumped and slammed my diary shut. I turned around to face Justice, who stood along the side of the bed, with a white towel wrapped around his waist and another one draped behind his neck and over his shoulders. I used to melt like butter when my chocolate thug-daddy stood before me, practically naked with his eight-pack gleaming and his pipe print bulging. Now I was aggravated. "Are you for real?"

He arched a brow, clearly taken aback. "For real about what?"

I twisted the lock on my diary and slid it into the nightstand drawer. "Why are you sneaking up on me?"

"How I'ma sneak up on you in my crib?" he asked, annoyed.

Boy, bye, this is not a crib; this is a cradle. "Look, what is it? Wassup? What do you want?"

Justice paused and completely took me in, from my sleeveless and oversized gray Gucci T-shirt and gray Gucci jeans to my bare feet. He looked over at the clock: 11:30 a.m. "Where are you going?" he asked.

"Out."

"Out where?"

"Outside."

He folded his arms across his chest, and his pecs pumped, like they always did when he was pissed. He took a step into my personal space, then took the tip of his index finger and mushed it into my forehead. "Wassup with you? All week you've been laid up in here with a funky attitude."

I pushed his finger away and spat, "I don't have an attitude."

"Really?" He arched a brow and pumped his pecs again.
"Then what would you call it?"

*Pissed off. Frustrated. Tired of you being broke, busted,
and disgusted.*

He carried on, "And in case you forgot, you can't afford to
be catching no attitude with me."

"*Bzzzz, annnnnt,* wrong answer, because an attitude is
the one thing I can afford. Can you say the same?"

He hesitated. "What are you tryna say?"

"I'm not trying to say anything, I said it."

"Yo," he snorted, "are you tryna call me broke on the low?"

"I didn't whisper." I rolled my eyes.

He arched one brow, then the other. "Last I checked, you
ain't have no dough. Yo' fat ass didn't have a job, and no
place else to go. So from what I see, you need me. Not the
other way around." He snorted and mushed his index finger
into my forehead again. "Gon' call me broke. For real, for
real, you need to learn to watch your mouth and get your
mind right. Because what you about to catch is these hands."

"Boy, bye, puhlease. We both got hands!"

He narrowed his eyes, and his gaze burned through me.
"You better shut your dumb behind up before I bust you
dead in the mouth. I can't believe you, yo. You really gon'
disrespect me where I pay rent? You ah ungrateful ass trick!"

"Trick?! Who you calling a trick?! You a trick and your
mama and daddy are two tricks!"

Justice took the palm of his right hand, placed it over my
face, and pushed me into the bed. "Say something else about
my parents, and see don't I take my Timb and stomp yo'
mouth shut! Now try me."

Silence.

"Thought so," he said.

"Whatever." I mumbled.

"Didn't I tell you to shut up?!" He stepped into my personal space, like he was looking for a reason to put his boot in my face.

I pushed him back and stood up. "Move!"

He reared a closed fist back, and immediately I ducked. He huffed, then put his hand down and said, "Know what, before I end up bustin' yo' fat nasty behind, I'ma do you a favor and step." He snatched a pair of True Religion jeans and a red T-shirt off the edge of the bed. "And to think I wanted to take you lunch today, but you know what, screw yo' retarded ass. You don't need to eat anyway." He threw on his clothes and slid his feet into a pair of worn Timbs.

I jumped up and blocked the doorway. "Where are you running off to, to see London? Kaareema, huh? Some slum-slut?! So we get in an argument, and you wanna run to the side ho?"

"Move, Rich!"

"No."

"A'ight." He brushed past me, causing me to stumble backward. I didn't fall, though. I caught my balance, turned around, and grabbed the back of his shirt.

He pushed me, and this time I fell to the floor. I hopped back up, and he snatched me by the collar. "Don't make me slap the ish out of you, yo! You think this is a game? You think I'm playing with you, yo? I'm laid up in here living with you, claiming you, loving you, and you're trippin' on me?! You buggin'. Instead of being worried about some side jawn, you need to take your fat behind and look for a job. 'Cause you eat up everything in here, you can't cook, and you don't clean. So the least you can do is stop stressing me and bring some money up in this piece! I should turn you out and put you on the track. That's all you good for anyway!"

"Justice!"

He didn't answer; instead he stormed out the apartment door, slamming it behind him.

Before I could figure out what to do next, the bell rang. I knew it was Gary, my old driver. I'm sure Logan sent him for me.

I snatched open the door and said, "Hey, Gary...I just need...a minute." I paused.

"Hey, Richie-Poo."

Dear goddess of all things surprise, what in the black Jesus was this?

It was my mother, dressed in a fitted, peach, and off-the-shoulders dress that hugged every one of her curves to perfection, and six-inch python-skin stilettos that made her gleaming milk chocolate legs look as if they went on forever.

And there she stood outside of Justice's apartment, bearing gifts.

My brown eyes beamed, my mouth watered, and my heart fluttered. In one of my mother's hands was an extra-large shopping bag from my favorite Parisian boutique. And in the other hand were two small red bags from my favorite jeweler.

Truthfully, all I wanted to do was fall into her arms and squeeze her.

But I had to be strong.

My mother gleamed as she reached into one of the small red bags, pulled out a red velvet box, and popped it open.

"A pink diamond choker!" I screamed, clutching my chest. "Dear goddess, yes, bish, yes! That has got to be at least three karats!"

I looked up at Logan, and she grinned from one yellow-diamond studded ear to the next. "In the other bag are the pink diamond studs to match. They will go well with your new coming home wears."

Fight, queen, fight! And do what's right! I threw on a fake frown and arched a brow. "So, what, you came here to bribe me? After you let your hoodlum son and his gang-bangin'

daddy come for me? My dignity is worth more than diamonds, Mother."

She smiled and practically sang, "Three-karat necklace.
Three-karat earrings—"

"That's nine karats!" I screamed.

"Three plus three is six, Rich. But no worries, I've arranged
for you to return to Hollywood High and receive tutoring."

Inhale.

Exhale.

Now let it rip! "You are real live tacky showing up here
like this, trying to buy my womanhood with gifts. First of all,
Shakeesha, you said to meet you at Sweet Teas."

She shot me a look, as if to remind me that she wasn't above
attacking me, her own child. She closed the red velvet box and
put it away. "That was two hours ago, Rich. And when you
didn't show up, I figured I'd come to you." She looked over
my shoulder and took Justice's apartment in. I knew she was
criticizing everything, from the blue tweed sectional to the
small sixty-inch, flat-screen TV. She asked, "May I come in?"

"No." Then I paused, blocked the doorway, and let her
marinate on that.

She swallowed.

I continued, "This is me and my man's home, which we
take pride in, and I don't need you judging our mod-del sur-
roundings."

"You mean modest?"

I sucked my teeth. "See, there you go."

"Look," she said as she softly reached for my hair and
twirled the end of a curl, "I have so many new things for you.
I've ordered you an entirely new wardrobe, new heels, new
bags, and all I want is for you to come home, Richie-Poo."

I wanna come home too, Mommy. "I am home."

She looked over my shoulder again. "This sweat box is not
your home! You are a château kind of girl."

I sure am. "First of all, this is not a sweat box. It's a one-bedroom-studio apartment-townhome. And just so you know, there are more important matters in life than material things, Logan Montgomery."

"Oh, please." She pursed her lips. "That's cowshit, and you know it. Your closet is the size of this place. And your bedroom alone makes two of this raggedy dump."

Amen! "It's not a dump. It has a balcony with a view!"

She clenched her jaw, swerved her neck, and pointed behind me. "A balcony?! First of all, that thing jutting from the living room to the outside is about as wide as a basement windowsill. And second of all, what view? The broken-down jalopy in the parking lot? Dear God! Have you lost all rhyme, reasoning, and class?!"

She looked me over, from my swollen feet to my round and chubby cheeks. "I know you, and I know that you miss Chef Jacque, and his specially made strawberry crepes, goose eggs with Gouda, and beer-mosas."

I'm dying for it! "No, I don't. I don't even like goose eggs. Gross."

"Then what are you eating? Wendy's, Burger King, McDonald's, Chinese food?!"

"No, I am not! I resent that! For one, I don't eat sushi, and for two, I'm not some low grade. My man cooks for me, and when, and if, we do eat out we don't eat fast food, we eat Chick-fil-A! Thank you!"

She hesitated. Then she blinked, and blinked again. "Look, I'm not going to keep standing here in my good heels, debating with you. I'm your mother, and you're only seventeen years old. I tell you what to do! And what you're going to do is gather your things, come home, and take a good and long bath to wash this hood-bugger stench off of you! Get your behind back to school. Go to therapy. Have a conversation with your brother and apologize to your father!"

This old ho is buggin'! "Shakeesha, you are straight out of order! Coming up in here disrespecting my man, where he pays rent, bearing gifts, like I can be bought! Then you're talking about goose eggs and strawberry crepes, which I have never liked! And therapy?! You need to send your pimp of a son to therapy!

"And apologize to your rolling stone of a husband?! Like, I did something to him when he came for me, while you sat there and watched it all go down! That was real gutter and grimy. Real slimy. If anything, the three of you owe me an apology!

"And now you wanna be all in me and my man's hallway, crappin' on Justice's name and trying to lure me home! Get this through your head: I am home, and I ain't leavin'! So what you can do is gather your gifts, your nose, and your good heels and march yourself out of my business!"

I slammed the door in my mother's face, and as the sinking thought of not being able to wear those pink diamonds stabbed needle pricks through my skin, I fell across Justice's bed and made tearstains on his cheap sheets.

51

Spencer

I sat at the kitchen table, staring out at the mountains through the wall of glass, my eyeballs bouncing back and forth from the magnificent view to the manila folder on the table, a folder that I'd gotten from my PI less than an hour ago.

"I had to search high and low for this," he'd stated when he'd handed the nearly empty file to me. "Someone wanted to make sure it was nearly impossible to find out anything."

I'd taken the folder from him, then rolled up my car window and sped off. It'd taken me weeks to dig up these goddiggitydang bones; now all I needed were the meat and potatoes to fill up the plate.

"Who is Cleola Mae, Kitty...?"

"Spencer, stop with this nonsense...Maybe she's some dead woman, some ghost your father sees in that little peabrain mind of his..."

"Who is Cleola Mae...?"

"There is no Cleola Mae. She doesn't exist. She's some crazy figment of your father's overactive imagination..."

"Tell me now, Mother. Who is Cleola Mae...?"

"Okay, fine, Spencer...she was some ole country bump-kin your father was once infatuated with..."

Absentmindedly, I ran my fingers along the edges of the folder. I was many things but one...two...three things I wasn't was dumb. Some bimbo. *Mmmph*. I could smell a pile of crappy mess a mile away. And all that mess Kitty was trying to stuff down my throat was some hog crap!

I flipped open the folder and stared. *This* was not some country bumpkin Daddy had been infatuated with. Inside were two photos of a crooked-toothed, cinnamon-colored girl with a wide nose and two unkempt, lopsided ponytails. The part in her hair looked crooked, and her roots needed a good scrubbing. She couldn't have been any older than twelve or so.

Her eyes.

Sad, hazel eyes with thick dark lashes.

They (those eyes) looked strangely familiar, yet very foreign to me.

I'd already gone upstairs to ask Daddy who this little girl was, but conveniently he wanted to play like his brain was all of a sudden freeze-dried. All of a sudden *he* didn't know of any Cleola Mae. "Don't go hunting in no empty nests," he'd warned, before shooing me out of his room. Well, goshdiggity-danggit. Mother*fudgepop* him and some ole dang empty nest! I wanted answers, and I wanted them *now!*

I picked up the black-and-white photo and studied the girl's face. It was the face of a child who could have easily ended up on the side of a milk carton. But it hadn't. And yet there was a caption that read:

MISSING.

CLEOLA MAE PICKENS

IF ANYONE HAS SEEN THIS CHILD, PLEASE CONTACT YOUR LOCAL
AUTHORITIES.

What happened to her? Was she kidnapped? Had anyone ever found her? And why was Daddy all of a sudden tight-lipped and senile about it?

I placed the photo back inside the folder, my jaw clench-ing as my gazed drifted over to the box of red dirt sitting up over on the island. Dirt I had my little dickie-dick bring back with him from his eight-day trip to some hick town in Emm-eye-crooked-letter-crooked-letter-eye-crooked-letter-crooked-letter-eye-humpback-humpback-eye.

When he'd told me he was in—I glanced at the white label on the bottom right corner of the folder—LEFLORE COUNTY, MISSISSIPPI...I insisted he bring me back a shoebox full of dirt.

"Strange request," he'd said. "But whatever. As you wish."

Mmmph. There was nothing strange about what I'd asked for. If this photo didn't nudge Kitty's memory about who that little girl was, then perhaps the box of red clay-dirt would.

They said LeFlore County was the home of cotton and cat-fish. Well, from where my booty cheeks were sitting, it was also the place for lies and dirty little secrets. And I planned on plowing through, excavating, every goshdang lie ever told, or, so help me sweetheavenlyjeezus, I was going to tear the roof off this mothersucker tonight.

I glanced over at the wall clock. *Kitty should be here soon. And then it's time to jumpstart this rodeo show.*

"Dear God. Where did you get this?" Kitty asked, her smooth-silky skin suddenly going colorless and gray.

I narrowed my eyes. "Who is she, Mother? Who is that missing girl?"

Kitty's hand shook. The photo dropped from her hand, flut-tering to the table. "You meddling little *bitch!*" she screamed, before lunging at me. She was quick, too quick, as her hands wrapped around my throat. "I should kill you with my own bare hands!" She shook me, her grip tightening.

I gasped for air, trying to claw her hands from around my neck. I kicked and wailed, knocking items off the table, as she continued squeezing. *"Why*, Spencer? Why did you have to go digging up that little girl's ugly past, huh, you little wretched *slut?!"*

I felt myself going light-headed as Kitty shook me like a rag doll. I tried to scream, but all that came tumbling out from the back of my throat were gurgling sounds.

"You have no idea what you've done!" She lifted one hand and slapped me, hard, across the face, while her other hand tightened around my neck, her nails digging into my flesh. She slapped me again.

"I spent my entire life burying that little girl so far down into the earth that no one would ever find her. And yet *you"—whap!—*"turn around and undo everything I buried with that girl!"

I had to figure out a way to get her off of me, before she strangled me on home to glory. The look in Kitty's eyes told me she was planning to make me the next girl missing if I didn't act fast. *Lordgodlordgodlordgodjeezus! Help me!*

I reached over and clawed at the table, trying to reach for the crystal tumbler until my hand wrapped around it. I swung with all my might, knocking my mother in the head until she finally let me go. Gasping, I leapt up from my chair, chest heaving, and my eyes full of tears.

"Aaaaah!" I screamed, wild and crazy like, charging her. "You tried to kill *me!"*

"I'm your mother!" she yelled. "And you had no business going behind my back, digging up—"

"I had every right, Kitty! You're a liar!" In my hysteria, I ran over to the shoebox of dirt and slung it in her face. Red soil flew out all over the place—in her eyes, her mouth, the table, and all over the floor. "You clay-eater! You told me there was *no* Cleola Mae!"

Kitty gasped and coughed, wiping dirt from her face. "Aaah! You hateful little trollop! I told you she was *dead!*"

"And you also told me she was a figment of Daddy's imagination. That he was crazy! You ole cotton-picking mud mouth! You snake sucker!"

Kitty charged me, and we both fell to the floor, rolling around in Mississippi soil, fighting each other like two rabid wolves, scratching, slapping, and punching each other, ripping blouses, and tearing at bras until we were both too exhausted to keep fighting.

After rolling around on the floor for what seemed like forever, we were finally exhausted and bloody and shredded to pieces with our boobs nearly exposed, breathing heavy, sore and bruised, muscles burning and backs aching, crawling.

I glared at Kitty as she held onto the table, before plopping down into the only chair that hadn't been knocked over.

I crawled my way over to the island and grabbed onto one of the barstools, hoisting myself up.

"Now tell me, Kitty, who is Cleola Mae. And one more lie," I warned through clenched teeth, "and we are both going to regret the day you gave birth to me."

Kitty's burning eyes met my face with a glare of her own. "I already do." She shook her head. "I should have dumped you in the ocean and let the whales raise you. I knew you were trouble, Spencer, from the moment you slid out into the world. Your entire seventeen years of breathing, you have done nothing but try to wreak havoc in my life. Well, my darling daughter. You have finally managed to unearth my entire world. Bravo to you! You—"

"Oh, shut it, Kitty!" I spat, my whole body shaking with anger. "Just tell me who the hell that missing girl is?"

"Fine, Spencer. She's *me!*" She reached for the photo and slung it at me. "*I'm* Cleola Mae! *I'm* the girl in that photo."

I stalked over toward the counter and pulled out a dish towel from one of the drawers, and then slung it at her. "Tell me everything, Kitty. Why did you go missing?"

We glared at each other. And for the first time in my life, I saw them. Wet. Streaks. My mother had tears streaming down her scratched face.

"I ran away," she said, closing her eyes. "I had to get out of that godforsaken hellhole of a life…"

Then, with tears falling heavy from her eyes, Kitty told me her whole life story: growing up dirt poor, with no money for food or clothes, or barely having a roof over her head, being called black and ugly and forced to sleep with a dirty old man just to keep her stomach from growling in the middle of the night.

"Momma knew what he was doing to me, but she'd let him keep doing it anyway. She said I had to earn my keep. Help feed my family. So I…" she choked back a sob, then shook her head again.

"And then he started in on Norma…I mean, Camille," she corrected.

I blinked. "You *knew* Heather's mother back then?"

"Yes. We were best friends. The little ugly black girl and the poor white trash girl in the dirty panties. Norma Marie and I were all we had. We were both broken. We looked out for each other. And then one day, I walked into Mr. Petey's rickety shack and found him on top of Camille. She was crying and begging him, 'Get off, get off…please, stop…'" My mother paused, and my heart stopped. "I stabbed him," she confessed in almost a whisper, "until he stopped breathing, until he stopped hurting Norma—I mean Camille—until he could no longer keep hurting me."

My jaw dropped when she told me how she and Heather's

mother set his lopsided shanty on fire with him still in it. Then—with a pinky swear—promised each other to never mention him *or* that night again.

"Two years later, Camille's father moved them to the hills of West Virginia. Her great escape from her horrid past—and mine. But I was the one left behind to relive the memories day after day after day. Momma had too many kids to feed. There were eight of us, and I was second to the oldest—the only girl. But I wasn't gonna let Momma pimp me out to some other dirty old man. I wanted out of that horrid life. So I ran. I ran until my chest burned and my legs ached. I slept in fields, under bridges, in Dumpsters, anywhere I could. And I did *what*ever I had to do, sleeping with anyone, turning tricks to get me what I needed..."

I blinked. Dearholyfathersweetjeezus. I had no idea. Kitty then shared how she'd finally made her way to Atlanta and danced in strip clubs, wearing wigs and dark brown contacts to disguise herself; she'd perfected a lie for a new life.

"And that's where I met your father. My biggest catch." She wiped her face, then offered a faint smile. "He was so big and strong, and handsome. And he smelled of money, lots of it. All the girls tried to work him, but I'd managed to snag his attention. He saw something special in me, something no one else ever wanted to see. He saw hope, Spencer. And I saw it in him. Ellington saved my life. He rescued me from my past. He took me with him and gave me hope. He gave me a new identity, and a whole new life."

She sighed, then closed her eyes. "He made me trust again. And over time I'd grown to love him because he'd found it in his heart to love a poor little *clay-eater*—as you called me—like me."

She looked down at the photo lying on the floor atop dirt from her past.

"I'm not that girl, anymore. She's gone. Cleola Mae Pickens died the first time Mr. Petey touched her in her sacred places. I buried her—or at least I thought I did—the day I left with nothing but the tattered clothes on my back. And, yet, after hundreds of thousands of dollars of plastic surgeries, getting my education, going to charm school to learn proper manners and etiquette, after years of erasing that horrid rural Mississippi accent, and amassing hundreds of millions of dollars, branding myself as a force to be reckoned with, *you* have managed to find a way to remind me that, no matter how hard I tried to erase my past, somehow, someway, someone would eventually dig it up and remind me that there is never any escaping it. I just never thought it would be *my* own child."

"Then maybe you should have told me the truth," I said tersely as I half-limped, half-walked over to the cordless phone. I lifted it from its cradle.

"Who are you calling at this time of night?" she snapped, shooting me a venomous glare.

"The police," I said.

"For the love of God, Spencer! Why on earth would you do that?"

I blinked. "Because you're a murderer, Kitty, *and* a..."

"Hello. Nine-one-one...what's your emergency?"

"I'd like to report a missing person," I said.

"Okay. Who is missing?" the dispatcher asked.

I looked over at Kitty, my eyes full of my own tears, and then said, "My mother."

52

London

I knew I had no business showing up here.
But here I stood...

Dressed in a nude-color, form-fitting sequined dress that draped off the shoulders with a hard-cased crystal-mix clutch and a pair of Jimmy Choo pumps that were killing my feet.

Out in a balmy, starlit evening.

Surrounded by lots of red carpet and velvet rope.

Alone.

At the marina, looking up at *Buff Daddy*: Anderson's three-level floating paradise. The American flag, along with the state flag of Texas, fluttered from its mast.

I gulped in a breath of night air. The luxury yacht was absolutely breathtaking. But then I swallowed, remembering the first time Anderson had brought me aboard. It had been a gift from his father, and he'd wanted to show it to me. Yet I hadn't been interested or impressed with its teak-planked decks, oversized Jacuzzis, the voile privacy drapes, or its beach-chic areas.

Now I panicked at the thought of not being able to climb aboard. I ran a hand along the side of my head; my hair was pinned up into an elegant French roll. And then I nervously touched my neck. I'd purposefully worn one of the diamond necklaces Anderson had given me one Christmas.

A knot coiled in the pit of my stomach as five photographers sprang from out of nowhere. I cringed. I should have known the paparazzi would be lurking, I thought, wishing I had worn a wig and dark shades or a huge floppy hat.

I turned my body slightly on an angle, hoping to not be noticed. So far, they were busy taking shots of a slew of Victoria Secret models posing a few feet ahead of me.

The waterfront was alive with yachts and partygoers, some dressed in cheesy gold lamé bikinis. And others were topless, wearing nothing but disgustingly short shorts (that showed more of their *ass*ets than fabric) with strappy high sandals. And then there were the more sophisticated bunch, the ones I could relate to, who were donned in the best designers their money could afford.

A tall, muscular, bald-shaven guy with a well-groomed beard held a clipboard in his hand, checking off guests before pulling back the rope and allowing them to climb on board the yacht.

I only hoped—

"Hey, there. I know you," a reporter said as he pointed at me. "London Phillips, right?"

I contemplated shaking my head no, but then forced a smile instead.

Click.

Click.

Click.

Camera shutters flicked, then came the near-blinding burst of flashes.

"Hey, London. Are you ready to get back on the runway?" echoed another reporter.

"You made quite a spectacle of yourself at Club Sixty-Six," shot another pap dog. "Do you plan on getting drunk tonight?"

"Will there be any begging tonight?" asked another reporter.

Oh, they were trying to provoke me into making a scene, but I refused to give them that even as the small crowd in back of me tittered. Still, I nearly died from the embarrassing memory. Yet I remained poised, despite the smile that was already on my face nearly cracking from the inside out.

"No, no, and no," was all I could say in response.

"Does Anderson Ford know you're here?" asked another reporter.

"Of course, he does," I said. "We're still good friends." Okay, that was totally a lie, but so what. They didn't need to know that Anderson hated my guts.

"Word has it," said another reporter, "that he plans to pop the question tonight to that hot Russian model he's seeing..."

My knees nearly buckled. *Is this an engagement party?* Nothing was mentioned of an *engagement* party on the Internet or any of Anderson's social media sites. I was now even following Ivina on Twitter and Instagram. And her pages said nothing either about some damn marriage proposal.

Click, click, click...

"Are you still hoping he changes his mind and takes you back?"

I swallowed. "Not if he's happy I don't," I said tartly. I refused to burst out into tears out here in fear it would land me on *Ellen* and on the cover of every tabloid and gossip blog known to man.

"I wish Anderson nothing but the best," I added for good measure. It was one big lie unless I was going to be the one ultimately ending up with the engagement ring and marriage proposal.

"There goes Jaden Smith," a reporter stated, causing all the other pap dogs to quickly scatter away from me to chase down the teen star. Clearly, they had grown tired with me for not allowing their mocking and taunting to get to me.

But it did.

I blew out a breath.

"Name, please," said surly Clipboard Man as I stepped into view.

"Umm. London Phillips."

He looked me up and down, his gaze slowly sliding along my frame before his eyes returned to my face. He flipped through the printout of the guest list, then raised a brow.

"Sorry. This is a private party. Your name isn't on the list."

"Please. Check again. There has to be some mistake."

Mr. Clipboard Man looked again, then said more forcefully, "Like I said, your name isn't on the list. Step aside. Next guest, please."

I stood planted in my spot. "Please, sir. I really have to get inside," I said in a voice that sounded whiny.

He grunted. "Not tonight you won't. Now step aside."

I knew this was a stupid idea. Who shows up at someone's party without an invite?

"Please, sir, can you—"

"This beautiful lady's with me," a rich, thick voice said, sidling up beside me. I blushed as he took my arm and looped it around his. "I'm on the list. Devon Blade," my mystery saver said to Clipboard Man. "She's my plus one." He flashed me a conspiratorial smile.

Mr. Clipboard Man gave Mr. Save the Night a look of skepticism, his glare going from me to him, before finally glancing down at his clipboard and skimming through the list and checking him off. He pulled back the rope and allowed us both through.

"Thank you," I whispered as he helped me up the ramp.

"No problem. By the way, I'm Blade."

I smiled. "Nice to meet you. And I'm—"

"London Phillips," he said. And then he flashed the prettiest white smile I'd ever seen on a guy. He was young, and handsome, and clearly very rich, judging by the large diamonds in his ears and his Jacob the Jeweler watch.

"I follow you on Twitter," he added, noticing the puzzled look on my face.

Oh.

"So what's the deal with you and Anderson Ford?"

I shrugged. "It's complicated." And then I laughed, surprised at my use of the word. He gave me a confused look. "I hate that word."

He chuckled. "Yeah. Me too. But listen"—he grabbed my hand as we reached the main deck—"if things with you and Anderson don't work out, give me a holla. I'll show you how a man treats a beauty like you. I'm the epitome of uncomplicated."

I smiled and then thanked him again for getting me on the yacht. I leaned in and kissed him on the cheek

He flashed me another smile. "Save me a dance," he said, taking a flute of champagne from a waiter's tray as he walked by. And then he was gone, leaving me to find the object of my desire.

Anderson.

I sauntered through the crowd of glam and glitter and all things expensive, my eyes sweeping the area as I moved. There were flickering votives everywhere, but there was no sign of Anderson, or his, his...*ugh*...that *girl* he was screwing—or not.

I found myself wishing for the *nth* time that I'd stayed home, that I'd never chosen Justice over Anderson. But I was here *now* (there was no turning back!), and I couldn't change the past (although I wished like hell I could), and I knew I couldn't control what happened next...

God, I needed a cocktail, or two. But I fought the urge to snatch two flutes from off a moving tray as another waiter whisked by.

"*London!*" a female's voice shrieked in a European accent

as heels clicked across the deck. I swung around to see a very blond, very blue-eyed, impossibly beautiful girl in a nearly see-through wrap dress and very high heels.

"*Annika?*" I said, shocked to see the teen supermodel here. Wondering what she was doing in L.A., and *here*, no less.

We'd done fashion week in Milan together, and the Swedish runway powerhouse had been so nasty to me—messy and condescending to the point that I wanted to step out of my heels and fight her.

"Ohmygod! *Look* at you!" she said, grabbing me in an unexpected embrace and then air-kissing me. "You look so... beautiful."

I flushed. "Thank you."

"I'm so sorry for the way I treated you during Fashion Week. I was being so bitchy toward you."

I tilted my head. "No. You were only being you. But apology accepted."

She laughed. "Well, okay. Still," she said, taking my hands into hers, "you didn't deserve it. I felt so awful about..." Her voice trailed off.

I gently squeezed her hand. "Don't be. I'm better," I stated, referring to my suicide attempt. "What I did was stupid and careless. Through it all, I'm glad to be here, alive and well."

Annika smiled. "So am I. I was wrong about you, London. Dead wrong."

I gave her a confused look. "About?"

"About not belonging at Fashion Week or on any runway. The runway is your world, London. I think you should embrace it."

"*From catwalk to crash cart! Model sensation, London Phillips, hit the runway in more ways than one when the teen socialite pony-stepped her way down the catwalk in a near bloody white gown...*"

That's how one blog had started off about me after my suicide attempt.

I shrugged. "I don't know. Maybe one day."

"Hopefully sooner than not," she said. She leaned in and then lowered her voice. "Imagine it, London. Ivina, you, and me...the three of us taking the fashion world by storm."

I recoiled. Firstly, I couldn't imagine it—me back on the runway. And, secondly, the mere mention of Ivina's name sent my nerves reeling. The only thing I could imagine at this moment was pushing her over the railing and then—

"London?"

My breath caught. It was Anderson.

I swallowed, praying that he wouldn't embarrass me in front of Annika or the rest of his well-heeled guests. My heart was beating fast. And hard.

"Let me have a word with you. *Now*," he rudely said, grabbing me by the elbow and ushering me off to a nearby room. He closed the door behind us once we were inside.

Anderson scowled. "London, what are you doing *here?*"

"I—"

"I don't recall your name being placed on the guest list," he stated emphatically. And then he gave me a look that teetered between a smirk and a sneer. "Are you stalking me now?"

I cringed. The word *stalking* sounded so, so creepy. Desperate.

Sadly, I'd somehow become both.

"Stalking you? N-no. Absolutely not, Anderson," I said nervously.

He raised a questioning brow. "I don't know. First you just pop up in New York out of the blue," he said, glancing over my shoulder, before looking back at me. "Then you happen to be at Club Sixty-Six—trashed. And now you're *here*. Uninvited, no less."

"I *was* invited," I lied. "I'm here with, with...*Blade*."

"Blade?" Anderson scrunched his face, then seconds later he raised a brow. "It's *Devon*. Not Blade."

I let out a nervous chuckle. "I know what it is. Blade is what I call him. I'm his date."

"Oh, really?" Anderson asked with a smirk. "Then why is he up on the sundeck dancing with three half-naked girls? And why did he tell me that you were outside begging to get inside?"

I swallowed. "I, um...I wasn't *begging*."

"Yeah, right. Cut the crap, London. Why are you here?"

"Are you and Ivina getting engaged?"

Anderson stared at me, long and hard, before finally answering the question with a question. *"Why?"*

"Because I need to know," I said, feeling myself slowly unraveling from the inside out. "Is this an engagement party?"

He shook his head, letting out a frustrated breath. "No, it's not an *engagement* party. It's a *private* charity fundraiser—for Big Brothers; I'm trying to raise money for inner-city kids. And had *you* been invited, you would have known that."

But nowhere on the Internet did I see that, so how was I to know? I didn't feel relieved. If anything, I felt more anxious. Anderson looked at me with disgust in his eyes. I was slowly peeling apart.

"But noooo," he said coldly, "spoiled London wants to try to bum-rush her way back into my life, disrupting my world, and then expects me to drop everything for her." He made a sound, like that of a buzzer, then said, "Wrong answer. Not gonna happen. You could have had a good man, but you wanted a leech. Now you'll have to go find yourself another sucker, because I'm all suckered out."

A lump formed in my throat. "Anderson, why do you hate me so much?"

Anderson flinched. Then he sighed, glancing down at his

watch. "Look. We're gonna have to wrap this up. I have a silent auction that's about to start. But I don't hate you, London. You hurt me. You chose a bum *nucca* over me. And I've had to get over that."

My lips quivered. "I made a mistake. I'm so sorry, Anderson." I closed the distance between us. "Choosing Justice over you was the biggest mistake of my life."

He gave me a doubtful look. "Oh, well. And now you'll have to live with that. We both will," Anderson said, but by the slightly sorrowful tone of his voice, I could tell (or at least I hoped) he didn't mean it.

Still, I choked back a sob, looking up at him. "Can't you find it in your heart to forgive me, Anderson, and give me— *us*—another chance?"

He shook his head forlornly. "Nah. I'm good on that. You can't be trusted, London. You're too wishy-washy. I can't trust that you won't hurt me again or trust that you'll ever be able to love me the way I used to love you."

Used to?

Past tense. As in he no longer did?

I wanted to burst into tears, but I didn't want Anderson to see me as the same weak, emotional girl. I needed him to see me as vulnerable, but not broken. Yet, I was on the verge of a full-fledged panic attack. I knew it, but I pushed through my words anyway.

"I *do* love you, Anderson. I've *always* loved you. I just didn't know it until you broke up with me and you were gone. I'm so lost without you in my life, Anderson. All I'm asking for is another chance. *Please*."

Anderson reached out, surprisingly, and cupped my cheek in his warm hand. I stopped breathing. I actually shivered as I tipped my face back up to his, hoping, wishing, praying for his lips to brush mine, just one kiss; that's all I prayed for.

Pleasepleasepleaseplease...

Anderson was staring at me, nearly expressionless, when he finally said, "There'll be no kissing and making up."

It took a minute for his words to register, and when they did, I felt like I'd been kicked in the heart. Anderson re-opened the door.

"Go home, London," he said, his face stony and resolute. "And have a good life."

"Please, Anderson," I gasped, fighting for breath. My whole world was going up in flames. And when Anderson walked out and I could no longer breathe, I broke down and cried.

53

Rich

My Dearest Justice,
I'm tired of pretending.
Plus, I'm no good at it.
*Yes, I love you. But I can't take love to the bank; it
only deposits air into my account. And this version
of Queen Bonnie and Low Budget Clyde against the
world has worn me out and will not work another
day. Clearly, I'm not the for-richer-or-for-poorer kind
of girl. I'm simply for richer.*

*And yeah, yeah, we fought the other day, and
when you came back home, we made up and tore
the sheets off the bed.*

But I'm done with that fix.
You can keep it.

*Or call London, Kaareema, or another one of
your hoes to come over and deal with your pipe-
slinging Band-Aid.*

*Unlike them, I'm experienced enough to know
that a hot and desirable woman like me can find a*

no-strings-attached, pipe-slayin' healer anywhere, all shade.

I have standards, Justice. And up until this evening, I thought you knew that. That is, until you came for me all sleazy and left a hundred-dollar bill on the nightstand, like I was some cheap ho, and a note that read, "Go to the grocery store, and while you're there fill out an application."

Clutchin' pearls!

Boy, you got me all the way twisted!

You don't send me on errands! That's what a house manager is for!

Furthermore, what the hell is a hundred dollars supposed to do for me?

And fill out an application?

How dare you?!

To think we've been together all of this time and all you know how to do for me is put me in a pretzel position! I am more than just the bedroom tigress, Justice.

I'm elegant!

Grand!

Da bomb.com!

But did you appreciate those qualities?

Nooooooo!

All you did was bring the petty out of me, which is exactly why I'm taking that hundred-dollar bill you left and using it to pay for my three Ubers so I can bounce up out of here!

So while you're at some dumb show for the broke and the talentless, trying to sing your heart out, I'll be moving out and going back where I belong! To my chef, my gold rainspout (where the hot water doesn't

*run out), my three-feet-high, four-poster bed, and my
brand-new pink diamonds!*
    Signed,
    Your ex-girlfriend!

"Is this it, Miss Montgomery?" asked one of the Uber drivers, who held one of my boxes in his hand.

I took one last look around the bedroom, ensuring that the only thing I left behind was the lingering scent of my perfume. "Yes, we have everything," I said as I lifted Justice's pillow and placed a lip-stained kiss on it, then lightly placed the letter over it.

On the way out of the apartment, I saw Justice's six-hundred-pound neighbor and flipped her the bird. Then I slid into the backseat of my personal Uber, my things were loaded into the other two cars, and I eased on my black, bumblebee Chanels, and rode off and into the sunset.

I lay my head back against the headrest, and it occurred to me that I needed to let my diary, the only thing I trusted, know that I'd been freed from Justice and released from the world of Brokedom.

I unzipped my red Hermès tote bag, and at first glance all I saw was my wallet, my eyeglasses case, and my makeup bag. No diary.

Look again.

I turned by bag upside down and dumped all of the contents out. Loose change scattered everywhere. My things were spread all over the floor and the backseat.

No diary!

Where is my diary! "Stopppppp!" I screamed. "Stop now!"

The driver slammed on the brakes, knocking me forward and into the back of his seat.

"Turn around!" I said in a panic. "Tell the other two they can go on and unload my things, but you and I have to go back!"

"What's wrong? What's the matter?"

"I gotta go back and get all my secrets!"

By the time I got to Justice's condo, I was frantic! I hurriedly punched in the security codes to get into the building. *Thank God, I didn't leave my key!*

I unlocked Justice's apartment door and was greeted by the dark living room. Before I could step all the way in, a lamp flicked on, and there stood Justice with my letter in one hand and my diary in the other.

The last thing I remembered, before everything went black, was being thrown to the floor and the thick rubber ridges of his Timbs hovering over my face.

54

Heather

"Good morning, Mr. Montgomery. There's a Heather Cummings here to see you."

"Very well, Cathy. You may show her in." His baritone voice poured evenly, with no hint of happiness, disappointment, or surprise, from the intercom that sat on his receptionist's desk.

He's really going to see me?

I was shocked.

Stunned.

Scared.

Nervous.

Unsure.

Didn't exactly know what I should want or expect from him.

Didn't really know why I was here, other than to say, "I'm your daughter. A part of you."

Which he already knew... for seventeen years... yet never gave a damn about.

Or maybe he did...

Cathy smiled and rose from her gray leather wingback chair. Her deep brown eyes soaked me in. I wondered if she could tell my anxiety was building nerve by nerve, sweat bead by sweat bead, heart jump by heart jump. "Follow me, please," she said.

I didn't move.

I couldn't.

Instead, I gasped for two gulps of air and stood there, looking stupid.

I felt the urge to purge, then run out the door.

You should've stayed home.

No.

Yes.

No, I have something to say.

Like what?

Like, what did I ever do to you...that was so wrong...? How come I was never good enough for you? Camille said you already had a daughter...but I'm your daughter too.

And you really think he's going to listen to that?

"Miss Cummings," Cathy said, as if getting my attention had been a struggle, "is everything okay?"

Why is she asking me that? "And what is that supposed to mean? I have a right to be here too!"

I shouldn't have said that. Now she's looking at me like I'm crazy.

"Okay." She hesitated, clearly unsure of what to say next. "Umm, Mr. Montgomery said he would see you now."

I bit the inside of my cheek.

Gasped for air again.

Look, girl, get it together. This is the chance you wanted. Just go in there and belt it out. Say, "Here I am, your disgrace in the flesh!"

I can't say that.

I'm not a disgrace.

Yeah, right.

I locked eyes with Cathy, "Where's your bathroom?"

She paused, then said. "The bathroom?"

I nodded, "Yeah."

"Okay, umm…It's behind you, down the hall, first door to your left."

"Thanks." I turned around and rushed away. Thank God, it was a single stall. I locked the door and fell against the blue suede wall. My nerves were a wreck. My stomach bubbled, strained, and cramped. And my mouth was so dry that my tongue felt brittle.

I walked over to the vanity, pressed my palms into the limestone counter, and stared into the mirror.

Nothing was going the way I wanted it to. The plan was to go into his office, look him in the face, and say, "Hey." Then stand back and pray that he at least offered me a smile.

A smile?

Psst, please, trick, bye.

You need to quit, and get out while you can.

You sound like one big bag of stupid!

That is not Rev. Run up in there!

That is Richard Montgomery, the deadbeat.

So what you need to ask him is why hasn't he been around? Didn't he think you needed a daddy too? Ask him what kind of dogmatic bullshit has he been puffin' on all of these years that he would dump you in Camille's drunk womb and never look back.

Step. To. Him.

Ask him what's his problem.

You are Heather Cummings, dammit!

And what does that mean? Who the heck is Heather Cummings supposed to be?

A star! On her way to being an iTunes icon. One of the greatest teenage idols out there. A badass who slays every day!

Yeah, right. That's Wu-Wu.

Heather Cummings is a woolly-haired, too fair to be black and too brown to be white, unlovable, ugly mutt!

Tears beat against the backs of my eyes. I dabbed at the wet corners in a speedy effort not to streak my makeup.

Chile, you need a bit.

No, I don't.

Yes. You. Do.

Now, take it out of your purse, and get you a li'l pinch. It'll help calm your nerves and make you feel better. 'Cause right now you're tripping.

I don't wanna go in there high.

You won't be high.

You gon' be nice.

Chilled.

Just right.

A li'l pinch of goodness will chip those nerves away. Besides, this is your chance, and you've been in here long enough.

I don't need a pinch right now.

Do you want him to change his mind and not see you?

No.

Then you know what you gotta do.

"Miss Cummings, you were in the bathroom for quite some time, and Mr. Montgomery is no longer available. He's in a meeting..." Cathy's voice trailed off behind me as I stormed my way to his office. I didn't care what she had to say or what he had to do. He hadn't seen me in seventeen years, but he was gon' see me today! And I put that on everything!

"Miss Cummings, stop! Miss Cummings!" Cathy called, her feet shuffling behind me.

I didn't even turn around, and when I got to a set of double mahogany doors with a gold nameplate marked RICHARD MONTGOMERY SR. GRAND RECORDS CEO, I flung open both doors. And there he sat behind his desk: upright, square-shouldered, dressed in a beige dress shirt and a lavender, pinstriped tie.

Lil Wayne sat in one of the chairs across from him, holding a contract in his hand, and someone else—I guess one of the record execs—sat in the other chair. All of their faces went from stunned to pissed.

"My apologies," my father said to everyone in the room, except me, the one he really owed the apology to. "Cathy, please show everyone to the conference room, and I'll be there in a few minutes."

Cathy let out a nervous huff of air. "No problem, sir."

Everyone stood up and looked at me nastily, as they walked past me and out of the office.

When the office was cleared, Cathy said, "Mr. Montgomery, do you want me to come back?"

"No," he said, "I'll be fine. Please close the door behind you."

She did, and there I stood before my father, a direct vision in his eyes and he one in mine.

He reared back in his leather throne chair and said, "Don't just stand there. You stormed in on my meeting for a reason. Thank God, I've already signed Lil Wayne or you would have scared him off. Now say something. Obviously, you've got a Montgomery heart and don't take no for an answer."

Montgomery... Did he say a Montgomery heart?!

I tried not to smile, but I couldn't help it.

"Time is money." He snapped his fingers. "Clearly, you've been waiting sixteen years to get here."

"Seventeen," I corrected him.

"Well, seventeen years is a long time. And as you can see, I'm a busy man, so whatever it is you need to get off your chest, didn't say onstage when you ruined my daughter's party, and didn't spit on your diss track, I suggest you say it now."

His daughter's party? Did he say his daughter? Well, who the hell did he think I was, the neighbor's kid?

Knots filed my stomach.

He continued, "I gotta give it to you, you have skills,

though, and I was proud when I heard your rhyme and saw
that you could rap."

Proud? Did he say proud? What the eff was he proud of,
me slicing my wrist on computerized wax behind his bullshit?! *Proud?!*

Before I could say anything, he said, "You seem to be quite
the lyricist. Something we're missing in today's rap. And if you
weren't so reckless, you could probably go somewhere with
that."

Reckless? "Reckless?" I said. "I'm reckless? You don't know
me like that! And anyway, who could be more reckless than a
man who runs up in er'body raw and never looks back to see
if his seeds bloomed. Reckless? Boy, bye!"

He shot me a crooked grin and said, "She speaks."

"Yeah, I can speak. I can walk. Run. Sing. Act. Rap. My favorite color is red. And I'm a hustler. But you wouldn't know
any of that because you haven't been around to get to know
your own child!"

"You're Camille's child," he said evenly.

I felt like he'd just sliced me across the throat. *Camille's
child?*

I spat, "Oh, so since I'm not that whore-bucket, Rich, I'm
not your daughter!"

"This isn't about Rich. This is about you."

"What did I ever do to you?!" I screamed.

"Nothing!"

"So why do you hate me?"

"I don't hate you. I just don't have anything for you. Your
mother knew what she was getting into when she was with
me. You aren't even supposed to be standing there. I gave
her a hundred grand for an abortion and four hundred
grand to stay out of my sight, because I couldn't stand to
look at her anymore.

"Yet, eight months later, she's on the cover of some magazine with you propped up in a pram. So before you try to emotionally hustle me about not having a daddy, go check Camille."

"What I need to check Camille for?! She's the one who has been there all of these years. You ain't never done shit!"

"Really? Well, tell me, who do you think has been paying for that expensive private school." He paused. "I'll wait."

I just stood there. Honestly, I didn't know who it was, until now.

He continued. "No response is a response, and I'll take that as you now knowing that I paid for it. But seeing as though you've quit school, my charity work is done."

My voice trembled, "All this time, I blamed and blasted Camille for keeping me away from you, but now I see that you really didn't want me. And obviously, you didn't even love my mother!"

"I loved your mother, but I was never going to marry her, if that's what she told you. We were never a couple. We were a situation that I chose to walk away from. She held on, and I guess she thought having a baby would keep me. Well, now she knows better."

His words were dizzying. Head banging.

I didn't know how long I could keep calm enough not to hop over that desk and drag his ass!

"You ain't shit, yo!" I spat, no longer able to contain myself. "Nothing! Here I've been living for your attention—no, I've been dying for it—and this is how you come at me! I never did anything to you!"

He shuffled a few papers on his desk and gathered them in his hand. "You're right, you've never done anything to me; we've already established that. And since you've appointed yourself to the head of the identifying shit committee, why don't you start with yourself. 'Cause from what I see, you inherited the not shit gene. Standing up in here tweekin' like a fiend. High as hell. What, you thought I couldn't tell? Little girl, I'm from the streets, and I run the music business, so I know a junkie when I see one. And you need help. Now if you'll excuse me, I have a meeting."

"I ain't going nowhere! You owe me!"

"Owe you?" He arched a brow. He pressed the intercom button on his desk. "Cathy, get security in here."

I couldn't believe this was happening. "I should sue you for a paternity test and child support!"

He laughed. "You don't need a paternity test. I know I'm your father. But understand this: If I would cut Rich off—my own flesh and blood, who I love and raised—what do you think I would do for you? And if you wanna sue me"—he stood up and slid his suit jacket on—"go on. But know this: My money is long. And from what I hear, between your druggin' and Camille's drinkin', neither of you can keep a job or pay your rent, so you certainly won't be able to afford an attorney to battle me. Trust me. 'Cause I'll have you tied up in court until your fiftieth birthday, and even then you still won't get a dime."

"Security's here, Mr. Montgomery," Cathy interrupted as she opened the door and two uniformed men walked in.

My father looked at me and said, "They will show you out."

"I said I wasn't leaving!" I took off for his desk, hoping to at least land a drop kick in face.

Whish!

Whash!

Bam!

Bang!

Ahhhhhhhhh!

Black.

Everything went black.

And all I remembered as I screamed and rushed toward him were the two security guards dragging me by my forearms and tossing me across the parking lot's asphalt. My skin burned as sharp pieces of the ground sliced it open.

I tried to get up and walk, but my body felt heavy. My mind lost. I had no strength.

I knew I needed to get to my car, so I crawled, my knees scraping the ground, Once I got to my car door, I lifted the handle and pulled myself into the driver's seat.

I needed a more than a pinch. I needed a few lines.

I reached into my purse and took out the foiled ball of China Doll: OxyContin, coke, and a sprinkle of potpourri. Unwrapped it and stretched it across my lap.

I rolled up a dollar bill and snorted one line.

Then snorted two.

Three.

Four.

Until all that remained on the foiled plate were powdered brown specks. I picked up the foil and licked it clean.

Finally, the invisible weight fell off my back, and now I could get the hell out of here!

I raced out of the parking lot. The sound of screeching tires and the smell of burning rubber filled the air. I swerved around two cars that were in my way and took off for the highway.

You're Camille's daughter!

A junkie.

A fiend!

I never wanted you!

I ain't got nothin' for you!

"Stop it!" I screamed at the painful voices crowding my head. I whipped along the highway's curves, doing my all to out run my thoughts and race up the mountain in front of me.

You're Camille's daughter!

A junkie!

A fiend!

I never wanted you!

Stinging tears blurred my vision. I did my all to wipe my eyes clear, but the more I wiped, the more the tears poured.

I couldn't focus on the road. I couldn't see. I couldn't hear anything more than the voices in my head.

You're Camille's daughter!

A junkie.

A fiend.

I never wanted you!

I gunned my engine and swerved around the mountain's curve.

That's when it appeared, out of nowhere...

The tractor-trailer.

Horns blared.

Tires screeched.

I lost control of the wheel. My car jumped the divider. And then twirled gracefully up in the air like a ballet screwdriver. Everything around me spun in slow motion.

And then the world stopped.

All I could do was close my eyes, and whisper, "Dear God, *nooooo!*"

EPILOGUE

Spencer

One year later...

"*Swing looooow, sweet charrrrrriot,*" *I sang in a low, whispery voice as I looked on in wide-eyed amazement at the seventy-five-inch flat-screen TV, with Mr. Westwick's big face stretched out wide and in color, his hands cuffed behind his big, burly back, as he was being escorted down the steps of Hollywood High.*

"Janice," the reporter said, looking into the camera while talking into her microphone, "we're live out here on the sprawling campus of Hollywood High. And it's a sad day for students and alumni. It's been confirmed. Rushmore Westwick—class of nineteen seventy-two—has been arrested on multiple counts of bribery, embezzlement, and numerous improprieties too scandalous to mention on air during his reign as the illustrious school's headmaster..."

"I'm innocent!" Mr. Westwick screamed into the camera as the police dragged him down the stairs.

"Samantha," the Janice newscaster said, "what do you

think this means for Hollywood High?" She swiped strands of hair out of her face as the wind blew.

"Well, Janice, we shall see. So far, no one on the board of trustees has been willing to make a statement. But from what I have gathered, the police, along with the FBI, acted on a series of tips from a reliable source who provided the authorities with everything they needed to begin the six-month probe leading to Westwick's arrest."

I pursed my lips. Then licked them. This was so juicy. Ooh, I loved me some juicy tea.

"Thanks, Samantha," Janice said. "Now back to you, Julie..."

"Swiiiiiiing looooooooow, goshdiggity-danggit. Sweeeeeeet..."

"In other news," bleach-blond Julie said. "Los Angeles County detectives seized more than twenty-five hundred packets of heroin, along with six thousand pills, including oxycodone, Xanax, Adderall. Also seized were steroids, one loaded handgun, and nearly one hundred thousand dollars in cash..."

In back of the reporter was an inset photo of Co-Co Ming and some tall, dark, chunky hunk of chocolate dipped in lots of heavy gold jewelry.

I tilted my head, and smirked. *Mmmph.*

"Co-Co Ming, son of five-star Sushi King, Ying Ming, was arrested late last night along with Kevar Reynolds—known as Dope Boy—in what authorities call a major California drug raid. The arrests took place at an abandoned warehouse, where the two men sold and manufactured dangerous street drugs to teens across the southern and northern regions of California..."

"Dope pushers," I hissed. "Dream killers!" And then I did a little nasty hip twirl and pumped my pelvis as I popped my fingers and sang, "Shut 'em down, shut-shut-shut-shut... 'em down..." I bent over and made my buttery-soft flapjacks smack.

Heeheehee.

The newscaster continued, "Authorities executed several search warrants throughout Los Angeles County as the result of the eight-month-long investigation. Investigators seized numerous drugs from multiple locations..."

"Serves you right," I spat at the television as the reporter stated that Co-Co and his cohort were both charged with possession of controlled dangerous substances and possession with intent to distribute. And they were both being housed at the Los Angeles County jail on million-dollar bails.

Mmmph.

I'd seen and heard enough. My charity work was done. I reached for the remote and clicked the power off. I had dropped three nickels and two dimes on those two drug-dealing coots. Shut their little candy shop right on down. They were lucky I hadn't greeted them with a canister of Mace and my two besties, *nun* and *chuk*, before doing them in.

Mmmph. Co-Co should have been charged with attempted murder after what happened to Heather. *God!* Heather—I shook my head, placing a hand up over my aching chest...It was too painful to even think about her. Her accident was horrible.

I cried like a—

"Damn, bae," RJ said, snatching me from my thoughts, walking up behind me and wrapping his arms around my waist. "You did that. You ruthless, baby."

I giggled. "Mmm-hmm. I sure am. Don't test my gangster."

He grinned, dipping his head low and planting a warm juicy kiss on my neck. "Remind me never to get on your bad side," he teased.

"Oh, you'll be wise to remember," I playfully warned, looking up at him. "That's if you want to keep your man parts intact."

"Ouch, bae. Daaaaaayum." He kissed me on the neck again, then nipped at my ear. "You drive me wild."

I slammed my fatty-pack into his groin and giggled. "And I'm about to drive you wildly into the mattress."

"Then let's do—"

Rihanna's "Man Down" interrupted RJ. I rolled my eyes, glancing over at my cell phone. It was Kitty. No, heeheehee—she wasn't calling from a jail cell. Although that was probably where that wild cougar needed to be—off the streets, caged and away from the playgrounds where she stalked her eighteen-and-up prey.

"I just shot a man down..." rang out again.

I sighed. Kitty was still my mother, so I stayed loving and kind. That horrid night after she'd spilled her raggedy guts out to me, I shouldn't have called the police on her; tattling on her would have not only ruined her, but Heather's mother too—and, most importantly, *me*.

When the police showed up, ringing the gate buzzer, I'd had to scramble around the house, smear my clawed-up face with face cream, wrap myself in a robe, then peer through the surveillance screen and tell them that it was one big mistake. That I'd thought Kitty was missing, but that I'd found her out in the pool house, drunk and passed out.

I wasn't one for telling lies, but one teensie-weensie lie to avoid public scandal was okay. Right?

Anywho, anyhow, anyway...

Kitty was back to being her messy self. And I promised to keep her horrible secret between us. I hadn't even mentioned it to RJ, my boo—because it's none of his beeswax. Besides, sometimes a girl had to keep a few secrets to herself.

Now moving along...

Oh, what's going on with me?

Heeheehee.

Well, you know. I'm starting my freshman year at the University of Oxford, majoring in law and international economics, while I host my own gossip-talk show *Sip the Tea*, airing on the Kitty Network next fall. It was Kitty's gift to me for not dragging her secret through the media. Besides, she thought being messy was my calling.

And the best part about of this was the fact that I'd be closer to RJ, while he headed up the A&R department for his father's label, Grand Entertainment—their UK division. Mr. Montgomery was grooming my sugar-boo-boo to take over the reins in the next few years, while he and RJ's mother traveled (eye roll!). That lady was already a well-traveled road, but I wasn't messy. So I wasn't going to spill tea on the queen of Ratville. But, ooh, I was so proud of my sexy chocolate-drop boo-daddy. Heeheehee. Besides, you had to know I didn't trust any of them British scallywag ho-dogs to not try to get their paws on my man's meat stick. Not on my watch.

I came prepared. Armed with a purse full of arsenal—brass knuckles, mace, nunchuks, darts, and my trusted jeweled flyswatter. I'd swat a hooka down if I had to over my RJ. Heeheehee. Ooh, Rich hated me more than ever, now that she knew RJ and I were madly in love. And I loved every second of her haterade. She really couldn't help herself. Hateful was that man-eater's middle name.

Rihanna sang out again. I frowned. And this time I pressed IGNORE.

Daddy passed on four months ago. I missed him. But I was relieved that he'd made his way up to those pearly gates in the sky. I didn't know the man he'd become. And he dang sure didn't know me. So saying bye was bittersweet. But I had my trust fund, and I had the boy of my dreams. I was young, rich, and in love. And I was on my way to becoming the next force to be reckoned with.

So watch out, world. Spencer Ellington, the Ace of Spades of Messy, is coming to get you!

Rich

"This way! That way! Look here! Look there! Stand straight! Yes, baby, come through for the camera! Come through, doll!" shouted Valentino, my celebrity photographer, as he whizzed from one side of the eighteenth-century ballroom to the other.

Click!

Flash!

Went the buzz of Valentino and his many assistants' cameras, followed by the shuffling of their feet as they angled for the best heat. Which of course was me, dressed in a custom-made Marchesa. A champagne-colored, strapless mermaid gown that gripped every ounce of my double melon-D's, my round middle, and my curvaceous hips, then swept into a bustling bottom and a fifty-foot train.

Yassss, bish, this Hollywood diva had arrived, and I was on my grown woman grind!

Click!

Flash!

And it doesn't matter what you may have heard, or what any of those other wannabes Spencer, London, or Heather may have already said or will open their lying mouths to say about me, I was still queen. I still reigned supreme. And I was the greatest success story Hollywood High's Pampered Princesses had ever seen.

And yeah, over the course of my high school years, you may have witnessed me as the sacrificial lamb, surrounded by phony friends. Disloyal relatives. Liars. Deadbeats. Users. Fake news. Even those who tried to strip me of my beauty... but no more.

Why?

'Cause God was good, honey! And black Jesus was not to be slept on! Now touch your neighbor and tell 'em that!

The last anyone knew of me, I was spotted under Justice's feet and left for dead. My nose was broken, my eye sockets fractured, and my right jaw collapsed. My face was a devastating bloody explosion.

I had to have emergency reconstructive surgery. And two days later, when I came to, I had one good eye I could flutter open...and are you ready for this?...I opened that eye and, honey, there was Logan holding a baby!

"Mommy," I asked, "whose baby is that?"

Before she could answer, the doctor rushed to my bedside and said, "Well, well, young lady. We are glad to see you have come around. You are quite a lucky young woman. And by the way, congratulations, you had a baby girl." He said this in a casual tone, like he'd just told me it was sunny outside.

"Lies and deceit!" I screamed. "I didn't bring no baby in here with me!" I looked over at my mother and asked her in a more forceful tone than before, "Whose dang baby is that?!"

"Calm down, Richie-Poo." She walked over to me and said, "Rich Gabrielle Montgomery, meet your daughter." She pulled the receiving blanket completely out of the baby's face. The baby looked to be at least eight pounds, with smooth milk chocolate skin and a full Afro of thick black curls. "Oh, Rich!" My mother gleamed.

All I could think was that I had died and was in the twilight zone part of hell. "Maybe you're not hearing me, but I did not come in here with no baby! I came in here with a footprint across my face, no eyes, and a missing jaw!'

I did my best to sit up in bed. "Shakeesha," I said, "you have already been in the slammer, and you know about that three-strike rule, don't you? So you better take that baby back where you got her from."

"Rich, you didn't know you were pregnant?" the doctor asked, now sounding concerned.

I snapped. "How the heck was I supposed to know I was pregnant?! I never been full pregnant before, just a little pregnant, so, no, I didn't know." Now all of my weight gain, heartburn, and cravings made sense. Still, I couldn't believe it.

But.

The more I stared at the baby, the more I knew she was mine. She had my eyes, my mouth, my hair, and my dimpled cheeks.

"Is Justice her father?" Logan asked.

"Yes." I rolled my eyes, pissed that here I was on my sick and shut-in bed and my own mother had called me a ho on the low. Instead of poppin' off, though, I held out my arms and asked to hold my daughter.

After my baby, who I named Rich Gabrielle Montgomery Number Two, of course, and I got out of the hospital, I found out that Justice had been arrested and the state of California had charged him with aggravated assault and battery for what he'd done to me. And to think I loved Justice. But he was a sick boy who needed help, my help. And I did just that.

I helped him go to jail by pressing charges, testifying, and doing my best to make sure the book was thrown at him. Which the court didn't do. All the judge did was find him guilty, bang her gavel, and sentence him to three years of boot-camp time. But not once did Justice get hit with a book, which completely pissed me off!

I got over it, though.

Besides, I had more important things to worry about, like my newborn chocolate sunshine.

Life was different, but I adjusted to being a mommy.

I also got my snap back. With the help of my bariatric surgeon, I lost a hundred pounds naturally. And thanks to my glam squad, cocoa-butter, and my plastic surgeon, all the scars left by Justice stepping on me were removed from my face, and my skin was cleared.

After seeing how I had bloomed, my mother, who finally got her mind right and became my bestie, taught me the score on how to get in heaven's door and turn my life over to God's loving and tender touch.

Rewind that: turn my life over to the mega super star, televangelist, make T. D. Jakes look like a traveling Wednesday tent, dumb-stupid and filthy-rich God's Loving and Healing Touch's founder and senior pastor's only child, Otis Stackhouse. *The* Otis Stackhouse, the one with three capital eyes behind his name. How boss is that, baby!

Chile, cheese!

Boo, please!

And how did I snag him?

Well...a tigress never panty-drops and tells. But I'll give you a little hint. Three months into the judge breaking me and Justice up, or something like that, I met Otis Three Eyes at his daddy's church and found out that our fathers grew up in Compton together and knew one another.

And that convo led to another, and on to another, and on to one lovely Sunday afternoon stroll that ended with him calling my name and clawing my back to heaven.

A month later I found out I was pregnant—with twins!

Bingo!

My mother said for once that I had knocked something out the park, baby! Two homeruns at once.

Otis had to marry me and, as per his daddy, quickly. Otis also agreed to adopt my little pudding-poo Richie Number Two and be her new daddy.

Yasssss, honey!

I was now the soon-to-be Rich Gabrielle Montgomery-Stackhouse, with three capital eyes behind my name.

And so what if this was a forced marriage with a little under-cover sin mixed in! I didn't give a damn!

I was on my way to being wholesome!

Plus, Otis loved me. And on top of that, I'd finally made

my parents proud. My daddy said he was happy to give me away, and my mother said she had faith that her legacy was finally safe.

And so, a year later, after Justice tried to do me, the double doors of the ballroom opened, I stepped over the threshold of my new Humbly Hills estate, and onto the white sands of my private beach.

There were hundreds of guests seated in white-fabric-covered chairs, on both sides of a hand-sewn and embroidered runner.

And with all eyes and camera flashes focused on me, my daddy and I walked arm and arm toward my perfect and well-played destiny.

London

Milan, Italy

"London, darling," my mother's voice rang out, "isn't this exciting?" She gripped my shoulders and then pulled me into a tight embrace. "I'm so happy for you, my darling." She kissed me on the cheek. And then took a step back. "You look beautiful, darling."

"Thank you," I said, smiling at her.

"London, love! Save the chitchat for later!" yelled one of the assistants, flamboyantly clapping his hands to move me along. "Let's go! Showtime in fifteen!"

"Well, my darling London," my mother said, "I'll let you get to it. See you on the runway." Then with one last hug, she was gone.

It was Fashion Week. And, yes, I was back. Right back where I said I never wanted to be again. But here I was, a slinky pink dress (part of Valentino's Pretty in Pink collection) being pulled over my head and down over my hips.

Ready to hit the runway.

I had nothing left back in the States. No life. No *real* friends. And no real purpose, just lots of painful memories. So right after graduation from Hollywood High, I packed my things and flew to Milan, never looking back.

Anderson and I, well...we eventually had our *talk*. Unfortunately, there was no reconciliation. And, interestingly, I was okay with that. Finally. Besides, I was *seeing*—sort of, kind of—someone else. Devon Blade. He'd recently signed a fifteen-million-dollar contract to play for the Portland Trailblazers. Who woulda known? I'd truly had no clue. Still, he wasn't Anderson. But he was the next best thing. And he was good to me. And like my mother had once told me when I hadn't wanted to be with Anderson: "You will learn to love him." And she was right. I was learning how to do exactly that. Love him.

As for my parents, let's see. They were still *not* divorced (shaking my head!). After having my bat-wielding, window-smashing meltdown, I'd swung the bat at Rich's mother, to only end up bashing out her car's headlight. She and I fought. She'd won, of course, because there was no way I was going to beat an ex-gang-banging street rat. And, yes, she and Mr. Montgomery were still married. She'd made it very clear that she wasn't leaving him. In fact, I'd learned (okay, overheard) later on that he'd been the one who encouraged her to go out and find her a side piece to keep herself busy and out of his face. Wow. Adults were sometimes more crazy than we were.

As for the recording of her and my father, well...I still had it. I wasn't sure why I held onto it as a memento, but I did. Anyway, after Rich's mother attacked me, things with her and my father became, well...*strained*...as he claimed.

Whatever. She would always be a man-stealing whore in my eyes.

"Places, dolls! We're live in five, four, three, two..."

It was almost time for the show to start. The atmosphere was crazy tense, but thrilling. Excitement and nervous energy hung in the air like a glittering lariat.

My mother had been right. *This* was my world. This *was* where I belonged.

On the runway, in front of the cameras...right smack in the spotlight.

Not for bad press—even though bad press sometimes came with the territory, but for the publicity and—*yes*, for the attention.

Rich, Spencer, Heather, and I were all attention whores for different reasons, and we all sought it in different ways.

For me, it was the runway.

I couldn't speak for the rest of the so-called Pampered Princesses. But I was a princess. And I was pampered. However, I never needed to be in a clique, with a group of girls who defined themselves by a title. Pampered Princesses.

Speaking of which, Rich and I were finally speaking—cordial to one another was more like it, but speaking nonetheless. Her daughter was adorable. I'd seen all the pictures of her on Instagram and Twitter all glammed—*no*, we still weren't social media friends again. She was "friends" with one of my aliases, Rokeeta. Nevertheless, I was truly happy for her, even though I still couldn't imagine *her* being trusted with a baby. The idea of Rich ever caring for anyone other than herself was frightening. Still, I'd reached out to her after she'd had the baby. And, for once, we were able to have a civil conversation. I apologized for everything that had happened between us. She didn't, of course. And I hadn't expected her to. Rich was Rich.

You could fill in all the blanks for yourselves.

I was done with the mean-girl life.

Spencer, well...she was still crazy as ever. But, at least, we'd found a way to dislike each other without being disrespectful toward one another. *I think*. Distance away from her was definitely for the best, even if that old saying "Out of sight, out of mind" didn't seem to apply. Spencer still "checked in" on me, as she liked to call it. I NEED TO MAKE SURE YOU'RE NOT DANCING WITH THE GRIM REAPER AGAIN, TRAMP, were her text messages to me once a week. Maybe she cared, in her own strange, annoyingly twisted way.

Or not.

Heather?

Oh, right. Heather. Well, after her tragic accident, we'd found—surprise, surprise—a way to put our differences to the side. I'd visited her in the hospital twice and sent flowers to her. I even apologized to her for judging her without ever giving myself a chance to get to know her. I was wrong for that. Turned out, she was really a cool girl. And funny. Who knew, maybe she and I would be able to be—um, on second thought. Nah. We really had nothing in common.

I blinked as several shoulders jostled me. No one apologized or gave a second glance. I didn't take offense. The madness wasn't personal.

"Let's go, ladies! Three minutes to showtime!" someone called out, and everyone started shoulder-bumping anyone who was in their way, out of the way as they scrambled to take their places.

I smiled, my eyes quickly sweeping around the organized chaos. Pouty-lipped models fluttered around the tent changing, while hair people, makeup people, and assistants buzzed around, preparing to transform us.

I took my place in the back of the line. God, I was so different from when I'd taken this spot the last time. I'd been so broken. I definitely wasn't that same girl, thanks to my therapist. Yes, I was still in therapy—well, via Skype these days.

But—

I blinked back to the present as another model stumbled off the stage, rushing to get changed for her next outfit. There were now only two girls ahead of me.

Dr. Kickaloo kept me grounded. She reminded me that we—Rich, Spencer, Heather, and I—were simply overindulged teenaged girls, all casualties of Hollywood, of the glitz and glitter. All addicted to the fame and the spotlight. Cursed by our birthrights.

As I stood among all the beautiful models, I found my breath and slowly exhaled. Yes. This was truly my world, my life, where I belonged.

Back straight. Chin lifted. Hip jutted forward. I stepped out from behind the curtain, focused on the photographers at the end of the runway. In my peripheral, I saw the people lining the edges of the stage—fashionistas and bloggers.

Flashbulbs went off, nearly blinding me. Yet I pushed through the white lights and served my signature strut down the catwalk. And this time, as I turned my head left and right so the photographers could get their pictures of me, I didn't have to pretend to be someone I wasn't.

I was fly, fine, and fabulous. A trendsetter. A diva. Born in London. Cultured in Paris. Molded in New York. A transplanted by-product of Hollywood High.

I was London Phillips.

A famous runway model.

Heather

Don't be nervous...you got this...
Deep breath in.
Deep breath out.
Now go...
"Hello, my name is..."
I froze.
Solid.
My heart thundered, and my stomach dropped to my feet.

Here I was, in the center of this packed room, looking and now feeling like I had two stones stuffed deep in my cheeks.

I couldn't do it.

But I had to.

It was the only way I'd truly be able to say, "Eff this shit. I've been carrying it around for way too long…"

There were at least fifty pairs of eyes on me.

I tapped the arms of my chair and eased out two breathing techniques. Hell, I needed something to shake my anxiety. I wasn't ready, but I was ready, if you know what I mean.

I looked to my left and surprisingly spotted Spencer. Then I looked to my right and spotted Camille. Camille smiled, a real smile. One that was proud. She winked, then took her right hand and lifted her chin: a sign for me to hold my head up high and be strong enough to tell everyone just who I was.

I closed my eyes and began, "Hello, my name is Heather, and I'm an addict." I exhaled, opened my eyes, and felt as if a ton of bricks had tumbled off my shoulders.

"Hello, Heather," everyone said, practically in unison, "Welcome."

I drank in another deep breath and blew it out. I continued, "Umm…I'm not sure where to start or where to end, but I'm going to do my best."

"Take your time," someone yelled out, and it brought about a calming chuckle from the crowd.

I said, "For as long as I can remember, I've either been drinkin', snortin', smokin', or poppin' something. I've never had one particular moment that I can pinpoint and say, 'Yeah, that's it. That's the first time I got lit. Or that's the high I've been chasing. As far back as I can remember I was sippin' my mother's scotch, sniffin' crazy glue, Listerine, cough syrup, crushing Sudafed, smoking weed, snortin' black beauty, bath salt, Xanax. You name it, and I have turned up on it.

"And sure, people would look at me and say, 'You got it all.

Fame and fortune, and people at your beck and call.' But the truth is, those people I hung with didn't give a damn about me.

"My fortune came and went, mostly went. And my fame, mmmph." I shook my head. "The only thing fame did for me was make me a well-known junkie with no place to hide.

"Truth is, I had nothing. My mother was an abusive alcoholic who berated me, and my father pretended I didn't exist.

"Well, one day, I got tired of the bullshit and decided that I was going to confront my father and let him know that I would no longer be ignored. So I stormed into his office. And you know what he did? He sat there, listened to me, and then told me he had nothing for me, called me reckless and a junkie. Then he told me to leave. When I wouldn't go, he had two of his security guards drag me out of his office and ban me from coming back.

"I was hurt, enraged, and out of my mind! I think I snorted five lines and took off for the wind, trying to outrun the sky, I guess. I raced up the highway, around curves, sped up the mountain, swerved in and out of lanes—and all of this on an open highway. There was this car in front of me, going too slow. I whipped around it, and by the time I spotted the eighteen-wheeler, it was too late.

"I woke up three months later with third-degree burns on my back, a broken femur, two shattered knees, an injured spine, and I couldn't feel my legs. That's how I ended up in this wheelchair.

"For months, I just wanted to die. Many nights I would think about how I needed to end my life. Would I blow out my brains or take a bottle of sleeping pills?

"But God had the last say. One of those low days, my mother, Camille, came to me and said, 'That's it. My drinking and your drugging has to end. We can't keep living like this. I won't have you give up. I love you and I need you. And I know that we can do this.'

"That was the first time my mother had ever said that to me. She asked me then if I would go to rehab, and I agreed. We've both been clean and sober for six months, three weeks, and two days."

The audience clapped and I felt like...like I could conquer the world!

I continued, "God has really blessed us. And just so you know, some mysterious donor—who I don't think is really all that mysterious—gave us fourteen million dollars...But more than money, we have each other, we have our sobriety and are able to live our lives the way they're supposed to be."

The crowd erupted into a furious applause.

"So anyway, I won't go on and on, I just wanted to tell you a little bit about me and let you all know that no matter how cold the world may seem, and no matter your circumstances, it's never too late to turn your life around and be whoever you want to be!

"Just look at me!"

DON'T MISS

Dear Yvette by Ni-Ni Simone
All sixteen-year-old Yvette Simmons wanted was to
disappear. Problem is: She has too many demons for that.
Yvette's life changed forever after a street fight ended in a
second-degree murder charge. Forced to start all over again,
she's sentenced to live far from anything or anyone she's
ever known. She manages to keep her past hidden, until a
local cutie, known as Brooklyn, steps in. Will he give her the
year of her dreams, or will Yvette discover that nothing is as
it seems?

Chasing Butterflies by Amir Abrams
At sixteen, gifted pianist and poet Nia Daniels has already
known her share of heartache. But despite the pain of los-
ing her mother and grandmother, she's managed to excel,
thanks to her beloved father's love and support. Nia can't
imagine what she'd do without him—until an illness
suddenly takes him, and she has no choice. And Nia's in for
one more shocking blow. The man who'd always been her
rock, her constant, wasn't her biological dad. Orphaned and
confused, Nia is desperate for answers. But what she finds
will uproot her from the life she's always known...

Available wherever books are sold.

Connect with Us